A ROGUE FOR ALL SEASONS

A Rogue For All Seasons

A Weston Novel

Sara Lindsey

A ROGUE FOR ALL SEASONS
Copyright © 2013 by Sara Lindsey.

Edited by Charlotte Herscher
Cover design by Janet L. Holmes.
Interior Design & Layout by VMC Art & Design, LLC

Print ISBN: 978-0-9860125-1-8
Digital ISBN: 978-0-9860125-0-1

This book is a work of fiction. Names, characters, places, and incidents either are the product of the author's imagination or are used fictitiously, and any resemblance to actual persons, living or dead, business establishments, organizations, events, or locales is entirely coincidental.

All Rights Are Reserved. No part of this book may be reproduced, stored in or introduced into a retrieval system, or transmitted, in any form, or by any means (electronic, mechanical, photocopying, recording, or otherwise), without the prior written permission of the copyright holder, except in the case of brief quotations embodied in critical articles and reviews.

First print publication: September 2013

*For Dad,
even though you repeatedly suggested*
No Pants Romance *as the title.
You're my champion* and *my companion.
I love you.*

*And also for the readers who asked for Henry's story.
You helped me remember what happily ever after
is really all about.*

ACKNOWLEDGMENTS

The biggest thank you has to go to my family. You stood by me, even on the days when I would have run as far away from me as I could get. I'd be lost without your love, your patience, your laughter, and your hugs. I must acknowledge, however, that we're one man—er, fish—down. Dorio, you took one for the team—swim free in the great blue beyond.

Huge thanks also to my friends, both for allowing me to retreat into the writing cave for long stretches of time and for dragging me out before official hermit status is declared. Lizy Dastin, you overwhelm me every day with your unflagging love and support, and you inspire me to do better and be more. Stacey Agdern, this book wouldn't exist without our brainstorming sessions and breadsticks. Elyssa Patrick, I know I can count on you, day or night. Jennifer Goodman, you read this book in all its incarnations—from some very exotic locations—and you provided invaluable feedback and friendship throughout this *long* process. Courtney Milan and Tessa Dare, I sure got lucky when they were handing out big sisters in Romancelandia! Marni Bates, you came along when I needed the final push, and you gave me the energy and enthusiasm to keep going. *Merci beaucoup* to Brenna Aubrey who helped me with some of the French translations—any mistakes are mine. I am also so grateful for the Vanettes and my other romance friends—you know who you are—who always take the time to listen and offer encouragement and advice.

The romance world has brought me into contact with so many incredible people. These individuals are not only masters of their crafts, but genuinely lovely people who all went above and beyond for me. I am indebted to: Charlotte Herscher, my editor, whose insight into the story and characters helped me to write a stronger book; Martha Trachtenberg, copy editor extraordinaire, who answered questions I didn't know I had and was marvelously patient with the barrage of emails I sent at odd hours; Janet Holmes, graphic design goddess, who worked tirelessly to create my perfect cover and surpassed all my expectations; and Victoria Colotta, designer and miracle worker, who saved me from all sorts of formatting folly and brought romance into every element of the book's design.

Finally, thanks to all of the readers who stuck by me through a difficult time. Writing is said to be a lonely business, but I've never felt that way with you around.

THE WESTON FAMILY TREE

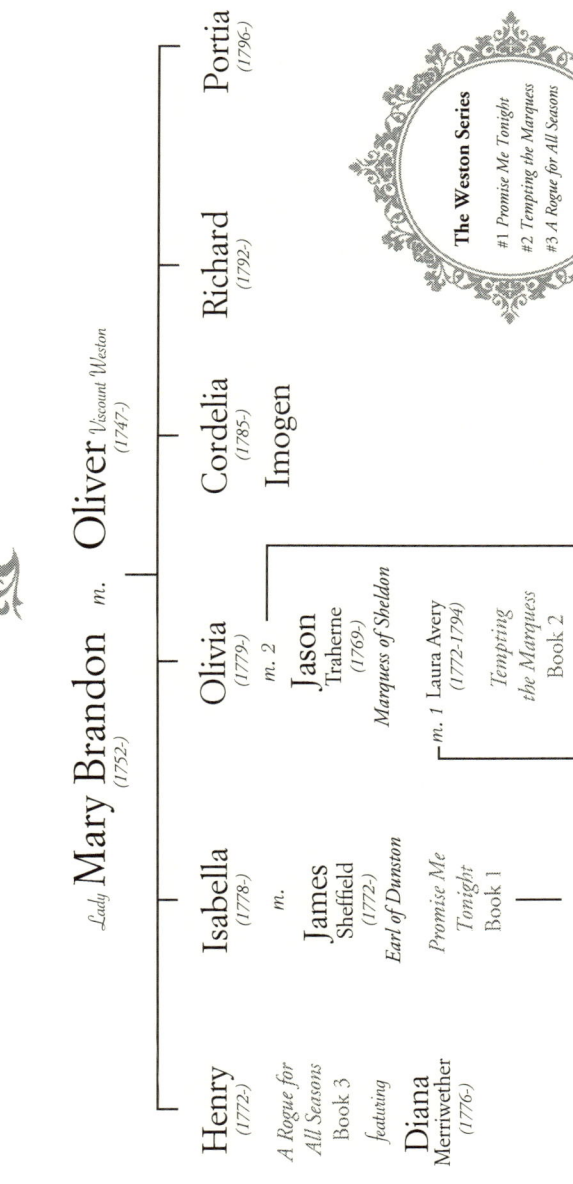

Lady **Mary Brandon** m. **Oliver** *Viscount Weston*
(1752-) (1747-)

Henry | **Isabella** | **Olivia** | **Cordelia** | **Richard** | **Portia**
(1772-) | (1778-) | (1779-) | (1785-) | (1792-) | (1796-)

A Rogue for All Seasons
Book 3
featuring

Diana Merriwether
(1776-)

m.
James Sheffield
(1772-)
Earl of Dunston

Promise Me Tonight
Book 1

m. 2
Jason Traherne
(1769-)
Marques of Sheldon

m. 1 Laura Avery
(1772-1794)

Tempting the Marquess
Book 2

Imogen

Bride | **Edward** | **Rosemary**
(1798-) | (1792-) | (1799-)

The Weston Series
#1 *Promise Me Tonight*
#2 *Tempting the Marquess*
#3 *A Rogue for All Seasons*

PROLOGUE

Suffolk, England
February 1784

For a girl of only eight years old, Diana Merriwether was very good at hiding. She hid in empty cupboards, behind thick drapes, and under accommodating pieces of furniture. She'd tucked herself beneath the big desk in the library today. She enjoyed hiding, but she loved the excitement of someone finding her.

Her parents were very good at finding her. They called her name throughout the house, with Mama pulling the drapes aside, and Papa searching beneath the beds and opening cabinet doors. Diana's nurse believed hunger would eventually drive any child out of hiding, so she saved her knees the trouble of looking. Nurse wouldn't have been good at finding in any case; she was old and didn't move much above a waddle. She also had Diana's little brother, Alexander, to watch over.

There weren't many good hiding places at Swallowsdale. Papa said the stables were too dangerous to play in, and Mama had forbidden her from going in the home woods alone since the time she got lost. If she were at Halswelle Hall, where her grandparents lived, she would never run out of places to hide. She had only visited once, but she remembered that The Hall was as big and grand as a palace. When Diana had said as much, her grandmother had explained that dukes and duchesses were only a step below royalty. Her grandparents had visited Swallowsdale when Alex was born, but now they just sent for Mama to come to them.

Her ears pricked as she perceived the faint rattle of coach wheels. Papa hadn't said anything about a visitor today. Could Mama be home? She had gone to The Hall almost a fortnight ago because the duke had taken ill. He and the duchess often took ill, and they always sent for Mama—just in case. In case of what, Diana wasn't sure, but she wished it didn't happen so often. She liked it best when her family was together. Papa was always grumpy when Mama went away; he missed her worst of anyone.

As the heavy tread of her father's footsteps sounded down the stairs, Diana considered leaving her hiding place beneath the desk. She didn't want to run into the entry hall if the person in the coach had come to do business. Papa wouldn't like that, since she was supposed to be reading quietly in the nursery. She caught her breath as the library door opened with its telltale squeak. Papa always promised to fix it, but the stud kept him very busy.

"Your messenger said only that I must come home at once." Diana nearly darted out at hearing her mother, but the strain in her voice kept Diana still. "You promise the children are well?"

"Did I not tell you so at the door?" Papa did not seem at all happy to see Mama. A bad feeling took up root in Diana's belly as the door squeaked closed.

"Oh, I have been so anxious," exclaimed her mother. "I was so frightened Alex or Diana had taken ill, or that you were hurt, or—"

"Would you care if I were hurt?"

"How can you ask me that?" her mother demanded.

"You leave so often, I don't know who you care for anymore."

This wasn't right. She wanted to tell her mother to leave the room, and then come back in and begin again. Her parents would find her hiding underneath the desk and they would all laugh. Papa would tell her that she was a clever puss, and then Mama would groan and say he shouldn't encourage her, but she would smile when she said it.

"Is this the urgent reason you needed me home?" her mother asked angrily. "I know there's no love lost between you and my parents. I don't blame you, and I don't begrudge you your dislike. You know why I go; we have the same argument every time I leave. Was it necessary to scare me out of my wits because you wanted to go over it again? For God's sake, I would have returned in a couple more days."

This was wrong, Diana thought, but if she told them, she would give away her hiding place. She had a feeling that whatever her parents were fighting about, it was serious. She curled herself into a tighter ball and rested her cheek on her knees, waiting for it to be over.

"No, that isn't the reason I sent for you," Papa said. "Before I say why, is there anything about your visit that you want to tell me? Is there anything you think I should know?"

"No, I don't believe so. The Hall was very dull—"

"Is adultery dull to you? Damn you, Linnet, if you wish to make a cuckold of me, couldn't you at least choose a smart man? He sent on a shift you left behind."

Adultery. Diana had heard that word before. It wasn't a good word. It was one of the thou-shalt-nots that the vicar liked to go on about come Sunday morning. But Mama—

"How dare you?" The sharp slap of flesh on flesh split the air.

"Don't do that again," her father warned. "You don't get to act the part of the outraged wife when I know you spent days at Peckford's house. I wouldn't ordinarily read your mail, but I wondered why Peckford sent a messenger with a parcel for you. Imagine my surprise when I unwrapped the paper and found your underclothes! I don't know why I bothered to read the letter but, the more fool I, some part of me hoped there might be an explanation." Diana heard the crinkle of paper. "He wrote how he enjoyed having you in his home, although he fears you did not get much sleep—"

"You *are* a fool. Mother and I went to dine at Folkham and, while we were there, the weather turned bad. Mother made such a fuss,

Malcolm felt obliged to let us stay the night. It must have snowed as much here as it did there. We couldn't leave for a couple of days, but it isn't as if I were alone with the man. I spent my time nursing his aunt since the doctor could not get through from the village. My shift needed washing after she was sick on me in the night. One of the maids lent me a clean one. Obviously, I forgot to retrieve mine before we left. I can't imagine why he would send it here rather than The Hall."

"You could make a man forget his own name, let alone his common sense. It's a tidy explanation, I must admit, but that hardly sounds like a dull visit. If it's all as innocent as you say, why would you feel the need to hide it from me?"

"I didn't tell you because I feared you would react like a jealous idiot. It seems I was correct. I am prepared to forgive you, after a proper amount of groveling, because if some woman sent home your smalls, I don't know which of you I'd kill first." She laughed, but Papa stayed silent. After a long moment, her mother whispered, "My God, you don't believe me."

"This isn't the first time you and Peckford have slept under the same roof. I remember, when you went to The Hall in December, you wrote in one of your letters that Peckford had stayed the night. You gave yourself away."

"Malcolm is my parents' nearest neighbor; he dines at The Hall regularly. The poor man had too much to drink one night. He wasn't fit to ride home, and The Hall can certainly accommodate another person."

"Unlike here, you mean?" He gave a bitter laugh. "I know this isn't good enough for you, that I'm not good enough for you. I tried as hard as a man can try, but I can't live like this. I thought I could steal you away, as Hades did with Persephone, but I should have known I couldn't keep you in my world."

"You are talking nonsense. Have you been drinking Bar's moonshine again? My world is wherever you are. I don't enjoy dancing attendance on my parents, but for the children's sake, I must keep them happy. You know I would rather be here with you. Your past has never mattered to me. I wouldn't care if you were a fishmonger.

You are the one who has always been concerned that you're a bastard. That's an accident of birth. You have no such excuse for acting like one right now."

Her father said a bad word under his breath. "When were you planning to tell me about the babe? I know you're with child, so don't think to deny it."

"Why would I deny it?" she returned hotly. "I would have told you before I left, but I wanted to wait until I was certain. I haven't felt sick at all, and"—her voice shook—"we've been disappointed before. I thought . . . I thought you would be happy."

Mama was going to have another baby? Maybe this time, Diana would get a little sister. She loved Alex, but a sister would make her so—

"Happy?" her father shouted. "You thought I'd be *happy?*"

Something hit the wall and shattered.

"Thomas! That vase was a wedding gift from the Prince of Wales," her mother exclaimed.

"And now it's broken. Just like my trust. Just like our marriage. Christ, do you even know if it's mine?"

Why was Papa being so mean? He knew how much Diana loved that vase. She was always so careful when she looked at it. She knew it was special, just as Papa always told her she was special. Why would he break something she loved?

"How can you say these things?" her mother whispered. "When did you stop loving me?"

"What do you mean?" Her father's tone was low and gruff; Diana had to strain to make out the words. "I dreamed of you, wanted you, from the first time I saw you. I fell in love with you that night you sneaked to the stables to watch over that foal. God help me, even knowing what I do, I still love you. I'll love you until I die."

"If you loved me, you would trust me." Mama's voice trembled as if she were trying not to cry. At first, Diana had been too surprised to cry, but now the surprise was wearing off. She bunched up her pinafore and pressed it to her face so no one would hear her distress.

"I don't know who you are," Mama said slowly. "There is a stranger in this room with me. You aren't my Thomas. You aren't the man I married, or the father of my children or"—she choked—"or the man I love. *He* is the father of this child. I don't know you, and I don't care to know you. I'll return to The Hall as soon as the horses are rested, and I won't come back. I pity you on the day you realize how stupidly you've acted."

"I don't know you, either. You say you love me, and maybe you did when we married. You chose me then, but now you run off to your parents at the first word. They treat you like a servant. They haven't forgiven you, Linnet, and they never will. They want Alex."

"I'm not an idiot. I know my parents' shortcomings, but at least their anger at me is justified. I wonder if you realize you've given them just what they want. You've driven the children and me straight into their arms."

"Diana and Alex stay with me. I won't have them raised in that shrine to wealth and privilege."

"You can't raise Diana alongside you in the stables. Do you want her to grow up to be a lady or a circus performer? And whether you like it or not, Alex is second in line to the dukedom. That 'shrine to wealth and privilege' might well be his someday. Will you deny our children their birthright?"

"There's nothing I wouldn't do for them," came her father's fierce reply.

"Then perhaps you're not completely lost, even if you are lost to reason."

Long moments passed before her father said, "Diana will have a better life with you than I can give her, but you must break with Peckford. I don't want him around my children. I want Alex—"

"I was never *with* him!"

Then there was only the sound of Mama crying. Diana cried with her. They would hear her soon. She couldn't keep quiet much longer. Mama was leaving, and Diana would go with her. Papa didn't even care. He only wanted Alex.

"There are times I've been so angry with my parents that I wished them out of my life, but however much I disagree with them, I have always understood them." Her mother sounded as if she had a cold. "I will never understand how you could doubt me. I didn't know I could love someone and hate him at the same time."

"Neither did I." Papa's voice was colder than Diana had ever heard it. "You will stay the night. Tomorrow—"

"No!" Diana shrieked, scrambling out from under the desk. "No, no, no, no!" She stamped her feet and flailed her arms around, trying to make it all go away.

"Diana. . . ." Her mother, ashen-faced, took a step toward her.

Diana screamed as loud as she could. If she couldn't hear her parents, then they couldn't say any more bad things. Or at least she couldn't hear them. So she screamed until she ran out of air, and then she was crying. She was crying with her whole body, crying so hard that it hurt and made it difficult to breathe.

Her mother's concerned face swam before her eyes. "Come now, you must stop. You will make yourself sick." She reached out a hand.

Diana backed away. "Don't touch me!"

"Diana, love," her father began.

"Don't call me that," she sobbed. "You don't love me."

"Don't say—"

"You *don't*!" she yelled. "You only love Alex. I hate you! I hate you, hate you, *hate you*!" With a fierce cry, she shoved everything she could off of her father's desk. The papers, the books, the inkwell—off it all went in a satisfying crash. She didn't wait to assess the damage, though. She ran from the study, then through the front door and out into the cold, dark night.

Diana heard her parents calling her name, but she ignored them. When her father came after her, she just ran faster. She ran and ran and ran, her heart pounding away in her chest and tears coursing down her face. Because if she ran long enough, and if she ran far enough, Diana was sure she could find a hiding place so secret, so safe that nothing bad would be able to find her. . . .

CHAPTER ONE

With you and Olivia now happily married, I can turn my attentions to your brother. I had hoped, as you may have guessed, he and Miss Merriwether would suit. I know you think her quiet and reserved, but your rogue of a brother needs a woman with maturity and strength of character—a woman to see beyond his looks and his flirtations to the man he has the potential to be. I thought to bring them into each other's company by pushing him to dance with her, but I should have known he would look askance at any female brought forth by his mother. All his life, I have only sought his happiness. As Shakespeare wrote, "How sharper than a serpent's tooth it is to have a thankless child!"

—from the Viscountess Weston to her daughter the Countess of Dunston

SIXTEEN YEARS LATER
LONDON

"Are you truly staying in town for the Season?" Isabella, Countess of Dunston, asked as she handed her brother a cup of tea. "I thought having the whole family here would send you running far and fast."

"I am keeping a valise packed in the event I need to flee in the night." Henry Weston regarded his sister with amusement. "Was that your subtle way of suggesting I leave, Izzie? Perhaps you should have considered how often I would visit your breakfast room before you married my oldest friend."

Isabella laughed, but Henry didn't miss the subtle tension that tightened her shoulders. James Sheffield, Earl of Dunston, the husband and friend in question, frowned as he set aside his morning paper. "I would wager you come for the food, rather than the company," he said dryly as he took Isabella's hand. They exchanged a fond, intimate look that had Henry averting his eyes.

Isabella leaned forward in her seat. "Hal, you must know I am always happy to have you with us," she earnestly assured him. "I even suggested to James that you ought to stay here. Now that I have redecorated, this is surely more comfortable than your bachelor's lodgings. However—"

"However," James broke in, "I persuaded your sister that her generosity was unnecessary."

"But James—"

Henry chuckled. "No, Izzie, he's quite right. 'Two is company, three is none,' isn't that the saying? Believe me, I have no desire to intrude on your, er . . ."

"Desires?" supplied James.

"Do you know, I believe we're long overdue for a round in the ring at Jackson's. I know I promised my sister I wouldn't call you out for seducing her, but I think I deserve the opportunity to blacken your daylights."

"Don't you dare think of fighting with James," Isabella warned. "And, just so you know, *I* was the one doing the seducing."

Henry and James groaned in unison.

"Hush, love," James told his wife. "I have a reputation to uphold."

"The only reputation you need to be concerned with upholding," Izzie maintained, "is that of the world's most faithful husband and devoted father."

"And if he slips up? Then can I pound him into the ground?" Henry asked hopefully.

"If he slips up, you are welcome to whatever is left once I've finished with him," his sister agreed, her blond curls bobbing in approval.

James winced. "You have nothing to worry about, my bloodthirsty little wench."

A tender smile curved her lips. "Then neither do you."

"What you should both be worried about is the spectacle Mother is going to make of you at her ball," Henry interjected. He wasn't looking forward to his mother's ball, but at least he wasn't the cause for the occasion. That honor fell to James and Isabella, along with Olivia, another of Henry's sisters, and her husband. In the past two years, two of his sisters had married, giving him two brothers-in-law and two baby nieces. At times, everything felt a bit *two* much.

Isabella grinned and glanced knowingly in his direction. "I don't think *we* are the ones who need to be concerned."

"What do you mean?"

Isabella sighed. "Have you learned nothing in all these years? What is our mother's main purpose in life?"

"Finishing her book?" Henry guessed. Their mother had been working on a collection of essays about Shakespeare's heroines for, well, forever.

"Yes, well, aside from that." Izzie waved a hand, brushing aside their mother's opus.

At his blank look, she gestured between herself and James, then held up her left hand, wriggling the finger encircled by her wedding band. How could he forget? Even more than finishing her book, his mother wanted to see all her children wed.

"The twins are a bit young for her matchmaking efforts. Lia and Genni are only twelve. Besides, they're more interested in books than boys."

"The twins are *fourteen,* and the books they're currently enthralled with are romantic tales. When they were over last week, Lia spent the better part of the visit rhapsodizing over one of the grooms at Weston Manor, and you know Genni will follow where Lia leads. Still, I think the twins are safe for now. Mama's current project is well past marriageable age."

Henry groaned. "Is she back to Miss Merriwether again?" His mother had a soft spot for that particular wallflower. "The chit has been out for at least five Seasons. She—"

Isabella stood and leaned over the table until her nose nearly touched his. "Not. Miss. Merriwether." She punctuated each word with a sharp jab to his chest. "You!"

"No." He tugged at his cravat, wondering if the temperature in the room had risen drastically in the past few minutes.

"Until the twins are out of the schoolroom," Isabella continued, confirming his fears, "you are the only child Mama has left to marry off. The real reason for this ball is so she can look over this Season's crop of debutantes with an eye to picking her future daughter-in-law."

"I'm too young to get married," Henry protested. "I still have wild oats to sow."

"If even half of what I hear is to be believed, you've already sown more than your fair share," his sister remarked dryly.

"Besides, I am only four months older than you," James reminded him, "and Izzie and I are about to celebrate our second anniversary. You're going to need a better argument than age to avoid the parson's mousetrap. There's no reason to avoid it, though. So long as you choose wisely—and I can't imagine your mother or sisters allowing you to do otherwise—I think you will find the wedded state most enjoyable."

"He certainly enjoys the bedded one," Isabella drawled. "Though I think all men—"

"Izzie, my darling, stop tormenting your brother. Will you see if the baby is awake? I'm sure Henry would like to see his niece."

"Very well," Isabella huffed, as she rose and headed for the door. "But there is to be no fighting while I am gone," she reiterated. "Just think how devastated Mama would be if Hal showed up to the ball with a black eye marring his pretty face."

Henry glowered at her back as she swept from the room. If Isabella was right—and he had learned that Weston women were nearly always right—his mother was intending to see him at the altar by the end of the Season.

CHAPTER TWO

Like all men, Hal wishes to be charge of his destiny. The trick lies in allowing him to maintain that fiction whilst guiding him in the desired direction. Should he meet the right woman, I do not imagine he will put up a great fight. Love has toppled far more determined bachelors than our prince. . . .
—from the Countess of Dunston to
her mother the Viscountess Weston

"Now that she's gone, tell me what's troubling you." James leaned forward, bracing his elbows on the table. "There's no use pretending otherwise. You haven't touched the food."

"I've lost my appetite. Hearing that your mother is single-mindedly pursuing the end to your bachelorhood has a way of doing that to a man."

"There was plenty of time for you to consume that entire plate of scones before Izzie brought that up."

Henry *had* actually considered the scones, but they looked a bit gray today . . . and lumpier than usual. Even so, he glared at his best friend, reached for a scone and shoved as much of it as possible into his mouth, an act he regretted as soon as he began trying to chew the damned thing. He had once eaten a handful of horse grain on a dare. That had been manna compared to this.

James hooted with laughter. "Perhaps," he said, once he had himself sufficiently under control, "I should have warned you. Our cook fell and twisted her ankle yesterday, and her assistant ran off last week with one of the footmen. We've had to resort to desperate measures in the kitchen."

Henry gulped his tea, hoping the crumbly mass in his mouth would congeal enough for him to swallow. Only by strength of will did he manage to choke down the foul mixture; it was only by even greater strength of stomach that he managed to keep it down.

"Whomever you found to replace your cook shouldn't be allowed anywhere near the kitchen," he grumbled.

"I prefer her in the bedchamber myself." James winked. "She's a comely wench."

Henry took a second to sort through the meaning of his friend's words, and then a wave of rage descended over him.

"You bastard!" he snarled, lunging at James.

"What are you—? Damn it, that hurt!" James protested as Henry hauled him out of his chair and landed a sharp jab to his side. James wrenched away and blocked the next blow, then snaked his leg around Henry's ankle. Henry tripped, staggered a few steps as he struggled to keep his balance and then lost the fight.

He didn't go down alone. One of the legs snapped off a spindly-legged side table when he landed on it the wrong way. Not that there was a right way to land on a table.

The pretty Wedgwood vase that had been on the table lay in pieces beside it, suggesting there wasn't a right way for pottery to land on the floor, either.

Isabella burst into the room and eyed the disarray. "Was I somehow unclear when I said there was to be no fighting?"

"Good God!" Henry exclaimed as he picked himself up off the floor. "You sound exactly like Mother."

James sighed and shook his head.

"I do *not*," she snapped, sounding more like their mother than ever.

A bark of laughter escaped from James.

As Isabella rounded on her husband, Henry grinned in anticipation. Unfortunately, she saw him and changed her course.

"I wouldn't smile just yet if I were you," his sister warned, planting herself in front of him with her hands at her hips. "I am certain this is your fault."

"He started it," Henry contended. "Damnation, Izzie, the— He is—" He grappled with how to tell his sister what he had just discovered. In most households in Mayfair, the tidings would hardly qualify as news. He had always found it distasteful, but a goodly number of men turned their attentions to the female staff. He suspected a fair number of wives were relieved their husbands did so . . . but Isabella wasn't going to be one of them.

"He's what, Hal?" she prompted.

He shook his head. "Given all you've been through, you don't deserve this, but it's only right you should know. James all but told me he's taking advantage of one of the maids."

"Oh, Christ," James muttered. "You misunder—"

"I did not misunderstand," Henry bit out. "I'll call him out for you, Izzie, or I'll hold him while you vent your spleen. I know the fire poker is one of your weapons of choice, but if you truly wish to punish him, force him to eat that plate of the girl's scones."

Isabella's eyes narrowed as she crossed her arms over her chest.

"You're being very calm about this," he blurted out, just as she demanded, "What's wrong with my scones?"

"*Your* scones?" Henry exclaimed. "Do you mean to say you were the one mucking about in the kitchen?"

"I told you it was a misunderstanding," James muttered, rubbing his side. "Damn it, Hal, will you get it through your thick skull already? I love your sister. I'm not going to be unfaithful, no matter how terrible her culinary skills. Oomph!" Isabella elbowed him in his other side. "Not that she's a terrible cook," he amended quickly. "I hope she makes scones for me every day."

As declarations of love went, this one was impressive, Henry had to admit. A man truly had to be in love to keep a woman around if she could not even produce basic sustenance. To offer to eat those scones again was nothing short of adoration. His sister apparently agreed, for she rewarded her husband with a quick kiss.

"Perhaps I overreacted," Henry admitted a bit sheepishly. "I have been a little out of sorts of late."

"Speaking of out of sorts," Isabella murmured as the high wail of a child's cry sounded from upstairs. "Can you refrain from destroying my home long enough for me to finish with the baby?"

James pulled Isabella close for quick hug. "We'll behave, love, I promise, and I'll replace what was broken."

"I shall write to Mr. Wedgwood about a replacement for the vase. As for the table . . ." She shook her head. "Apologies to Mr. Chippendale, but I never liked it much. The legs were positively spindly."

She turned to Henry. "May I offer a word of advice, Hal? I'm not certain our mother has the right of it this time. It's not a wife you need to find, but yourself." She rose up on her tiptoes to press a kiss to his cheek before giving him an impish grin. "And while you find yourself, Mama will find a wife for you."

Content that she'd had the final word, his sister swept from the room. He and James seated themselves, and silence grew in the space between them.

Finally, James ventured, "Come now, it won't be that bad. There are benefits to the married state. I know these virginal misses seem all milk-and-water, but wives are every bit as lusty as mistresses are, and even more possessive."

A strangled growl rose up in Henry's throat. "Please remember that your wife is my sister. I am not having this conversation with you."

"You and I have always discussed females—"

"That was before my sister became one of them, er, one we talked about. She's always been a female."

James's lips twitched. "That wasn't something I ever questioned, but your reassurances on the matter are comforting nonetheless." His expression turned earnest then. "I apologize if I said something amiss. I want everything between us to be easy, for us to be as we were, but I don't suppose we can be."

He knew James spoke the truth, but the truth was so damned unfair, he wanted to smash a dozen spindly-legged tables. Of all the men his sister could have married, why had Izzie gone and fallen in love with his best friend? He was happy for them, he really was, but that didn't mean he wasn't also feeling the tiniest bit sorry for himself. Still, that didn't excuse his little tantrum.

"I must apologize as well. My actions were unwarranted, and I—"

"Consider the incident forgotten."

Henry raked a hand through his hair and sighed. "I would my sister were so understanding."

"She might surprise you. The two of you have more in common than blond hair and blue eyes; you're both fiercely protective of those you love. Isabella understands that the reason for your outburst today was concern for her. She also knows the difficulty of letting go the past and rebuilding trust. For the moment, it's enough that Isabella trusts me with her heart, and I trust her with mine."

"I do trust you," Henry said, surprised by his friend's words, "but sometimes my brain is a bit slower to react than my body. I never thought I would say Isabella was right about something, but ever since your marriage, perhaps even before then, I've been at a loose end. You and my father have families and estates; there are people dependent on you. That sort of responsibility gives direction to a man's life, keeps his feet on the ground."

"Let me be certain I understand you correctly. You *want* responsibilities?"

Henry scowled. "You needn't sound so shocked."

"Sorry, Hal, but you must admit this is a change for you. Your idea of the perfect day is to sleep in, spend the remainder of the morning at Jackson's, pass the afternoon at Tattersall's, put in an appearance at some respectable *ton* event, and then enjoy being disrespectable until the early hours."

"Is that all you think I am capable of being—some sort of self-absorbed sybarite?" His voice rose sharply on the last word.

"Of course I think you are capable of doing, of being more than that. I realized it a long time ago. I didn't realize you wanted more. It's horribly selfish, but part of me hoped you would always be *Hal*. That you wouldn't . . ."

"Grow up?" Henry gave a short, humorless laugh. "I think we all have to do it at some point, but I'm hardly about to take my vows."

"That would be rather drastic," James agreed. "This may take some getting used to, this idea of Hal Weston as a serious adult, but I daresay we'll all adjust. Have you considered what you want to do?"

Henry drew in a deep breath. "I want my own stud."

His guts twisted as he waited for his best friend's reaction. If James didn't believe he could do this, what chance did he have of succeeding?

After a moment, James's face split into a wide grin. "That's a damned fine notion. You have as good an eye for horseflesh as Old Tatt had, rest his soul, and the bloody beasts respond to you as well as to any Gypsy. This is ingenious, Hal! Who came up with this idea?"

"If you can believe it, I did," Henry said, but his words lacked heat. Over the years, Henry had more than justified James's insinuations about his intelligence, or lack thereof. What Henry truly cared about was James's enthusiasm for the stud, which he had in abundance. As his friend's energy washed over him, Henry jumped to his feet and began to pace about the room, skirting the wreckage of his earlier outburst.

That, if nothing else, proved how badly he needed this. For some time now, he'd been drifting along; while he wasn't unhappy, neither was he particularly happy. He simply was. And he wanted more than that. His life had become a monotonous stream of excitements that had long since ceased to excite him. The mere thought of the stud invigorated him more than all of the debaucheries he'd committed in the past three months combined.

"I've already found the perfect place," he told James. "Do you remember the Ravensfield stud?"

"How could I forget? Our first year at Oxford and, instead of studying, you dragged a group of us to Epsom for the Oaks. Then you wanted a souvenir, and we had to visit every breeder in the vicinity. I recollect Lord Parr was somehow involved."

"His younger son, Jack, was the owner."

"Was?"

"You must have been in Ireland when it happened. He was in the wrong place at the wrong time, and he took a kick to the head that killed him. It wasn't the horse's fault. He was a good racer, but Parr said he was too dangerous to live." Henry shook his head in disgust. "In any event, Jack's widow and daughter went to live with Parr. The old man sold off all the stock and closed the place up. For whatever reason, he's kept it all these years." He shrugged. "Perhaps Fate was lending her hand."

Fate. The notion had crossed his mind more than once since partnering with Parr's heir in a game of whist one evening at White's. The man had been in his cups, which neither helped him at cards nor impaired his ability to talk . . . and talk . . . and talk. And when he began to express his frustration at trying to convince his father to part with Ravensfield Hall, Henry had listened.

He'd remembered the place, and he'd remembered, too, a dream that had grown in his heart between boyhood and becoming a man. He had discarded most things from that in-between time in his life, forgotten them or buried them away out of embarrassment, but now he began to dream once more of neatly fenced paddocks and airy stable blocks housing the finest horseflesh in England. His heart raced at the possibilities spread before him like endless acres of fresh green grass. . . .

"Fate?" James arched one dark brow. "Perhaps the property is entailed."

"It isn't and, from what I gather, neither Parr nor his heir has any interest in horses. Parr is holding on to the place out of sentiment. He'd do better to let go of the past and look to the living. His granddaughter is making her come-out next year; the money Parr could get from selling the estate might go toward her dowry."

"An excellent idea," James agreed. "Of course, if he were out to catch the future Viscount Weston for the girl, he could always offer the estate *as* her dowry."

"Bite your tongue! My interest is in bridles, not brides."

"Are you certain?" Isabella asked as she entered the room, her daughter, Bride, in her arms. "Would you like to hold your niece?"

She didn't wait for a response, just pushed the little one into his arms. Henry took her easily, bade his perfectly tied cravat farewell, and wished his waistcoat buttons luck. Despite her very tender age, Lady Bride Sheffield was winning handily in the ongoing war she had waged upon her uncle's vestments.

Henry gazed down into a pair of thickly lashed blue eyes, the same shade of blue as his own, and simply marveled. "She is more beautiful every time I see her."

"She *is* pretty, isn't she?" remarked James.

"She's perfect," Henry declared.

Isabella laughed. "Not in the middle of the night when she screams loud enough to wake the whole house, she isn't. Someday you will understand."

Henry grimaced. "*Someday* is an agreeable thought."

"For you, perhaps. For Mama, tomorrow would not be soon enough."

"Mama!" Bride shrieked, triumphantly waving one of Henry's waistcoat buttons.

"Oh, dear." Isabella fought a smile. "James, will you—"

Even as she spoke the words, James was out of his seat, lifting Bride from Henry's arms and taking her to Isabella. While Isabella held the squirming child, James pried the button from her tiny fist. Bride was *not* happy about the forceful removal of her prize, which she had fairly won, and she made her displeasure known. Loudly.

James sighed. "The price of visiting," he said, handing the button back to Henry.

Henry laughed and got to his feet. "Well worth it, but I won't trespass on your hospitality any longer." He hugged Isabella and kissed the top of Bride's head. "I have some business in Surrey that will occupy me for a few days, so I doubt I'll see you before Mother's ball next week."

She wished him a safe trip, and then James walked him to the entrance hall. Henry looked at his best friend. "Do you believe I can really do this? The stud, I mean."

"Of course you can." James clapped him on the back. "Provided you can come up with the blunt."

Henry winced, partly because he was feeling the effects of his tussle with that damned table, but mostly because James was right. The stud would be a costly venture, more than he could fund on his own.

"I don't suppose you would consider a loan?"

"And make this easy on you?" James laughed and shook his head. "Not a chance, old friend. Not a chance."

CHAPTER THREE

Had I prevailed upon you to return my missives from Seasons past, my letter writing now would be wonderfully uncomplicated. I should simply send them back to you, perhaps with a few names scratched out and new ones scribbled betwixt the lines. The date must change as well, but that is all. You do not care for gossip any more than I do, and my little world shall go on this Season just the same as the year before, and the year before that, and the year before that....

—from Diana Merriwether to
her brother Alexander Merriwether

"Do try to smile, Diana."

Miss Diana Merriwether gave no indication of having heard her mother's hushed admonition, but she curved her lips into what she hoped would pass as a smile. She had been to enough balls to know that effusive smiling so early in the evening would have her cheeks aching by the time she sat down to supper.

"Much better," Lady Linnet whispered approvingly, delicately fluttering her fan before her face to mask their conversation. Diana was tempted to grab the fan out of her mother's hand and put it to good use. There were at least two hundred people packed into a space comfortably able to hold half that number and, as always, the dowagers had chosen to hold court as far away as possible from any source of fresh air.

Where those grand dames went, other respectable chaperones followed, and with them, their charges: dreamy-eyed debutantes, woebegone wallflowers, and soon-to-be-spinsters. Diana had passed through those ranks over the years. She wasn't sure exactly when she had advanced from wall-flower to soon-to-be-spinster, but surely anyone who was in her seventh Season had passed into the realm of imminent spinsterhood.

"You have a lovely smile, my dear," her mother said, patting Diana's shoulder with her free hand. "I only wish you showed it to the world a bit more often."

Diana nodded absently, shifting in her seat as strains of the musicians tuning their instruments drifted in from an adjoining room. Liveried footmen bearing silver trays laden with fluted glasses of champagne expertly navigated the crowded room. Diana accepted the glass pressed into her hand, relishing the slight chill that seeped through her glove.

The ballroom was uncomfortably warm, but she expected that tonight. No one lucky enough to receive an invitation would willingly forgo this ball. Lord and Lady Weston's enduring popularity aside, this particular evening boasted three of the *ton*'s most talked-about gentlemen, all of whom were currently making their way to the head of the room where their hosts waited.

The Earl of Dunston was married to the Westons' eldest daughter. He'd been all the rage since the gossip papers had reported about how he had secretly joined the navy and been wounded in battle. Rumor had it that Lord Nelson had personally commended Lord Dunston on his patriotism. His wife was one of those women who was so beautiful that Diana wanted to despise her but couldn't, since Isabella had always been kind and friendly when she and Diana had chanced to meet. She was radiant tonight, standing between her handsome husband and her younger sister, Olivia.

Olivia's husband, the Marquess of Sheldon, was another of the evening's honored men. As the widower had lived in near isolation until their marriage a year ago, the *ton* had been abuzz with the romantic tale. Watching Lord Sheldon smiling down at his petite wife, his arm around her shoulders, Diana knew without a doubt that they were very much in love.

Near his sisters and parents was the third man of note. Of the three, he was the only one who remained single. He was also the only one who made Diana's heart race like a filly in the final stretch of the Derby.

Henry Weston.

Tall, handsome, and heir to a viscountcy, he was the *ton*'s favorite rogue.

Lord Weston held up a hand. A muted rumble moved through the sea of guests as everyone hushed each other. The viscount waited until the room was silent, or as quiet as a room packed with gossiping aristocrats was likely to get.

"Dear friends, my wife and I would like to welcome you to our home and thank you for being with us on this happy occasion. The last time we hosted a ball here was for Isabella's come-out. Tonight we present our daughter unto you again, along with her husband, the Earl of Dunston. They recently celebrated their second anniversary."

Cheers and good wishes rang out. Again, Lord Weston waited until the crowd quieted. "A year ago this month, in the beautiful chapel at Weston Manor, we welcomed another son-in-law into our family. The Marquess of Sheldon wisely captured the heart and the hand of our daughter, Olivia, before the scoundrels here in London had a chance."

A handful of boos burst forth, and the crowd laughed. "To add to our blessings," the viscount continued, "we have rejoiced in the births of two beautiful, healthy granddaughters." He raised his glass. "Now, please join me in a toast. To love, happiness, and family!"

"To love, happiness, and family!" The refrain echoed loudly through the room as the guests lifted their glasses.

The words stuck in Diana's throat. In her experience, the three words did not go together. She raised her glass to her lips and let the chilled wine slide down her throat, noting that her mother hadn't repeated the toast either.

There was a great shuffling of bodies as the crowd redistributed to clear the center of the room. A number of the guests, with the ratio leaning heavily in favor of the men, cleared the room entirely, heading off to play cards or admire the rest of the house. Once everyone settled, Lord and Lady Weston took the floor, followed by their daughters and their husbands, and the musicians began to play. After the couples had progressed through a set of figures, others began to join in the dancing. In response, those left lining the walls of the room shifted their attention from those currently dancing to the task of locating a partner for the following dance.

No one came looking for her, but that was hardly surprising as Diana considered herself something of an expert on the art of hiding. She hid her boredom at sitting with the doting mamas and dotty dowagers. She hid her pain and anger when she overheard the whispers about her parents. She hid her loneliness, schooling her face into a polite expression as the dazzling diamonds and dainty debutantes around her were asked to dance.

Diana knew she didn't measure up—her red hair, hazel eyes, and freckled complexion were far from the current standards of beauty; or rather, she measured too far up, because she towered over many of her prospective dance partners. But when Henry Weston came looking for her, even if it was because his mother forced him, Diana had difficulty remembering why she wanted to hide in the first place. That was a problem. A big problem.

And she did mean *big*. He made Diana feel tiny in comparison, which was no mean feat. Everyone knew that he put in a goodly number of hours in the ring at Jackson's Salon, and she—along with the rest of her sex—was most appreciative of the results. His excellently tailored black tailcoat and knee breeches displayed his impressive physique to perfection. She could easily see him as a barbarian leader of old, ruthlessly invading foreign lands and victoriously claiming the spoils.

Why she found this thrilling, she could not say. He wasn't going to be plundering her, after all. Nor did she want plundering. And she did not spend a great deal of time in contemplation of Henry Weston's pugilistic pursuits, because that would be exceedingly improper. And she certainly never considered what he might wear—or not—when he boxed.

Very well, it was possible her mind wandered those forbidden paths—and her eyes traced the definition of those impossibly broad shoulders—on a regular basis. She couldn't help herself. The man drew female attention like lit candles called moths. He reminded her of Apollo, with his golden hair, strength, and vitality. He looked the part tonight, with the candlelight gilding his fair hair, but everyone knew he had more of the devil in him than of any god.

Seduction stamped the hard angles of his cheekbones. Temptation marked the square set of his jaw. Desire defined the curve of his lips. When those lips parted in that charming, slightly crooked smile of his, Diana knew it was only natural to feel the bottom of her stomach drop away and hear her mother calling her name. . . .

No, the bit about her mother wasn't right.

"Diana!"

Her mother's sharp rebuke finally penetrated Diana's mental wanderings. She snapped to attention to discover the man himself standing before her as though her thoughts had somehow drawn him over. Diana felt her cheeks heat, which only served to further her embarrassment as pink cheeks clashed horribly with red hair—a vicious cycle, really.

She scrambled to stand and nearly tripped. Her mother, who had risen as gracefully as she did everything else, shot her a worried frown. Diana risked a sideways glance at her grandmother. The Duchess of Lansdowne did not look pleased. This wasn't unusual, but she usually attempted a more neutral expression in public.

"Good evening, Your Grace. Lady Linnet." He bowed. "Miss Merriwether, will you do me the honor of a dance?"

"Thank you, Mr. Weston." She dropped a flawless curtsy that she hoped made up for a bit of her prior clumsiness. "I would like that very much."

They walked toward the lines that had formed for a country-dance, and Henry led her to the top, where Lord and Lady Dunston stood. They made space so she and Henry were the second couple in line, which made her uneasy. She wasn't concerned about her dancing abilities; her grandmother had insisted she have a dancing master, so she knew she could acquit herself passably on that account.

Even so, she didn't like to place herself at the center of attention. From the moment she'd made her debut, Society had been waiting for her to follow in her mother's footsteps. Though Diana was *not* sorry to disappoint them, she had no thought of running off and marrying the stable master. Not, she reflected, that her grandfather's stable master, or any other man, wanted to run off with *her*.

When she'd first come out, she'd had some suitors. Though her looks weren't fashionable, and though she stood under the cloud of her parents' scandal, there were men willing to overlook those failings for a generous dowry and ducal connections. Most of those men hadn't come up to her grandmother's rigorous standards. The duchess deemed any suitors flush in the pockets but lacking titles, upstarts. Men with good breeding and no money were, of course, fortune hunters.

Those few men who had met with her grandmother's approval had not suited Diana. Though she did not seek a love match, she didn't want a husband, whatever his wealth or title, with one foot in the grave, or a fondness for drink, or a penchant for heavy gambling, all qualities of the men the duchess had proposed as suitable candidates. Their battle of wills had continued through her second Season.

They might have compromised in Diana's third Season, but both her grandparents took ill and the doctor advised their family to remain at Halswelle Hall, her grandfather's country estate. The following year, Diana had discovered that men had little interest in a girl in her fourth Season, no matter her dowry or relations. After three Seasons, there was an understanding that a girl hadn't "taken," or was disinclined to marry, and she would no longer have to suffer the constant round of balls, masquerades, Venetian breakfasts, and musicales expected of a young lady single-mindedly fixed on matrimony.

The Duchess of Lansdowne did not ascribe to this understanding. Her desire to see Diana wed increased with each passing year, which meant she forced Diana to attend every possible event where she might encounter a prospective husband. When Parliament finally called a recess and the *ton* departed London for their country estates, Diana was as unattached as ever and utterly exhausted.

She promised herself that this would be the last year. She would rather spend eternity leading apes in hell than spend another Season hunting for a husband. The apes might even be preferable. Supposedly, *they* could be trained.

The dance wasn't complicated, and her attention strayed to Lord and Lady Dunston. Love was evident in every look they shared. Passion was almost palpable in the air between them. Diana thought them either very brave or very foolhardy, perhaps a bit of both. The more one had, the more one had to lose.

"So grim," Henry murmured as he turned her. "The other women will refuse to dance with me if you make it look so unpleasant."

His words amused her, and she was grateful for the distraction from her dark thoughts. "Every woman in this room hopes to dance with you."

"You flatter me," he said. "Surely, as a gentleman, that is my responsibility."

She shook her head. "We both know your mother has given you enough gentlemanly responsibility where I am concerned."

He recovered himself quickly, but she could tell she'd surprised him. She'd surprised herself. If there was one thing she had learned in all her Seasons, it was that pretense was everything. Society would cease to function without the pretty lies that passed for polite manners.

"Miss Merriwether—"

"I was not taking you to task, Mr. Weston," she said softly. "I only meant that, with me, you need not exert yourself to be charming. I am grateful enough for the opportunity to dance."

No further words passed between them for the remainder of the dance. As he escorted her back to her mother and grandmother, Diana wondered if he would defy his mother and refuse to stand up with her again. That would certainly limit her opportunities for dancing this Season.

Henry paused a few feet from their destination. She glanced at him, noted the solemn expression on his face and braced herself not to react to whatever he had to say.

"I have already danced with you this evening for my mother's benefit," he acknowledged, "so when I ask you to dance again, it will be solely of my own accord."

Then he smiled at her. Not his practiced heart-melting, knee-weakening smile. Not his slightly crooked grin that was at once boyish and wicked. This was a genuine smile, crinkling the corners of his eyes and revealing white, even teeth. This smile put the others to shame.

"Miss Merriwether, will you save me a dance after supper?"

Perhaps she ought to refuse and suggest he save that dance for some other lonely wallflower, but Diana wasn't that selfless. If she had to suffer through this Season, she wanted to pretend for a night—just one night—that she was the sort of girl Henry Weston wanted to dance with twice in an evening.

She smiled back at him. Not the smile of polite disinterest she used to keep the world at arm's length, but a true smile.

"I will," she promised, as they took the remaining steps to where her grandmother was holding court.

"Until later, Miss Merriwether." Henry bowed, his blue eyes twinkling up at her as he gave her gloved hand a quick squeeze.

She managed a curtsy despite knees that felt distressingly weak, then seated herself beside her mother and watched as he walked off. A thrill raced through her at the knowledge that tonight he would be back.

For her.

That was when Diana knew she was in trouble . . . or she would be, but for one thing. She didn't intend to lose her heart, least of all to a rogue.

CHAPTER FOUR

I feared the stable block would not live up to my memory, but I am exceedingly pleased. To be sure, the paddocks and hovels need mending and painting, and there are more repairs wanted inside, but the quadrangle's plans are superior in every way. Though the design is not new, it is unusually forward thinking. The stalls receive plenty of light and air, and there are a number of spacious loose boxes, perfect for birthing or housing the injured. I was unable to keep from smiling as I looked about the place. I am certain I looked quite the fool...
—from Henry Weston to
his brother-in-law the Earl of Dunston

After returning Miss Merriwether to her family, Henry danced with two more women of the variety found in his mother's garden of wallflowers and shrinking violets. Considering his duty done for the night, he decided to escape until supper. He beat a gradual retreat from the ballroom and headed to his old chamber; his parents had made the room into an informal family parlor after Henry had moved to his bachelor's quarters.

As the room wasn't part of the suite of public rooms on display to the guests, Henry collected a candle as he made his way from the brightly lit spectacle on one side of the house to the quiet privacy of the family quarters. He relaxed with each step away from the grating buzz of too many voices whispering *on dits,* from the distinct aroma of mingled perfumes and overly warm bodies.

He was a social creature by nature, and he enjoyed the company and amusements that town life offered, but he found it trying at times. Of late, he was more often unimpressed. He had the sense that his life was a series of installments, as in the novels his sister Olivia devoured. He knew there was more than what he had at present, but he wasn't sure of the plot's direction. He had waited, partly because he was certain the next chapters would present themselves in time, and partly because he was comfortable with the story. Perhaps he felt a little caged at times, but better that than the unknown, which might be worse.

Waiting hadn't offered any answers, though, and he wasn't sure it ever would. He had put a good face on, but maintaining that pretense was growing increasingly difficult. He had always considered himself even-tempered and, for years, he had boxed for the pleasure of the sport. These days his temper lurked just beneath the surface, and he boxed to give voice to the restlessness and frustration growing within him.

He recalled the stricken expression that had crossed Miss Merriwether's face as they danced. She was generally very composed in her demeanor—a little too much so—but tonight she had temporarily lost control of herself. He had seen her inner turmoil and recognized so many of the emotions he had struggled with over the past couple of years: the loneliness, the worry, the dissatisfaction, the exhaustion . . .

All had been writ large on surprisingly expressive features, and her distress struck a chord with him. For a moment, he'd been certain that this woman understood how he felt, would understand *him*. The thought should have been comforting, but he found it unsettling. Unsettling and undeniably intriguing.

She'd reined herself in quickly but, having caught a glimpse of what lurked beneath that poised façade, Henry suspected Miss Merriwether was a woman who felt deeply. Intensely. *Passionately.* The thought was almost enough to make him wonder if that passion would carry over into . . .

No. Christ, what was wrong with him? Miss Merriwether was . . . *Miss Merriwether*. He didn't think of her that way. He reprimanded himself until he reached his destination. Upon opening the door, he found he wasn't the only one who sought refuge there. At least he wouldn't be alone with his strange thoughts.

"Rather unsporting to desert your guests, sir."

His father laughed. "Were you sent to find me, or have you turned tail as well?"

Henry blew out his candle before seating himself opposite his father at the large, round mahogany table that dominated the room. "I wasn't sent to find you," he said, setting his candlestick down.

"I am most relieved to hear it. I shall rejoin the fray presently, but a temporary escape was necessary. I believe it's also considered unsporting to strangle one's guests?"

"Indubitably," Henry told him. "I very much doubt they'd ever accept another of your invitations."

"Or anyone else's. Death does tend to limit a person's social engagements. However, as I intend to refrain from all murderous impulses this evening, let us speak on another, more lively matter. I read your proposal for the stud."

Henry's nerves stretched tight. Following his discussion with James, he'd visited Ravensfield Hall. Near Great Bookham in Surrey, the stud sat only twenty miles or so south of London, which would allow him to conduct regular business in the city. As the estate was only a handful of miles from Epsom—one of England's racing capitals—he'd have a steady influx of clients. Each June, everyone interested in horses and racing made their way to the area for the Oaks and the Derby.

Plum location aside, the manor house itself gave him a moment of pause. Parr had closed up the house, but the buff-colored brick building bore signs of neglect and disrepair; ivy snaked up the walls, and where there had once been rose beds along the perimeter of the house, only dried, prickly clumps remained. If a steward were overseeing the place, the man wasn't earning his wages.

Another look at the stables convinced Henry that the house—and whatever renovations and refurbishments it might require—wasn't important. He could almost hear the pounding hooves echoing in the covered riding house, and the whinnies and neighs as the stable lads brought round buckets of oats. With nary a doubt in his mind, he had ridden back to London and compiled his ideas regarding the stud into a proposal for a business venture, which he gave to his father.

As the heir to the viscountcy, Henry was in the somewhat uncomfortable position of needing his sire's financial support. He received a generous quarterly allowance, much of which had been successfully invested on the Change, which allowed him to live in a comfortable manner. Purchasing the stud and quality stock, not to mention the additional money for building, repairs, and dozens of other smaller concerns, would require a sum far greater than he had at hand.

"Your proposal impressed me, Hal," his father said slowly, "and I cannot deny that your mother and I are pleased to see you displaying an interest of a more serious nature, but perhaps you ought to approach this slowly. You might spend a year or two working out of the Manor to be certain you truly enjoy the business."

Henry's gut clenched as he felt Ravensfield begin to slip from his fingers. "Please, sir, I realize the sum I am requesting is not inconsequential, but I will have earned back the money and more within a few years."

"Hal," his father began.

"I remember, when I was a boy, you told me that I could do anything I put my mind to. I *know* I can make the stud a success."

"I don't doubt your ability." His father sighed. "Do you recall that shortly after I told you that, you decided that your greatest ambition was to be an artist? I hired Mr. Edwards from London to come tutor you. After less than a fortnight, you sent him packing. He never even started work on the mural for the library ceiling."

Henry scowled. "The man was an idiot, and an indifferent artist."

"You do realize he is a member of the Royal Academy?" said his sire.

"That hardly precludes idiocy. He expected me to sit indoors and draw drapery all day long. *Drapery!* I never so much as saw a paintbrush, let alone a box of paints."

"Practice is generally a component of training. You imagined you had only to put brush to canvas and produce a masterpiece. You didn't want to spend the time on drawing lessons."

"I would have spent the time, but it was apparent, even to me, that I have no inherent artistic talent. When I showed you and Mother some of my drapery studies, she sighed and said something to you about my duckies being handsome." He shook his head. "There were no ducks in the drapes I was drawing."

"Hal, she said—" His lips twitched. "Never mind it. So you're not an artist. What about your music lessons? You asked to learn to play the violin. I persuaded Herr Cramer that teaching would be more fulfilling than performing for their majesties. That lasted all of a month."

"You can't blame me for not being able to tell one note from another. I was willing to keep trying. Herr Cramer was the one who threw up his hands and left."

"After you broke his bow, and your own, using them to fence with James," came the parental protest.

"I still maintain the fencing was James's idea."

His father rubbed at his temples. "What about all the letters I received from Headmaster Davies at Eton, or when you were sent down from Oxford? The only way you applied yourself in school was in finding opportunities for mischief."

"I prefer to think of my extracurricular activities as creative endeavors."

His sire sighed and got to his feet. "My point is that you have a history of giving up when something doesn't come easily to you. Naturally, you can understand my reluctance to hand over a large sum of money for you to invest. What if some difficulty arises? How can I be certain you won't turn your back on the project and hie yourself back to town and your, ah, creative endeavors?"

"I need to do this. I'm *meant* to do this."

"But you believed you were meant to be an artist and a musician and any other number of things, too. I know how grand this all seems in your head, but a great deal of time and hard work are required on your part. I don't doubt that you're capable of putting forth both. However,

I can't help but worry whether your desire will subside after the initial excitement is past."

Henry gripped the arms of the chair and took a deep, steadying breath. "I know I can do this, and I'm not going to give up on it. I understand how much work will be required of me, and I look forward to the challenge. I hoped my proposal would show you I've changed, but you appear determined to think the worst of me."

His father walked over to him and laid a hand on his shoulder. "I don't think the worst of you, Hal. You're a fine young man, and any father would be lucky to have you for a son. That doesn't mean I am blind to your faults. Still, I found your proposal impressive, and I certainly can't deny your abilities with horses."

The tightness in Henry's chest eased a mite. Cautiously, he asked, "Is this your circuitous way of telling me that you're not going to be tightfisted with the purse strings?"

"I'm afraid not, but I've spoken with Lord Parr, and I'll counter your proposal with one of my own."

"You spoke with Parr? When was this? Is he willing to sell to me?" Henry shot out of his chair as he fired off the questions in a single breath.

His father's lips twitched. "Yes, the night before last at the Standish musicale, and possibly."

"At least he is considering the notion. I hope you offered a fair price."

His father began to fiddle with his watch chain. "I do not think Parr is considering the money so much as he is considering *you*."

"What do you mean by that?"

"Parr has, as you know, a strong sentiment for Ravensfield, largely because his son loved the place. He knows there is little sense in holding on to the property, and he likes the idea of keeping his son's memory alive. I am afraid he has seen your name once too often in the gossip rags, and he is concerned that Ravensfield will become a . . . What did he call it? Oh, yes, 'a place of licentious revelry where young men cohabitate with women of loose morals and engage in all manner of sin.' His words, not mine."

Henry gaped at his sire. "I . . . But . . ." He began to pace across the room, then suddenly stopped, turned back and demanded, "Do you mean to tell me Parr believes I will turn the place into some sort of brothel?"

A choked laugh escaped his father. "A brothel? Heavens, no. A den of vice, perhaps—"

"I am glad you find this amusing," Henry said tightly.

His father's face grew serious. "I beg your pardon. I should not have made light of something so important to you. I will be frank: Parr is willing to sell the estate on the condition that the buyer is a respectable gentleman who will run the place in a respectable manner. I have convinced him to give you until the end of the Season to prove your worthiness.

"As to funding this venture, use these upcoming months to approach potential investors. You are well-known and well-liked; I am certain you can find men willing to fund you in exchange for a share of the profits or for breeding privileges. If you can raise half of the money you need to purchase the stud and your starting stock, I will gladly give you the rest and cover whatever other expenditures arise."

Henry nodded. "If investors will convince you of my commitment, I don't think I'll have too much difficulty there. Ravensfield is perfect, Father. If you see it, you will understand."

"I believe you, but if I simply give you the money, Parr's opinion of you will not change. Once he sees you have turned respectable, or at least discreet, and have the trust of well-connected men, his concerns will vanish. I am certain the old man will soon feel foolish to have ever doubted you."

"Thank you, sir. I will not disappoint you."

"You have never disappointed me, Hal. You have worried me at times and given me and your mother some sleepless nights, but I have always been immensely proud to call you my son."

As his father spoke, a lump began in Henry's throat and grew until it threatened to choke him. He suspected any attempts at speech would come out sounding like a croak, so he opted to cross the room and hug his father instead.

"Enough. You will break my ribs, boy. Come. We had best get

back to the ball before your mother sets the servants to looking for us." He paused for a moment, eyeing Henry up and down, and then shook his head. "Sometimes I wonder from whence you sprung."

"Mother has told me on more than one occasion that I am my father's son, so you should not have to look far," Henry said as he relit his candle, and then blew out the tapers in the candelabra on the table. A quick glance at the fire assured him it would keep until one of the servants banked it for the night.

"I've always known where I came from," Henry murmured as he opened the door and stepped past his father into the hall. "It's where I am going that took some time to figure out."

"What are you mumbling about?"

Henry cast a glance over his shoulder. "Nothing of any import."

"Go on, then. I will be right behind you."

The words eased something in Henry. Although his sire only spoke of walking through the town house, Henry knew his family would stand by him in whatever he attempted. He was, he thought, a very lucky man.

And then he saw his mother waiting for them at the door to the drawing room.

"Do you know what time it is?" she hissed at them. "Supper should have started five minutes ago. We have two groups sitting down. Livvy and Sheldon will sit with the first, and Izzie and James will take the second. Both of you"—she pointed a menacing finger first at Henry and then at her husband—"will sit with the first group. When you are not eating, I expect you to be circulating amongst the guests, not hiding on the other side of the house. Do not look so dumbfounded. We have been married for thirty years, Oliver. I know you better than you know yourself. Now please, go in so the guests can line up and go down to dinner. I will send Hal along in a moment, but first I want a quick word with him."

"Yes, dear." His father winked at him. "Remember those words, son. They are the secret to a lasting marriage." He bussed his wife's cheek and headed into the drawing room.

"Impossible man," his mother muttered, gazing after him

fondly. She turned back to Henry. "As for you, you have rather surprised me."

Henry raked a hand through his hair. "I am quite capable of asking Miss Merriwether to dance without your constant reminding."

"Of course you are, dearest." Her eyes sparkled. "I was referring to your interest in starting the stud."

"Oh," he said weakly, the wind not so much leaving his sails as entirely changing direction.

"A mother cannot help but fret about her children and wish to solve their problems. For some reason, you have not been happy, and I have not known how to help. There is a sense of purpose about you now, as if you have found yourself and finally know which direction to go."

"My life is up in the air, and yet I feel more grounded than I have in years." He put his arms around her. "I regret that I caused you to worry. You should have spoken to me."

She laughed up at him. "You are my *son,* Hal. You have but one purpose in life, and that is to worry me."

"I am sorry for it, all the same."

"I can think of some way for you to make it up to me if you like," she suggested, reaching up to adjust his cravat. "For instance, I was very pleased to see you dancing with Miss Merriwether tonight. As you noted earlier, I did not have to remind you of your gentlemanly duty to dance with the less popular girls as well as the pretty ones."

"Interesting," Henry mused, "how often Miss Merriwether's name comes up in these delightful little conversations of ours."

"I freely admit to being fond of her," his mother said, her look daring him to oppose her, "and you make such a striking couple, what with both of you so tall. You need not slouch when you dance with her, and you know how I despise poor posture. Then there is that glorious hair of hers. . . ."

"Glorious?" Henry's lips twitched. "It's red."

His mother gave a despairing sigh. "It is no surprise you did not take to painting. You clearly lack an artist's appreciation for true beauty."

He frowned. "I thought you *liked* my ducks."

"Your what?"

"My ducks. When I showed you and Father my drapery studies, you told him my duckies were handsome."

She stared at him for a long moment, clearly puzzled, and then she began to laugh. "I said it was *lucky* that *you* were handsome. A mother does not like to speak poorly of her child, but there was nothing redeeming—or recognizable—in any of your drawings. I think you took years off poor Mr. Edwards's life. You were such a trial to him."

"I tried my best," he joked.

"Not then," she said softly. "I do not mean to imply that you are averse to hard work, but our family has been very blessed. Your father and I did not deliberately spoil our children, but you have never had to fight for something you want. Perhaps it is because you are the eldest, but you hold back. I think you doubt yourself, but you must remember what Lucio tells Isabella in *Measure for Measure*."

He looked at her blankly.

"He says, 'Our doubts are traitors and make us lose the good we oft might win by fearing to attempt.' You fear failure, Hal, and you believe that if you do not try, you cannot fail. The truth is that if you do not try, you cannot succeed. So long as you try your best, as long as you fight for what you want, you could never be anything other than a great success in my eyes. I hope you know that, for all you try my nerves, I love you very much."

"I love you, too." Then, because the atmosphere had grown so serious and theirs was a family of laughter, he said, "I think you forget how devoted I am to certain activities. There is one in particular where I know I have never held back. Some may call my appetite sinful, even greedy, but I—"

"That is enough! I will not have such improper talk in my house."

"Mother!" Henry tried to sound shocked. "You cannot think I meant anything other than eating?"

Her eyes narrowed. "When you decide to marry, do not have a long engagement. You do not want to give a prospective bride time to realize how bothersome you truly are. Now, go and sit down to supper."

As Henry moved to go, he heard her mumbling something about him being his father's son. He bit his lip to keep from laughing, relieved she couldn't see his face and just . . . relieved. Change was good, but a man needed to have stability too. There was comfort in knowing some things would always stay the same.

Like his parents.

And handsome ducks.

He was a lucky man, indeed.

CHAPTER FIVE

I am convinced what transpired this evening must have been a dream. Miss Merriwether stood up twice with Mr. Weston, who is every bit as dashing as you would think from the gossip columns. He did not dance at all with Miss Hill, who is just as much the catch this Season that she was last! As if that were not wondrous enough, my dearest Lucy— Oh, I hesitate to put down what happened to me on paper for fear I will wake at any moment now . . .

—from Elizabeth Fothergill to
her sister Lucinda Fothergill

"I'm not certain this is a wise decision," Diana murmured as Henry claimed her for their second dance of the evening. "You shouldn't dance twice with me when there are so many other women with whom you have not danced at all. It isn't proper."

Henry chuckled, a deep, rich sound that warmed her even as it sent a shiver of feminine awareness through her body.

"I begin to understand my mother's fondness for you, Miss Merriwether. While I am much obliged for your concern, I very much doubt anyone here expects propriety from me."

"Even when you act outrageously, the *ton* still dotes on you," she agreed, "but we are not all so fortunate as to be universally admired. By singling me out in this manner, you will earn me the enmity of three-quarters of the women in this room. It won't matter to them that you have no real interest in me."

Blond brows drew together like gathering storm clouds. "Perhaps you will be so good as to tell me what you mean by that," he said as they joined three other couples for a cotillion.

As though he didn't know.

"Humor me," he drawled, lips quirking, and she realized she'd spoken aloud.

She regarded him a moment, trying to determine if he were serious, but she couldn't tell. Her own lips twitched. "Far be it from me to deny you further flattery, Mr. Weston." She saw her words took him by surprise, but she shook her head when he would have spoken.

"I can tell you what all of the women in this room are thinking at this moment, watching us together," she said, pitching her voice so she wouldn't be overheard. "Your sisters and both of our mothers are confused. My grandmother and Miss Fothergill, I think, are pleased. I don't think Mrs. Ellison or Lady Kilpatrick care; the former has eyes for no one but her husband, and the latter dislikes your entire sex. Every other woman here, whatever her age or marital status, is irritated that I am standing here because she would like to be in my place. If not, she would at least prefer to have been passed over for a diamond like Miss Hill."

He couldn't have looked more shocked if she'd just told him the sun rose in the west. Then again, she'd never spoken so many words to him before, and certainly not in so free a manner. The sun rising in the west might have come as less of a surprise.

The musicians began to play then, and the opening steps of the dance gave them no further opportunity for private conversation. Her reprieve was short-lived, however, because as soon as they began to promenade about, arm in arm, Henry tilted his head toward hers and whispered, "I hardly think my company is as prized as you seem to believe, Miss Merriwether, but my vanity thanks you all the same. I must correct you on one point, though. I am certain my mother is also pleased."

"Your mother is a very kind woman," Diana replied.

"She can be," he muttered.

At least, that was what it sounded like he'd said. She was already joining hands with the other women to form a circle. For a short time, she forgot everything but the excitement of the dance and the joy of moving her feet to keep pace with the music.

"For someone who has earned the enmity of so many, you look surprisingly happy," Henry remarked when he took hold of her hands again. "Now tell me, who is Miss Featherbill, and why is she pleased for you?"

Diana wasn't surprised he didn't know Eliza, despite this being her third Season. She wasn't the sort to catch Henry Weston's eye, but neither was she so totally lacking in dance partners as to require Lady Weston's kind intervention. As they turned in the dance, Diana inclined her head in the direction of the far wall. "See the brown-haired girl wearing pink who is seated near my mother? That is Miss *Fothergill*."

"Yes, yes, Fothergill. Why is she pleased for you when none of the other women are?"

"We have become friends over the past few years," Diana told him. "Neither of us dances a great deal, so we have time to talk at events such as this."

Diana thought of the conversations she shared with Eliza, which consisted mostly of Eliza talking and Diana nodding. As Diana wasn't particularly comfortable sharing her secrets, she didn't mind. Besides, she found the younger girl's chatter and boundless enthusiasm charming. That Eliza's conversations had, for the past two Seasons, focused exclusively on one subject was slightly less endearing. But, as that subject wasn't Henry Weston, Diana knew Eliza wasn't jealous.

"There's something else," Henry accused. "I can see it in the smile you are trying to hide. Is your friend another hater of men?"

"Certainly not. She speaks of nothing but him— er, them. Men. She speaks of nothing but men."

Interest lit his eyes, and she knew she hadn't been successful in covering her slip. He looked in Eliza's direction, and Diana could only watch helplessly as he tracked the girl's love-struck gaze to the dancing couples.

He turned his attention back to her, clearly bemused. "Gabriel?"

Diana gave a slight shrug. Half of the ladies in London were infatuated with Mr. Gabriel's dark good looks. As Lord Blathersby's nephew and heir, the young man had, or would eventually have, a fortune as fair as his face.

"Please, you understand the matter is somewhat delicate—?" she began anxiously.

"You can trust me." His wink did little to reassure her.

"I don't suppose she believes she could ever win him," Diana confided as she and Henry circled each other. "We don't think that way—"

"We? Are the two of you in league?"

"Oh, there are more than just us two. Have you not heard of the Ape-Leader Army?"

He looked at her in alarm.

"Perhaps you know us better as the Squadron of Spinsters?"

He laughed, but there was a touch of desperation in the sound. He eyed the women seated around the perimeter of the room. "You *are* jesting?"

Diana imagined he was trying to calculate his odds of survival should she be in earnest. "Jest about the Militia of Old Maids? Never!" She gentled her tone. "Don't be alarmed, Mr. Weston. We wallflowers have no grand conspiracy afoot. Besides, if there are wronged women in your past, I doubt they number among our ranks. But I do wish Mr. Gabriel would do his duty as you do. One dance with him would probably be enough for Eliza."

He made a noise that sounded suspiciously like a snort but, surely, Henry Weston didn't snort. "That it would, if she has any sense. Gabriel is a nice enough fellow, but unfortunately"—he grimaced—"he shares his uncle's interests."

Oh. That *was* unfortunate. Lord Blathersby's consuming passion was sheep. He confined most of his woolly charges to his country estate, but he always had some living in the garden of his London residence. He counted them before he slept, wore no cloth but that spun from their wool, and while she wasn't sure whether he ate them, given his substantial girth, she wouldn't be surprised if a fatty haunch of mutton was a staple of his menu. His own sheep were the preferred subject of conversation, but Lord Blathersby was perfectly happy to converse at length about any or all ovine-related subjects.

"Well," she said brightly, "I believe Miss Fothergill's family is involved in the manufacture of textiles. They might have a common thread after all."

He made a noncommittal sound as the dance separated them once more. Diana wasn't sure if he thought her pun too awful to remark on, frowned upon the Fothergills' involvement in trade, or had simply lost interest. He looked pensive when they next faced each other, and they finished the little that was left of the dance in silence.

Henry held out his arm so he could escort her back to her mother since they both knew no other gentleman waited to claim the next dance. They were halfway across the room when he abruptly stopped and, mumbling incomprehensibly under his breath, craned his head about. After a few moments he spotted whatever it was he was looking for and began leading Diana in that direction.

Lady Weston was talking with Lady Hayvenhurst and Mrs. Campbell, but she turned away at their approach. "Henry." She beamed with a mother's love as he embraced her and kissed her cheek. "Miss Merriwether, what a delight."

Diana bobbed a curtsy.

"Excuse us, Mary," Lady Hayvenhurst broke in. "Augusta and I must go check on the gentlemen. I must commend you on another lovely ball, not that I expected anything otherwise, and extend my felicitations."

"You must be very proud." Mrs. Campbell had perfected the art of speaking in a confiding manner while managing to address everyone within earshot. "Such good fortune. Two well-heeled, titled son-in-laws . . . and you didn't even have to go to the trouble of giving Olivia a Season."

"Fortunate, indeed," Lady Hayvenhurst tittered, fluttering her fan in time with her flapping tongue. "My Annie took three Seasons to decide on a husband. *Three!* Hayvenhurst and I despaired of her ever marrying."

"Sally!" Mrs. Campbell jostled her friend with her elbow as she inclined her head ever so slightly in Diana's direction.

"Oh, I beg your pardon, Miss Merriwether. You must know I meant no offense. Not all women are meant for marriage, after all, and I'm certain your continued presence is a great comfort to your mother given, ah, well . . ." Lady Hayvenhurst's voice trailed off as her fan ceased its movement.

"Lady Hayvenhurst, I believe I see your husband looking for you," Henry said, his tone so chilly Diana nearly shivered.

"I had best go to him," she replied weakly. "Good evening, Lady Weston. Mr. Weston. Miss Merriwether."

Whatever politeness had been lacking in the conversation, it returned tenfold in the curtsies and bows exchanged as the women took their leave.

"Good riddance," Henry muttered as they walked away.

Lady Weston halfheartedly hushed him. "To what do I owe the pleasure of your company?"

"Miss Merriwether and I have come on another's behalf to beg your assistance. Mr. Gabriel is desirous of dancing with Miss Fothergill. Will you make your way over to her vicinity so that someone is on hand to perform the proper introductions?"

"It would be my pleasure."

"Thank you." Henry pressed a kiss to his mother's cheek. "Miss Merriwether and I will go inform Mr. Gabriel of his, ah, impending good fortune." He winked at Diana.

"How are you going to get Mr. Gabriel to dance with Miss Fothergill?" she whispered as Henry led her over to the refreshment table where the gentleman was engaged in earnest conversation with his uncle.

Henry turned to look at her, his head tilted to one side and a quizzical expression on his face, as if he were not quite sure her question was serious. "I'm going to tell him to do it," he said, as though telling someone to do something was enough to ensure their compliance. Then she realized for him, it *was* enough.

"Oh, I see. Just like that." She smiled tremulously, a slight unease growing in her stomach. She wondered if, like Aladdin in *The Thousand and One Days*, she had unwittingly summoned a powerful genie to do her bidding, though she was under no illusions that she could control the force of nature that was Henry Weston.

"Just like that."

His grin turned the unease in her stomach to something else entirely. Something heated and forbidden and, just like that, the time had come for her to flee. She pulled away slightly, and he instantly tightened his arm against his side, effectively trapping her arm in the crook of his.

"Oh, no," he warned under his breath. "Don't even *think* about abandoning me with Blathersby."

"I wasn't—" she tried to protest, but he shushed her as they drew near their quarry. They sidled up to the refreshments table pretending interest in the food. At least on her part, the interest was feigned. Henry had a glove off before they reached the table. As soon as his long arms were within grabbing distance, he snagged a ginger cake and popped it into his mouth. As he chewed, a blissful expression came over his face that set her insides fluttering.

"Want one?" he asked, reaching for another.

"It's not worth the trouble of taking off my gloves. You men have no idea of the exertion required to wear long gloves," she huffed.

"I've never put them on," he agreed, a mischievous gleam in his eyes, "but I'm quite proficient at taking them off."

Her eyes widened as his meaning sank in. He laughed, a low, easy sound that skipped along her nerves like rocks on water, the ripples echoing through her entire body.

"Have I shocked you, Miss Merriwether?"

"I—"

He bit into the ginger cake he was holding, and then pushed the other half between her lips.

"There." He smirked at her as he licked the crumbs from his fingers. "Problem solved."

Thankfully, her mouth seemed to know what to do when presented with food, for Diana's brain refused to function properly. She couldn't blame the poor, overwhelmed organ. Sometime during the course of the evening, she'd ceased to be herself. Miss Diana Merriwether lurked at the periphery of social events, danced when pity or parental coercing managed to overwhelm a gentleman's natural inclinations, and always maintained a calm, collected demeanor in public.

Miss Diana Merriwether didn't participate in matchmaking adventures, certainly not with Henry Weston. She wasn't the recipient of knowing smiles, especially not from Henry Weston. And she never ate morsels of ginger cake, or any other dessert for that matter, from anyone's hand—most definitely not Henry Weston's.

Oh, heavens above, his fingers had touched her lips. The barest whisper of a touch, but still . . . her *lips*! Things like that simply didn't happen to her. Then another thought struck her, and her heart began to pound.

Had anyone seen?

She slowly turned her head, half-expecting to see a crowd of pointing fingers and accusatory glares, but she found nothing out of the ordinary. She exhaled a sigh of relief, knowing how lucky she'd been. She turned her attention back to Henry, prepared to scold him for his improper behavior, and found him downing yet another ginger cake. Her scolding turned to an exasperated smile.

Henry grinned back and patted his flat stomach. "Fortifications," he informed her. Then, in a louder, jovial tone, he said, "Lord Blathersby, Gabriel, so good of you to come."

The two men turned and greeted Henry.

"You both know Miss Merriwether?" Without waiting for an answer, he threw her to the wolves—or rather, he threw her to the sheep. "Lord Blathersby, Miss Merriwether has just been expressing her admiration for the wool of Swaledales, so I insisted—"

"No, no, my girl, Swaledales are not the thing at all. Coarse wool, you know. For superior wool you cannot beat Lincolns. . . ."

Diana gritted her teeth and tried to look interested as Lord Blathersby launched into a lengthy explanation about the various breeds of sheep best suited for wool production. She watched out of the corner of her eye as Henry engaged Mr. Gabriel in close conversation. The young man frowned, then shrugged and headed off. Henry helped himself to yet another ginger cake and leisurely donned his gloves, a smile lurking around his mouth, before coming to her rescue.

"Excuse us, Lord Blathersby," he interrupted, taking Diana's arm. She tried to brace herself against the thrill that raced through her at his touch. "I see Miss Merriwether's mother looking for her. I suggest you try the ginger cake. Our cook adds just the right number of raisins—makes all the difference, you know."

"Is my mother truly looking for me?" Diana asked as Henry led her off.

"No, but I suspect she will be soon enough. Mothers grow concerned if their daughters wander out of sight whilst in my company. My father informed me earlier that I have the devil's own reputation to live down." His words had a faintly bitter tinge to them.

"I believed men took a certain pride in that."

"Yes, well . . ." He grimaced. "Apparently there are some who find me utterly without conscience." Then, as if he realized he'd grown more serious than he should, he adopted a blatantly flirtatious tone and asked, "Do you think me wicked?"

"Oh, at least," she retorted, the words out of her mouth before she could halt them. Her cheeks flamed. "I beg your pardon. That is, you do have a certain reputation that precedes you, but a man without a conscience wouldn't do as you have just done for Miss Fothergill. Thank you for that."

"It was nothing," he said brusquely.

"On the contrary," she insisted. "What you did was very kind."

"I'm not kind."

She shrugged. "How would you describe your actions?"

"Madness," he grumbled. "I did it because . . ."

"Perhaps you did it for yourself," Diana suggested.

"What do you mean?" He looked lost and uncertain. Surprisingly vulnerable.

"Maybe you needed to prove to yourself that you *are* a good man."

He shook his head, and Diana wasn't sure if he was rejecting her reasoning or the idea of himself as a good man. She saw, with not a little relief, they were close to where her mother and grandmother were sitting. The evening had been so peculiar; she needed time to sit and consider everything that had happened.

Thinking was all but impossible in such close proximity to Henry. She *felt* too much around him for her brain to function properly.

"What I did. . . . I didn't do it for myself." His sigh ruffled the curls at her temple. "I did it for you."

"For me?" she exclaimed. "Why?"

"I have no idea," he admitted bluntly. "As a rule, I try to avoid matchmaking."

Diana laughed. "That, I can well believe. My mother and I called on Lady Weston last week." She lowered her voice to a whisper as they took the final steps to her seat. "I do believe your mother is nearly as put out by your unwed state as my grandmother is by mine."

"I see." A thoughtful expression came over his face.

What he saw, Diana wasn't certain. She saw nothing but the brilliant blue of Henry's eyes. The deep cobalt reminded her of the blue and white Chinese vase that had been in the library at her childhood home.

The piece had probably been worth a small fortune, but her father had allowed her to hold it. She remembered sitting by his feet, tracing the flowers and swirls with her fingertips, listening to the scratching of his quill as he made notes in his studbook.

A simple memory, but a happy one.

"Do you plan to attend the Keltons' soiree?"

Henry's question brought Diana back to the present. "Ah, yes, I believe so."

"Good. I shall look forward to seeing you there. Thank you for the dance, Miss Merriwether." He bowed to her, then acknowledged her grandmother and mother before walking away.

Watching him go, Diana almost felt as though she were holding that Chinese vase again. It had been, she recalled, a wedding gift to her parents from the Prince of Wales. Fit for a princess. Those had been her father's words. And since she was the Princess Royal of

Swallowsdale Grange, just as long as she was careful and her mother didn't see, Diana could hold it.

She had thought herself so special when she held that vase. She'd had the power to capture fairies and conjure magical potions. Nothing had been beyond her reach.

But no matter how particular his attentions had been this evening, Henry Weston was beyond her reach. And no matter how he made her heart pound, Diana knew better than to reach for him. Or rather, *because* he made her heart pound, she knew better than to reach for him.

She remembered what had happened to that blue and white vase. Yelling. Crying. Breaking.

The porcelain shards had lain on the floor alongside the pieces of her parents' shattered marriage. She would never risk that kind of hurt for herself. She ought to run far from Henry and hide herself away. That's what a smart woman would do. Unfortunately, Henry had a way of stealing her wits, and she knew nothing would keep her from the Keltons' soiree.

"Quite a crush tonight," Henry remarked as he joined his sisters and James in the small garden off the ballroom. His parents were ushering the remaining few guests off to their own homes. He could have left earlier. He didn't live there anymore, and he wasn't one of the guests of honor, but leaving hadn't crossed his mind. Besides, he'd promised to take some of the remaining sweets upstairs for his siblings who were too young to attend the ball.

"Indeed," agreed Olivia, fanning herself. Though the temperature outside was noticeably cooler, the night air was warm and heavy. "Jason went to fetch some champagne."

"Unfortunately for you, Hal, he's only bringing four glasses," James pointed out, "though perhaps that's for the best. I'm not certain you should be allowed anything more to drink."

Before Henry could ask what he meant, Sheldon strode through the French doors that led into the garden. He held a glass of champagne in either hand; a footman followed him bearing two more.

"Beg pardon, Weston," his brother-in-law apologized, handing a glass to his wife. "I didn't realize you would be joining us."

"Shall I fetch another glass, sir?" the footman volunteered.

"No, thank you," Henry replied. He waited until the servant had gone inside before arching an inquiring brow in James's direction. "Why do you think I'm in my cups?"

James gestured in the direction of the ballroom. "Unless my eyes deceive me, you danced with Miss Merriwether twice this evening."

"I did." Henry shrugged. "What of it?"

"Is there some reason he shouldn't?" Sheldon whispered to Olivia.

"He hates dancing with Miss Merriwether," Olivia whispered back. "My mother was friends with Miss Merriwether's mother when they were younger, and she believes gentlemen have a duty to dance with the wallflowers, so Mama forces Hal to dance with her."

Henry winced at her choice of words, though he'd likely used them on more than one occasion. "I don't *hate* dancing with Miss Merriwether. I asked her to dance a second time because I wanted to"—he gave a pointed look in James's direction—"and I had all my faculties about me when I did so."

"Are you feeling quite well?" Isabella reached out to touch Henry's forehead.

He stepped backward, out of her reach. "What is the matter with all of you?"

"I could have sworn you just said you wanted to dance with Miss Merriwether," James said slowly, as if testing out the words.

"So what if I did?" Henry crossed his arms over his chest. "One dance means nothing."

"Oh, no," James agreed. "But surely you can understand our surprise given your usual moaning and groaning about being made to dance with her. I thought perhaps this had to do with your project."

At the word "project," Isabella and Olivia snapped to attention, like two hounds scenting prey.

"Project?" Olivia probed, taking a step toward him.

"What project?" Isabella queried, taking two steps in his direction.

Henry sighed. He'd hoped to keep the stud a secret for a bit longer, but he knew his sisters—they wouldn't rest until they knew everything.

"I mean to purchase a stud," he told them. "I figure I ought to do something more with my life than attend balls and hunting parties but, unlike present company, I'm not ready to settle down and start a family just yet. A stud seems like a natural fit, given my interests."

"Yes, it's a definite combination of your two great loves," Isabella said, a devilish grin lurking about her mouth. "Sex and horses."

Sheldon choked on a mouthful of champagne. Olivia giggled and pounded him on the back.

"I've tried to instill some sense of propriety in her, without much success," James said by way of apology.

Olivia gave Henry a quick hug. "I think it's a very good plan. You're certain to be a great success."

"Indeed!" Isabella agreed.

Olivia's lips quivered. "We already know all the fashionable ladies will come see you when seeking a g-good m-mount." She dissolved into laughter.

Isabella shrieked, and then clapped her hands over her mouth.

Sheldon shook his head, trying to mask his amusement behind disapproval. "Clearly my efforts have been similarly unsuccessful."

Henry glanced back and forth between his brothers-in-law and sighed.

"Oh, pish. As if you have any great regard for proper behavior," Olivia accused Jason. "Besides, if I have any improper thoughts, you are certainly to blame for them. Well, you and the Minerva Press," she conceded.

"Careful," Isabella warned. "Hal is starting to get that look in his eyes. It was there just before he tried to destroy my breakfast room."

"I would like to hear more about your project," Olivia said quickly in an obvious effort to distract him. Obvious, but successful. He unclenched his fist. "How exactly does dancing twice with Miss Merriwether fit in?"

Henry was about to tell her that he hadn't the faintest idea when Isabella grabbed his arm. "Oh!" she breathed, her eyes growing wide. "You will need money. Father will advance you the sum, and if he will not, James will. There's no need to marry—"

Henry shrugged her off. "Izzie, calm yourself! I have no intention of marrying anyone."

She eyed him suspiciously before turning to her husband. "Why did you say Hal was dancing with Miss Merriwether to further his project?"

"Miss Merriwether's father is a well-respected breeder," James explained.

"My understanding has always been that Miss Merriwether and her mother are entirely cut off from the man," Olivia said.

"Let me assure all of you," Henry stated firmly, "especially the two of you who are incapable of restraining your wild imaginations, my interest in Miss Merriwether has nothing to do with her dowry and even less to do with her estranged father."

Olivia pounced. "Then you *do* have an interest in her?"

Before he could say anything, Isabella laughed. "Livvy, you read too many novels. Can you imagine Hal courting Miss Merriwether?"

Perhaps Isabella couldn't imagine it. Maybe Olivia didn't see it. But Henry could. A plan was quickly taking shape in his mind. He didn't have everything worked out, but enough to know that courting Diana Merriwether was, at this particular moment, less of an impossibility than a probability.

One he found himself looking forward to, oddly enough . . . but there was no need to tell his sisters that just yet.

CHAPTER SIX

The household is asleep, and so should I be, but the baby is most decidedly nocturnal, and she prefers to have a companion sit up with her. Thus, I shall subject you, dear aunt, to my late-night ramblings, starting with my thoughts on a phenomenon so incredible that I know you must believe my words a hoax. After all these years, my brother has taken an interest in Miss Merriwether! Naturally, Isabella and I plan to meddle. I do not doubt Hal will kill us if he finds out but, oh, I do believe it will be worth the grave discomfort of being dead!

—from the Marchioness of Sheldon to
her aunt the Dowager Marchioness of Sheldon

Diana was in high spirits when she and her mother set off in the carriage for Lord and Lady Kelton's dinner party. Her grandmother was feeling poorly and had elected to stay home, and her grandfather never attended Society events unless forced, so the evening was off to a fine start. It wasn't that Diana wished her grandmother ill, but to say the Duchess of Lansdowne was critical was a bit like saying Alexander the Great had been ambitious.

Diana was constantly aware of being a disappointment, but tonight she was free of her grandmother's watchful eye, which meant she might have some small chance of enjoying herself. Of course, there was another reason Diana was looking forward to this evening.

An impossibly foolish reason.

An impossibly handsome reason.

Henry.

Just thinking his name sent a ridiculous, giddy rush through her. Not only had he gone out of his way to do something kind for Eliza, he'd asked Diana to dance of his own accord. He might not do so again. He had probably come to his senses, but as she had yet to come to hers, the bubble of hope within her had not yet burst.

She knew nothing could come of her infatuation. Henry wasn't the sort of man to settle down, while she was ready—past ready—for that. In truth, she was ready to settle. She wanted her own home and a child, and she needed a husband for that.

He didn't have to be athletic or terribly handsome. As her grandmother was also willing to settle, he need not have a grand title or a great fortune. Diana wasn't even that particular about his age or intellect. All she asked in a prospective spouse was that he be even-tempered, treat her and their offspring kindly, and inspire no more than modest affection in her heart. Was that really so much to ask?

Still, no one would be *hurt* if she danced with Henry again. . . .

"Oh, the endless waiting!" she fretted to her mother. The Kelton residence wasn't very far from Lansdowne House, but the line of carriages moved at a snail's pace. By the time their carriage neared the front of the line, Diana could have walked there and back at least half a dozen times.

Her mother tweaked one of Diana's curls. "You are unusually eager tonight. I thought you would beg off once your grandmother took to her bed."

"Then I might have been summoned to read to her." Diana wrinkled her nose. "Do you know, she even objects to the way I read?" She imitated the duchess's haughty tones. "'No, Diana dear, you are speaking too quickly. You must learn to e-nun-ci-ate your words. You have had the best governesses money can buy, granddaughter, yet you still sound like a shop girl. That must be your common blood showing.'"

Her mother drew in a sharp breath. "She said that to you?"

"No," Diana admitted. "She's never said those precise words, but I know that's what she's thinking."

"Oh, my sweet girl." Her mother wrapped an arm around Diana's shoulders. "Believe me, your grandmother found just as many things wrong with me when I was your age. Age has actually gentled her tongue somewhat."

"But you're so perfect!"

"Hardly." Her mother laughed bitterly. "I made mistakes, and now my children are made to pay for them. I don't worry so much about your brother. Alex is happy away at school, or at least he always seems well on those rare instances when we get to see him. As I doubt my brother will marry, or return to England for that matter, it's likely he will someday inherit the dukedom. No, it's you I—" She broke off as the coach door opened.

Diana said nothing as she accepted the footman's proffered hand and stepped down to the ground, but as they made their way up the front steps she whispered, "Don't worry, Mama. I have a feeling about tonight. Something good is going to happen."

She wondered at her words—wondered if she'd inadvertently cursed herself—when the guests proceeded from the drawing room downstairs to the dining table. Diana had no expectations of sitting next to the most eligible bachelors—no, that honor fell to her hostess's youngest (and only unmarried) daughter—but she considered mutiny— or perhaps she ought to say *muttony* —when she found herself seated beside Lord Blathersby.

Baron Finkley was on her other side, and Diana could not say which man she was less pleased to see. Finkley was eighty if he was a day, and when he spoke to her, his eyes never ventured north of her chest. Being next to either man would have been bad enough; together, they bordered on cruel and unusual punishment.

She was never so glad of the practice of leaving the men to their port and politics as she was tonight. It was all she could do not to rush ahead of her hostess as Lady Kelton led the women upstairs. Diana glanced around, looking for the least conspicuous place to sit for the remainder of the evening, as she felt a hand on her shoulder.

"Diana!" Her mother's face glowed with excitement. "Oh, my dear, I think you were right about something good happening tonight. I sat next to the nicest young gentleman—"

"That makes one of us," Diana muttered.

"Sir Samuel is a cousin of Lady Kelton's, recently arrived from Wiltshire. He is just turned thirty—"

"Oh, tell me you did not ask his age!"

Her mother didn't even have the good grace to look guilty. "The information came up naturally in the course of our conversation. Sir Samuel came into his title a few years ago, but he wanted to spend some time modernizing his estate before setting out to look for a wife."

"So far, he sounds too good to be true. Does he have warts on his nose? A passel of incorrigible younger siblings? Is he losing his hair and running to fat?"

"Nothing of the sort. He has one brother, a little younger than Alex, and a sister still in the schoolroom. As for his looks, Sir Samuel is not, I grant you, the sort to turn ladies' heads in the street, but he is pleasant looking. I haven't told you the best part." She dropped her voice to a conspiratorial whisper. "I mentioned I had a daughter and— Oh, you will never believe his response. He said, 'My lady, while I'm sure any daughter of yours must be exceedingly lovely, I pray, do not think to match me with a young girl in her first Season. My head is as apt to be turned by a pretty face as the next man, but I want a woman ready to be a wife and mother.'"

Diana shook her head in disbelief. "Are you certain this paragon is real?"

"You shall see for yourself when the gentlemen come in."

They found a group of empty seats and, before too long, Lord Kelton led in the gentlemen. He stopped to speak with his wife before making his way over to them. Diana looked a question at her mother who shook her head, clearly just as puzzled as to why their host would seek them out. They stood as he neared them.

"Good evening, ladies." He bowed, and they curtsied in response. "Lady Linnet, I have come with a message from Sir Samuel. I believe he sat next to you at dinner."

"He did. Is everything all right, my lord?"

"A messenger arrived just as you ladies left us. There is some pressing matter on Sir Samuel's estate that requires his immediate presence. The poor fellow has not been here a week. What good is a steward, I ask, if he wants your advice every time the roof threatens to cave?"

Neither Diana nor her mother had a response to that.

"He has gone upstairs to pack and will leave straightaway," Lord Kelton continued. "He asked me to impart both his regrets at being called away and his hope of renewing your acquaintance upon his return to London."

"Thank you, my lord." Though her mother kept her voice even, Diana could sense her disappointment. "If you see Sir Samuel before his departure, please convey my wishes for a speedy resolution to his troubles."

Lord Kelton promised to relay the message and excused himself. Diana took her seat, unaccountably deflated by the turn of events. In all likelihood, she and Sir Samuel wouldn't have been a good match, but she felt cheated at not getting the opportunity to meet him and ascertain their unsuitability.

"It seems fate is already conspiring against you and Sir Samuel," her mother said with false cheer. "I'm certain this business that takes him away will soon be dealt with, and in the meantime, we must see about having a new dress or two made up for you."

Diana bit back a sigh. Her mother believed Sir Samuel was a gallant knight sent to rescue her near-spinsterish damsel-self. "I'm not going to object to new gowns, but please don't go planning the wedding quite yet. I do not even know the man's last name."

"New gowns? Weddings? I beg your pardon. I was quite shamelessly eavesdropping."

Diana looked up to see Henry's sisters, Lady Dunston and Lady Sheldon.

"If you are having new gowns done up, you simply *must* go to Madame Bessette," Lady Dunston continued. "The woman is more than a modiste; she is an artist. She almost never takes on new clients, but she's very fond of our brother. She says Hal flirts as well as a Frenchman. Once she learns you've caught his interest, she will insist on dressing you."

Diana's cheeks burned, and the heat spread over her face and neck. She probably matched Lady Sheldon's cherry-colored sash. "I'm certain you are mistaken."

"Please, may we join you?" asked Lady Sheldon, shooting a hard glance at her sister. "Our husbands have retreated to the card room in an effort to avoid dancing."

"Oh, yes, of course." Her mother appeared as overwhelmed by the vivacious pair as Diana felt. She placed her hand on Diana's shoulder. "My dear, there is Lady Downes. Now that Lady Dunston and Lady Sheldon are here, you will not mind if I leave you?"

Diana shook her head. "Please give her my regards."

As the women seated themselves to either side of Diana, a flash of bright red caught Diana's eye, then again. One after the other, the tips of Lady Sheldon's red satin shoes emerged from beneath the skirts of her demure white silk gown.

"Bold, aren't they?"

At the wryly spoken words, Diana jerked her gaze from the shoes up to the face of the woman sitting next to her. Lady Sheldon smiled warmly. "The shoes were a gift from my husband. I never would've bought them myself, but he knows me too well. These"—she wriggled her feet—"make me daring. They remind me to take chances and find joy in unexpected places."

Such love, Diana thought, *such devotion showed true daring.* No one knew what the future held, and love didn't always conquer all. But Lady Sheldon would not want to hear that. A polite smile in place, she retreated to safer ground.

"Please accept my belated felicitations on marriage and motherhood. Your ball was truly lovely, not that I would expect anything less from Lady Weston."

Lady Sheldon studied Diana as though she were a particularly perplexing puzzle.

"Thank you, Miss Merriwether," Lady Dunston responded

when her sister did not. "My sister and I both had small weddings, much to our mother's dismay, so we had to agree to let her plan something grand. My poor brother shall not get away with less than St. George's. Speaking of the devil, where is—? Oh, dear. Lord Blathersby has trapped him into conversation again."

Diana couldn't suppress her sympathetic groan. "I sat next to him at dinner," she explained, then added, "Baron Finkley was on my other side."

"Whatever did you do to win the enmity of Lady Kelton?" Lady Dunston questioned.

Diana laughed and shook her head. "I wondered the same thing." She worried at her lip a few moments before adding, "Your brother looks quite miserable."

Lady Dunston nodded, though she did not seem overly perturbed by his distress. "Someone ought to rescue him." She looked pointedly at her sister.

"Yes, someone ought." Lady Sheldon's reply made it clear that she would not be doing the rescuing.

"I will."

Diana wasn't sure where the words came from, but once she said them, she had the undivided attention of both women.

Lady Sheldon looked thoughtful; Lady Dunston appeared bemused.

"Miss Merriwether, my brother doesn't truly need to be rescued," Lady Dunston said.

Diana took a deep breath. "I know," she said softly, "but he has rescued me often enough over the years. This is the least I can do."

Before she could change her mind, Diana quickly got up, excusing herself as she did so, and made her way over to the two men. She waited for Lord Blathersby to draw breath, which was the closest she would come to a break in the conversation.

"I do apologize, Lord Blathersby, but Lady Dunston requests that her brother attend her directly. She has a most pressing need to speak with him."

Henry groaned and mumbled his excuses. "What have I done this time?" he asked as he escorted her across the room.

"Nothing." She shrugged. "You seemed in need of rescuing, and one good turn deserves another, don't you think?"

"Miss Merriwether, you have my sincerest gratitude. After five minutes of conversing with Lord Blathersby about his sheep, I begin—"

Her lips twitched. "—woolgathering?"

"Exactly." He gave her an assessing look. "Why do you never show this side of yourself?"

"What do you mean?"

"You've a quick wit, and I can sense there's mischief within you, but you've buried it. There's laughter in your eyes right now and a real smile pulling at your mouth; it's far more appealing than your usual unapproachable mask of propriety."

She stiffened. "It's not a mask, and proper behavior does not make me unapproachable."

"No." He chuckled. "What scares everyone off is that tight-lipped smile you've perfected. Ah, there it is. Yes, yes, quite intimidating."

"It doesn't seem to have affected *you*," Diana muttered.

"Ah, but I am fearless," Henry boasted, gesticulating broadly with his free arm.

She shook her head. "Everyone is scared of something."

"And what are you afraid of?" His voice was a silky purr in her ear.

She turned her head and looked into his blue eyes, clear as a summer sky. She ran her tongue over her dry lips and watched, fascinated, as his eyes darkened a shade. "You," she whispered.

"Me?" A frown creased his brow.

"Well, not *you,* but men *like* you."

Looking at him, no one would know her words had affected him, but Diana felt his muscles contract beneath her hand and heard the slight hitch in his breathing. He had himself under control an instant later. She wished she could say the same. His words had unsettled her, frightened her . . . touched her.

"Men like me," he repeated softly. "And what kind of man would that be?"

"You are a rogue."

His loud bark of laughter set heads whipping around in their direction. Diana grimaced as the weight of their gazes settled over her like a suffocating shroud. She waited for the whispers and the pointed fingers.

. . . her mother ran off with the stable master—bad blood, if you ask me . . .

. . . she'll never be a beauty, that one . . .

. . . If she were my daughter, I would never have taken her back. Did you hear Lansdowne took the girl as well? That is taking Christian charity too *far . . .*

What had possessed her to think Henry wanted her rescue? No one wanted her. Not her grandparents. Certainly not her father. . . . An insidious gray fog hazed over her mind, trapping her in a past she didn't want to remember but couldn't seem to forget.

She ran and ran, endlessly onward, and not just because she'd lost her way. She always ran. She had no choice. She couldn't turn back and go home. She didn't have a home.

Beads of sweat chased each other over goose-pimpled flesh as she pushed herself to go faster, farther. The only sound she could hear was the heavy beat of her own heart. The woods were vast and filled with shadows that snatched at her hair and clothes. Her lungs were tight, burning from exertion and fear.

She'd been lost here before, but she'd known someone would look for her if she waited long enough. She had no one to depend on now save herself. No one was coming to find her.

Without any warning, a wall loomed up in front of her. Before she could turn in another direction, the wall reached out and held her in place. Then it began to rumble.

"Why are you running from me? Miss Merriwether? *Miss Merriwether!*"

The urgency in Henry's voice managed to break through to her, and the past retreated. She lifted her head and found his concerned face looming over her; his hands gripped her shoulders as if he feared she might collapse at any moment. Diana drew in a deep, shuddering breath as she drank in the sight of him. The warmth of his presence drove away the lingering chill about her heart.

"Why did you run from me?" he demanded.

Run from him?

Her attraction to him terrified her, but she wasn't smart enough to run from him. No, she sought him out like a moth drawn to a flame, unable to keep away despite the risk of getting singed. He was so close she could smell him—a heady mixture of soap on skin mingled with port and some earthy, masculine scent that was simply Henry.

His scent swirled around her, clean and crisp as a country breeze, yet crackling with the leashed energy of a coming storm. The muscles in her stomach tightened and released in shivery delight. Heat built inside her and spread through her body until she burned.

Run, run, run, her mind urged, but her body wanted to burn.

Burn, burn, burn.

Perhaps she was a little afraid of him. He was dangerous to her health. If she stood there long enough—just stood there with his hands on her—he would burn her alive. She would go up in flames, right here in . . . She glanced around in confusion as she realized they stood in the courtyard. "What are we doing outside?"

"I hoped you would tell me. You called me a rogue, and then ran off. Are you unwell? Shall I fetch your mother?"

For a moment, she could not answer. Her feminine senses were overwhelmed, paralyzed at having somehow captured the interest of such a giant force of pure masculine energy.

"Forgive me. I just . . ." Heavens, he had the bluest eyes. In the light of the lanterns, they sparkled like brilliant sapphires. "I just became a trifle overheated, and I needed some air. There is no cause to upset my mother. We can return inside." She took a small step back, trying to shrug out of his grasp, but his hands tightened about her shoulders, preventing her retreat.

"Hold a moment." For all they were a command, the words were gentle. "You're trembling," he noted with concern.

She would continue to do so as long as he held her close. Diana turned her head, darting a glance at the other couples who had ventured outside. "Did I cause a scene when I ran out?" she asked worriedly.

He gave a short laugh. "No, but I'm certain everyone is wondering what I said to set up your bristles." Keeping one hand on her shoulder, he guided her to a bench a few feet away. "Sit," he told her. "You look as though you're about to faint."

She was still a little unsteady, so she did as he asked. The position put her eyes level with the hands that braced on his hips as he asked, "What happened in there?"

Perhaps because he'd rescued her once again, she felt as though she owed him at least a partial explanation. She had to look up, way up, to deliver it. "Sometimes I . . . I don't know how to describe it, exactly. All of a sudden, my heart races, and I can't catch my breath. It's almost as if I'm in a dream or a trance. Most people run from their ugly memories in a less literal sense, but when I'm in that state, I have no control. I don't . . . I don't even remember running out here." She ducked her head and hunched in on herself. "You must think me mad."

"If you are mad, Miss Merriwether, there is very little hope for the rest of us. Does this happen often?"

She sighed and forced her gaze back up. "When my past catches up with me."

Henry's brow wrinkled.

"I wasn't running from you," she explained. "When you laughed and everyone turned in our direction . . . I couldn't wait and risk seeing all those disapproving stares, overhearing the whispers . . ."

"I apologize. I never meant to distress you."

"I know, and it wasn't you that made me uncomfortable."

"Even though I am a rogue?" he teased.

Diana blushed. "Well, you *are*!" she insisted.

"I assure you, at least half of what is reported in the gossip columns is entirely made up, and the other half is greatly exaggerated."

"Yes," she said bitterly. "I know just how much liberty newspapers take with the truth. All they care about is selling papers—making a profit—no matter how many lives and reputations are ruined in the process."

His blue eyes were gentle, his expression thoughtful as he seated himself beside her. "You haven't had an easy time of it, have you?"

She shrugged, disconcerted by this tender side of him. "I never lacked food to eat or a roof over my head."

"I think I would rather face the elements than most of the spiteful old biddies at Almack's. Going hungry, however? I'd have to think harder on that."

A chuckle escaped her.

"Ah, now that's better," he said with satisfaction. "You have a beautiful smile, Miss Merriwether."

His words flooded her heart with pleasure and her cheeks with heat. It didn't matter whether he truly meant them, or if he'd said them to all the women in London. When he said them to her, she felt like the prettiest woman alive . . . which just brought her back to the fact that Henry Weston was a very dangerous man.

"And you have a way with women, Mr. Weston."

"Although I'm certain it was not meant as such, I will take that as a compliment."

"In truth, I envy you," she admitted. "I am ill at ease with strangers, and I am no good at making polite conversation. You could charm an entire village without being uncomfortable. That is a gift."

He shifted uneasily beside her, and Diana suddenly under-stood that this master of compliments had difficulty accepting them. She glanced away to hide her amusement.

"Of course, I must point out that you have taken no little advantage of this gift with regards to the female gender. I daresay that, despite your protestations otherwise, you have charmed every woman you've ever met and put far too many of them at ease."

He relaxed and leaned in, giving her that roguish half-grin that made her heart skip a beat. "Do I charm you, Diana?"

"Not at the moment." She lied without hesitation. "Nor have I given you permission to use my given name."

"No, you have not," he agreed. "Not yet. You will, though. But, I must point out, *Diana*"—the sound of her name on his lips sent chills tingling up her spine—"daring is part of a rogue's attraction."

"Attraction doesn't last," she replied, stiffening her spine—and her mind—against his potent allure. "And, though you may find this difficult to believe, not all women are attracted to rogues."

"You, for one?"

She nodded. "When I was in my first Season I made a list of desirable attributes, and—"

"You have a list?" His expression hovered between horror and interest.

"It has grown shorter over the years, but no roguish qualities were ever included."

"I can't say I'm surprised. I can imagine precisely the man you would seek. You want a quiet, studious country gentleman. Someone totally dependable, utterly predictable, and unbearably dull. Well, have I got it right thus far?"

She refused to take his bait. "As I am quiet, studious, and prefer the simplicity of country life to the pleasures of town, you have indeed described my perfect match. He must also be of a steady disposition and an even temper, guided by logic rather than emotion."

"You haven't made any mention of your heart. Is this to be a love-match?"

And risk the jealousies that could tear a marriage apart? Her parents' separation hadn't only devastated her mother. The man Diana had loved and trusted most in the world had betrayed her, and she would never open herself to that pain again.

"No," she whispered. "I know love is a game to you, but it isn't to me. People get hurt—" Her voice broke.

He gently lifted her chin until she met his gaze. "You are safe with me, Diana," he promised.

His fingers spread shivers across her skin, and she jerked her head away. "I know." She smiled wryly. "I'm not a woman to stir a man's passions."

"That's not what I—"

"But you needn't worry that I will fall in love with you, either." She reached over to pat his hand in reassurance. "You are safe with me, too, Mr. Weston."

CHAPTER SEVEN

I cannot ask this over the breakfast table, since we both know Izzie will make a fuss. She will tell my mother and Livvy, and then I may as well forget the idea. You are my oldest friend, so I hope I may trust you to be honest with me. Am I insane to consider courting Miss Merriwether? I realize this may be a question from one madman to another. You married my sister, after all, which surely makes you a candidate for Bedlam....
—from Henry Weston to his
brother-in-law the Earl of Dunston

Henry frowned at Diana. He didn't expect every woman he met to fall for him, but . . . Well, perhaps he did. Not that he wanted *this* woman to fall in love with him, but it intrigued him that she seemed so sure she wouldn't.

"Because I'm a rogue," he clarified. "That's why you won't fall in love with me."

"One of many reasons, Mr. Weston."

"Please, call me Henry."

She shook her head. The movement sent the curls around her face dancing like little flames. In the moonlight, her hair shimmered with all the colors of a summer sunset, from russet to gold and every shade in between.

What had his mother called her hair?

Marvelous? Gorgeous? *Glorious.* That was it. Without stopping to think about what he was doing, Henry reached out and captured a curl between his thumb and forefinger.

"W-what are you doing?"

The little quiver in her voice prodded at something inside him, something male and primitive that would have been best left sleeping. Now the beast stirred awake.

"I'm trying to decide the color of your hair." The words emerged on a husky whisper.

He met her startled gaze and found her eyes were the colors of his dreams. Chestnut stars flecked with gold overlaid a field of rich green—a glossy Arabian streaking across the turf. As their eyes held, her breath caught. He kept hold of her silky curl, but his gaze dropped to her mouth.

He looked at her then, really looked at her. Though he'd danced with her countless times, if asked to describe Diana Merriwether, he would have said she was tall with red hair. He would have had to guess at her eye color. In all the years he'd known her, he had never really seen her.

How had he never noticed that she had a mouth made for sin? In the landscape of her serious face, her mouth was a folly, surprising and sensual. She likely thought it a bit too wide, her lips a shade too full. Women had the oddest notions about these things. From a male point of view, Diana's mouth was perfection. Lush, naughty perfection.

That bothered him. He was bothered because he hadn't noticed before, bothered because he noticed now, bothered because the bothersome mouth in question belonged to Diana, and mostly bothered that he was feeling . . . *bothered*. And hot.

He released her hair to tug at his cravat.

"My hair is the same unfortunate color it has always been: red." Her brow furrowed as she patted at her curls. "You asked why I wouldn't fall in love with you. Mr. Weston, I'm not a young girl wishing for a handsome gentleman to sweep me off my feet. I am determined this will be my last Season. If I haven't found a husband after this many years of looking, I doubt I ever shall. I'm not averse to the notion of marriage—I should like to have my own household and children—but I want nothing to do with love and less to do with scandal. My family has been subject to enough pointing fingers and wagging tongues. Thus, I think it unlikely I'll succumb to your charms."

Henry got to his feet and extended his hand to her. "Come. Walk with me."

After a slight hesitation, she stood and took his arm. "I don't see how I can refuse"—she flashed him a smile—"given that you didn't bother asking. We shouldn't stay out too long, though. Half of the guests likely saw you come after me, and they'll talk if we linger here too long."

Henry wasn't used to caring if people talked about him, but given what his father had said earlier, he must learn to care. In order to convince Parr to sell Ravensfield, Henry had to become respectable. He could learn from Miss Merriwether. As she said, there was scandal in her family history, but the lady herself was propriety personified.

They walked the length of the courtyard in companionable silence. The musical notes of the pianoforte and the chatter of polite conversation spilled down from the open windows above. He found himself noticing little things about her.

The way she carried herself, tall and regal. The long, graceful line of her throat. The pale copper freckles decorating her porcelain skin. The faint scent of orange blossoms, fresh linen, and *woman*.

He wondered if he'd overlooked her because his mother was always pushing her at him, but in his heart, he knew the truth, which was far less palatable. Society had deemed Miss Diana Merriwether beneath its notice, and Henry was nothing if not a member of society. He bedded its widows, gambled with its men, flirted with its matrons, and danced with its maidens. He loved society, and society loved him right back.

He and his siblings had many blessings, and his parents had always encouraged them to share their good fortune. Henry listened with one ear to the reminders, thinking his parents were speaking of taking baskets to their tenants and treating servants well. It dawned on him now why his mother always prompted him to dance with spinsters and wallflowers, and he was ashamed at what a burden he'd made it out to be.

He found he wanted to help Diana. Again. He was a man who helped himself, but she brought out some nobler impulse in him. That was, admittedly, a little worrisome, but in helping her, he could help himself. Parr needed to be convinced Henry was a respectable gentleman, a family-minded man like his son had been. If Henry was on his very best behavior and he courted a very proper lady like Diana, he thought he could sway Parr in his favor.

Diana would benefit from his attention. She wanted a husband, and if he displayed an interest in her, he felt certain other gentlemen would follow suit. Most importantly, they'd already established there was no risk of either of them falling in love with each other.

"Have you a plan?" he asked.

"I beg your pardon? A plan?"

"You need to find a husband this Season. I wondered whether you had a plan."

"My plan is no different than it has been any other year: I shall attend as many events as possible in hopes of meeting an eligible man. I can't say it has worked terribly well for me thus far," she said drily. "Have you a better idea?"

"As a matter of fact, I do. I have a proposition—an arrange-ment I believe would benefit us both." He saw a flash of interest in her eyes, so he pressed on. "You may have noticed that men generally follow each other's lead. If I begin to court you, others will take notice."

She stopped in her tracks and turned to face him. "You wish to court me?"

"I wish to pretend to court you."

She shook her head. "I don't understand."

"You are in need of a bit of popularity. My presence by your side can give you that."

Her eyes narrowed in suspicion. "What do you get out of this?"

Clever girl. He liked that about her.

"To say that my dear mother is anxious to see me wed is an understatement of epic proportions. I can think of only one way to ensure she won't spend all Season parading eligible misses before me. I must be engaged in a courtship with someone she likes, and she likes you."

"I like her as well, but—"

"The only people I wish to court this Season are investors for the racing stud I plan to open. Lord Parr, whose stud I hope to purchase, finds me a bit too, ah, *roguish* for his taste. Time spent with you can't help but make me more respectable. When you find the man you want and decide to throw me over, preferably close to the end of the Season, surely Lord Parr will not add to my heartbreak by refusing to sell me the stud. Isn't it a perfect plan?"

He was quite pleased with himself. Not only had he solved his own problem, he'd solved Diana's as well, or as close to it as he could get without actually marrying her.

"Madness is what it is, Mr. Weston." She worried at her bottom lip.

He found himself unaccountably transfixed by that succulent swell of flesh. "Genius is what it is," he corrected, unable to lift his eyes from her mouth, "and you must call me Henry." The sudden, unwanted attraction he was experiencing was untenable between Mr. Weston and Miss Merriwether. Between Henry and Diana, it was slightly more palatable.

"Using your Christian name would be improper."

He laughed. "I could have a great deal of fun teaching you the joys of impropriety."

"You're very kind to want to help me, but if you think on it, you will see there's no way your plan could ever work. We should go inside. My mother will be wondering where I am."

Henry refused to give up so easily. But if he couldn't persuade Diana with logic, he would try a different tack.

"You're right," he said and began leading her toward the house. "Forgive me. It was a foolish idea. It could never possibly work."

"Yes, I believe I said that," she replied cautiously, obviously thrown by his quick capitulation.

"I'd forgotten the most important part of such a courtship," he explained.

"Which is?"

"Believability."

Her shoulders hunched as she shrank into herself. "No one would believe you would be interested in me."

Henry ushered her inside, but instead of heading for the stairs, he took a chance and opened the nearest door. The library. As luck would have it, the room was empty. Well, he'd always had that rogue's knack for finding empty rooms in strange houses at opportune times. He tugged Diana inside and moved to shut the door.

"Mr. Weston! Have you taken leave of your senses?" Diana's hand shot out, bracing against the door. She was going to bolt.

He lifted his hand from the door and stepped back a few paces into the room, holding both hands up, palms out. "Wait, Diana—Miss Merriwether," he corrected himself. "Please, wait. You misunderstood me. I meant that it would be impossible for *you* to maintain the illusion of interest in *me*."

She turned on him, her expression shocked, all thoughts of the door and propriety forgotten. He'd succeeded in removing her mask. How long until she noticed and put it back on?

"Do you take me for a fool, Mr. Weston?" She crossed her arms over her chest. "You know very well you are a catch. Most of the women upstairs would give their eyeteeth to have a chance with you."

"Then I'm sure they could hold up their half of the courtship very well. I could convincingly play the part of a besotted fool. But you . . ."

She shook her head in disbelief. "You believe your plan wouldn't work because I couldn't affect infatuation?"

He nodded, trying to look dejected.

"I could, but no one will believe you've taken an interest in me."

"Why not?"

"B-because you are you, and I am me," she stammered.

"I see." He smiled and took a step toward her. "You know, you're quite pretty when flustered."

"I am not flustered."

"You're not used to compliments, are you?"

"I'm not accustomed to being lied to, no."

"I'm not lying." He wasn't. Though it had escaped his notice all these years, Diana was actually a very pretty girl.

No, not a girl—a woman—and pretty wasn't the right word. Fresh-faced English roses were pretty. Diana was a lily—tall and slender, pale and elegant. Hers was a quiet beauty, one easily overlooked in the loud glitter of a packed ballroom. Even he, who considered himself a devotee of the fair sex, hadn't seen her beauty until tonight.

His attention would take the blinders off the gentlemen in their circles, and by the end of the Season, Diana would have suitors aplenty. She would gain every bit as much from his scheme as he would, maybe more. Besides, he didn't have ingenious ideas very often; he wouldn't give this one up without a fight.

The kid gloves were coming off.

"It seems we're at a crossroads," he said, taking another step closer. "Neither of us believes the other is capable of pretending sufficient attraction for a convincing courtship. We must conduct an experiment."

"An experiment?"

He moved close enough to reach around her and pushed the door shut. He braced one arm on the wood panel, caging her in. "A kiss."

"A kiss?" she squeaked. She tried to step away, but the door was at her back.

"Are you always so repetitive?" He'd cornered his prey, and now anticipation lit a fire in his blood.

Her spine stiffened. "Are you always so brazen?" she tossed back, chin lifted in defiance. Her eyes darted to the door handle, and his lips quirked in amusement. He had escaped from an amorous pursuer a time or two, but a woman had never run from him.

This one wouldn't either.

Just to be certain, he took a step back, giving her a bit of space. He pulled off his gloves and tucked them in his waistcoat pocket. He captured one of her hands in his, interlacing their fingers, and waited to see her reaction. She was watchful, a little wary, but she didn't try to pull away.

He gave her hand a gentle squeeze. "I don't think a kiss is too great a sacrifice to make. If this courtship is going to have any chance at succeeding, we need to be able to convince society of our mutual attraction. If I can make you believe I desire you, then I will have succeeded on my part."

He leaned in and spoke against her ear. "And if you can convince me that you want me in return, you will have succeeded on yours."

A tremor ran through her body.

"Shall I kiss you, Diana?"

"I didn't think rogues asked for permission."

Henry was unsure whether she meant to question him or challenge him with her words, but issued as they were in a breathy, unwittingly seductive voice, everything in him responded.

"You're right. Rogues don't ask for permission. We take what we want."

"Oh?" Her tongue darted out to wet her lips.

He tensed at the sight of that pink tongue flicking over those luscious, full lips.

"I want to kiss you now." His words were barely more than a whisper.

She swallowed hard and inclined her head ever so slightly, either giving him permission or signaling her understanding that he would take what he wanted. He didn't care which. At this point, a kiss between them was as unstoppable as the changing seasons or the turning tide. At this point, their kiss was fate.

The hand holding his turned to a vise as Henry settled his free hand around Diana's neck. Her body stiffened, eyes squeez-ing shut, at the first brush of bare flesh against bare flesh. Against his palm, he felt the frantic pulse in her throat.

He feathered his thumb against the rigid line of her jaw, soothing and stroking. As her heartbeat began to slow, he luxuriated in the sensation of skin softer than swansdown beneath his fingertips. After several long moments, she released a shaky breath, inhaled deeply and tilted her head back, waiting for his kiss.

The movement exposed the slender column of Diana's throat, an expanse of ivory skin patterned with those intriguing freckles. She was so pale, he could see the fine network of veins running beneath the surface of her skin; the faded blue lines mapped the way to her heart. She was fragile, he realized. He needed to be careful, or he might hurt her.

He lowered his head, appreciatively noting that he didn't need to stoop. He touched his lips to hers gently, almost in greeting, trying to remember the last time he'd kissed such an innocent. He couldn't recall. As he had no wish to end up caught in the parson's mousetrap, he deliberately restricted his attentions to widows, actresses, and other women of questionable virtue. He lifted his head, smiling at the realization that the territory of this kiss was as uncharted for him as for her.

Untangling his hand from hers, Henry cupped the back of her head. His hands looked enormous in comparison with the delicacy of her features, and he reminded himself again to be gentle with her. Angling her head back further, he twined his fingers in the silky curls at the base of her neck and pressed a kiss to the base of her throat. She arched her head to the side, and he felt her hum of approval against his lips.

The quiet vibrations passed from her body into his, sending a pleasurable thrill reverberating through him. He pressed lingering kisses up her throat, inhaling the light scents of orange blossoms and soap, and beneath—pure, intoxicating woman. He dragged his mouth along the line of her jaw, letting her feel just the barest touch of teeth. Her breathing, already fitful, became audible. When he flicked his tongue against the velvety patch of flesh hidden behind her ear, she gasped.

That was all the invitation Henry needed. He returned to her mouth, slanted his lips over hers, and began to kiss her in earnest—sweet, slow, and steady. He wrapped an arm around her waist and pulled her closer, flush against his body. She fit him perfectly, all soft and lithe where he was hard and demanding.

Her mouth surpassed all his expectations. He ran his tongue over the soft fullness of her bottom lip, then caught it in his teeth and sucked it into his mouth. She tasted of the ratafia served with dessert, mostly sweet but with a hint of spice. Another taste lurked beneath, luring him in deeper—*her* taste. He wanted more.

Like the rogue she accused him of being, he took it. Taking advantage of her parted lips to deepen the kiss, he eagerly thrust his tongue inside her mouth. Her taste washed over him, dark, wild, and sensual, and an untamed heat rose up in him in response. He was desperate for more of her taste, more of her touch—more of *her*.

Henry fought to retain some vestiges of control, but he was losing the battle. Unable to help himself, he pressed his body into hers. She shivered in response and clutched at him.

So good.

She felt so good with her body arching into him, pressed to all those places certain to drive a man mad. A primal, male part of his brain bade him to cover her, conquer her . . . claim her. He wanted to haul her skirts up, unbutton his breeches, and wrap those long, sleek legs of hers around his waist. He would take her right here, the sound of her harsh pants filling his ears like the most glorious music as he surrounded himself, sated himself in her.

When was the last time he'd felt so urgent? Something about her called to him, demanded his response. It was her innocence, he told himself. She was untried, untutored, and that was a novelty for him. The women he played with were well versed in this game.

This wasn't a game, though, and he couldn't play with her.

He lost his tenuous grasp on that thought as she began to kiss him back, tentatively at first, and then with increasing daring. A little moan of pleasure rose up in her throat and traveled across their fused mouths into him. It raced through his body, and moved south, straight to his cock.

He skimmed his hand down her back to cup her bottom, fitting her more closely to him. She tore her mouth from his, a breathy cry escaping at the intimate caress, and turned her head to the side. A denial. He'd be damned if he would allow that. He caught her earlobe between his teeth and bit down just hard enough to punish her for the sensual torment his body was undergoing.

"Henry!" her low cry was loud in the silence. Loud enough to shock him back into some semblance of sanity. Christ, he was kissing (more than strictly kissing, if he wanted to be honest, which he wasn't sure he did) Diana Merriwether (something, or someone rather, he wasn't sure he wanted to think about) in the Keltons' library where anyone might discover them.

And he really, *really* didn't want to stop.

Diana—no, it would be better for both of them if he thought of her as Miss Merriwether—looked deliciously disheveled and more than a little bewildered. She looked ripe for dalliance. Unfortunately, he could not afford to dally with this particular woman.

He stepped away from her, thinking of cold lakes, curtain studies, the St. Crispin's Day speech from *Henry V* that his mother had forced him to learn as a boy . . . Anything to cool his blood.

Anything but her.

"I think you did tolerably well," he said, pleased at the level tone to his voice.

She blinked at him, slowly coming out of her sensual haze. "You kissed me," she said slowly, disbelievingly. She raised her gloved fingers to trace her mouth, as if she could still feel him there.

"You kissed me," she said again, this time a bit more firmly.

"And you kissed me. You were very believable, too. You nearly convinced me."

"Nearly?" Her brows winged up.

Henry bit the inside of his cheek. They both knew she'd all but devoured him. And he'd done the same. That thought sobered him. Having never experienced desire before, Diana's sensual surrender wasn't surprising. His loss of control, however, was inexcusable.

"Given your natural aversion to rogues, it was only to be expected that you would maintain some . . ." He gestured broadly, searching for the right words. "Some emotional distance."

"Emotional distance," she repeated, a faint frown creasing her forehead.

"Well, there wasn't any physical distance, if you recall." He grinned as a charming flush rose up in her cheeks. "Since you nearly convinced me, I think we've a fair shot of persuading the *ton* that we're taken with each other."

She held up a finger. "I could convince everyone that I'm taken with you. Given your popularity with my sex, no one would be surprised if I kissed your feet and vowed my eternal devotion."

Henry chuckled. "If you are vowing your eternal devotion, there are better places to kiss than my feet."

"However," she went on, ignoring his innuendo or, more likely, not understanding it, "your plan is still flawed. No one will believe that you've suddenly taken an interest in me. As I told you earlier, I am hardly a woman to stir a man's passions, while you are . . ."

Henry stopped listening to Diana's nonsense. Not a woman to stir a man's passions? Where had she been just moments ago? She hadn't merely stirred his passions; she'd awoken, challenged, and inflamed them. His breeches were still uncomfortably tight.

How could she doubt his interest? For whatever reason, however, she did, and that was unacceptable. His gaze centered on that incredible mouth of hers. His kiss had plumped her full lips and darkened them to the color of pomegranates. Unaccountably, Diana had proved as rare and delightful a delicacy. He wanted another taste.

"You appear to need further convincing," he told her. "I am happy to accommodate."

Diana didn't have long to ponder the meaning of Henry's words. He covered the distance between them in a flash and hauled her back into his arms.

Oh. So this was what he meant by convincing.

One of his big hands cupped her scalp, tilting her head back, and then his mouth descended on hers. There was no gentle seeking this time, no coaxing, just him taking and demanding. Insisting she acknowledge the sparks between them. The fire that roared to life.

The searing heat that flared in his blue eyes, burning every inch of her it touched.

Oh . . .

A sigh escaped her as her arms rose to twine round his neck. Whatever difficulties her mind was having accepting the situation, her body had no such reservations. Her body was convinced and very partial to a courtship involving these false affections. If all rogues kissed as well as Henry, she might have to revise her position on rogues leading women astray. Given the chance, women probably dragged these scoundrels into their bedchambers.

Oh, saints preserve her, what was she thinking? She broke the kiss and buried her face in his shoulder, struggling to control her breathing. It was a mistake. His scent surrounded her, filled her with each shaky inhale, drugging her nearly as effectively as his kisses.

"Tell me again I do not desire you?" His breath was hot against her ear as he pressed himself against her. She felt the hardness of him through the layers of her skirts and his breeches.

"Believe me," he groaned. "My body's reaction is real. This attraction is unfeigned, and I haven't yet decided if it will work to our advantage. For now, just know this: I want you. I want you every bit as much as you want me."

Diana lifted her head at his words. "I thought I had only *nearly* convinced you."

The infuriating man had the gall to laugh at her. "You *nearly* convinced me to take you right up against this door."

He thought her wanton. The realization struck her like a slap in the face. She knew her mother hadn't committed adultery, but her parents' separation had been as good as an admission of guilt in the eyes of society. Over the years, Diana had found that where the mother's morals were suspect, so were her daughter's. After years of careful propriety, of never stepping out of line, she'd behaved as badly as all those mean-eyed, clucking dowagers had always expected. She sniffed, fighting back tears.

"That was uncalled for— My God, are you crying? Did I hurt you?" Henry looked stricken.

She shook her head, her throat too tight to speak. He had hurt her, but not physically. He had released something in her that frightened her.

"I scared you." He began to reach for her, stopped himself. "I forgot myself tonight. I lost control. It will not happen again."

She wiped at the tears that had escaped.

Henry swore under his breath. "I meant to go easy with you," he said against her hair, and this time when he reached for her, he didn't stop. He held her gently against him and rubbed her back. "You responded to me so perfectly, I forgot this is all new to you."

His tenderness very nearly undid her, but as much as she wanted to let herself fall to pieces, Diana knew this was neither the time nor the place. She'd been gone from the party too long as it was, though she doubted anyone but her mother had remarked upon her absence. They would have had to notice she was there in the first place.

"It would be best if we went back upstairs separately," she said, somehow finding the strength to pull away from him.

"Yes, indeed," he murmured. "I'll go ahead, shall I? That will give you a few minutes to compose yourself. I shall call on you tomorrow."

"That isn't necessary," she began.

"I disagree. Calling on you is the first step in making my interest known."

"You might send flowers instead," she suggested, trying to think of some way to prevent him from showing up on her doorstep tomorrow. She would not agree to his absurd plan.

"What are your favorite flowers?"

"Day lilies. My mother planted them in the garden where I grew up. My fath—" She stumbled over the word, swallowed and tried again. "My father called them 'Di lilies.' He said they were sunny and freckled, just like me." Her throat ached at the bittersweet memory.

"Tomorrow, when I come to call, I will bring you day lilies." The mischief in Henry's eyes helped to ease the tightness in her throat.

"But—"

He reached out and placed a finger on her lips. "No more 'buts,' no more excuses," he told her, opening the door. "We both know you want to say yes."

Before she could respond, he stepped into the hall and shut the door behind him, leaving her alone with muddled thoughts and a racing heart.

The man was maddening, but he was also right, and therein lay the trouble. Where Henry Weston was concerned, it was all too easy for her to say yes.

CHAPTER EIGHT

My offer still stands to double Diana's dowry. My money may not be as old or respected as that of your family, but I am now a wealthy man. My daughter should benefit from my prosperity. All I wish is to see her. I have no right to ask you to intercede on my behalf, but I beg of you, help me. . . .

—from Thomas Merriwether to
his wife Lady Linnet Merriwether

Linnet spent the coach ride back to Berkeley Square quietly observing her daughter. Diana claimed she had a headache, but Linnet didn't believe her. Or rather, Diana's head might pain her, but something—or someone—had caused that hurt. Shortly after Diana had gone to "rescue" that Weston rogue, Linnet had lost sight of her.

In truth, her daughter was probably safer with Weston than most of the men who'd been present. If what his mother said was true, he shared Diana's lack of enthusiasm for the married state. But Weston's disinterest stemmed from a reluctance to give up his wild bachelor ways, and he would come around eventually. Diana . . . might not, and Linnet carried the blame. She and Thomas had fought a desperate, losing war against each other and for each other, and their children had borne witness.

Alex had been too young to know what was happening, but Diana had been understandably distressed. She began having terrible night terrors and, for a time, Linnet had feared the strain was too much for her daughter's young mind. Diana had outgrown the nightmares, but the scars from childhood had only faded. Linnet knew they would never disappear completely, and she would face the devil himself to keep Diana from further hurt.

When they arrived back at Lansdowne House, Linnet announced her intention to retire, though she didn't intend to go to bed just yet. Something had upset Diana, and Linnet would not rest until she assured herself of her daughter's well-being.

She prepared for bed as usual, and then dismissed her maid for the evening. After donning a wrapper and slippers, Linnet headed across the hall to her daughter's room. Diana was in bed reading, but she laid aside her book at Linnet's entrance.

"I wanted to see if you were feeling any better," Linnet ventured.

"I'm certain I will feel better shortly." She laughed. "One can't sit between Lords Finkley and Blathersby for the duration of a meal and expect to come away unscathed."

Diana's laughter would have fooled anyone, Linnet thought. Anyone save her mother.

"Were you able to enjoy yourself at all tonight?" Linnet asked. "I know you dislike going to these parties, but—"

"It isn't the parties I dislike as much as the people who attend them."

Linnet seated herself on the end of the bed. "You like Mr. Weston well enough."

Her daughter gave a noncommittal murmur.

"He is very handsome," Linnet prompted.

"Yes," Diana agreed.

"You danced twice with him at the Weston ball. I heard Lady Endersby remark upon it."

Diana bristled. "Lady Endersby is an old gossip. She'd do better to concern herself with her son's excesses than my dance partners."

"That may be true, but people still listen to her. You must be careful of your reputation."

"Why?" Diana exploded, throwing her hands up. "What good has it done me?"

Linnet understood her frustration, but the loss of her reputation would not only ruin Diana's chances for marriage, it would make her a social pariah. "I know what it's like to have your reputation destroyed. Even after all this time, I sometimes hear whispers when I enter a room, and they still hurt. My heart has withstood a great deal in my life, but I think it would break if you were hurt that way."

"Because Mr. Weston must be toying with me," Diana said softly, plucking at the bed covers. "That's what you are trying to say, isn't it?" She raised her head to meet Linnet's eyes.

Linnet leaned forward and reached for Diana's hand, but she tugged away.

"Diana, you are a beautiful young woman with a good head and a kind heart. Mr. Weston would be lucky to have you. My doubts have nothing to do with you and everything to do with him. I am certain he is an amiable young man, but he's shown no indication that he is looking to marry. If you think sensibly, you will not believe his interest any more than I do."

"Perhaps I don't. Did you consider that? Perhaps I wanted to feel desirable for one evening. Can you not even let me have that? You're not the only one who still hears the whispers!" Diana clapped a hand over her mouth.

Linnet saw the immediate remorse in her daughter's eyes, but she bore the painful lashes of Diana's words as her due. Knowing she deserved them didn't lessen their harsh sting. "I beg your pardon," she whispered, scrambling off the bed.

"Mama, I—"

Knowing she was going to cry, Linnet fled the room and hurried toward her own chamber. Once inside, she collapsed back against the door, overcome with hating herself and with what her life had become. Her breath came in shaky, shallow pants as she sobbed into her hands. Where had she gone so wrong?

Unbidden, her mind raced back to a long ago winter's eve at Halswelle Hall, her family's country estate. . . .

She sneaked out after everyone was in bed. Her heart pounded with the fear of discovery, but the need to see Thomas spurred her on. She trudged through the snow around the back of the stables to the small cottage built to house the stable master. The darkness would have frightened her once, but now she was glad of its cover. She didn't need light to see the way when she had the path etched on her heart. When Thomas opened the door, she hurled herself into his arms.

"Linnet? Why have you come?"

"I had to see you."

"You shouldn't come out in such ill weather for that, love. I'm not worth it," he teased as he shut the door and gathered her close.

She snuggled into his heat. "When you hold me, I think everything will be all right." She raised her arms and threaded her fingers through his thick, red-gold hair. She tugged his head down to hers, and they both groaned as their mouths met. He kissed her until her toes curled and she had trouble remembering her own name.

"Make love to me," she pleaded. It wasn't the first time she'd made the bold request. But just as he'd done every time before, Thomas stubbornly shook his head.

"Don't ask me, Linny." He stepped away from her and prowled around the small space. Even from across the room, his blue eyes burned her with icy fire. "You know how badly I want you, but not like this. I won't dishonor you, and I won't betray your father's trust by stealing your innocence like a thief in the night."

"Mother brought up the Season tonight. It's only January, but she's already fixed on it." The words poured out of her in a panicked rush. "This year she won't let me come home unattached. The only reason I escaped before was that the Duke of Inwood was still in mourning, and she thinks I have a chance at him. I thought if I had a Season and refused all my suitors, perhaps my parents would accept you as my choice. We couldn't cause a worse scandal than a duke marrying the daughter of the King's horse trainer."

"Yes, we could. She brought him a great fortune. I can only give you all I am and all I hope to become. Society will forgive a duke

who marries a commoner for money. They won't forgive me for daring to love you. You deserve to be a duchess, and I would take that away from you."

"I deserve happiness, and Inwood can't give that to me." She swallowed hard. "My parents will never give us their blessing, will they?"

"No," he said softly. "I don't believe so, but even if we kept in good with them, we wouldn't have an easy time of it."

She sank to the floor in despair. "What are we going to do?"

He picked her up and carried her over to the chair before the open hearth, settling her on his lap. "I love you, Linnet. You know I want to marry you, with or without your parents' approval. This is your life, though, and this needs to be your choice. I will love you whether you pick a life with me or a life with them."

"I don't want to have to choose." She buried her face in his chest and wept.

"I know." His tone was gentle as he stroked her hair. "I hate that I'm the one making you choose, but I can't let you go, even when I know I should." He patted her back. "Please, no more tears, Linny. It breaks my heart to see you unhappy. You don't have to decide anything just now. There's time yet before the Season."

Linnet looked up at him, her choice suddenly made. "I may be forced to choose because of loving you, but my parents are the ones who are forcing me to make the choice. If they care about my happiness a fraction as much as you do, they will come to accept you." Her smile was at once tremulous and tender as she brought a shaking hand up and splayed her fingers over his heart. "You, Thomas. I choose you."

A soft scratching at the door brought Linnet back to the present. She dashed away her tears with the backs of her hands. "Yes?"

"*Pardonnez-moi,* my lady." Though her mother's lady's maid had lived in England at least as long as Linnet's parents had been married, Martine had never entirely given up her native tongue. "*La duchesse,* she wishes to see you."

"Tonight?"

"*Oui, maintenant.*"

Linnet sighed. It did not matter that she had no desire to see her mother just now. A summons from Her Grace was not a request; it was an order.

"Very well, Martine. I will be along in a few moments."

The washstand was in the small closet attached to her room. Linnet splashed some water on her face, washing away the salt from her tears, and then tidied up her bedchamber. There was no need. One of the chambermaids would see to any clutter the following day. But in the early years of her marriage, when there had only been enough money for a maid-of-all-work, Linnet had learned to clean up after herself. She hadn't minded, but Thomas had been distraught over her work-roughened hands.

Oh, Thomas. She had loved him from the first. Even with the years of separation, and in spite of all the hurt and anger, she loved him still. But the price paid for that love—by her, by Thomas, by her children, by her family . . .

She wanted better for Diana. She wanted safety. Marrying for love was foolish, especially in their class. She had followed her heart, and it had only brought her pain. She'd been so certain that love was enough to span the gap between their stations, to bridge their differences, and for years, it had seemed to work. And then her world had fallen apart, everything crashing down at once, collapsing like a house of cards caught in a tempest gale.

She'd been so shocked. She'd believed her marriage was as enduring, as stalwart as a fortress. But she and Thomas had built on rocky foundations, and tiny cracks she hadn't thought worth noting had accumulated over the years.

There were some larger cracks, too, and when they became impossible to ignore, they patched them as best they could and went on with their lives. Each of those repairs had weakened her marriage a bit more, but she never realized how fragile it had become. Not until it crumbled at the slightest push.

The tears welled up again, and she let them come. When she felt she had herself sufficiently under control, Linnet headed to see her mother. The duchess sat before the fireplace in her bedchamber.

Like the rest of Lansdowne House, the room was formal and grand, opulent and . . . oppressive.

"Good evening, Mother." Linnet pressed a kiss to her mother's wrinkled cheek. "Lady Kelton sends her regards. Are you feeling at all improved?"

The duchess shrugged. "At my age, one becomes accustomed to feeling poorly. I doubt I shall feel improved until I am dead."

Ever the optimist, Linnet thought wryly. Aloud she said, "Please don't say such morbid things. I am sure you have many years left on this earth."

"All I ask is to see my granddaughter wed."

"I want that as much as you do," Linnet reminded her. "As it happens, at dinner I was seated next to a very promising suitor for Diana."

"His name?"

"Sir Samuel Stickley. I understand he is a cousin of Lady Kelton's."

"A baronet," the duchess said with distaste. "At this point, we cannot afford to be particular. Did he seem taken with Diana?"

"Unfortunately, Sir Samuel received a summons home before he and Diana could meet, but I believe he means to call upon his return to London."

"We shall have to wait and see, then." The duchess motioned for Linnet to sit on the footstool by her chair. "Martine," she called, "bring the hairbrush from my dressing table." She untied the strip of linen from the bottom of Linnet's braid and unplaited her hair.

Taking the silver-backed brush the maid brought over, she began to brush Linnet's hair. This was a familiar ritual, one Linnet usually found calming; tonight she found it cloying. She was still a child in this house, no matter that her own child was grown and of marriageable age. She would always be a child in this house. Like a child, she couldn't escape punishment for her mistakes.

Despite assurances of forgiveness from her mother—her father refused, then and now, to speak of his daughter's fall from grace—Linnet knew the truth. Her parents had accepted her back into their household, but they would never forgive her. Neither would they forget, or let her forget, the failed marriage that had predicated her return. In what time she had left after regretting the past, Linnet worried for the future; she preferred either to dwelling on the present.

"Go on," the duchess urged. "Who were Diana's dance partners?"

"She spent a good deal of time with the Weston boy."

"He is a handsome fellow. Being seen with him can do her nothing but good."

"I'm worried she is too taken with him," Linnet fretted. "His reputation . . ."

"He is a young man." Her mother dismissed Linnet's concerns. "He is from a good family and will inherit a viscountcy. As the wife of the oldest son of a viscount, Diana would take precedence over a baronet's wife. She cannot depend upon her father's rank as you can."

There it was—a not-so-subtle jab at Linnet's socially inferior choice of husband.

"Henry Weston may be from a good family, but he isn't right for Diana," she insisted. "Why should he suddenly start paying her attention now?"

"Perhaps he is ready to do his duty by his family."

The "unlike you, you undutiful child," went unsaid. Linnet decided to change the subject. "Diana asked me the other day if this could be her last Season."

"Perhaps it should be. If she does not make a match this year, there is little reason to think she will make one next year or the year after."

Linnet blinked. "I thought you were determined to see her wed."

"If my determination were enough, she would have wed years ago, but I do not intend to give up. If Diana has not managed to bring a gentleman up to scratch by the end of the Season, and you know as well as I the unlikelihood of that coming to pass, we must consider other possibilities. Perhaps we should spend a few months in Bath or Brighton. Such places force one into much more mixed company, which is distasteful, but some men of good breeding must be there. Then again, I have thought for some time now that an older gentleman would suit Diana nicely. I shall ask Lansdowne to make a list of his acquaintances that are in need of youthful companionship."

"No!" Linnet leapt to her feet. She would sooner see Diana in a nunnery than married to some lecher old enough to be her grandfather.

"I beg your pardon?" The duchess's voice was soft—Linnet could not recall having heard her mother speak in anything other than this carefully modulated, ladylike tone—but steely.

"I would not wish to put Father to all that trouble just yet," Linnet lied, sitting back down. "The Season is only just beginning, after all."

"You have a point," her mother agreed as she resumed brushing. "And there are worse things in life than Diana remaining unwed. She would be a comfort to you in your old age, just as you have been to me."

But I want more for her than that, Linnet wanted to yell. *I don't want her living my life. Unlike you, I care about my child's happiness more than my own comfort.*

Her parents' selfishness had ruined her marriage and any chance of happiness she might have had. No, that wasn't entirely fair. Her marriage had fallen apart for other reasons, but her parents' refusal to approve of the union had not helped matters. They had worked to drive a wedge between their daughter and her undesirable husband, and it had worked.

The duchess set aside the hairbrush and began to braid Linnet's hair. "Have you any news of my grandson?"

"None since last I told you."

The duchess made a sound of annoyance. "That was nearly three weeks ago."

Linnet laughed. "I would have news of him every day if I could, but young men at university have better things to do than write their mothers. I am certain you need not worry. Alex has always been sensible and even-tempered; he has never given me a moment's worry."

"I cannot help worrying about my grandson. What with your brother off in India, refusing to come home and take some of the burden of running the estates off your father . . ."

She had heard this diatribe against her older brother so often she could have recited the words along with her mother. Linnet hardly knew David. Eight years her senior, her brother had gone off to school before she could talk. She'd seen him during school holidays, but he hadn't wanted much to do with her. Once he finished at Cambridge, he'd sailed off to India on some business, apparently never-ending, for the British East India Company. Though she didn't know David well, Linnet certainly understood his actions. There were times when she wished herself as far away as possible from her parents.

". . . I am fortunate to receive a letter every six months letting me know he is still alive. As David seems ill-inclined to do his duty," the duchess continued, "Alexander is as good as the heir to all of this." She waved her hands in an encompassing gesture.

"I am aware," Linnet said tightly. Her parents had cut her off after her marriage. They had only tried to reconcile after Alex's birth. Linnet had known what they were after and, to some extent, she even understood. Her son might someday wear the Duke of Lansdowne's coronet and mantle; in order to wear them at all comfortably, he needed to grow up with certain privileges.

She'd tried to explain as much to Thomas, when her parents had arrived at their house shortly after Alex's birth. They'd come with a retinue of servants and carriages full of extravagant gifts. Thomas had wanted to close the door in their faces, but she'd swayed him, hoping to mend the rift between them and finally earn their approval.

"Don't try to make this into some outpouring of familial love, Linnet. Your parents are only here because they chased off your brother, and Alex looks like a welcome replacement."

She wrapped her arms around him, trying to ease some of the tension pouring off him. He resisted, standing stiff and unyielding as one of the tall elm trees lining the drive. Lord, how she loved this strong, stubborn man.

"I know," she agreed, "but once they begin to know the children they can't help but love them, and Diana and Alex should be allowed the chance to know their grandparents. My parents haven't always behaved well, but they are *family. You have no kin to take the children if, heaven forbid, anything should happen to us. And you can't deny that my parents' acceptance*

will give the children certain advantages. One day, when Diana is grown and ready to be married, she will be able to make a better match as the beloved granddaughter of the Duke and Duchess of Lansdowne. Alex—"

"Alex doesn't need five nursemaids to powder his bottom, or velvet nappies, or a damned ducal cradle. I see your mother's face when she looks around our home. We might as well live in squalor. She couldn't decide which was the worse, Swallowsdale or the village inn."

"The cradle was a bit much, but they did bring it here. I half expected them to demand to raise Alex at The Hall." Her laugh came out forced and shrill.

He gave no answering smile. If anything, his face grew stonier.

"I know this is difficult for you," she said. "But it's difficult for them—"

"I don't give a damn about their feelings!" He raged around their bedroom. "Your parents lost my respect forever when they forced you to choose between us. Now they want to sweep back in and take what's mine. Alex is my son, Linnet, my son, and I'll be damned before I let those unfeeling monsters you call parents have the raising of him."

Linnet stepped in front of him and took his face in her hands. "Thomas, please, I wasn't seriously suggesting the possibility. Alex is staying here with us, where he belongs."

Rather than calming him, her words seemed to ignite some wild terror in him. He gripped her wrists, his big hands closing around her flesh like shackles. "It isn't only Alex they want." His voice was little more than a ragged whisper. "They want you, too. They want to take you from me. They never meant to let me have you."

"Hush, my love. I'm not going anywhere."

"I won't let you go, Linny."

As always, her knees felt a bit weak at the use of his pet name for her.

"You are mine—my wife. You chose me over them. Damned if I know why, but—"

She stopped him with a kiss. When they finally came up for air, she placed her hand over his heart. "I chose you because I love you. My place is, and always will be, with you and our children. If I were forced to choose again right now, I would still choose you."

He nodded, not meeting her gaze. His uncertainty, even after so many years of marriage, fractured her. "I know—" His voice wavered and cracked. He wet his lips, drew in a shaky breath and tried again. "I know you love me and the children, but you gave up so much when you chose me. You lost more than your family; you lost your entire way of life."

"I made a new family, a new life—"

"I used to hear you crying in the night, and I'd lie there, saying nothing, just hating myself for being too selfish to let you alone. . . ."

If only Thomas knew how often she cried in the night now, Linnet thought. She pressed the heel of her hand against her chest trying to drive away the ache that surfaced every time she thought of her husband.

"Are you unwell?" her mother asked.

"A bit of indigestion is all. I'm certain I shall feel better in the morning." That was what she told herself. Perhaps one of these days it would be true.

Diana stared into the darkness and listened to the clatter of horse hooves on paving. Most of the rooms in Lansdowne House boasted views of the large garden out front, or of Berkeley Square, or of the sweeping landscape of Devonshire House. Her bedchamber, though spacious enough, sat at the back of the house's west wing and faced Lambeth Mews. Should she ever question her position in this household, she need only open her window and breathe deeply.

With her thoughts scattered from her argument with her mother, she'd made the mistake of doing just that. There was nothing like the fetid odor of equine droppings to jolt a person awake. Not that she could have slept in any case. There were too many questions racing about in her head.

Had Henry been similarly distracted tonight? Had he just been going through the motions he always went through? Had he smelled some horse dung and come to his senses since then? Did he regret proposing that mad scheme or . . . kissing her? But regret implied he cared at all, which she knew he didn't. He'd kissed so many women. A kiss that had meant so much to her was commonplace to him. A wave of guilt washed over her as she acknowledged her mother had every cause for concern.

She tensed as she heard her door open. She stayed on her side, her back to the door, undecided if she should feign sleep or admit she was awake. She knew she ought to talk to her mother and apologize, but she couldn't handle any more emotional upset tonight.

Light footsteps whispered across the rug as her mother approached the bed, her movements perfuming the air with the calming scent of lavender. Her mother always kept bunches of dried lavender in her clothes press. In the past, the two of them had spent happy, sunny days gathering the fragrant flowers in the garden at The Hall. Now they spent those days in London, husband hunting.

Diana flopped over on her back with a sigh. She much preferred the flowers.

Her mother perched on the edge of her bed and made shushing sounds as she drew the disheveled coverlet up over Diana. "I didn't mean to wake you."

"I was awake," Diana admitted. "I couldn't get to sleep. I apologize for what I said. I didn't mean—"

"I know. Our minds often lose control of our mouths when we are hurting. Your unhappiness is what truly hurt me. You are my child, and I want to protect you. Mr. Weston has a reputation with women. You would do better to spend your time with a man like Sir Samuel."

At that, Diana sat up and took her mother's hand. "Sir Samuel isn't here, Mama, and for all we know he may never return. Even if he does, there's a possibility that he could take one look at me and run screaming for the hills."

"He would not!"

Diana couldn't help but laugh at her mother's outrage. There was something truly lovely in knowing at least one person believed her the catch of the Season. Her thoughts turned to Henry's offer. Again. She couldn't think of much else. Well, perhaps the actual offer featured less prominently in her thoughts than Henry's persuasive tactics.

Could he possibly do what he claimed? Only her mother would ever consider her the catch of the Season, but might Henry's attentions convince a few gentlemen that she was, indeed, a catch . . . or at least a fish worthy of closer inspection? Perhaps she shouldn't have been so dismissive.

In all likelihood, Henry would change his mind. When he awoke, he would probably think the night's events but a strange dream. They would never speak of their private interlude, and everything would be as usual. That was for the best. Although, as she had mentioned earlier to Henry, she'd gone on the same way every Season and had nothing to show for it. Maybe she did need a bit of change.

"Mama, what you said earlier about Mr. Weston . . . You're right. He's not truly interested in me."

"Dearest, I never meant to suggest the man wouldn't be attracted to you, only that you should be wary."

"Yes, well, I spoke with him tonight. He—" She took a steadying breath. "He suggested we enter into a mutually beneficial arrangement of sorts. Nothing improper," she added quickly at her mother's startled gasp. "He wants to court me, or pretend to court me at any rate, which he believes will have the result of attracting the interest of other gentlemen."

She shrugged through the tension weighing down her shoulders. "I can't say if it would work, but I can't imagine what I have to lose. His reputation is wild, I know, but no woman in the *ton* would refuse him as a suitor. I feel certain he'll take very good care with my reputation. He doesn't wish to marry me any more than I wish to be bound to him."

Her mother looked unconvinced. "Aside from the pleasure of your company, how is courting you beneficial to Mr. Weston?"

"He believes that if he's courting me, his mother won't spend the Season pressuring him about getting married. He means to involve himself in a business, and I won't make too many demands on his time since we won't truly be courting."

Her mother looked far from convinced.

"He also wishes to improve his reputation," Diana continued. "He likes that I'm proper." She was glad of the darkness in the room, for it hid the color staining her cheeks. She hadn't been at all proper earlier that night.

Those kisses. That heat. The hard strength of his body pressed against hers. The sighs, groans, and rasp of harsh, heavy breathing. The taste of him . . .

Enough. Diana fisted her hands in the coverlet and fought to bring her rapid heartbeat back under control.

"In what business does Mr. Weston mean to involve himself? Something respectable, I presume, or he wouldn't be concerned about his reputation."

"Yes, of course," Diana assured her. She hesitated a moment before admitting, "He wants to purchase a stud."

"Like your father," her mother mused.

"He is nothing like my father!"

Jagged shards of anger and hurt had embedded deep in her heart when her perfect world shattered. Time had worn them down, like pieces of glass in the sea, but it hadn't removed them. The slightest pressure brought painful memories and left her aching. Sometimes, not often, she could go an entire day without thinking about her father or of how her life might have been. . . . But she wouldn't let herself think of that right now.

"He wrote to me again about your dowry," her mother offered.

"I don't want his money," Diana snapped. "He can't buy forgiveness."

Her mother sighed as she reached out and laid a hand on Diana's shoulder. "True forgiveness must be freely given," she agreed, "but perhaps it's time you consider doing so. You aren't only punishing him with your continued refusal to see him. You're punishing yourself as well." She gently squeezed Diana's shoulder, pressed a kiss to her cheek, and got off the bed.

Diana sat unmoving as her mother left the room. Her mother's suggestion shocked her too much to do anything else. She didn't think she would ever be ready to forgive her father.

As for Henry . . .

He wasn't like her father. He couldn't be. She'd worshipped her father, loved him with her whole being, and his rejection had broken her heart. Henry could never be like her father because she would never give him that power.

CHAPTER NINE

For once, Rosie does not keep me awake, but my own nerves. What amused me but days ago now ties my stomach in knots. I fear what is between Hal and Miss Merriwether will end badly. I glimpsed a deep sorrow in her. Hal could heal her, or he could break her, and I have not my mother's certainty they will make a match of it. I have made a list of everything that could go wrong, beginning with the possibility that Miss Merriwether is not truly a Miss, but secretly married. Her husband, exiled to the Continent for some scandalous reason, will hear of Hal, return to England and they will duel, just like in The Mysterious Courtship....
—from the Marchioness of Sheldon to her aunt the Dowager Marchioness of Sheldon

From his rooms on Jermyn Street, Henry had an easy walk to Lansdowne House, which stood at the southern end of Berkeley Square. Actually, the garden of Lansdowne House *was* the southern end of Berkeley Square. A high brick wall surrounded the property, and a liveried guard opened the gate at Henry's approach. Once inside the opulent mansion, he gave his card to the butler.

He wasn't certain just what reception he expected upon his arrival, but he *had* expected to be . . . expected. From the surprised expression on the butler's face, however, Henry quickly surmised this wasn't the case. The butler quickly recovered and, after dispatching a footman to inform Miss Merriwether of her caller, he escorted Henry to an extravagantly gilded and painted room.

"Extravagant" described Lansdowne House perfectly, and Henry was a man accustomed to excess. He'd been inside the ducal mansion a time or two, along with several hundred other guests. Now, alone in one of the rooms, he saw the true scale of the place, and the luxury evident in every detail. Perhaps he should have dressed for a royal audience rather than a ride in the Park.

As he waited, he realized the butler wasn't the only one surprised by his arrival. He glowered at the flowers in his hand for close to twenty minutes before a rosy-cheeked Diana hurried into the room and dropped a curtsy. "Mr. Weston, I apologize for keeping you waiting. I wasn't expecting to see anyone."

Henry stood and bowed. "I did say I would call on you, did I not?" He held out the bouquet of day lilies.

"Oh, how lovely!" A genuine smile graced her face as she came forward to take the flowers. He felt a stab of jealousy that her happiness was due to the flowers, rather than his presence, but he told himself that was ridiculous.

Diana's eyes closed as she lifted the bouquet to her face and inhaled. "Thank you," she said softly when she lowered the flowers. "I should have readied myself, but I believed you would come to your senses."

"Come to my senses?" Henry didn't like the sound of that.

"Mr. Weston, what a pleasant surprise." Diana's mother glided into the room.

"Lady Linnet." Henry bowed in greeting, his expression giving away none of his aggravation at her untimely entrance. "Will you persuade your daughter to walk in the garden with me? We discovered last evening that we are reading the same book, and I hoped to continue our conversation." He gave Lady Linnet the grin that never failed to charm women, but there was no answering smile.

Instead, Lady Linnet regarded him with disbelief, which he supposed he deserved. The probability of Diana and him reading the same book was highly unlikely, given that he hadn't read a novel since *The Monk*. What a disappointment that had been! It contained enough debauchery and damnation that he could overlook the ridiculous plot, but there hadn't been any illustrations—not a single erotic etching or wicked woodcut, and that was inexcusable. What was the good of an immoral book without pictures?

As if she could tell the direction his thoughts had taken, Lady Linnet narrowed her eyes. "Provided you stay within sight of the house, I see no reason why you and Diana may not take a brief turn outside. Run upstairs and fetch your straw hat, Diana."

Diana was clearly hesitant to leave him alone with her mother. She cast worried looks over her shoulder as she went out of the room.

"You and my daughter have grown quite familiar of late, Mr. Weston." Displeasure rang through every word.

Belatedly, Henry realized Diana's concern hadn't been for her mother, but for him.

"Your daughter is an excellent companion, my lady. Any gentleman would be fortunate to spend time with her." He spoke the words with absolute sincerity.

Lady Linnet unbent a trifle. "Very true. I understand it's your plan to make other gentlemen realize this as well?"

Henry choked. *She had told her mother?*

"Do not die on my account. Yes, Diana told me something of your scheme, but she was convinced you would think better of it. May I understand from your presence here that you wish to go ahead with this courtship?"

"I do. My lady, I wouldn't have asked Miss Merriwether to help me if I didn't truly believe I could help her in return."

She sighed. "I can't say whether your plan will work, but neither can I dismiss it outright, much as I might wish. Gentlemen of your reputation are not the company a mother wishes for her daughter."

"Whatever you have heard—" Henry began.

She held up a hand. "Mr. Weston, I know not to blindly believe whatever gossip is spread around, but I also know most rumors have some shred of truth at their core. They rarely grow from nothing. You are an attractive young man. It would be surprising if you had no misdeeds to your name. I simply wish to keep my daughter from being one of them."

Henry no longer questioned his mother's friendship with this woman. Terrifying, the both of them. "I will concede that my reputation is not wholly undeserved, but I'm a man of my word. I promise you I would never intentionally do anything to hurt Miss Merriwether."

She regarded him for a long moment and then nodded. "I believe your intentions are good. Let us hope they do not pave the way to hell."

Diana came back into the room then, saving Henry from having to reply. She tied the ribbons of her wide-brimmed hat under her chin, her gaze darting back and forth between him and her mother, as if looking for visible signs of a fight.

Henry smiled reassuringly and extended his arm to her. "Shall we, Miss Merriwether?"

Diana laid her hand on his arm, her touch as light and delicate as that of a butterfly. He placed his free hand over hers, anchoring her to him. He inclined his head in Lady Linnet's direction. "My lady."

"Good day, Mr. Weston. Take care that you're not in the sun too long, Diana."

Henry remained quiet until he and Diana were in the garden, strolling along a winding path that skirted the oblong drive. "I wish you hadn't told your mother about our arrangement."

She shook her head. "We have no arrangement, Mr. Weston. I have not agreed."

"Yet," he amended her statement. "You haven't agreed *yet*."

"Yes, and before I do, *you* must agree to something."

"Go on," he urged.

"No other women. I've spent enough of my life as the subject of pitying glances and hushed whispers. I won't be humiliated that way again if I can help it."

"I can be discreet—"

"No." She tugged her arm from his. "If you can't go without a woman for a few months, you should find another woman to pretend to court."

For a moment, he was tempted. There had to be another woman

in London who would agree to his plan without making him take a vow of abstinence. But he couldn't ignore the challenge she unwittingly posed. He was perfectly capable of going months without feminine companionship. That he hadn't done so in over a decade meant nothing.

This wasn't painting or music; he would not fail here. He would succeed if he truly tried, and he wanted the stud badly enough to try. Diana Merriwether would solve his problems with both his mother and Lord Parr, Henry reminded himself. Finding another woman or a different solution altogether would take time he didn't have. Besides, he found he very much wanted to prove Diana wrong.

"Very well, no other women," he agreed, bidding a silent farewell to the little dancer who had recently warmed his bed. He'd already begun to lose interest in her, and she likely wouldn't have lasted much longer, even without Diana's edict. "Have you any other concerns?"

She cocked her head, peering up at him from under the wide brim of her hat. "Have you considered that our courtship might not contribute to my popularity as much as irreparably damage yours?"

He considered the scenario she presented for the barest moment, and then dismissed it. "That won't happen. Before I forget, you're to pay a call on one of my sisters in the next couple of days. You have your choice of Isabella or Olivia, though I suspect you will see both, whomever you pick."

She kicked at a stone in the path. "The Weston family will not only provide me with the pretense of a suitor, but the illusion of friends as well."

He ignored the little show of temper and walked on. "Between the attentions I mean to pay you over the next several evenings, combined with my call this afternoon, and your upcoming visit with my sisters, people will take notice. Within a week, all the gossip columns will have reported our courtship and, within a fortnight, you won't know what to do with all of your suitors."

"You think so highly of your charms?"

"I think so highly of *yours*. And I'll have you know," he said archly, "that both Isabella and Olivia are most impatient to speak with you."

"Do they know about us? Our arrangement, I mean."

"More or less." He had spoken with them briefly last night, before leaving the Kelton party. "They want to be certain your intentions are good and you will not wound my male pride or break my tender heart."

"I doubt I am capable of even bruising your male pride. As for the other, we agreed there would be no broken hearts, did we not?"

He smoothed his thumb over the back of her hand. He meant the gesture to be comforting, but her sharp intake of breath sent his thoughts racing back to the previous evening. To their bodies, so perfectly aligned, every inch of her pressed against him. To the sweet, rich taste of her. To the images of her long legs wrapped around him that had filled his mind, even while he had been buried in another woman. He snatched his hand away.

She looked at him questioningly. "Is something the matter?"

"No! I— I need to check the time." He patted his fob pocket only to realize he hadn't worn a watch. And something *was* the matter. He'd lusted after Diana Merriwether.

Again.

Last evening, he'd thought it a fluke. Even a second lapse was excusable, he'd told himself as he gathered his clothes in the dark and left the small, sparse room in the Haymarket for his own cold, empty bed. But this lusting was becoming routine, and that worried him. What worried him even more was the way his chest felt tight when she worried that his being with her might harm his reputation.

"Do you have somewhere you need to be?" she asked.

"No. Why?"

"You were looking for your watch."

"I wanted to be certain not to keep you too long in the sun," he claimed. "Your mother likes me little enough as it is."

Diana wandered to the side of the path and stared down at the flowers. "You remind her of my father," she said softly. "He owns a stud. You've likely heard of Swallowsdale Grange." She spoke the name wistfully. "That was where we lived before . . ." She faltered.

"Before your parents separated."

She nodded and faced him. "Like you, he is tall, handsome, and too charming for anyone's good. He was a performer, you know, before he worked for my grandfather. He traveled on the Continent doing trick-riding. His tumbling gave my mother fits. She said he took five years off her life with every headstand." She fiddled with the wide ribbons beneath her chin. "Whatever rumors you've heard, I swear to you, my mother was never unfaithful."

"I believe you," he said solemnly. In truth, he had no idea if Lady Linnet was innocent, but the evidence existing against her couldn't have been too damning or, duke's daughter or no, Society would never have taken her back.

"I thought, because of last night . . . because of what happened . . . between us . . ." Her cheeks were as crimson as the roses they walked past. "I don't wish my behavior to reflect poorly on my mother," she said in a rush.

Henry caught hold of her hand. "I'm not entirely certain what you just said, but I'm prepared to forget it since I suspect it will only make me cross. I'm not particularly pleasant when I'm cross, Miss Merriwether, so think carefully before you answer. Are you ashamed of kissing me?"

Henry had long ago accepted that women were more emotional creatures than men were. He expected, therefore, that when he kissed a woman, though he might experience only one emotion, namely lust, she could feel a wide range of emotions, all in close pursuit. But he did not expect shame to be one of those emotions. Women were not *ashamed* to kiss him.

He would accept Diana's shock and confusion at what had passed between them. He would even accept that she might feel embarrassed by her passionate response to him. But shock and embarrassment were different from shame. Shame was like guilt. It ate away at the soul, and he wouldn't accept it from Diana.

Her gaze fixed on his hand, holding hers. "I ought to be. I behaved terribly."

"No worse than I," he pointed out. "Then you're not ashamed?"

She looked up, meeting his eyes. "I comfort myself with the knowledge that given the legions of women you've seduced, I had little chance of resisting your charms."

"Legions?" He burst out laughing. "You greatly exaggerate my prowess. I have not seduced above half the women in London."

"*Half?*"

He nearly kissed her then, but a movement in one of the upper windows of the house caught his eye. A near save. He reached out and tweaked her nose instead.

"I'm teasing you, Diana." He shook his head. "Half the women in London," he muttered. "Come along. I daresay you've been in the sun long enough if you believe me capable of that."

"Why do you call me Diana sometimes and other times Miss Merriwether?" she asked as they started back toward the house.

"I can't make up my mind as to who you are," Henry answered truthfully. "I've known Miss Merriwether for years, and she's a shy, proper miss who wouldn't say boo to a goose. Diana, on the other hand, is something of a vixen. She accuses me of being a rogue and seducing half the women in London, and I'd wager there's a temper lurking beneath that red hair."

"Miss Merriwether sounds exceedingly dull, and Diana sounds like a termagant," she huffed.

"Don't speak ill of Diana," he scolded. "I'm growing fond of her sharp tongue. She keeps me on my toes. I like Miss Merriwether, too. Something about all that buttoned-up propriety makes a man wonder what is hiding beneath. It's exciting, really, courting two women at the same time."

"You are incorrigible." She tried to sound disapproving, but the amusement in her eyes gave her away. "Are we truly courting?"

"No, we are pretending to court," he corrected her, "which is a very good thing. If we were truly courting, I would feel obliged to behave as a gentleman. As we are pretending to court . . ." He stared at her lush mouth. "As we are pretending to court, and as I am denied other women, I think it only fair for me to kiss you as often as I like."

"Oh!" She was flustered and flushed, every inch the proper Miss Merriwether. Then, as if by magic, she transformed into Diana. She resolutely met his gaze, the gold flecks in her hazel eyes gleaming with interest. He felt her attention slide down to his lips. "Yes," she agreed.

"Yes?" he croaked, wondering if he possibly could have heard her correctly.

"I am determined this will be my last Season. I shall be five and twenty come November, and if your plan doesn't work, yours may be the only kisses I am ever to experience. You are a rogue, but I trust you won't damage my reputation, if only for fear of winding up alongside me in the parson's mousetrap. So yes, Mr. Weston, do your best."

From demure to daring, all in the blink of an eye. Henry was almost reluctant to turn her loose on the men of the *ton*. A tall oak stood alongside the path a few feet ahead. As soon as they reached it, he stopped her, using the thick trunk to shield them from the house.

"If you agree to call me Henry, I'll do better than my best." He lifted her hand and pressed a kiss to her palm, then gently nipped the fleshy bit at the base of her thumb. He had heard the spot called the mount of Venus; the size of the mound indicated whether a person was of a passionate nature.

"Henry!"

She exhaled his name on a shivery breath. Her eyes were unfocused, the pupils wide with arousal. Without taking his gaze from her face, he licked the spot he'd bitten. A shudder rippled through her body.

Unable to resist, he backed her into the tree and demanded her mouth—hard and wet, fast and hot. When he stepped back, he noted with satisfaction that she swayed on her feet. He steadied her and waited for her dazed expression to recede before indicating they should resume their walk.

Yes, Diana Merriwether most definitely possessed a passionate nature, and for the length of time she was his to pleasure, Henry would do better than his best.

He would do his worst.

CHAPTER TEN

You cannot possibly consider this Season the same as previous ones, but why did I not hear the news from you? Instead, I received congratulations that my sister had secured the interest of Henry Weston. I adore you, Diana, but I question this match. Are you well? Also, will you ask Weston his opinion on the proper amount of starch for a cravat?

—from Alexander Merriwether to
his sister Diana Merriwether

Henry was wrong. The newspapers, fearing libel suits, took longer than a week to run the unbelievable story of her courtship. By that time, word had spread to all of London, down to the lowliest ragpicker, and bets were entered into the books at Brooks's and White's. And though she did indeed have suitors by the end of a fortnight, she knew exactly what she wanted to do with them....

Nothing pleasant.

They gathered in her drawing room, but it wasn't as if any of them were there for her. Well, perhaps one of them came for her. Sir Samuel Stickley's business at home had been quickly resolved and, as he'd promised her mother, he had called at Lansdowne House. He was as amiable as her mother had described, and he hadn't taken one look at her and run screaming for the hills. Admittedly, he had potential.

But as for the rest . . . They were merely the fawning courtiers of the golden prince of the *ton*. Wherever he went, they followed. She wished she could blame them, but after so many years spent standing in the shadows, she found herself just as drawn to Henry's light. He was all levity and good humor, though their morning rides tested the latter.

Just being with him tested her.

"Why is it only at this ungodly hour that a body can ride without trampling someone?" he grumbled as their horses ambled down Rotten Row following an exhilarating race.

"It must be near noon," she protested.

"I had a late night of it." He chuckled. "What with Bess's games, I didn't seek my bed until five o' clock this morning. I must remember to rest up before my next visit. . . ."

He kept talking, but she stopped listening. He'd been with a woman all night. Anger rose up, along with hurt and the harsh sting of betrayal. Real or not, their courtship had rules and, after only a fortnight, Henry had broken them without a care. Without a care for her.

Of course, he doesn't care for you.

Her mare sensed her inattention and jerked the reins out of her hands.

"Have a care, Diana," Henry admonished. He urged his horse close to hers and leaned down to grab her reins. She refused to look at him as he handed them to her.

He sighed. "I've angered you. Come, berate me, and have done with it."

"How could you?" she whispered.

"How could I what?" He sounded sincerely confused. "I didn't realize you were truly upset. Diana, please, tell me what's wrong."

"*Bess.*" She nearly choked on the name. "You promised there would be no other women."

He cursed before leaning close. "I want you to listen carefully to me." His voice was low and rough. "I spent last evening in the company of Rutland and *his wife,* Elizabeth. She is my cousin through my mother's family, and His Grace plans to invest in my stud. Bess is nearing her confinement and feeling poorly. Playing piquet until dawn to amuse her was the least I could do."

"I thought—"

"I know what you thought. You were wrong. Look at me, Diana."

She obeyed and got lost in those boundless blue eyes.

"You believe I'll disappoint you," he continued. "You believe that men are destroyers, not protectors. That's not the usual way of the world. Trust me to take care of what's mine and keep you safe. I want to lighten your burdens, sweetheart, not add to them."

Her heart tripped at the easy endearment, began to fall at what he promised, but she pulled herself back. Henry didn't understand. Her father had carried her world on his shoulders, and he had dropped it. She couldn't allow another person to hold her happiness, no matter how strong and capable.

She shook her head. "I'm not yours."

"You are for the length of our courtship." His blue eyes were serious, searching, and then they crinkled at the corners as that crooked grin came out to play. "When we're together, I want you to practice setting your cares aside and taking pleasure in the moment. We're each seeking something out of this courtship, and I'm determined we shall both get what we want. In the meantime, you, my dear Miss Merriwether, are in desperate need of amusement. Fortunately for you, I am extremely qualified to teach you about enjoying life."

He was.

They set about exploring London like strangers to the city, fiercely determined to experience all the metropolis had to offer. They marveled at the Egyptian mummy at the British Museum. They argued over the merits of the artworks presented in the Royal Academy exhibition at Somerset House. Henry dragged her, along with his younger brother and his nephew, to the Leverian Museum. Diana found the cases of dried insects and deceased animals repulsive, but she found pleasure in the obvious excitement of the boys—all three of them.

Henry made countless introductions as they walked along the best shops on Mount Street and drove in the Park during the fashionable hour. He invited her to Covent Garden, where his brother-in-law had taken a private box for the Season. They went to Vauxhall, chaperoned by his sisters and their husbands, where they passed a glorious April evening. Henry even secured a subscription for Almack's and danced with her on Wednesday nights under the fierce stares of the Lady Patronesses.

He asked her to dine with his family, an occasion she enjoyed tremendously as laughter and lively conversation dominated the meal. Diana issued a return invitation, and despite the ensuing affair being far more dismal, he seemed content. She suspected that his contentment had everything to do with her grandfather's French *chef de cuisine*.

He won over her grandmother by virtue of his courtship. Her grandfather only said that Henry's grandfather had been a good man, and Henry had the look of him—high praise, as the duke rarely said anything to anyone. Her mother remained cool toward Henry, but then, she knew the truth.

Her mother determinedly championed Sir Samuel. He, too, came to dinner. The baronet called on Diana regularly, walked with her in the Park, and danced with her at balls. She thought he would propose by the end of the Season. If he did, she would accept. She liked him well enough, liked the safety he represented.

Diana never felt *safe* with Henry, but her comfort with him had reached a place she had never found outside her mother and brother. Though they had little in common save a mutual love of horses, they never lacked for conversation. He made her laugh with stories about his days at Eton and Oxford. She told him terrifying tales of life under the reign of Her Grace, the Duchess of Lansdowne. They wove dreams of Henry's future stud, and he held her hand when she ventured to talk about her past. He teased her when she became overly concerned with proprieties, while she appealed to his better nature when he forgot them.

Mostly.

When he forgot propriety with regard to her, she forgot everything but the pleasure she found in his arms. She could have no doubts about his roguish past; he seduced her far too often, and far too easily. In the mix of all the couples dispersing after a dance, he would whisk her out of the ballroom and onto the terrace, or behind a potted palm or a marble column.

Those were hasty, stolen kisses. Just enough so his wild taste clung to her lips, so his wicked scent of masculine skin and approaching storm lingered in her every breath. Those kisses haunted her days, but at night, alone in her bed, she allowed herself to relive his other kisses.

The ones where he hurried her down the hall to a deserted room, an empty alcove—the man had a diabolical knack for locating unoccupied spots. And who but Henry could turn a linen closet into a perfect site for seduction?

"Henry!" She laughed as he pushed her inside the tiny room. "This is a lin—"

His mouth came down on hers as he pulled the door shut, blanketing them in darkness. Her lips parted, welcoming him, as she let the first burst of pent-up desire rush over her. He wrapped his arms around her, clasping her tightly to him—one of his hands splayed across her back, the other indecently lower—as if any distance between their bodies was too much. As if she could go anywhere in the tiny space. As if she wanted to be anywhere else.

She raised a hand to Henry's jaw as she sucked on his upper lip. She wanted more than the encouraging sound of pleasure she got. Ever so slowly, she lightly traced his upper lip with the tip of her tongue. Diana sensed the need rising in him, but he held still save for the fingers clenching her behind. She let him feel a hint of teeth.

He tensed, groaned, and then, after gently nipping her lower lip in retaliation, he seized control. As he devoured her mouth, he pulled both her arms behind her back and held them there, restraining her wrists in one big hand. She opened her eyes, but she could see nothing in the pitch-blackness.

At his mercy.

She gasped when his other hand molded over her breast. He tightened his hold on her wrists, but he eased back from her mouth, letting her breathe as he dropped soft kisses over her face. She barely noticed them. Her entire being centered on where his palm cupped her. Her breasts felt full and heavy, and her nipples strained against her corset. She arched against him, rubbing restlessly, trying to ease the ache.

Henry slowly made his way back to her mouth as his hand moved higher. He traced his forefinger across the sensitive swell of her breasts. Back and forth, back and forth, Diana floated between the intoxication of his kiss and the rhythmic caress. Distantly, she realized his finger skated progressively lower, easing under neckline of her gown, and then lower still. Sweeping beneath the layers of her corset and shift, he grazed the tip of her breast.

She jolted out of her dreamlike state, the light touch spearing pleasure through her. Henry took her choked cry into his mouth as he pressed her body into the wall of shelves. Her knees buckled as he rubbed over her nipple in slow, deliberate circles. Desire spiraled low in her belly, throbbed between her legs. She clenched her thighs together, too conscious of the emptiness at her core.

Her virginal state didn't preclude some knowledge of sexual matters. She'd grown up on a stud in the country, and her grandfather collected ancient statues. She ate dinner every night with nude men looking on, though there was a definite difference between cold marble and heated flesh. From what pressed against her, there existed another, er, sizable difference between the statuary and Henry. Her hips jerked at the thought.

"You steal my wits," he whispered against her ear.

The loss of her sight sharpened Diana's other senses. She heard the husky catch to Henry's voice, the rough sounds of their breathing, the heavy drumming of her heart. She savored the faint taste of sugar clinging to his lips, drank the brandy from his breath. She caught the subtle smell of the lavender and rosemary folded away in the linens and the sweet fragrance of the rose water she had dabbed on earlier that evening. Stronger than both, the deliciously masculine scent she had come to associate with Henry wrapped around her. Each time they came together, the scent darkened as the storm built.

Closer and closer, the storm approached. Soon, she wouldn't be able to outrun those tempestuous clouds. Soon, the storm would break. *It would break.*

Diana's breath caught as Henry scraped his nail over her nipple.

The vase shattered in a burst of blue and white. One of the pieces landed near her hiding place. Diana hugged her knees tighter underneath the desk.

"Thomas! That vase was a wedding gift from the Prince of Wales," her mother exclaimed.

"And now it's broken. Just like my trust. Just like our marriage...."

"No," she whispered. She pushed at Henry's chest until he removed his hands and backed away, as much as he was able to do so in a space not meant to hold one person, let alone two.

"Di?" Confusion and a hint of regret colored the syllable.

"I— I shouldn't . . ." She swallowed hard. "I have to get back."

"Of course, you mustn't keep Sir Stick-in-the-Mud waiting," he grumbled.

"I wish you wouldn't call him that. Sir Samuel is—"

"Stickley is a duller-than-dull stick in the mud with atrocious taste in cattle."

That was true, Diana thought. She'd barely managed to hide her dismay when Sir Samuel had proudly showed off his newly acquired carriage horses, an ugly, mismatched pair of gray nags.

"I'm not marrying the man for his taste in horses," she said quietly. "I may not be marrying him at all, but he's my best chance at the moment. This behavior isn't helping you get your stud, and it could very well hurt my chance at a husband. Sir Samuel is exactly the sort of man I want. *This*—" She gestured between them. "*This* is . . ."

Wonderful. Terrifying. She took a breath. "This is more than kissing. For both our sakes, we must remember what we stand to lose if we were found like this." She wedged herself past Henry and exited into the hall, which was blessedly empty, and closed the door. A downward glance had her hastily rearranging her bodice, but even properly dressed, Diana feared her *im*proper behavior would be all too obvious. She fanned her hot cheeks and smoothed her hands over her hair.

She tried to find her composure as she returned to the party, but her thoughts kept circling to a dark, passion-filled room and a man who threatened her prized control. Henry always made her forget herself, but tonight, he'd also made her remember her past. Even more reason to hurry back to Sir Samuel.

Henry stood in the dark, angry and frustrated, wondering how he'd lost control. Again. Since that first night, he'd been careful not to let things get out of hand, but tonight he'd lived up to Diana's low expectations and acted every inch the rogue. She'd come to her senses, thank God, but what if she hadn't?

Guilt settled on his shoulders, an unaccustomed, unwanted weight. Whatever she thought, he was no seducer of innocents. She was the granddaughter of a duke, damn it all, and he was a gentleman. A gentleman didn't fondle a well-bred young lady's breasts, no matter how tempting, and he didn't continue reflecting on how they had felt in his hands or how they might taste—

He cut off the thought, swearing as his already uncomfortably tight breeches got a bit tighter. He was fit to burst with wanting her, and all from touching her breast. Touching. Her. Breast. He hadn't taken her soft flesh in his mouth and tasted her, or sneaked a hand beneath her skirts and found her damp with wanting him, or—

Christ. He passed a shaky hand over his face. Perhaps he should leave town for a short time. He could find a small village inn somewhere with a lusty tavern wench and take her until this damnable lust abated. Diana need never find out. He'd be protecting her, really. She'd challenged him to go without a woman for the length of their courtship and, by God, admitting defeat would be better than the alternative.

If he kept along his current path, he would ruin her. He didn't have much to start with in the way of brains. What little he had ceased functioning in her presence, likely because all his blood congregated south. Had she not stopped him tonight, he didn't know if he would have controlled himself. He thought it more likely he would have greedily accepted everything she had to give . . . and then taken more.

Despite being perilously close to "on the shelf," Diana was an innocent. She wasn't, thanks to him, quite *untouched,* but she was a virgin, and a virgin she must remain for her future husband. That was the reason she'd agreed to this courtship. She wanted a husband, a boring country gentleman like that starchy Sir Samuel. If Henry ruined her, or was caught trying, she would still get a husband—him. That would be disastrous.

Well, maybe not *disastrous.* He could imagine himself in worse situations. Hell, maybe he *had* lost his mind. He didn't want to marry Diana. This desire he felt for her was the result of spending too much time with her and not enough time with other women. Celibacy didn't suit him.

True, the past two months hadn't been as challenging as he'd expected, but he'd been busy meeting with investors, teasing Diana, planning improvements for Ravensfield, kissing Diana, considering horses to purchase for the stud, and pretending to court Diana. If he were truthful with himself, he hadn't needed to pretend. He enjoyed spending time with her. She amused him, challenged him, understood him, believed in him, and brought forth a gentler side of him. A softer side. Maybe even a *better* side.

There had always been more than lust between them. Even before they'd begun their arrangement, she'd made him want to help her wallflower friend. What was the girl's name? Miss Featherbill? Whatever her name was, he'd wanted to help her dance with Gabriel to please Diana. He'd arranged to have a bouquet of day lilies delivered to Lansdowne House every week because he knew the flowers would make Diana happy. He'd spent more time with her than with any past lover, and his interest in her hadn't waned.

He sighed. He needed to find her a husband. If he found her a husband, he could think of her as unavailable. He might be a rogue, but he had his morals, and he did not carry on with married women. Yes, he must get her married off and soon.

There was that toad-eating Sir Samuel, but Henry couldn't like the man. He doubted Stickley had ever broken a rule, or a bone . . . or a spindly-legged table. Diana didn't really want to marry an uptight prig like Stickley. She couldn't. There was too much passion in her. And Stickley didn't deserve her.

He would never make her laugh. Diana was too self-possessed to laugh easily or often, but Henry knew how to break through her reserve. And how she rewarded him! Her hearty, open laughter wrapped around a man's insides and coursed through his blood like fine brandy. Stickley wouldn't know what to do with that rare, precious sound. He wouldn't be driven, on hearing it, to kiss her breathless.

Diana was already too proper by half. Marriage to Stickley would wither her spirit. She needed someone who would keep her from being too serious. Someone who would coax out the passion she tried so hard to suppress and teach her to revel in those desires. What she needed, Henry decided, was a rogue.

Someone like him.

No, not someone *like* him.

Just him.

Henry leaned back hard against the wooden shelves as he allowed himself to consider the possibility. Him. Diana. Marriage. The words hovered in his mind like dandelion seeds adrift on a gentle current of air. He waited for a fast rush of denial to blow the mad notion away, but none came. Instead, the little bits of fluff drifted down and put out roots. With each one, new pictures grew in his mind. Teasing. Talking. Touching. Laughing. Helping. Engaging in all the libidinous acts allowed between married persons. . . .

"Marriage." He spoke the word softly, testing out the taste of it. "Married. Married to Diana." The words were new and strange, but he liked them. He decided to try a variation as an experiment. Who was considered the catch of this Season? He had to think for a moment before he recalled Miss Sibylla Hill, an uncommonly pretty, uncommonly silly girl with a gift for setting his teeth on edge. "Married to— Dear God, I'd rather be hanged," he muttered. "It might come to that if I had to listen to her day in and day out."

He realized, somewhat abruptly, that he was talking to himself in someone else's linen closet . . . not that the situation would necessarily be less objectionable were he in his own. He squared his shoulders and opened the door, praying that the corridor was empty and he wouldn't have to come up with an explanation for his presence there.

As it happened, the object of his recent thoughts was exiting the ladies' retiring room just opposite. He stepped into the hall, just managing to close the closet door before she caught sight of him.

"Mr. Weston!" She giggled. "My goodness! You appeared so very suddenly. Whatever were you doing in—?" She frowned. "Where were you?"

"I—"

No sooner had he opened his mouth to speak than Miss Hill took care to show him she was more than capable of holding up his half of the conversation as well as her own.

"No, I shall not make you say it. You were waiting for me. Oh, it is too wicked of you!" she trilled and rapped his arm with her fan. "You nearly waited too long. I almost gave away the dance I saved for you. You are a devil to keep me in such a state of anticipation. My nerves are too delicate— Oh, I do not mean to scold you. I shall be generous and forgive you."

She batted long, dark lashes at him as she came close. "My uncle says men prefer generous women. You would need your wife to be very . . ." She twined both her arms around his, despite the limb not having been proffered, then afforded him a gamine smile. "Very *generous,* would you not say?" She rubbed against his arm, pressing her breasts into him.

Henry regarded her coolly. "You, Miss Hill, are playing a very dangerous game."

"Oh, you look so cross," she pouted. "I only wished to . . ."

"Extend your generosity?" he drawled.

She nodded, clinging even more tightly to his arm.

He wasn't the least bit tempted. He had no interest in Miss Hill. He wanted Diana, and only Diana. As he accepted his fate, something in him calmed and settled. Diana was right. There was more than kisses between them, and he was through fighting it. She was right, and she was right for him.

His dear Miss Merriwether had best prepare herself because he was changing the rules of their arrangement. Henry didn't fool himself that getting her to the altar would be easy. Their time together had given him a very clear understanding of Diana's thoughts about men and marriage. She didn't think highly of either. She thought even less of rogues.

That explained her preference for Stickley. Diana didn't think of the deplorably dull baronet as a *man;* she wanted a marriage of convenience that left her invulnerable to any emotional upset. That was what she *thought* she wanted. Diana's body told Henry that she wanted *him.* He couldn't promise they would always be in perfect harmony, but he could promise that they would always enjoy making up.

He wouldn't enjoy what he was about to do, but if seeing Miss Hill in his arms caused Diana even a small fraction of the frustration he incurred on seeing her with Stickley, the price his ears paid would be well worth it.

"Miss Hill, may I escort you back to the ballroom? I trust you will not be so cruel as to deny me a dance."

She flashed him a brilliant smile, but he would swear she was annoyed with him. They were equals, then. He didn't have time to play Miss Hill's games. Keeping a step ahead of Diana presented enough of a challenge for him. Diana might not want a rogue, but she had one all the same, and he wasn't letting her go.

If he had to fight a little dirty . . . His mouth curved into a slow, anticipatory smile. He could teach Diana how enjoyable being a little dirty could be.

CHAPTER ELEVEN

I told myself I would be content if only I could dance with him, but having done so, I find I want more. Now I tell myself, if he will but call on me, I will be content. How easily we lie to ourselves! I wish you were with me, my dearest Lucy, that you might speak sense to me. Too many dreams cloud my perspective. . . .

—from Elizabeth Fothergill to
her sister Lucinda Fothergill

Henry awoke the following morning filled with purpose and anticipation. His good humor lasted until his manservant, Jasper, entered his bedchamber and informed him that a message had come round from Weston House. His father wished to see him at his earliest convenience. The news cast a pall over a day previously bright with possibility.

As Henry dressed, he racked his brains for something he might have done to deserve this summons. His behavior in the past weeks had been exemplary, and the only woman he'd kept company with was Diana. Christ, had his father found out about his arrangement with Diana? Or worse, the way he had very nearly taken advantage of her last night?

He felt like a man headed for the gallows as he walked the short distance between his bachelor's lodgings and the family residence.

He entered his father's study with not a little trepidation. "You wanted to see me, sir?"

"Hal." His father sat before the fireplace, his expression serious. He gestured to the chair beside his. "Come and sit down. I want to speak with you."

That sounded ominous. "Oh?" Henry asked, cautiously moving forward.

"When you first came to me about the stud, I gave you something of a rough time, and I apologize."

Henry shook his head as he settled into the wingback chair. "There's no need for an apology, sir. I understand your hesitation, and I've taken all of your advice to heart. Several investors are ready to write bank drafts, and though I can't manage to keep my name out of the papers, there's been nothing lascivious."

"I know, and I'm pleased with the direction you have shown of late. You have proven very committed to this business of the stud, and you've surprised me with your pursuit of Miss Merriwether." His father laughed. "I never thought you'd take a wife to convince Parr you've changed your wicked ways. Or have you realized that your mother is always right, and there is little use in fighting her? Either way, I commend you on your choice."

Henry shifted in his seat, uneasy with his father's praise since his initial motivation for the courtship had been to escape his mother's matchmaking and reassure Parr just long enough for him to sign over the deed. Marriage had only occurred to him last night. It wasn't that he doubted his sudden decision to wed Diana—once he'd opened his mind to the possibility, he'd known marrying her was the right course for him—but Diana didn't even know his intentions were real yet. And he wasn't entirely sure she would be happy about the change.

"She hasn't yet agreed to marry me," he pointed out. He tried to joke, but the words came out wooden. "She thinks I'm a rogue, and I'm not certain how to convince her I'm serious in my attentions."

"So your wild past has caught up to you? The right woman will reform a man, but convincing a woman of that . . . I don't envy you. A word of advice: A woman will have difficulty believing you've changed when you sneak her off and misbehave at every opportunity."

Christ. "Did anyone else see us, or only you?"

"See you?" His father frowned in confusion, and then chuckled. "Ah, no, I spoke from my own experience. I had the damnedest time convincing your mother—"

Henry groaned. "I don't want to hear this."

His father grinned. "Someday you will have this conversation with your own son. Lord, what a thought! Now, in preparation for this grandson you will give me, I have some things for you." He reached into his waistcoat pocket and pulled out a ring. A cluster of diamonds gleamed as he held it out to Henry.

"Your mother asked me to give this to you. It would please her if you gave this to Miss Merriwether as a betrothal ring. It belonged to your grandmother. Your mother's mother," he elaborated. "She died only a few months after you were born, but she was so delighted to have a grandchild. We were all so excited for your birth." He shook his head, laughing a little as he remembered.

"Your mother said you would be the most adored child in all of England, a veritable little prince, what with all of us fawning over you and scrambling to do your bidding. That's why she named you Henry. You've always been her prince, Hal."

"How is it that I am a mere prince while Richard, who has not yet had his eighth birthday, is a king?" Henry asked, taking the ring. Eight smaller diamonds were set around a larger stone, like a flower of brilliants.

"Prince Hal matures into King Henry. You would know that had you applied yourself—"

"—to my studies. Yes, yes, I've heard it before. Everything was just so dull. All that Latin and Greek. . . . At least there wasn't any Shakespeare."

"I won't tell your mother that you said that."

"I appreciate that. I very much appreciate the ring as well, but why isn't Mother giving it to me herself?"

His father leaned forward, bracing his hands on his knees. "We both know that if your mother gave you this ring, she'd cry and make a big fuss."

Henry nodded.

"And we both know she'll cry and make a big fuss when you announce your engagement."

Again, Henry nodded.

"I offered to give you the ring in order to keep the crying and fussing to a minimum."

"And she agreed?" Henry asked, astonished.

"I simply suggested that too much maternal excitement might send you fleeing in the opposite direction from the altar." He rose and walked to his desk. "There is something else I have for you—an early wedding present, if you will." He picked up a large document and brought it over to Henry.

Henry looked at the first words and was glad he had remained seated. "This is the deed to Ravensfield," he said incredulously.

"The indenture is written up. You can arrange with Parr to sign it. I spoke with him last week, and he agreed the stud would be in capable hands. You have done everything I asked of you and more, and you will need a place to set up once you're married. I thought you should have a home to offer your bride when you speak to Lansdowne."

Henry stared at the vellum sheet, still in shock.

"I never doubted your ability to succeed, Hal, but you haven't always been willing to work hard. You felt the pressure of being the oldest and the heir, and you chose not to try rather than chance failure. No one is expecting you to be perfect. Your mother and I will always be proud of you, win or lose, so long as you try your best. I hope you know that. Now, I expect there is someone with whom you'd like to share this news."

"Yes, sir," Henry answered dazedly. "I can't begin to thank you en—"

"Thank me with a grandchild." At Henry's eager nod, he added, "One conceived *after* the wedding." He strode to the window and looked out. "The day is very fine. A clever man would celebrate in the Park with a pretty woman. A very clever man would ask Cook if she has some strawberries left over from last night's tart to take along as a snack."

Henry joined him at the window. "Is this a jest, or are you truly giving me romantic lessons?"

His father raised a brow. "Are you not one of seven children? Your mother and I will be married thirty years come December. I do have some knowledge of the way a woman's mind works."

Henry relaxed. "Just as long as you only plan to talk about her mind."

"A woman's mind is the key to the rest of her. Once you learn a woman's mind—discover what she wants—you can begin giving her what she needs."

Henry pondered his father's words as Cook packed a basket for him. He knew Diana wanted Sir Samuel. At least, she wanted to want the baronet. But she needed *him*. He'd planned to court her a while longer, seduce her a bit more, but a need for action filled him.

Though he could scarcely believe it, Ravensfield Hall belonged to him. He was thrilled, no question, but he couldn't help feeling as though he'd been given the place under false pretenses. He shook off the doubts. He'd secured the investors, hadn't he? And though he hadn't intended to change his ways when he started courting Diana, such a circumstance had to be insignificant in light of his intention to wed her.

Henry walked home and asked his manservant to have his phaeton readied. He was anxious to show Ravensfield to Diana, but as he couldn't imagine Lady Linnet approving that particular excursion, that would have to wait. They'd talked many times of what he imagined for the stud, discussed the changes he planned to make. He'd shared his hopes and dreams. Now he would ask her to share his life. He pictured her shock, the delightful crimson flush sweeping over her fair skin. She would come up with a thousand and one reasons why they shouldn't marry, but he would put her fears to rest, one by one, until she said yes.

He whistled as he climbed into his phaeton, stowed the basket, and steered his team toward Berkeley Square. He was too early to call, but what, he wondered, did one more transgression matter? The butler, Snellings, knew him by now; he showed Henry into the drawing room to wait, though the pompous arse made his disapproval clear.

Henry paced around the room, trying to expend some of his restless energy, and thought about the improvements needed at Ravensfield. He'd concentrated his plans on making the place habitable for horses. He needed to extend that concern to humans. The house wanted a good cleaning and fresh paint. Staff. A good cook. Food was important, but he also needed . . . a bed.

A large, comfortable bed.

Henry jumped at the sound of someone clearing a throat. Diana had entered the room, along with her mother.

"Mr. Weston, to what do we owe the pleasure of your company?" Lady Linnet's inflection implied just how little pleasure she took in seeing him.

"I apologize for the early hour, my lady, but I hoped to be the proverbial early bird and—"

"Are you calling me a worm?" Diana rounded on him, her hazel eyes flashing.

"Diana," her mother gently rebuked.

"Miss Merriwether, I meant no offense. Will a ride in the Park and a visit to Gunter's suffice as apology?"

Diana's eyes lit with pleasure. "How lovely!"

"I hope so. Can you think of a better way to celebrate?"

"What is the occasion?" asked Lady Linnet.

"I am now the proud owner of Ravensfield Hall, my lady, and I wouldn't have my estate without your daughter's help."

"What?" Diana gaped at him. "When did this happen?"

He grinned at her. "My father gave me the deed this morning."

"Oh, how wonderful." She beamed at him, and he knew she was genuinely happy for his good fortune. "You're right. We must celebrate."

"Indeed, you must," her mother echoed. "I hope you will have a very pleasant day together. It's already mid-June; there will not be many more like it."

Henry caught the meaning behind Lady Linnet's words. She thought he would end his arrangement with Diana today. He supposed she was right, in a way. The old arrangement had served its purpose—it had brought them together—but the time had come for a new one. Ravensfield Hall was his, and by the end of the afternoon, he hoped Diana would be as well. He patted his pocket and felt the slight bulge of the betrothal ring. His future mother-in-law could say what she wished. This afternoon would be more than pleasant, and he planned to have a lifetime more like it.

Shortly after setting out, Diana realized two things, neither of them pleasant. First, while most phaetons could comfortably hold three people, those phaetons did not include Henry Weston. Squashed between him and her maid, Diana endured jostling, jarring, and jouncing before they reached the Park. Her physical discomforts mattered little, however, in light of her second realization. In her earlier excitement, she hadn't considered the consequences of Henry's acquisition.

Now that he had his stud, he didn't need to continue with their arrangement. With Sir Samuel waiting off in the wings, neither did she need Henry. He would end their arrangement today. That explained her mother's good cheer.

Henry drove to an inch, his perfectly matched roan mares responding to the lightest of touches as he guided them on the path running along the Serpentine. When the road began to veer toward The Ring, Henry pulled up his team. His groom jumped down from his perch at the back and came around to help her maid down.

Henry got out next, handed the reins to his groom, and held out his hand to her. "I wish to speak with you about something. Will you walk with me?"

"That sounds serious." Her voice only wobbled the tiniest bit as he assisted her descent.

"It is serious," Henry agreed. "More serious, even, than food."

He lifted the phaeton's seat and removed a wicker basket and a folded blanket. Tucking the blanket under the arm holding the basket, he gestured toward a group of trees near the river. "Shall we?"

They left her maid with Henry's groom and walked until they found a shady spot. As Henry turned his attention to laying out the blanket and unpacking the basket, Diana watched him, her heart in her throat. He'd removed his hat, and patches of sunlight filtered down through the leaves to dance in his golden hair and across his broad shoulders. She ached to touch him.

More than anything, she wanted to trail the pad of her finger back and forth over the fullness of his lower lip. His eyes would take on that sensual slant she had come to know, darkening to a rich sapphire. His tongue would dart out to taste her skin, causing her to gasp in surprise. How she could be surprised in her own daydream, she didn't know, but as it *was* her daydream, she allowed herself that tiny gasp. She would try to pull her hand away, but his hands would come up and hold it in place, trapping her as he nipped the tip of her finger. He would gaze up at her from beneath heavy, lowered lids.

"Di?"

She shivered, helpless to respond when he turned her name into a deep growl of a question. Taking her silence as assent, he drew the digit into the hot cavern of his mouth. His tongue swirled over her flesh, rough and soft all at once. He made a noise, a hum of appreciation, pleased by her taste. The vibrations from his throat traveled through her hand and exploded throughout her body.

"Di? Diana?"

She blinked owlishly at the glass of wine Henry held out to her.

"Are you too warm?" he asked in concern. "You are all flushed, and though I enjoy nothing better than seeing you in this state, I have not done anything to provoke it. Come and sit."

Yes, she was too warm—hot, in fact. And no, Diana thought, he hadn't done anything other than being himself. Her own wicked imagination had done the rest.

"I am perfectly well," she assured him, sitting on the blanket and taking the wine he offered. "Tell me about the stud. I know you have many eager investors, but I thought Lord Parr would not make a decision until the end of the Season."

"I thought so as well, but my father saw him and talked him around. Our courtship has proven very convincing, which is why I wanted to speak with you."

"You needn't say anything. I understand. Truly," she said, her throat was thick with unhappiness.

"You sound hoarse. If you feel ill, I'll take you home."

"No!" she shouted, the ferocity of her outburst surprising them both. "I apologize," she said more softly. "I appreciate your concern. I may have a touch of something"—the Henry Fever—"but there's no need for me to go home, not yet. Please, I want to stay here with you." She would not willingly give up this afternoon, the magical time spent alone with Henry. Certainly not if, as she suspected, this was to be her last.

"There's no need to take on so." Henry laughed as he reached over and chucked her under the chin. He lifted her face and frowned. "Before you were redder than these strawberries, and now you're so pale I could count every last freckle."

She ducked her head in embarrassment.

"I think about it, you know," he continued. "Counting your freckles. Not really counting them so much as kissing them. Good, now you have a bit of color again. Yes, sometimes I lie awake at night imagining kissing your freckles. Every last one."

"But I have freckles all over my body," she blurted out, daring a glance at him.

He regarded her with undisguised hunger. "Yes." He nodded slowly. "So I imagine."

Unsure how to respond to that, Diana sipped her wine. After a glance in the direction of their servants, Henry shook his head. "If we were truly alone right now . . ." He sighed. "I may as well see you are fed."

There wasn't much, only some strawberries, a loaf of bread and a round of cheese, but with Henry handing her every bite, it was a feast. They both had their gloves off, so their hands brushed with each bit of food that passed between them. His fingers touched his lips and her fingers touched her lips; in a way, they kissed every time their fingers met.

She stared as he licked his fingers after eating a juicy strawberry. He caught her watching him, paused, and then began again in a more deliberate manner. He laved and sucked at his fingers, holding her gaze all the while. Her body tightened with need.

Henry took one last lick, and then handed her a strawberry. Fortunately, her unconscious mind knew how to chew, swallow, and breathe, because she could not think past the frantic pounding of her heart. She licked at her thumb, then sucked the tip of her finger into her mouth. The tugging sensation migrated to her breasts before lodging in her core. Henry's eyes blazed blue fire, so much hotter than she had imagined in her daydream.

And after today, he would return to being a dream. Diana lowered her hand and looked away from Henry. He allowed her to retreat and began to talk about his estate, going on at length about the stables, which he knew would interest her. In addition to her father's height, red hair, and freckles, she had inherited his love of horses. Some of her fondest memories were of the days before her parents separated when she had spent long blissful, dirty hours helping her father and the grooms in the stables. Most of her other happy memories were with Henry.

Think about that later, she told herself. She set aside her worries and memorized the sound of his voice, how he gesticulated with his large hands, and the way the dimple in his left cheek showed when he was excited. And then, since she was with him, she simply let herself be.

The afternoon passed all too quickly, and Henry drove them back to Berkeley Square. Since Gunter's was the sole place where she could go without a chaperone, Diana dismissed her maid. Given the popularity of the confectioner's shop, Diana expected the crowd of carriages drawn up around the railings of the central garden. Under the shade of the plane trees, fashionable ladies sat in their equipages and savored their sweets while their escorts stood and did the same.

Someone waved, and Diana absently waved back before recognizing Eliza Fothergill. The man accompanying her turned to see who had caught Eliza's attention. Good heavens, was that Mr. Gabriel? He bowed in her direction before turning back to Eliza.

Even from a distance, Diana saw the look of pure adoration on his face. A flash of white-hot jealousy tore through her, leaving her ashamed and not a little shaken. She gathered her composure as Henry gave their orders to the waiter who had dashed over.

"Look!" She nudged his shoulder. "Do you see Mr. Gabriel and Miss Fothergill?"

He followed her line of sight and broke out in a wide grin. Diana's gaze flitted upward, half expecting the clouds to part with rays of golden light.

"Confound it all, will you look at that!"

Diana began to point out that as *she* had shown *him,* she must already be looking at that, or rather them, when he clapped his hands in delight.

"You know, I think I have a knack for matchmaking."

"Surely I deserve some of the credit," Diana insisted, "though one couple hardly qualifies as a knack."

"Not only them—" The waiter delivered their ices, interrupting him. She had chosen the orange flavor, one of her favorites; today, it tasted sour. She set the ice down beside her on the seat of the phaeton.

"Are you certain you are well?" Henry asked, eyeing the sweet.

"Well enough, but my appetite has deserted me," she replied, her stomach churning. The time had come for them to talk—to part ways. Better now, before . . .

Before he broke her heart?

A bitter laugh escaped her. She'd told Henry she wouldn't fall in love with him. She hadn't lied. She hadn't *fallen* in love with him. She had been a little bit in love with the man for years. The time spent with him during their courtship had only strengthened her feelings. She needed him out of her life before he stole any more of her heart. She would not allow him to break her.

"What?" Henry prompted.

"Hmm?"

"You laughed at something."

"It's just that we're both thinking the same thing, but neither of us wants to speak first."

Henry took a bite of his chocolate ice. "Tell me what you're thinking. If I'm thinking the same thing, I will tell you. If not, I'll have a taste of your ice."

"I won't make a game of this with you. You may have my ice; I told you, I've lost my appetite."

"Diana—"

"I release you. Is what you want me to say? There's no need for our arrangement any longer. You are in possession of your stud, and I think it likely that I will soon receive a proposal of marriage."

"Stickley," Henry muttered darkly.

She nodded. "Sir Samuel is most attentive. I believe we are well-suited."

"He is not right for you," he bit out.

"I think I am the better judge of that." She tried to keep her voice light and teasing, but an edge of hurt cut through.

"Diana, you won't be happy with him. Any fool can see that."

"Then I must be particularly foolish because I think he would make a very good husband."

Henry stabbed his spoon into his ice and shoved it into the hands of a passing waiter. He braced both hands against the side of the phaeton as he leaned in close. "I'm sure he will be a good enough husband for some woman, but he's not right for you. Why are you willing to live a life without love and passion?"

Her hands clenched into fists. "All I want is a steady, comfortable marriage."

"But *why*?"

He had poked the scab one too many times, and the flesh underneath was still angry and raw.

"My parents had love and passion," she hissed at him, "and they turned to anger and jealousy. They destroyed each other and our family. I wouldn't wish that on my worst enemy."

She realized she was crying when he lifted his hands to her cheeks and wiped away her tears. She glanced around, fearful she had drawn attention to herself, but no one appeared to have noticed.

Henry pressed on. "You can't imagine all marriages are like your parents'?"

"Of course not," she scoffed. "Many marriages are a great deal worse."

He shook his head. "My parents have been happily married for three decades. My sisters are both happily married, admittedly not for very long, but both couples have already weathered hardships and come through stronger."

"Most marriages, most families, are not like yours."

"Perhaps they're not like yours," he countered. "I understand that you're scared. When you embrace passion, when you open your heart, there's always an element of risk. You could get hurt," he acknowledged, "but you could also find joy."

"I would rather not take the risk, if it's all the same to you."

His body was rigid beside her, nearly vibrating with tightly wound tension. She didn't understand him. He should be grateful she wasn't holding him to their arrangement until Sir Samuel proposed.

"It's not," he said gruffly.

"I beg your pardon?"

"I said that it's not all the same to me, but my opinion doesn't matter to you, does it?" He gave her his slightly crooked smile, the one that always made her heart flop around in her chest, but it didn't reach his eyes. No, those bluer-than-blue eyes were hard, and rather than doing its customary acrobatics, her heart dropped straight to her stomach. "I'm a rogue, as you are always so quick to point out, so naturally I have no feelings worthy of your consideration."

"Why are you making this so difficult?" she demanded. "You have your stud. I know you have no more use for me. And, though we both know you had little to do with it, I have a suitor whom I expect to propose. I will accept, we will be married, and all will be as it should. You see, I have no further use for you either, Mr. Weston."

Henry's face was ashen. "Di, I—"

"Miss Merriwether!"

Diana saw Sir Samuel quickly striding toward them.

"I just called at Lansdowne House, and your mother suggested I seek you out here."

"How fortunate you spotted us," Henry drawled.

"Weston," a tight-lipped Sir Samuel acknowledged.

They eyed each other like a pair of dogs with but one bone betwixt them. Her temples began to throb.

"Sir Samuel, what a pleasant surprise." Diana tried to look happy. "Forgive me, gentlemen, but I fear my head has started to pound."

"Delicate creature," tutted Sir Samuel. "You have taken too much sunlight, no doubt. Will you allow me to see you home?"

Henry straightened to his full height, though even slouching he was able to look down his nose at the other man. "I am quite capable of taking Miss Weston home."

This was ridiculous, Diana thought. Lansdowne House was *in* Berkeley Square. She could see herself home. But that wouldn't solve her problem. For whatever reason, Henry hadn't ended their arrangement, so she had to be strong enough to let him go. She had no future with him. She had the possibility of one with Sir Samuel.

"Nonsense." She smiled brightly at Henry. "You have a number of—of *friends*"—she stumbled over the word—"you have been neglecting at my request. I shall not keep you away from them any longer. You deserve to spend the remainder of the day celebrating, not playing nursemaid. Mr. Weston has come into some property," she informed Sir Samuel. "As we are old friends, I'm very pleased for his good fortune, though I fear his new duties will prevent him from calling on us as often as he has in the past."

"What a shame." Sir Samuel's words were at odds with the delighted manner in which he said them.

"Thank you for a most enjoyable outing, Mr. Weston. Sir Samuel can see me home, if it's not too much trouble?"

"None at all, none at all," the baronet assured her. "Come, let me help you."

Henry crossed his arms over his chest as Sir Samuel handed her down from the phaeton. "Sir Samuel, it appears the lady has made her decision. Miss Merriwether, I regret I will not see you tonight at the Winthrop musicale as planned. As you so obligingly reminded me, I have acquaintances to renew. Good day to you both." He touched his fingers to the brim of his hat and got up into his phaeton. His groom handed him the reins before clambering onto the tiger's perch at the back. Without so much as a glance in her direction, Henry clucked at his team and drove off.

Diana gladly accepted the support of Sir Samuel's arm as they walked the short distance to Lansdowne House. The day had left her confused and off-balance, but beside Sir Samuel's unflappable demeanor, she regained some semblance of the calm and order she craved.

"Do you plan to go to the Winthrop musicale tonight?" she asked. "I hear Signora Bolla is engaged to sing. Her voice is not as good as Miss Dixon's, but she is very talented."

"I received an invitation, but I hadn't made up my mind. I confess I care little for opera. It is pleasant enough to listen to, but I find nothing enjoyable in dramas of unfaithful, jealous lovers."

Diana stumbled, aghast at his outright condemnation of her parents.

Sir Samuel steadied her. "Are you all right, my dear?"

She opened her mouth to berate him for his unfeeling words, but she stopped herself when their gazes met. His brown eyes were earnest, and his expression spoke only of concern for her well-being. He hadn't been alluding to her past, merely expressing honest distaste at the storyline of many operas.

"I took a small misstep. I am in agreement with you about the opera, but perhaps it would prove more tolerable if we suffered through together?"

Henry could spend his evening being as roguish as he liked, Diana decided savagely. She was determined to enjoy herself without him. She looked at Sir Samuel, trying not to notice that she didn't have to tilt her head up as far as she did with Henry. No matter. Height clearly had no influence on moral rectitude.

"Will you think me forward, Sir Samuel, if I say that I hope to see you tonight?"

"On the contrary, I am glad to hear it. I won't disappoint you, my dear."

His eyes were kind, thought Diana. Comfortable. He wouldn't disappoint her, and that was what mattered.

CHAPTER TWELVE

Pray forgive me if I presume too much, but I thought you would wish this news. Of late, our daughter has formed an attachment to Henry Weston, eldest son of Viscount Weston, a young man given to all sorts of roguery. I believe his interest in Diana is suspect as he intends to start a stud. If you wish to protect your daughter, seek out this man and ascertain his true motives. . . .
—from Lady Linnet Merriwether to
her husband Thomas Merriwether

Thomas Merriwether shifted uncomfortably in his seat at the dining room at Tattersall's. He couldn't blame his chair since the room boasted very elegant accommodations. The wealthy aristocrats who idled away their days here must feel at home, what with the decorated ceilings and fine paintings on the walls. As he was not, nor had he ever aspired to be, one of them, the rich trappings left him ill at ease.

Also, he admitted to himself, his body no longer considered a visit to the capital—a ride of sixty miles from Newmarket—an easy jaunt. This was the third Monday in a row that he'd come to the weekly sale, and if he didn't run his quarry to ground today, he might just stay in the city until he found the scoundrel.

That might appease his joints, but a week here would do nothing for his bad humor. It was breeding season, there were upcoming races and horses to train, and the Marquess of Cheston's mare would foal any day now. He hated being away, even though Bar was perfectly capable of managing the place. Very few things could have brought him to London.

He ran his fingers over the folded piece of paper in his coat pocket. He'd been shocked to receive his wife's letter. Shocked was an understatement. He gave in to temptation and pulled out the letter, his eyes drinking in the graceful script of Linnet's hand. He lifted the paper to his face, certain that he could detect a whiff of lavender. The scent raked talons across his heart, but he would bear the pain, gladly, for that little taste of her.

For his children, Thomas would do anything. He'd given his daughter up so she could have a life where viscounts' sons courted her. He didn't know if she'd ever understood his motives. She'd not forgiven him, not for that or the rest. He didn't blame her. He would never forgive himself for what he'd done.

The moments, the times one wished to remember least, were often those that remained in perfect clarity. The happiest moments in his life—the births of his children, making love with his wife—those memories were blurred at the edges. He only wished he had some relief from *that* day. He didn't deserve to forget what had happened, but everything remained in such damned sharp, horrifying detail. . . .

Linnet had fled to her parents, taking both children, since Diana had refused to leave without her brother. He'd lost his mind about three minutes after they'd left. He drank until he was numb. Bar could run the stud without his direction, but the place could go to rack and ruin for all Thomas cared. His butler, Ingham, ran the household and, as long as he provided copious amounts of liquor, Thomas found no complaint.

After about three months, Bar had had enough of his wallowing and drunken outbursts. He'd taken the key to the wine cellar from Ingham, and then informed Thomas that there would be no more spirits forthcoming. Infuriated, Thomas had fired both him and Ingham, along with everyone else he'd encountered on his way to the public house in Newmarket.

Once he got there . . . He'd been so damned angry. With Bar. With Ingham. With Peckford. With the duke and duchess. With Linnet. And with each drink, his sense of outrage and betrayal grew. They had all conspired against him. They had made a fool of him.

The main room began to empty. The men here had to wake up and work come sunrise. He couldn't face going to sleep, knowing that nothing would have changed tomorrow. He'd wake in his too empty bed in his too empty house. He drained his glass and waved the serving girl, Marjorie, over for more.

Walt Crofter had been a good trainer, but his recklessness had killed him, and he'd left his widow with nothing. Marjorie appeared to do well enough without him. She always had a smile on her face whenever Thomas took a meal here. She wasn't smiling as she came to him now.

"Do you intend to drink yourself into a stupor, sir?"

"That is none of your business, Mrs. Crofter." The words emerged slightly slurred.

"Marjorie, please. Mrs. Crofter will always be my mother-in-law." He inclined his head. "Bring me another drink, Marjorie."

"I think you've had enough, Mr. Merriwether." She leaned in close and pried the glass from his hand. She smelled fresh and sweet, like the first hint of spring after a harsh winter. "Why don't you go upstairs and sleep this off? I'll ask for a key to one of the rooms."

As he watched her lips move, he remembered the other sure way to oblivion. He realized Marjorie hadn't stepped away. He met her gaze and found a combination of desire, loneliness, and need.

He had a brief recollection of kissing her on the staircase and stumbling into a room with her, and then nothing else until the morning when he woke to find himself alone in bed. He put all the money he had on his person on the table, and then hastily dressed and left. Whether it was the drink, the knowledge of what he suspected he'd done, or some combination of the two, as soon as he reached the street, he cast up his accounts.

His head throbbed to the rhythm of the horse's hooves as he rode home, stopping every mile or so to be ill. The physical discomfort mattered little compared to the agony tearing through his heart. He prayed he'd been too inebriated to do anything the previous night, but, whether or not he'd slept with the woman, he'd betrayed Linnet. He'd committed—or intended to commit—the very crime he'd accused her of, and now he wondered if he hadn't made a terrible mistake in accusing her at all.

If Linnet had gone to another man's bed, she must feel at least some of the wretchedness clawing at him, but she hadn't acted the slightest bit guilty when he'd confronted her. Oh, God, what had he done? He'd allowed his fear of being unworthy of Linnet to transform him into a man who *was* unworthy of her.

He didn't know how he would go on without her and the children. He certainly couldn't go on the way he had been. If Linnet could see him now, she would be disgusted. He didn't imagine Linnet could ever forgive him—hell, he would never forgive himself—but perhaps if he threw himself at her feet and begged. . . .

He lost count of how many times he fired Bar and Ingham over the next fortnight, as he fought off the craving for drink. The early days were the hardest, especially since he refused to take laudanum to dull his senses. As he paced the grounds on sleepless night after sleepless night, he told himself that this was but a small part of his penance. He would pay any price to have his wife and children—Diana, Alex, and the tiny one he'd yet to meet—back home with him.

At last, the day came, and Thomas arrived at Lansdowne House prepared to reclaim his family. He elbowed aside Snellings, who looked as sour and scrawny as ever, and stood in the marble entrance hall bellowing Linnet's name. The duchess arrived first.

"Go home to your horses, Thomas," she commanded. "You have no business here."

"My wife and children are here. I will not leave without them."

"They do not wish to go with you." The duchess's voice was like ice.

"Bring them here and ask them," he challenged her with more bravado than he actually felt. "This won't be the first time Linnet has been forced to choose between us. Given the choice to stay here—"

"Stay here?" The duchess's barked laughter chilled his blood. "After she allowed you to ruin her? His Grace and I cast her out."

Thomas's head spun as he tried to make some sense of the duchess's words. "Linnet told you I ruined her?"

"Oh, yes, she came to see us after it happened. Very contrite, she was, weeping and begging our forgiveness. She assured us the two of you meant to marry. I tried to persuade His Grace to send Linnet away for a time while we waited to see if any lasting misfortunes would result, but Lansdowne would not hear of it. You say you were Linnet's choice; in truth, she had no choice once you ruined her."

"No," he whispered, and then louder, "I didn't ruin her."

"Come, there is no need to shout. The past is in the past. His Grace and I have forgiven Linnet."

"She lied! I swear to you she was untouched on our wedding night. Linnet!" he yelled again.

She appeared at the landing at top of the stairs but made no move to come any closer. She was too thin and too pale, and she was still the most beautiful creature he had ever seen.

"Why have you come, Thomas?" Her voice was exhausted, pained almost. She gripped the banister with one hand; the other rubbed at her lower back.

"I came here for my family," he told her. "I convinced myself you were telling the truth. I told myself there were no lies between us—" His voice cracked. "Why? Why would you tell your parents I ruined you?"

She moved slowly down the stairs toward him, tears streaming down her face. "I was afraid they would come after us. If they believed me ruined, they wouldn't have bothered. I chose you," she yelled, then swayed and clutched the banister as if the act of raising her voice had sapped her strength. "I chose you. I gave up everything to love you, be with you, bear your children, and—"

"You never gave them up," he spat out, striding to the base of the stairs. "You told them lies so they would give *you* up. When they came back into our lives after Alex was born, you welcomed them without a word of reproach. Whenever they send word, you run off for weeks at a time to dance attendance."

"I do it for the—"

"Don't tell me you do it for the children because they don't give a damn about any of this. You are the one who misses this life."

"No!" she insisted.

"Then come away with me right now." He started up the stairs. "Prove to me once more that you love me as I love you. We'll take the children, go home, and put them out of our lives forev—"

"They are my parents," she sobbed.

"I am your husband!"

Movement above Linnet caught his eye. A frantic maid reached for— Christ, Diana and Alex sat on the upper landing, their arms around each other. He only caught a glimpse of their terrified faces before the woman began hurrying them away. He had to get to his children and ease the fear in their eyes.

"Not any—" An anguished cry broke from her lips as she doubled over, clutching her abdomen.

"Linnet!" He lunged for her, catching her just as she collapsed. Thomas cradled her against him as she moaned and writhed in pain, and then her body went limp. He looked around helplessly, his eye catching on the duchess. She stood utterly still and as white as the marble statues decorating the entrance hall.

"Do something!" he demanded.

With a tiny shake, the duchess moved into action. "You, fetch the doctor. You, bring linens to Lady Linnet's room." She doled out orders to the group of servants who had gathered at Linnet's scream. Then, imperious as ever, she marched up the stairs and gestured to him. "You, follow me."

Thomas shifted his wife into his arms and followed the duchess up another flight of stairs to a bedchamber, which he supposed belonged to Linnet. The counterpane lay on the floor beside the bed where maids spread clean white linens over the mattress.

"Lay her on the bed," the duchess instructed.

Thomas hesitated, not wanting to let his wife out of his arms. He had the terrifying notion that if he let her go, he would never get her back. Linnet twisted in his arms as a spasm wracked her frail body. A rush of wetness soaked through his coat on the arm that hooked under her legs.

Thomas's heart turned over in his chest. "She's losing the babe, isn't she?" He looked to the duchess for confirmation.

"I believe so." Her voice was eerily flat, emotionless.

Thomas gently eased his wife onto the bed. Her face had little more color than the snowy sheets upon which she lay. He knelt beside the bed and clutched her hand, but it was cold and limp in his grasp.

Two maids removed her shoes and stockings. Another untied the wide ribbon sash at her waist.

"You can go now, Mr. Merriwether," the duchess informed him.

Thomas shook his head, never taking his eyes from Linnet. "If you try to make me leave, you'll live to regret it." He released Linnet's hand only long enough for the maids to draw her arm through the sleeve of a clean shift.

"I feared this would happen," the duchess continued as she smoothed a sheet over her daughter. "She has not been taking proper care of herself."

Linnet whimpered as her body arched in pain. The hand that had lain lifeless in his suddenly gripped him with inhuman strength. Her eyes opened and focused on his face.

"Thomas?"

"I'm here, my love."

Her gaze moved beyond him, taking in the worried faces clustered around her bedside. "Am I dying?" she whispered.

"No!" He squeezed her hand. "Listen to me, Linnet. You're not going to die."

Another contraction wracked her body, leaving her sweaty and weak. The duchess dabbed at her brow with a wet cloth. One of the maids gasped. Thomas followed her line of vision and saw with horror the crimson patch that had blossomed on the sheet between her thighs.

Ages passed before the doctor and his nurse arrived. An elderly gentleman, he quickly took in the situation and ordered everyone from the room.

"She's my wife," Thomas protested as the nurse urged him away from the bed. "I can't leave her."

"If you stay, you will only be in the way," the nurse explained patiently. "Come along, sir. The doctor and I will see to Lady Linnet." She gave him a comforting pat on his shoulder as she pushed him out the door. "The doctor is very capable, but I will come for you if the situation worsens."

Numb with shock, Thomas allowed a footman to lead him to a small parlor. Small by ducal standards, that was. The sunny yellow room was larger than any room at Swallowsdale Grange. Unable to stand the sight of the cheery walls, he buried his face in his hands. He made bargains with God, the Devil, and every saint whose name he could remember along with some he couldn't. He prayed, cursed, and wept.

He knew his children were somewhere in the house, likely scared and confused, but he could not go to them. When he'd asked to see them, the footman brought a response from the duchess that she had calmed the children and, after what they had witnessed, his presence would only upset them. The old bitch might be lying, but another argument under this roof would help no one.

The light in the room faded away as night fell. A maid came in to light the candles and tend the fire. He began to wonder if the duchess had forgotten him. The other alternative, that no one wanted to face him with bad news, he refused to consider. When the candles had burned halfway down, he stood, ready to demand answers, but before he had taken a step, the duchess entered the room carrying a small wrapped bundle in her arms.

"Linnet?" he croaked.

"She is alive but weak. She lost a great deal of blood, but the doctor is hopeful for a full recovery."

He wet his lips. "The child?"

She shook her head, then walked purposefully toward him. Thomas wanted to close his eyes as the duchess drew back the top layer of cloth, but he forced himself to see the babe.

"Your daughter," the duchess said tonelessly.

She was impossibly tiny and beautiful, like a sleeping angel. In the candlelight, the barely formed crescents of her eyelashes and eyebrows glinted copper. There was no mistaking that she was his daughter.

Thomas wasn't a man of science. He did not know what held his heart together or caused it to beat, but he knew they failed at the sight of his baby girl, pale and lifeless. A sob tore from his throat, a howl of pain so intense he could not contain it. He reached out, but the duchess stepped back, drawing the cloth back into place.

"Listen well, Mr. Merriwether. Years ago, you stole my daughter's rightful place in society. Months ago, you broke her heart. She had finally found some measure of peace before your arrival. Are you so determined to ruin her life?" She sneered in contempt. "You should have stayed away. Today you took this innocent child's life and very nearly Linnet's as well. If you truly love her, you will leave now and keep your distance."

He'd fled, but he hadn't been able to hide from her accusations. He'd had a glimpse of that small, perfect face, and the sight was forever impressed on his mind. He saw her when he closed his eyes at night, relived that accursed day countless times, and he could never escape the crushing grief and guilt that came with the memories.

He'd done as the duchess had asked. He'd kept his distance. He'd kept his distance for sixteen long years. Linnet had been the one to break the years of silence between them.

Thomas sighed as he refolded his wife's letter and placed it back in his pocket. He would do as she asked, and not only for her sake. He had failed to protect one of his daughters. He'd protected Diana as best he knew how, by leaving her with her mother and putting as much distance as possible between them.

"Mr. Merriwether, the gentleman you asked about is here."

Thomas looked up to see Old Tatt's son, Edmund, who had taken over his father's business after his sire's death a few years ago. Edmund led him outside to the stalls.

"There he is." Edmund pointed a finger. "The tall, fair one, looking at Derby's colt. Usually turned out a bit neater, I must say. Do you want an introduction?"

"No, thank you. I'll let you be about your business."

He made his way over to the young man. Weston's attention was on the horse, which gave Thomas time to observe him. He saw nothing to allay his wife's fears. The scamp's hair was in rakish disarray, but not from a valet's careful styling. He was still in his evening dress, rumpled and much the worse for wear, indicating that he'd come to Tattersall's straight from the previous night's dissipations. Henry Weston appeared capable of every vice known to man and then some.

Thomas sidled up beside him. "Beautiful colt," he noted appreciatively. "Sir Peter's get, unless I'm much mistaken. If I were Derby, I wouldn't let him go."

Weston turned to see who had addressed him.

Thomas held out his hand. "Allow me to introduce myself. Thomas—"

"Merriwether," Weston finished, clasping Thomas's hand in a brief, crushing grip. "I know who you are. I daresay everyone here knows you. I saw your Penelope win the Oaks last year."

"Ah, Penny, my faithful girl. I hope you had the good sense to bet on her."

"Oh, I did." He grinned. "And a pretty sum I made off her, too."

While gambling wasn't a quality he sought in a son-in-law, Thomas found it difficult to judge the man too harshly when he'd wagered on his prize filly. "Word is, you're starting your own stud," he said casually.

"I make no secret of it."

"I also hear you're courting my daughter."

Weston shrugged. "I make no secret of that either. All of London knows." The hand he ran through his hand looked a bit unsteady.

Thomas's eyes narrowed. "Are you foxed, Mr. Weston?"

The young man let out a loud sigh. "Not anymore. I must remedy that."

Thomas bit the inside of his cheek, reminding himself all young men of Weston's class were spoiled and took their privileged lives for granted. He dealt with men like this all the time.

"I'll be frank with you. I find no fault in your taste for horseflesh, but your reputation leaves much to be desired. You're not the sort of man I want around my daughter."

"Is that so?" Weston regarded him with languid insolence. "I think that's her decision."

Thomas noted the tightly clenched fists at the younger man's side. Everything else in his body proclaimed him relaxed and carefree, but those hands gave him away.

"You say you saw my Penelope race?"

Weston frowned at the abrupt change of subject, but he nodded.

"I'll give her to you if you agree to stay away from Diana."

Surprise gave way to anger on Weston's face. He curtly shook his head and turned on his heel.

"Weston, wait!"

The young man halted, then turned back to face him. "I don't believe we have anything more to say to one another."

"On the cont—"

Weston took a menacing step toward him. "Before you insult me again, sir, I warn you that I'm in a foul temper." His voice was low and furious. "The only thing keeping my fist from rearranging your face is that the resulting talk would upset Diana, and she's been hurt enough. So much, in fact, that she would rather shroud herself in propriety and consign herself to a loveless marriage than risk being hurt again."

Thomas began to see the young man in a new, much more favorable light. "You care for her." He didn't say *love,* though given Weston's miserable state, there could be little doubt the man was very much in love. But if Weston hadn't yet come to that realization, Thomas didn't want to scare him off. Henry Weston might be the answer to his prayers.

"Yes." Anguish filled the solitary word.

"I misjudged you," Thomas admitted, "and I'm sorry for it. If you truly care for Diana, you have my blessing, though it's not worth much. Diana has refused to let me give her a dowry, but I'd like you to have Penelope. I put her to my Zephyr recently. She'll give you champions."

"Mr. Merriwether—"

"Starting a stud isn't easy going. No one knows that better than I do. I would ask, though, that you bring Diana to see me after you wed. There are things that need to be said between us."

"If you're willing to sell Penelope, I'll see if I can meet your price, but I would no more accept your bribe in this than I would when you offered it to keep my distance. That's of little consequence, however, as Diana has no wish to marry me."

The weight that had eased slightly from Thomas's shoulders slammed back down again. "I had to try," he said sadly. "A word of advice, and then I won't bother you further. Diana was a mischievous child, always running about and hiding places. She changed after . . ." Christ, how could it still be so hard to say the words after all these years? "After her mother and I separated. I've watched her through the years, and even from a distance, I can see the difference. She keeps herself apart."

"Perhaps your daughter is not as different as you believe," Weston said. "She's still very proficient at running and hiding."

Thomas raised his brows at the level of frustration he heard in the man's voice. Linnet had written to him to ascertain Weston's intentions, and the young man appeared to love his daughter. Weston could be the saving of him . . . of his family. Thomas wouldn't allow the boy to be as stupidly stubborn as he himself had once been. He needed to give him one final piece of encouragement.

"I told you that, as a girl, Diana liked to hide, but her favorite part of the game was when someone found her. You're the first person to find her in a long while. She's been hiding for so long, she's scared to do anything else. If you care for my daughter, then for both your sakes, fight to keep her. Regrets are the very devil to live with."

CHAPTER THIRTEEN

By the time I finish and post this, you will have seen reports about the shocking attempt on our sovereign's life at Drury Lane. None of the family attended that night; you know how my mother feels about Cibber. The royal family stayed through the play, but in the midst of such turmoil, I cannot believe anyone found much humor in the farce playing out....
—from the Countess of Dunston to
her aunt the Dowager Marchioness of Sheldon

While Henry would have been quite happy to accept advice of an equine nature from Mr. Merriwether, whose accomplishments in that vein he greatly admired, he had little trouble dismissing the man's romantic counsel. Given the sorry state of the other man's amatory affairs, Henry considered doing the opposite of what Mr. Merriwether suggested and letting Diana alone. He'd nearly convinced himself to do just that before the encounter at Tattersall's, but he found he couldn't stay away.

That explained his presence at the Countess of Langley's soiree, an event certain to be dull, ten days after Diana had made it clear she wanted nothing to do with him. He'd tried calling at Lansdowne House, but Diana wouldn't see him, which left him no choice but to seek her elsewhere.

He wasn't spying, Henry told himself, leaning against the wall as he surveyed the scene before him. He'd received an invitation. There was a chance, albeit a small one, he would have attended even if Diana hadn't been there. He was a social creature, a man of town. He liked balls, damn it.

He hadn't commanded his valet to cozen up to one of the Lansdowne House maids to learn which events the family was planning to attend. That would be unscrupulous and a touch desperate, which was why he had only *suggested* the scheme and left Jasper to decide whether to implement it. There were other ways for the man to come by the information if he so chose.

Spying sounded so devious. Henry was . . . protecting Diana. He still hoped Stickley would prove to be an unsavory, unsuitable character, but his initial inquiries had met with little success. The baronet had no wife or light-skirt stashed away, he hadn't fought a duel, and his finances weren't in disarray, any of which would have exceedingly pleased Henry. Sir Samuel's worst quality was having execrable taste in horseflesh and, having apprised Diana of this grievous shortcoming once before, Henry knew that wouldn't dissuade her from marrying the man.

Henry couldn't force her to marry him, not that she'd ever given him the chance to propose. No, he couldn't force her, but if someone found them in a compromising situation, she'd have to marry him. He dismissed the idea as soon as it occurred to him, since Diana would never forgive him, or herself, for the resulting scandal.

He just needed to make sure she was happy. And he needed to ascertain that Stickley was worthy of her. If she was truly content and Stickley was all he appeared, Henry would consider letting her go. Short of trussing her up and abducting her—a delightful idea he allowed himself to dwell on for far, far too long—what else he could do?

But even after a week of—very well, damn it, he was spying on her, and even after a week, he couldn't be certain how she felt. Her mask of polite reserve was firmly in place, revealing nothing of her true feelings.

Then, last night at the Tiverthorne rout, her mask had finally slipped. He'd sneaked up beside her at the supper buffet and selected a strawberry tart. Their eyes had met, and in that brief second before she glanced away and pretended not to see him, he'd glimpsed so many conflicting emotions, he couldn't begin to guess which was strongest. But happiness wasn't among them.

If Diana had been happy, he might have found the strength to leave her in peace. As he had not, he'd followed her again. Tonight, she *would* see him.

Henry glowered as a flushed Diana finished a dance with Lord Brantley, whom Henry fully intended to trounce the next time they were in the ring at Jackson's. If Henry was a rogue, Brantley was an out-and-out rakehell. The devil only knew what the bastard had been saying to put the color in Diana's cheeks. The man had no interest in her, or any other marriageable female, apart from goading Henry, in which he was succeeding admirably.

Brantley knew it, too. He shot Henry a mocking smile as he returned Diana to her mother, who was deep in conversation with Stickley. Henry's blood heated at the sight of the baronet. Diana whispered something in Lady Linnet's ear before heading in what he assumed was the direction of the ladies' retiring room. She would be more than a moment in returning, Henry decided, as he slipped through the crowd. Fortunately, he'd become very good at following her.

Without looking, Diana knew Henry followed her as she made her way upstairs. They'd played at this for months, and even if her mind understood the game was up, the rest of her hadn't caught on. She knew what would happen if he got her alone, and her body thrilled in anticipation.

She stopped in front of the retiring room, and he came up close behind her. "I took myself on a tour earlier," he said. "Three doors down on the right is a small dressing closet. We may speak now," he said, "or if you wish to refresh yourself first, we may speak after."

"And if I do not wish to speak to you at all?" she asked breathlessly.

"That is not an option." He walked past her and disappeared into the room he had described.

Diana hesitated a moment, then followed him. He was right; they needed to speak. She hated the way things had ended between them. She'd gone over their argument a hundred times during the past week of sleepless nights. She'd thought of what she could have said differently, of what she might have told him if Sir Samuel hadn't arrived, but she couldn't change the past. Now they could part as . . . as friends.

After checking that no one was around to see, Diana pushed open the door to the dressing closet and darted inside. The room was larger than the linen closet, but not by much. Moonlight poured in through the sole window, illuminating what little there was to see: a small desk and a chair, a high chest of drawers, and a low bench beneath the window.

And Henry.

In his shirtsleeves.

His coat and gloves lay discarded on the bench. Her heart fluttered. Without his coat, he seemed bigger somehow. She swallowed, her mouth suddenly gone dry. "You've made yourself very much at home," she observed.

"I didn't know how long you would make me wait. This room wasn't designed with ventilation in mind, and opening the window might draw notice from outside."

"What do you want?" she asked as he stepped around her to lock the door.

"You know what I want." The husky timbre of his voice wrapped around her like a caress, but there a slight edge to his tone that almost sounded like . . . need?

Impossible, she told herself.

Henry wanted her, but he didn't need her. And she didn't want him to. Need was a dangerous emotion that bordered too closely on other feelings. She shook her head slightly, trying to banish the unwanted thought.

His hands were at her waist, drawing her back against him. The scent of summer storms and male musk surrounded her as he wrapped his arms around her and rested his chin on her shoulder. "Do you wish me to tell you?" His warm breath against her cheek sent a shiver rippling through her.

"Well?"

"I beg your pardon?" Diana struggled to remember what he'd asked.

"I asked if you wished me to tell you what I wanted, but I think you know." He pressed a chaste kiss to the side of her neck.

A little sigh of longing escaped her. "I don't—"

"You *do,*" he insisted. "Because you want me, too."

Yes, she wanted him. He tempted her to throw caution and propriety to the wind, but people often wanted things that weren't good for them. She wanted Henry, but he wasn't what she needed. She was old enough, had seen enough, to know the difference. She just had trouble remembering that whenever he was near.

He raised a hand and settled it over one of her breasts. As if he'd ordered the response, her nipples tightened to stiff points.

"Don't," she pleaded.

"Don't what?"

"Don't make me want you." Her voice caught as her throat tightened with emotion.

"What would you have me do?" A humorless laugh escaped him. "I can't help wanting. I want you to burn as I burn. I want you to lie awake at night thinking of me. If you sleep, I want you to dream of me. I want you to tell me that you can't stand the sight of me dancing with another woman. I want to know this last week has been as miserable for you as it has been for me. Why did you refuse to see me when I called?"

Shaken, Diana twisted out of his arms and turned to face him. The heated desire flaring in his eyes burned through to the dark places in her heart. The parts that had worried no man would ever truly desire her.

"I didn't think we needed to say anything more."

"You didn't think—" he muttered. "I do nothing but think about you. You are driving me mad. All day long, you are in my thoughts. I dream about you at night. I can't concentrate on anything for wondering what you're doing, who you're with . . . whether you're happy. Are you happy? I need to know, Di."

"I—" She swallowed. "I am as happy as you are, I imagine. You have your stud, and Sir Samuel has intimated that he wishes to speak with my grandfather."

"He's going to ask for your hand," he said expressionlessly.

"Yes, I imagine he will."

"After spending close to a week in his near constant company, do you still plan to accept? Or dare I hope you've come to your senses?"

She glared at him. "The only time I take leave of my senses is when I'm with you."

"Good," he growled, and then his arms were around her and his mouth was on hers in a carnal, desperate kiss. She understood and kissed him back with all the passion and wildness that had built inside her. She wrapped her arms around his neck and tightened her fingers in his hair, holding him as if something was about to tear him from her.

She knew something would. Whatever was between them couldn't last. He would remember that this was all an act, and she was Diana Merriwether, a near-spinster in her seventh Season. Each kiss between them was a stolen treasure, a moment in time that should never have happened, and she hoarded them greedily. She knew she should push him away, but instead she clung to him, trying to impress every detail on her senses so she would be able to relive the experience in years to come.

They were both breathing heavily when he lifted his head. She didn't protest as he carried her across the room to the bench beneath window. He sat down, settling her sideways on his lap. Diana spared a moment of distress for the bench, which didn't look like it could support Henry, let alone the pair of them, but they didn't go crashing to the floor, so she turned to a more pressing matter.

Through the layers of her skirts, she encountered the undeniable evidence of Henry's interest. She tensed, uncertain whether she ought to leap off his lap or act oblivious to the hard length beneath her backside. While she debated, he tightened one of his arms around her waist and brought the other up to her face.

With more gentleness than should have been possible for a man of his size, Henry traced the sweep of her forehead, the line of her nose, the curve of her cheek. . . . When his fingers feathered over her lips, she surrendered to the urge to taste. She flicked her tongue over his skin, exulting in the way his whole body stiffened in response.

"God, Diana," he groaned.

She combed her fingers through his hair, then ran her hand down the strong column of his neck. She slowly smoothed her palm along the path to his shoulder, memorizing each magnificent inch of him. Through the fine linen, she felt every inch of hot skin over strong muscle. She wanted to touch him without his shirt and waistcoat in the way. Her palms itched to smooth over the solid breadth of his bare chest.

"Do you feel what you do to me?"

"It is, ah, rather hard to miss," she remarked.

His laughter, strained and hungry, pulled at her insides. "Not just that. I have missed *you*. Kissing you. Holding you. Talking with you. I've even missed being scolded by you."

"I have missed you, too," she admitted.

"I want you." He pressed an open-mouthed kiss to the spot just below her ear. "And you want me."

She inhaled sharply as he caught her earlobe beneath his teeth. Tugged. "Yes," she agreed.

She'd been wrong, she thought. Their last kiss hadn't been desperate. *This* was a desperate kiss. *This* was a fierce, wet, heart-pounding, toe-curling, get-close-as-you-can-and-then-get-closer kiss. *This* was more than a kiss.

She felt his hand at the hem of her skirts and tensed. Henry lifted his head. "I have to touch you." The words were part plea, part apology. "Don't push me away, Di. I swear not to go too far, but I need you now." She didn't have time to examine his words because he was taking her again. Tasting her. Touching her. And she was losing the will to push him away.

"Stop worrying," he murmured against her lips.

"How?" She jumped as his fingers brushed her ankle.

"Right here, right now, you are only allowed to *feel*." As he spoke, his hand moved along her calf and over her knee, drawing the skirts of her dress and petticoat up.

"What if that—" Her breath hitched as he passed her garter and toyed with the edge of her stocking. "What if that's what concerns me?"

His hand stopped its ascent. Diana shivered as his thumb brushed back and forth over the sensitive skin on her inner thigh.

He nipped her lower lip. "You don't like to let anyone close, do you, Di?"

How could he say that given their current position? He was close. So close to where she ached. Where she needed him—

She shook her head. No, where she *wanted* him. She could want him, but she couldn't need him. She couldn't *need* anyone.

Henry leaned his forehead against hers. "You will let me in."

His hand pressed between her thighs and covered her sex. Just the weight of his hand sent a shock of pleasure through her. Diana clamped her legs together, and she wasn't sure whether she aimed to stop him or to trap him there.

"Let me in," he murmured. "Open to me." He cupped her more firmly as he made the sensuous demand. She obeyed with a whimper.

Diana pressed her forehead against the side of his neck as he searched out her entrance. A fine sheen of perspiration covered his skin, and his pulse pounded as frantically hers. She still felt his desire, hard and unrelenting against her backside, but now she also felt his desperation. The knowledge thrilled and awed her. He was as excited by this as she—

She gasped as he circled the opening and pushed the tip of one finger inside.

"Your body wants me," Henry rasped. "So hot and wet. Your body knows you are mine."

His brazen speech shocked her, but her protest vanished as he slicked his fingers over her swollen folds and found a spot at the top of her cleft that made her writhe. Her existence narrowed to that place, to the sparks of pleasure that burst with each feather-light brush. She moaned, a muffled sound against his cravat, as he began to work his finger inside her again.

"I don't think—" she panted.

"No thinking," he admonished. "What do you feel?"

Diana lifted her head and met his gaze. "Aching. Fevered. Shivery. Like my skin is too tight, but somehow empty too. Like I need . . ." She looked helplessly at him. "Like I *need*."

"What do you need?" he asked softly.

She knew what he wanted to hear, but she couldn't say the word. She wouldn't even let herself think it.

"I need . . . more," she whispered.

She thought she glimpsed disappointment in his eyes, but the emotion disappeared so quickly she couldn't be sure. In the next moment, his eyes were so heated, his smile so wicked, her sex clenched around him.

"Christ," he groaned. "What did I do to deserve you? Now kiss me, Di."

She grabbed the back of his head and pulled him down. She kissed him as he'd taught her, teasing and tasting, entreating him to kiss her back. He thrust his tongue into her mouth as he stroked her intimately, matching the rhythm of his caress to their kiss.

She couldn't decide whether she wanted him to set her free or control her completely. Both, maybe. Her breathing came faster as the tension built higher and higher. Instinct had her arching her back and rocking her hips, fighting to reach whatever lay on the other side of this summit she was climbing. She was close to something. She had to be. She couldn't stand much more of this.

Henry rubbed the pleasure-packed spot at the apex of her sex harder and faster. Diana knew she would have been screaming if he hadn't locked his mouth on hers. Releasing him, she clawed her fingers into the bench.

Everything was too much. She feared she would explode into a million tiny pieces. What would happen if she couldn't put herself back together?

She would not break.

"Let go, sweetheart. I have you," Henry said against her lips.

She shattered.

CHAPTER FOURTEEN

I have received your request—another vase of blue and white jasper with the decoration again after Barry's Jupiter and Juno on Mount Ida—and I am most eager to accommodate your ladyship. All of us at Etruria are grateful for the earl's brave service to our nation. Pray, do not fret overmuch about this. I do not mean to sound self-deprecating, but it is only a vase. They break, we sweep up the pieces, and life goes on....

—from Josiah Wedgwood II to
his patroness the Countess of Dunston

Henry would never know if his words had pushed Diana over the edge, or if her body had simply been ready in that particular moment, but he couldn't bring himself to care. He swallowed her cries as he helped her ride out the pleasure, taking a fierce enjoyment in the way she twitched and trembled, and then finally collapsed against him in a shuddering, boneless heap. She'd given herself over to him completely, surrendering her need for control and propriety, and that told him everything she couldn't say.

She needed him every bit as much as he needed her.

And now that her need was sated, he was painfully aware of his own. He wasn't a clod; he was a passionate lover, and he always saw to a woman's pleasure first. With Diana, he wanted to give her pleasure not simply because it gratified him to bring a woman to her climax, but because her pleasure *was* his pleasure.

He eased his finger from her, trying to think of anything but the tight, hot clasp of her inner muscles, still pulsing with little tremors, reluctant to release him. Impossible. She squirmed at the friction against oversensitive flesh, her movements grinding her pert bottom into his swollen cock.

"Di?"

"I like this feeling," she told him in a breathy voice filled with languor and wonder.

"Good," he grunted.

He gritted his teeth, fighting his body's impulse to take her. It would be so easy, so damned easy to tumble her to the floor, but Diana deserved his care and respect. The first time he took her, they would be in a bed—*and they would be married,* he amended quickly, as the devil inside him insisted there was a perfectly good bed in the adjoining room.

But if he claimed her here, now, she would have to marry him and accept that she belonged to him. With him. She would realize that soon enough, if she hadn't already. He wouldn't push her any further tonight. There would be time aplenty for that after the wedding. They were out of time here.

Henry pressed a kiss into her hair. Would he ever be able to smell orange blossoms without getting harder than a horse's hoof? Probably not, he decided as he smoothed her skirts back into place.

"I could happily stay in this stuffy little room with you for days, Diana mine, but they'll wonder what's become of you downstairs."

"Oh, heavens!" She scrambled off his lap, nearly falling in her haste. He steadied her, watching in resignation as passion fled in the face of propriety. "How long have we been here?" she fretted. "Never mind it. Too long, I know. My mother has likely already looked for me."

"Tell her you were ill," he advised, "and you didn't wish to be sick in front of anyone, so you sought another room."

Diana shook her head. "She won't believe me."

"She might." A smile tugged at his lips. "You wouldn't be lying if you said you've been fevered." He picked up his coat from where it had fallen on the floor and shrugged it on. "If she does guess, I daresay she'll forgive us once she knows the circumstances. How early may I call on the duke tomorrow?"

How long did women need to fuss before a wedding? He liked the idea of a special license and, say, the day after next, but he didn't fool himself that might happen. His wedding would be as proper a wedding as Diana, Lady Linnet, and his mother could wish. Just as long as the event took place before the end of the Season. He refused to wait longer than that.

His smile widened as he noticed Diana had been speaking to him while he'd been daydreaming. "Beg pardon?"

"I asked why you wanted to see my grandfather," she said tonelessly.

She had her damned mask back in place, he realized. After everything they'd just shared, she was shutting herself off from him. She wanted to pretend that what they'd shared meant nothing, to go on with life as though tonight had never happened. That was too bloody bad.

"Why do I want to see the duke? Perhaps that has something to do with my nearly having ravished his granddaughter. Damn it, Diana, I know you believe me a rogue and a scapegrace, but I draw the line at debauching innocents. You can't imagine I meant to walk away from you." He caught her hand, held it when she would have pulled away. "Di, I want to marry you."

Henry had always thought he would marry for love, but he didn't tell Diana he loved her. He didn't want to send her running, for one thing, and he didn't want to say the words until he was certain he meant them.

He wanted Diana to the point of madness, and she wanted him. She hadn't realized it yet, but she needed him. He thought he might need her too. Just the tiniest bit. He cared for her as a dear friend—the best friend he had apart from James—and when he looked into the future, he saw her with him. But did all of that add up to love?

Love was sudden. Instant. Consuming. The French described it as a bolt of lightning. Henry had been standing next to James when he'd first seen Isabella as an adult. The man had looked like he'd taken a fist to the gut. His other brother-in-law admitted that the moment he'd laid eyes on Olivia, he'd known his life would never be the same.

Henry hadn't experienced anything like that with Diana. He couldn't recall his first meeting with her. At some point, years ago, she'd entered into the periphery of his life, and there she'd remained, save for those obligatory dances at his mother's insistence.

Well, perhaps there hadn't been sparks at their first meeting, but now the mere thought of her lit him up like a bonfire. And somehow, even after so many years, she'd still been waiting for him. Lightning hadn't struck him, but divine intervention must be at work to give him this second chance.

No, this was anything but sudden. This was a sweet, slow seduction. Their path had been longer, their pace slower, but as long as they were together, he was exactly where he needed to be. Yes, he decided, this was love.

Christ.

He pulled out the chair at the desk and sat before his knees gave out. Terrible manners when the lady in the room still stood, but it was the least of his transgressions this evening.

He loved her.

"Henry?"

He loved Diana.

"Henry, what is the matter?"

"I l—" *Not yet.* She wasn't ready. "You haven't answered my question."

She crossed her arms over her chest. "I don't remember you asking me one."

"Then let me rectify that." He ought to kneel, he thought. He needed to do this properly for her. He went to her and began to lower himself, but she grabbed the lapels of his coat and urged him back up.

"Please," she whispered. "I need to marry Sir Samuel."

The baronet's name on her lips infuriated him. "What can he give you that I can't?" he demanded. "The man doesn't love you, and I know you don't love him. Why are you so determined to marry him?"

"He will never break my heart."

"I won't—"

Before he could say anything further, Diana touched her fingers to his mouth. He spoke to her with his eyes instead, conveying all his hurt, his frustration, and his confusion in turbulent shades of blue. She trailed the backs of her fingers over his cheek and cupped the hard line of his jaw.

"You *would*." She had to close her eyes as she acknowledged, "You *are*."

"Di—"

She silenced him by rising up on her toes and pressing her lips to his. She stayed like that for several long moments as she tried to reconcile her heart with the plans she had made for it. Though she could never regret any kiss between them, she came closest to regretting this one. Because *this* kiss was good-bye.

Eventually she found the will to pull away.

"I wish you only the best, and I—" She swallowed past the knot in her throat. "I know your stud will be a great success."

"Don't, Di." His big hands clasped her shoulders. "Don't do this. I won't let you go."

"You will. If you care for me at all, you will," she said miserably as she ducked out of his grasp. She fled the room before he stole her wits again with his sweet words and sweeter kisses.

Tonight, Henry had breached her defenses. He'd battered the protective walls she had constructed until she lost all control, came undone in his arms. But however much he tempted her, she couldn't give in. Henry deserved a woman who would give herself to him wholly and unreservedly, and he would demand everything from his woman.

Diana refused to take that risk. She preferred the surety of safety to the possibility of pain. If that made her a coward, so be it. She blinked rapidly as she hurried down the hall to the room set aside for the use of the female guests. She needed a moment—more like an eternity—to regain her composure before returning downstairs to face her future.

The servant girl on duty in the retiring room took one glance at Diana and exclaimed, "Are you ill, milady?"

The mirror revealed that Diana looked little better than she felt. Her distress was evident, and that, combined with her disheveled hair and pale, clammy skin, gave her the appearance of a sick woman. Either that, she thought a bit hysterically, or a mad one.

"May I get you some tea, milady?"

Diana turned to the girl. "No, thank you. If you would just help me put my hair to rights, I will be fine."

She *would* be fine, she told herself, as she made her way downstairs.

She would be *fine,* she told herself, as she sat in the carriage on the way home. Her mother hadn't questioned Diana's sudden illness since she thought the crab served at dinner had spoiled and predicted several more hasty exits as the evening progressed.

Her sickness was of the heart, but she would be fine. She needed Sir Samuel to propose. They could marry quickly with a special license. Then she would go to Wiltshire, far from the dangerous temptation Henry posed to her heart.

But though the baronet had promised to call and inquire after her welfare, she didn't see him for several days. Sir Samuel, along with a dozen or so other guests at Lady Langley's soiree, had partaken of the aforementioned crab, covering it with too much of the fish sauce to detect anything amiss. They regretted their indulgence, but none suffered more than the countess (who was in disgrace) and her cook (who lost her place).

Diana's spirits remained low, but the doctor thought her quick return to health nothing short of astounding. He might have revised his opinion had he known the crab had never reached her end of the table, but she decided no one needed to know that insignificant detail. Sir Samuel, poor man, sent word through Lady Kelton that he would be indisposed through the end of the week. That gave her far too much time to think.

She began reading *A General View of the Agriculture of the County of Wiltshire,* which her mother had bought for her, but only managed the Introduction. Six pages in six days. She ought to tell Henry. He stupidly believed his disinterest in books signaled a lack of intelligence. The only books he'd ever enjoyed had pictures, he'd told her. Pictures of—

Best not to think about that. Best not to think about *him.* And yet, she did little else.

She'd been such a fool. From the night of the Weston ball, she had inched closer to the gate in the wall she had built to protect her heart. When she got close enough to see Henry, she'd reached through the bars and touched him. So long as she kept the gate locked, what harm could there be? But while she had stood transfixed, cracks had formed in her wall. She'd never intended to let him in—never welcomed him—but Henry had slipped through nonetheless and laid claim to her heart one moment at a time.

A wicked smile as he coaxed her into impropriety at Lady Galloway's masquerade ball. A fiery kiss stolen at Vauxhall that burned brighter than any firework. Those early morning races along Rotten Row. Every time he called her "my dear Miss Merriwether" in that teasing, tender way of his. The conversations about nothing that meant everything because he listened to her. The *look*—part lust, part amusement, and all male challenge—that brought every inch of her to life.

Something about Henry made her dare, dream, and, God yes, desire. She found that thrilling and terrifying. She'd spent years waiting for a proposal from a perfect country gentleman like Sir Samuel. Someone proper, considerate, and traditional. Three months with Henry—a Season with a rogue—and she'd discovered parts of herself she hadn't known existed, but she'd lost her way.

Diana's feelings for Henry scared her so much that, for once, the announcement of Sir Samuel's arrival at Lansdowne House relieved her. He shone like a beacon on the path to safety. If he reached out, she would grab on to his hand.

She wasn't condemning herself to some terrible fate. She liked the baronet. He enjoyed reading and spoke eloquently on many topics. He talked fondly of his family and took genuine interest in his estate. She became a little alarmed when he described his flock of Wiltshire Horns, but, thankfully, he did not go on at length; if he'd proven another Blathersby, nothing could have induced her to marry him.

What she liked best about the baronet was that he hadn't much more affection for her than she had for him. Oh, he'd proven a kind and solicitous suitor, and no one could doubt his enthusiasm for the match, but she fit his set of stipulations as perfectly as he fit hers. He had probably decided to marry her before he met her.

Though Sir Samuel lived but a half a day's journey from Bath, he had prevailed upon his cousin's hospitality and come to London to look for a wife. Diana interpreted this to mean that he aspired to a spouse with money and connections. Despite the scandal, she had both. From the first, he'd told her mother that he desired a sensible, family-minded woman; in other words, he wanted a woman content to live in the country, running his household and raising his children. Diana met those conditions as well.

There were no heated looks or longing glances. She didn't expect him to make an improper advance—he was too much of a gentleman—but he didn't appear to be exercising restraint. That suited her perfectly. The only advance she wished him to make was from the drawing room to her grandfather's study. That day, however, the only offer he made pertained to Drury Lane.

Two nights later, Sir Samuel escorted Diana, along with her mother and grandmother, to a box on the dress tier. She said a silent prayer of thanks that he'd bought the costlier tickets; her grandmother would certainly have complained if forced to bear the indignity of more plebian seating. Diana insisted that her mother and grandmother take the chairs, which left her sitting on the velvet-covered padded bench behind them, next to Sir Samuel.

She'd sat just so beside Henry on a few occasions. Maybe not *just* so. Henry had sat so close their shoulders brushed and whispered in her ear throughout the performance. Sir Samuel sat an appropriate distance from her and appeared content simply watching the play, rather than those around him. Though she was usually of the same mind, Diana had no interest in tonight's comedy about a feuding married couple. She fiddled with her program, folding and unfolding the paper, until her mother reached back and snatched it out of her hands.

A commotion in the theater distracted her. Mr. Townley, obviously drunk as a wheelbarrow, leaned over the side of his box and shouted at the actors. A number of people in the pit and gallery began yelling back. His niece—Good heavens, what had possessed Miss Hill to wear such an indecent gown?—looked on in mortification. Nearby, sitting uncustomarily alone, Lord Brantley glowered in their direction before leaving his box.

Diana spared a smile for Eliza, who sat with her parents, Mr. Gabriel, and Lord Blathersby. As she moved on, the hairs on her nape rose. Her breath caught as a familiar blond head came into sight.

Her heart slammed against ribs. *He shouldn't be here.*

Now that he had his stud—now that they were through—he ought to be drinking, wenching, and playing cards again. Or he ought to be in Surrey overseeing the renovations at Ravensfield. He shouldn't be here, with his sisters sitting in front of him, their heads craned around as if Henry provided better amusement than the play.

He kept his opera glass fixed on her. Even with a theater full of people between them, she felt his hunger and determination. A matching desire rose within her, and she couldn't look away. She heard the audience roar as the onstage couple launched into another silly spat. They were nothing but strutting actors reciting ridiculous words. They played out fiction, not fact.

But weren't they all actors, each with their roles? She slipped effortlessly between daughter, sister, granddaughter, and wallflower. What was she to Henry? More than a friend, certainly. Less than a lover, regrettably. She was . . . *his*. The word rose up from deep within her.

She shoved it right back down. She'd performed in a tragedy once before. She wouldn't chance it again.

Henry pressed the opera glass more firmly against his face, as if doing so would render Diana in closer detail. He'd spent the past week at Ravensfield, but he might as well have been in another country for all he'd accomplished. He'd thought of her constantly, yet he was no closer to figuring out what to do with his very stubborn, very lovely, very dear Miss Merriwether.

He drank in every freckle, every copper curl . . . and every disapproving frown. His lips twitched. Diana *would* frown during a comedy. Sir Stick-in-the-Mud should have thought before bringing her to a play about a marriage that proved disastrous in just three weeks' time.

She hadn't noticed him yet. She would, though, even if he had to make as big a nuisance of himself as Townley.

He knew the instant she spotted him. Her body tensed. Her eyes widened. Her lips parted, giving him the barest glimpse of white teeth.

He swallowed hard. He did it again when she bit down on her lower lip. The things he wanted to do with that mouth. . . .

You can't deny this, Di, he thought at her. *You can't deny* me.

She proved she could as she looked away and spoke to Stickley.

Well, damn it, he *couldn't*. He couldn't play when this was no longer a game. He couldn't look at her when she'd moved out of his reach. He couldn't watch her turn away from him to another man. He stood, handed the opera glass to Olivia, and walked out.

James followed him into the passage.

"Leaving, Hal? Or dare I hope that you're about to act like a barbarian and haul your woman off somewhere until the two of you come to rights?"

"Just let it alone."

"So it's the former." James crossed his arms and lounged against the wall. "Pity. Shall we take this conversation to the saloon? Misery may love company, but it's damned fond of drink."

"There's no conversation to be had. She refused me, damn it all. She'd rather have that blasted fool of a baronet."

"A woman who doesn't want you," James mused. "So, one exists after all."

"She *wants* me," Henry growled. "She doesn't want to *marry* me."

James laid a hand on his shoulder. "Come along. I need the drink, even if you don't."

They made their way to the nearest of the elegantly appointed saloons and found only a dozen or so people in the room. That would change come the intermission between the evening's two plays. Henry found a pair of chairs in an empty corner while James procured the liquor. If they were going to do this—*this* being two grown men discussing feelings—then they definitely needed alcohol, and at least some semblance of privacy.

James brought over two glasses and handed one to Henry. He swallowed half the contents in a single gulp. "Brandy would've been better," he grumbled as James seated himself.

"So," James said. He sipped his port.

"So?"

"So you say Miss Merriwether prefers the baronet to you. I find this . . . surprising. I may be unfairly prejudiced, but you *are* the better catch."

Henry raised his glass in acknowledgment, then drained it and set it on the floor. "Diana cares little about titles and wealth."

"I've seen the way she looks at you," James went on. "She cares about you."

"I know she *cares* about me. *She* knows she cares about me, and that scares her."

"I see." James tapped his fingers on the arm on his chair. "Have you spoken with her about her fears?"

"I've tried. She won't listen to reason." He had tried, hadn't he? He'd tried to make her see reason that day at the Park when everything had gone hellishly wrong. He'd told her he wouldn't break her heart. But had they discussed what lay at the heart of her objections?

"Perhaps you should try harder to listen to her reasons. Or are you willing to let her go?"

"If I thought she'd be happier with him—" Henry reached out, took James's glass, and finished what was left of the sweet wine. "Even then, I'm not certain I could. She sees something in me, believes in me, even when I doubt myself. And I see her, all of her. Everything she tries to hide. We . . ." He sought for the right word. "We balance each other."

"Setting aside your present distress, you're far more settled than at the start of the Season," James agreed.

"She's everything I never knew I wanted, never knew I needed. She's the part of me I didn't know was missing, but if I lose her now, I'll forever have a Diana-shaped hole in my heart. There's something comfortable, something enduring between us. I lust after her, God knows, but it's different with her. Better. Christ, I sound like—"

"—like a man in love," James finished. "Have you told her?"

"That I love her?" Henry sighed. "Even if I thought that would help, which I don't, she won't see me. Damn it all, how can I convince her of anything when she won't let me get near her?" His voice rose as his temper flared, earning him a few quizzical glances. The saloon had quickly begun to fill, which signaled both the end of the first play and their privacy. He inclined his head in the direction of the door and lifted a brow.

James nodded, and they headed back toward the box. "Why not ask your sisters for help?" he asked. "They enjoy intrigues and making devious plans. I think Izzie gets nearly as much pleasure from meddling as she does from se—er, surprises."

Henry glanced sideways at James. "I didn't think Izzie liked surprises."

"She likes nice surprises. I'm fairly certain our boyhood pranks can't be characterized as such."

"We never did anything worthy of the retribution she and Livvy extracted."

James chuckled. "They certainly were inventive."

Yes, they were. His sisters were inventive, devious, and meddlesome, and for the first time, Henry found himself grateful. "I'll listen to anything their scheming minds can dream up. Lord knows, it has to be better than what I have in mind."

"Do you have *anything* in mind?"

Henry shrugged. "I've thought about kidnapping her."

"Delightful in its own way, but abduction is a felony, isn't it?"

"Not a hanging offense, but I'd rather only use that plan as a last resort, all the same."

When they reached the box, they found only Sheldon. Henry surveyed the half-empty boxes, but he couldn't spot his sisters. For all he knew, they'd come into the saloon and he'd missed them in the crowd. He glanced across the theater to Diana's box, but she was gone. So was Stickley. Henry's hands balled into fists. It was a good thing he knew the baronet wouldn't attempt anything improper, or he might have taken James's initial suggestion and played the barbarian.

"Did they say where they were going?" he asked Sheldon tersely.

His brother-in-law shook his head. "They left whispering to each other, thick as thieves. Those two are planning something. I only hope Livvy knows I'm serious about not wanting a birthday celebration. Turning thirty is frightening enough without a party."

"There's no stopping either of them when they put their minds to something," James said, clapping a hand on Henry's shoulder and urging him to sit. "The girls will return soon enough. Now, tell me how you're getting on with the stud. . . ."

The curtain had already risen and the actors were just coming onstage when his sisters returned to the box. As they settled into their chairs, Henry tapped each of them on the shoulder. They looked at each other, and then back at him.

"I need your help. Diana is refusing to see me, and if I can't speak to her, she's going to marry that dull sod sitting beside her."

A little sigh escaped from Olivia. Such a romantic, she was. She would help him, and he suspected that, of the two, she was behind their most outrageous plots. He needed Isabella, too. She provided the daring and determination to follow through with Olivia's mad plans.

Isabella shot Olivia a quick frown before turning back to him.

"Are you simply against Diana marrying the dull sod, or do you hope to take his place?"

"The latter." He would set aside his pride to ask his sisters for help. He didn't need to trample it by telling them he'd proposed to Diana and been refused. They'd know soon enough. Isabella would insist on knowing everything he'd told James tonight, and she'd tell Olivia.

"Very well," Isabella agreed. "We'll help you. Come to the house tomorrow, and we'll decide what your next step should be. Three o'clock?"

"I can come in the morning," he offered.

"No," Olivia said quickly. "Not in the morning. Mama is coming to Izzie's to, ah, help with . . . with something, and she will only ask you questions. Don't come before three."

He nodded. Sheldon had the right of it; those two were definitely up to "something," as Olivia had so eloquently described it. He glanced back at his brother-in-law. Poor bastard. Henry knew his sisters too well to imagine Sheldon had a chance of dissuading them. When Isabella and Olivia put their minds to something, there was no stopping them. He was counting on it.

CHAPTER FIFTEEN

Jason believes I am planning an elaborate fête as a surprise for his birthday. The poor man is terrified, and I suppose the last list I left on his desk—by accident, of course—might have been excessive. I shall reproduce some of the items here for your amusement:

> *—Decorations still needed for Egyptian theme room— sarcophagus ice sculpture?*
>
> *—See Mme. Bessette about harem girl costume . . .*
>
> *—Fireworks, fireworks, and more fireworks!*
>
> *—Ask Lord Blathersby about loan of sheep for the evening . . .*

Can you guess which one I actually mean to do? This will be a memorable birthday indeed!

> *—from the Marchioness of Sheldon to her aunt the Dowager Marchioness of Sheldon*

At promptly two o'clock the following day, Diana grasped hold of the ring on the door of Dunston House. The brass lion head above it regarded her with solemn, inquisitive eyes. She questioned her presence there, too.

During last night's intermission, she'd sent Sir Samuel to fetch a glass of lemonade for her, and then she'd stood in the corridor outside their box. She'd hoped for a few minutes alone, but only moments after Sir Samuel headed off, someone called her name. When she looked up, she found Isabella and Olivia (as Lady Dunston and Lady Sheldon insisted she call them) descending on her like hounds on a fox.

"Diana!" they chorused, smiling brightly as they flanked her, each taking an arm.

Though she topped both of them by several inches, she suspected resistance would be futile. She couldn't imagine what they wanted with her . . . unless they didn't know she'd ended her arrangement with Henry. Her stomach dropped as she imagined telling them—women who had quickly become her friends—and seeing hurt and anger fill their eyes.

"We've seen neither hide nor hair of you of late," Isabella complained.

"I took ill at Lady Langley's."

Not precisely true, but what should she say? *Your brother gave me such extreme pleasure I thought I should die of it, and then he proposed marriage. I refused. My refusal won't break his heart, but my acceptance would eventually break mine. My future is with Sir Samuel, but until it's secure, I don't dare risk seeing Henry. I don't know if I have the strength to turn him away a second time. . . .*

"Oh, dear!" Isabella clucked. "You were among those unfortunate souls? You poor dear! How curious that Hal didn't say anything."

"He's been away this past week," Olivia countered.

Diana's chest contracted at her words. Foolish, as she'd just wished him away, but she wondered where he'd been . . . and whom he'd been with.

"He wasn't gone for a week," Isabella argued. "He must have returned to London by Sunday evening because James went with him to the sale at Tattersall's on Monday." She groaned. "I didn't see Hal, but I was forced to listen to a long recitation about the horses he purchased."

"No one cares about that, Izzie," her sister responded.

Actually, Diana *did* care. She cared both about Henry's whereabouts and the stock he'd selected, but she knew better than to say so.

"Did you enjoy the play?" Olivia asked her.

"Not particularly," Diana admitted. "I find little humor in a husband and wife fighting, especially over something insignificant."

"It's too ridiculous," Isabella agreed. "To think of ending a marriage over a card game! At least if he'd thought she was having an affair, there would have been cause."

"Izzie!" Olivia hissed.

"Oh!" A pained expression crossed Isabella's face, and Diana imagined she was remembering that Diana's parents had separated for just that reason. "I meant no offense—"

"As I've taken none, all is well," Diana reassured her.

Sir Samuel came back then with her lemonade, and Diana disentangled herself from Isabella and Olivia on the pretext of taking the drink. Before Diana could excuse herself and Sir Samuel and return to the box, Olivia asked Sir Samuel how he found London.

Isabella tugged Diana a little ways away. "As dreadful as the couple in the play are, three weeks into my marriage I would have traded places with them in a heartbeat."

Diana shook her head in disbelief.

"I couldn't fight with James because he wasn't there," Isabella explained with a thin-lipped smile. "I battled an old mattress instead, but I imagined it was James when I vented my spleen with some choice words and a fire poker."

"Good heavens," Diana gasped. She must remember not to anger Isabella.

"Livvy and Jason were smarter," Isabella continued. "They got their fighting out of the way before the wedding."

"I see," Diana said, though she didn't really. "Is it family tradition for newlywed couples to argue?"

Isabella laughed. "All couples, newlywed or otherwise, have their disagreements." She gestured to Diana. "The night of Lady Langley's, I believe you quarreled with more than the crab. Hal left for Ravensfield the following morning."

"He has work he must see to." The knowledge that he'd been at his stud eased the tightness in her chest.

"True, but his estate isn't so far as to preclude spending a night in town. Tonight is the first I've seen of him since before he left and he . . . He's not himself. Hal's a relatively simple man."

"No, he's smart—"

Isabella held up a hand. "Calm yourself, Diana. I don't mean he is simpleminded, though he is unbelievably thickheaded at times. Hal is simple in that he doesn't lose sleep over the complexities of the universe or parliamentary reforms. If he's unhappy, the cause isn't difficult to discern. Hal's world centers on two things right now: the stud and you. As he claims the stud is progressing steadily, logic points to you."

Diana took a deep breath. "You're aware that Henry and I had an arrangement. Our courtship wasn't real."

"Stuff! I know you care for my brother, and he cares for you. Your relationship may have begun as an act, but as you spent time together, true feelings grew between you. That is a real courtship."

Diana flushed. "I— It's complicated."

"Life is complicated," Isabella said bluntly.

Diana's mother came into the corridor then to inform them that the curtain was rising for the second play.

"I apologize. I never intended to have this conversation here." Isabella spoke softly as Olivia and Sir Samuel joined them. "Oh, dear," she exclaimed, pitching her voice to include everyone. "We've been here the whole of the interval without accomplishing our purpose."

"My sister and I are having an intimate gathering of like-minded ladies tomorrow afternoon," Olivia explained. "Do say you'll join us, Miss Merriwether. Unless you have a previous engagement?"

"You are coming to call tomorrow, are you not?" Diana looked pleadingly at Sir Samuel.

His complete misinterpretation of her plea was, she supposed, not terribly surprising. The look he gave her was fond, almost indulgent as he said, "I wouldn't dream of standing between women overdue for a gossip."

"Before you protest," Isabella murmured, "I should warn you that I will not take no for an answer. If you don't come to me, I'll call on you."

"I'll join you tomorrow," Diana told Olivia.

"I'm so pleased," Isabella said, as if she'd given Diana any choice. "We'll leave you to enjoy the play now, and we'll see you tomorrow at Dunston House at two o'clock."

So here she was, questioning her sanity as she faced the lion. Squaring her shoulders, she rapped the polished brass ring against the back-plate. The door opened a moment later and she stepped into the beast's den. Somehow she doubted she would leave as unscathed as Daniel.

She followed the butler to the drawing room. As she'd suspected, only Isabella and Olivia were present. They greeted each other, warmly on their part, warily on hers.

As they sat, Diana remarked, "This certainly is an intimate gathering, but I don't believe we're like-minded. As I told you last night, matters with Henry are complicated."

"We're willing to listen," Olivia offered. "Perhaps things aren't as complicated as you think. We *are* like-minded. All of us in this room want what is best for both you and Hal."

Diana shook her head. "I understand your concern for your brother, but why should you care about me?"

Isabella rose from her chair and moved to sit beside Diana on the sofa. "We care because we are friends."

"Will we remain friends after I marry Sir Samuel?" Diana challenged.

Olivia sighed. "If that's what you truly want, we will support you in your decision. Neither you nor Hal would be happy together if you honestly preferred another man. Having seen you in the presence of both men, I have difficulty believing that is so. Do you love the baronet?"

"No, but one doesn't need—"

Isabella reached over and held one of Diana's hands. "Do you love my brother?"

Diana hesitated.

"There's a measure of relief to be found in unburdening yourself," Olivia said. "You need have no concern of our discretion. I swear on the lives of my children, the words spoken between us today will never travel beyond the three of us."

"I would never endanger Rosie or Edward," Isabella added, "but if you wish further assurance...." She tilted her head back and looked up. "On my daughter's life, I swear not to repeat what is spoken of today."

That these women would make such promises in order that she might feel comfortable spilling her troubles to them.... They overwhelmed her, both with their kindness to her and their close bond with each other. Would a similarly special relationship have developed if her mother hadn't lost the baby following her parents' separation?

When they'd first come to live with her grandparents, her mother had told her the time in London was a long holiday. They'd gone to Gunter's for ices and to Astley's to see the clowns and trick riders. Diana had wept through the performance since everything reminded her of her father.

Alex had been too young to understand, but Diana had known the truth about how long their holiday would last. As the bump in her mother's stomach grew larger and firmer, she funneled all her love into her new sister. She just knew the baby would be a girl. Maybe she wouldn't hurt so badly inside once she had a sister to love and to love her in return.

Then her father had shown up at Lansdowne House, banging the knocker on the front door hard enough to rattle the pictures on the walls. She and Alex had run out of the nursery to see what was happening. Like the last time her parents were in the same room, she heard yelling, crying, and protestations of love. But the wreckage they left behind this time was far worse than a broken vase. There was no replacing a sister, and there was no glue strong enough to hold together broken hearts or a broken family.

Diana started at the soft brush of a handkerchief on her cheeks. She realized she was crying, and Isabella was blotting her tears. How long had she been lost in the past? She reached up and took the handkerchief. "My apologies," she murmured. She didn't bother wiping her damp cheeks. The heat of her embarrassed flush would dry them quickly enough. "I got caught in an unhappy memory."

"There's no need to apologize for tears in this house," Olivia told her. "Our mother cries at every small thing and, since having Bride, so does Izzie."

"As if you are much better," her sister returned tartly.

But Diana was, or she should be. The duchess frowned upon displays of emotion, and Diana had learned to keep her feelings to herself. She'd had self-containment down to a fine art . . . until Henry. She'd been prim and proper Miss Merriwether for so many years that she'd forgotten the little hoyden she had been as a child.

With Henry, she *remembered*.

He reminded her how to feel. How to laugh and weep, want and need, and . . .

Love.

She loved Henry Weston.

Little by little, he'd burrowed into her heart, and now he was too deeply entrenched for her to force him out. Even if she could, she wouldn't. The years spent under her grandmother's roof had left Diana serious and quiet—the perfect young lady. She'd resigned herself to quietly watching from the shadows and even had found a measure of contentment there, but she hadn't been happy. Not until Henry had coaxed, teased, and, on occasion, pushed her into his world of light and laughter.

With him, she remembered she'd once been brave and bold. She'd pushed away her painful past, but in doing so, she'd pushed away part of herself. She'd made herself forget the young Diana who always made too much noise and whose pinafore never stayed clean past midday. That Diana had been so courageous and confident, she'd tried balancing on one leg on her father's black gelding. She had fallen off Troy and knocked her head, but after the doctor saw her and her parents scolded her, she'd declared it the best adventure of her life.

That little girl hadn't known what it was to love a rogue.

Henry was, and always would be, the adventure of her life.

"I love him," she whispered. She wrapped her arms around herself. Saying the words aloud was thrilling, but also terrifying.

Though the words would never leave this room, they were real now. They existed outside of her, and she couldn't take them back.

Isabella and Olivia looked at her, and then at each other, before their gazes settled back on her. Satisfaction lit both their faces, but Olivia appeared particularly smug. "You owe me ten quid, Izzie."

Diana jerked her head toward Olivia. "You wagered on whether or not I love your brother?"

"No." Isabella squeezed Diana's shoulder. "We would never wager on that."

"We know you love Hal." Olivia moved to sit on Diana's other side. "We wagered on whether or not *you* know you love him. As you do, we're back to the complications standing between the two of you."

"Isn't it enough that he's Henry Weston and I am, well, *me*?"

"Do you believe people will think less of you for marrying Hal?" Isabella asked.

"Of course not! Everyone would marvel at my luck. Don't you remember the outcry when our courtship began? If we married, everyone would speculate about the reasons."

"Then let them speculate." Olivia waved an impatient hand. "I don't think there's any question that Hal values his own happiness above the public's good opinion, and everyone who matters will know the truth. Now, what other complications stand between you?"

There was a knock at the door, and then Lord Dunston entered with his daughter in his arms. "I thought Aunt Livvy and Miss Merriwether might like to see our little darling before she takes her nap." Olivia immediately claimed the baby from him and started fussing over her, while Isabella walked her husband to the door.

Diana gazed at the pretty child in wonder. She'd met the little one on previous visits to Dunston House, but she'd never before thought there was a possibility Bride might be her niece. If she married Henry, Lord Dunston would have said "Aunt Livvy and Aunt Diana." Perhaps even "Aunt Di." Isabella and Olivia would be her sisters. She could have her own baby with Henry's blond hair and beautiful blue eyes.

But what if Henry decided he no longer wanted her? What

would happen to that sweet child then? Good heavens, what was the matter with her?

"Kiss, Bride," Lord Dunston called from the door.

The cherub smacked her hand to her mouth, then flung her arm toward her father. They both laughed as he pretended to catch the kiss she'd thrown him. As she watched them, Diana's lungs constricted, and her heart began to pound. She blotted her sweaty forehead with the handkerchief still clutched in her hand.

She closed her eyes and fought for control. She had been so much better these past months. Just breathe, she told herself. Breathe. Don't think about anything but breathing in and out. After a couple of minutes, the tightness in her chest eased and her heartbeat slowed. She opened her eyes cautiously, expecting stares, but Olivia's attention remained on her niece and Isabella stood in the doorframe talking with her husband.

"Oh!" Olivia exclaimed. "I just remembered I need to speak with James. Will you excuse me for a moment?"

"Yes, of course." No sooner had the words left Diana's mouth than Olivia shifted the child into Diana's arms. Diana began to protest that she didn't know how to hold a child, but Olivia was already halfway across the room. Diana's arms seemed to know what to do. They fitted themselves just so around the soft, warm body, cradling the little one to her chest. Bride laid her head against Diana's shoulder and yawned. The last of Diana's tension eased as she rubbed her cheek against Bride's wispy blond curls.

"You look very natural," Isabella remarked as she returned to sit beside Diana. There were only the two of them now, and the baby, as Olivia had left with her brother-in-law.

"She's an easy-mannered child," Diana countered. "She didn't fuss when Olivia gave her to me."

Isabella laughed. "Yes, so long as someone's holding her and paying her mind, Bride is content, but let her alone too long. . . ." She shook her head. "I fear she's becoming quite spoiled. She has only to call for her papa, and James races to pick her up."

"She is lucky to have a father who loves her so much."

"He adores her, and yet there was a time not long ago when my husband refused to consider fatherhood. Every child is a gift, but Bride is something of a miracle for us." Her voice wavered, and she reached for her daughter.

"Why was he opposed to children?" Diana asked, reluctantly handing Bride to Isabella.

Isabella pressed a kiss to her daughter's head, drawing a deep breath as she settled Bride against her. "There's no scent more soothing to a mother than that of her child," she murmured. "As for James's reasoning . . . My husband had an unhappy childhood. His grandfather raised him, but the old man made it clear that James's only value lay in being his heir. James felt that ending the family line would be proper revenge.

"He'd convinced himself that was his reason for not wanting children. That was the reason he gave me, and I'm sure there was some truth in it, but buried beneath the desire for revenge lurked a very real fear. James believed that because his mother died in childbirth, the same fate awaited the next woman he dared to love."

"Oh!" Diana gasped. "That's dreadful!"

"Yes," Isabella agreed. "Our pasts, especially our past hurts, can't help but affect how we live in the present. For some, the past determines the future. My husband loved me enough to face his demons, but we came very close to losing everything. Perhaps you should think on whether you want to allow the past to determine your future." She sniffed and grimaced. "Oh, dear, our little miracle needs changing. Will you forgive me if I abandon you for a minute while I take her to the nursery?"

"Please, go ahead. My thoughts have been in such a jumble since I arrived, a few minutes alone wouldn't come amiss."

Isabella stopped and glanced at the clock. "I'll do my best, but I suggest you think quickly." With those cryptic words, she left the room and closed the door. Somehow, though, Diana didn't feel alone.

CHAPTER SIXTEEN

I daresay you are much prettier than I am and will take at once next year, but as you have so patiently endured my troubles, you must also share in this triumph. Oh, Lucy, my heart is so full of happiness I believe I shall burst!

—from Elizabeth Fothergill to
her sister Lucinda Fothergill

"You look terrible, sir," the butler said as he took Henry's hat and gloves. "Shall I prepare my usual remedy?"

"Hal," James strode into the entry hall. "Good. You're on time. MacGowan, you may try to poison him some other day."

"I suppose I must be grateful for small mercies," Henry mused as the butler walked off.

James looked him over. "MacGowan was being kind," he stated bluntly. "You look like you've been to hell and back since last night."

"I slept poorly," Henry muttered.

He'd dreamed of Diana as a child, a wide-eyed imp with bright copper hair. They stood together at the entrance to a maze. As he knelt to see her better, she smiled and she danced away, scampering off to hide in the hedges. He followed her into the maze, the sound of her laughter serving as his guide, but she always stayed ahead of him, out of his sight.

Without warning, her laughter turned to sobs. He ran, frantically yelling her name, but he only ever seemed to go in circles. Finally, when sheer exhaustion slowed his steps, he saw that there was a gap in the bottom half of the hedge, just large enough for a child. Had he gone more slowly or stopped to think from the child's perspective, he would have noticed long before now.

He dropped to his hands and knees and wedged himself as far into the opening as he could. She sat on the other side, no longer a child, but a grown woman. Relief poured through him at finding her, and then alarm; the hedges enclosed her on all sides, and as she was no longer a small child, they trapped her there. She regarded him with sad, reproachful eyes that cut him to the core.

"I'll get you out, Di," he promised her. He began snapping branches and ripping at the leaves around him, tearing at the hedgerow like a man possessed. After a time, he realized he no longer heard crying. He glanced toward Diana only to find she had vanished, and he knew with awful certainty that she'd moved beyond his reach forever. He'd woken gasping for air, his body covered in a fine sheen of perspiration, and a chill in the region of his heart that had lingered for hours.

"*You* slept badly?" James shook his head indignantly. "Just wait until you're a father. Bride has a tooth coming in, and she cried all night. These walls are no match for my daughter's lungs."

"You expect me to believe Bride cried in another room while you listened?"

James scowled. "You would go to her too, if she called for you. The night nursemaid swears she's better when I hold her."

Henry imagined the night nursemaid would say anything to hand off her squalling charge, but he only said, "I hope Izzie isn't too tired today. I need that devious mind working at full capacity."

James laughed. "Fear not. She and Livvy both seem very confident. You'll have to give them a few minutes. Izzie just took Bride up to the nursery, and Livvy has cornered me in the library to discuss some secret project. We'll be along to the drawing room shortly."

Henry headed upstairs. As he knew everyone else was busy elsewhere, he didn't bother knocking. He was halfway across the room before he noticed the woman sitting with her back to him. He didn't need to see her face to know her. He didn't even need so much as a glimpse of autumn sunset hair. He knew the exact curve of those tiny ears, the precise shape of the wine-colored birthmark at the base of her neck, and the unique patterns of her freckles.

He rubbed at his eyes. He hadn't thought he was tired enough to hallucinate. Christ, what if he was still dreaming? Perhaps he should drink one of MacGowan's vile concoctions after all. He took another step toward the sofa.

The dream, hallucination—whatever she was—suddenly came to attention. She took one look at him, shrieked, and then leaped off the sofa. "Henry! W-what are you doing here?"

Before he could answer, two sets of throats cleared themselves behind him. Isabella and Olivia stood in the doorway.

"His presence is our doing," Olivia explained. "He didn't know you would be here."

"Diana, I sent your carriage home, along with a message that you are to stay to dine with us," Isabella said.

"You presume too much," Diana bit out. "I will take my leave now."

"Not just yet. You two must talk." Isabella held up a key. "Let us know when you reach an acceptable agreement." With that, she stepped back and Olivia pulled the door shut. He heard the unmistakable metallic scrape of a key in a lock.

"They're mad!" Diana exclaimed.

"I'll not argue with you on that count."

Diana hurried to the door and yanked on the doorknob. Unsurprisingly, the door didn't budge.

"You should count yourself fortunate that my sisters took it upon themselves to interfere," Henry said as he approached her. "This is far nicer than the kidnapping I had planned for you."

Diana glared at him as she pounded her fist against the door. "That isn't funny. Make them unlock the door."

"I have never been able to make my sisters do anything. They will open the door when they are ready. Until then . . ." He placed his hand over her fist and lowered it to her side. "Until then, will you listen to me? Will you at least give me that much?"

Diana walked to the sofa and sat down, her movements stiff with displeasure. She clearly blamed him for their current situation. As he would have done far worse, he accepted it.

He slipped the privacy bolt on the door, just in case his sisters were ready before he was, and then moved to stand in front of Diana. If he touched her, it would all be over. Just having his hand on hers had sent a surge of desire through him. He wanted her willing, though, not compromised and sated on his sister's Axminster carpet. Damnation, he needed to get himself under control before he leaped on her like some slavering beast.

He cleared his throat and clasped his hands behind his back. "The last time you and I were alone together, you stopped me from asking you an important question, possibly the most important question of both our lives. Today, I will not be stopped."

"Please—"

He shook his head. "I'll not make this easy on you. You will hear me out."

"There is nothing you can say."

She believed that. This wasn't an attempt at playing coy or a display of stubbornness. Henry heard her resignation, her grim acceptance of the truth as she saw it. He strove for patience and understanding.

"If there is nothing I can say, perhaps you should do the talking," he suggested. "Give me every reason you believe we cannot be together. For each one, I will give you a reason why we *should* be together. We will see who has more reasons."

"You can't be serious."

"I can, though not often, and I am," he said, deliberately misunderstanding her. "You are too serious. You need me to make you laugh. That was too easy. Give me another reason."

She crossed her arms over her chest. He thought she would argue, but instead she offered, "You're a rogue."

"Ah, so we're back to that? You underestimate your good influence on me. I wouldn't declare myself completely reformed, but I've restricted my roguish attentions to one woman, and I find myself more content than ever before. It's not only my happiness at stake, though. While you've been taming me, I've been unleashing the wildness in you. You will never be satisfied with an indifferent lover." Her deep flush sent a surge of white-hot lust down his spine. "God, I want to kiss you," he muttered.

"That's not a reason."

He hadn't meant that last remark as one of his reasons, but the interpretation had definite possibilities. "I think it's a very good reason. In fact, I shall count each of the things I want to do to you as reasons we should be together. Now we have at least ten thousand reasons why we should be together—"

"Wanting is not enough for a marriage," she insisted.

"I agree," he said. But it wasn't a bad place to start. He moved to sit beside her on the sofa. She tensed and scooted as far away as the cushions permitted. He chuckled. "Di, if I decide to have my wicked way with you, do you really think an extra foot of space between us will save you?" Before she could answer, he grabbed her waist and hauled her back. The little squeak she let out set him to wondering what other interesting noises she might make for him.

Damn it, he needed to concentrate. He wrapped his arm around her shoulders and settled her against him. After a dozen heartbeats, the tension left her body and she leaned into him. "I like having you beside me," he told her. "I enjoy spending time with you, and I believe you feel the same. I agree that wanting each other isn't enough, but there's more than lust between us, isn't there?

"As I'm going about my day, I'll see something that brings you to mind, and I'm happier just for thinking about you. I go about, collecting these little pieces of you that I find in the world; they keep me company until I see you again, but they're a poor substitute for reality. I can't imagine not seeing you, not talking with you, not knowing where you are, or what you're thinking . . ."

"You have many friends. I can't be the only one whose company you enjoy." She tilted her head to look up at him. "You would marry for friendship?"

"I wouldn't marry without it, but friendship alone isn't enough to satisfy me." He shifted and caught her face in his hands. He could stare into her eyes for hours trying to memorize all of the shades of green and brown, the way the colors shifted with her dress or her mood. Right now, he only wanted to see one emotion in those hazel eyes, and he prayed his next words brought it forth.

"Listen to me, Diana, and know that I mean every word I speak. I don't want to marry you because I desire you to the point of madness. I don't want to marry you because I will still enjoy speaking to you over the breakfast table in fifty years. I want to marry you—only you, my dear Miss Merriwether—because I love you."

He saw a flash of pure joy cross her face before she closed herself off. He allowed her to tug her face out of his hands, but when she made to get up from the sofa, he held her back with a hand on her shoulder.

"I love you. Have you nothing to say to that?" For long moments, he heard nothing over the hammer of his heartbeat. "You feared I would break your heart. Are you so determined to break mine first?"

Her breath caught. "You promised not to." Her words were so soft, anguished.

"When was I so foolhardy?"

She seemed surprised he didn't remember. "We promised each other we wouldn't fall in love before you suggested our arrangement."

He thought back. "No, sweetheart, you said you wouldn't fall in love with me. I promised you were safe with me." He cupped her cheek and drew her back to look at him, willing her to see the truth in his eyes. "I promise you will always be safe with me. I can't change my past, but if you let me, I will promise you my future. I will promise to honor and cherish you. I will promise to worship you with my body, to forsake all others, to care for you and comfort you."

His heart clenched as he wiped away the tears that had begun to run down her cheeks. He would make similar pledges on their wedding day, but although a holy man and all their loved ones would witness those vows, Henry knew he would remember these. Alone with Diana in his sister's drawing room, these promises were no less sacred or meaningful.

"What has you so scared, Di?"

Her face tightened and her lips quivered with the effort not to cry. Christ, she was killing him. With a sigh, he tugged her close. "Just let it out, love." She shuddered as he tucked her head beneath his chin. The first sweep of his hand up and down her back drew forth a whimper. A moment later, the dam burst. Though he hated seeing her upset, he knew she needed this. Knowing it didn't stop him from wanting to put his fist through a wall—or Thomas Merriwether's face.

He expected her to quiet after a few minutes, but every time her cries began to subside, they started up again. "Diana, please talk to me. What can I do to make this better?" he begged. "Tell me why you're so upset."

"B-because I l-love you," she sobbed.

The words were muffled against his coat, but he heard them. Yes, he heard them. "Thank God," he murmured, lifting that stubborn chin as his mouth descended on hers. He lowered her back against the sofa, letting the weight of his torso press her into the cushions. Instinct urged him to subdue this woman—*his woman*—who had tried to rebuff his claims. He kissed her, time and time again, the intimacy soothing his heart even as it inflamed his body.

His hands tangled in her hair, holding her captive though she offered no resistance, her mouth and body yielding to him. He didn't want her passive, damn it. He lifted his head and studied her. Eyes glazed with desire. Lips red and lush from his kisses. Wet cheeks, pink nose and blotchy skin. His lips twitched. If she saw herself in a glass right now, she'd have hysterics. Foolish woman, but she was *his* foolish woman.

At her inquiring look, he dropped a kiss on the tip of her nose. "Do you have any idea how beautiful you are?"

She squeezed her eyes closed, but more tears leaked out the corners. "Di?"

She slowly opened her eyes and gave him a tremulous smile. "You make me feel beautiful." Her arms came up, one hand gripping the collar of his coat, the other reaching to twine in the hair at his nape. He pressed soft kisses to her forehead, the salty tear tracks on her cheeks, and that damnably stubborn chin.

"Henry." She exhaled his name, at once a plea and a command. Her fingers tightened in his hair, trying to draw him back to her mouth.

He willingly obliged, nibbling and sucking on her lower lip. A whimper of pure need escaped her when he lightly scraped his teeth over the sensitive flesh. He meant the kiss to be brief, but he forgot everything when she flicked her tongue against his lips and his world narrowed to their joined mouths.

He opened to her with a groan of surrender; no man had ever been so happy to concede defeat or to offer himself up to the victor. He'd taught her well, perhaps too well, or mayhap the fierce need growing between them overrode her usual inhibitions, for there was no shyness this time, no moment of hesitation. She tasted him as though she were starving for him, as though she were a sinner and he her salvation. Lord knew she was his.

Their kiss wasn't delicate or gentle. They were beyond that. This kiss was about hunger. Desperation. Fear. Relief. This kiss had something to prove. That what was between them wouldn't—couldn't—be denied. That in spite of their differences they were right together. That he wasn't above ravishing her in his sister's drawing room—

Henry summoned all of his willpower and ended the kiss. He was breathing harder than after a grueling session in the ring at Gentleman Jackson's. He pressed his forehead against hers, shaken by the intensity of his response. Christ, he wasn't sure his heart could handle bedding her.

A series of images flashed through his mind like lightning. Diana writhing beneath him. Gloriously abandoned and astride him. Her head thrown back and her long, long legs locked around his waist as he took her up against a wall. His cock strained against his breeches, more than happy to engage in any or all of the imagined acts. Before that could happen though . . .

With a groan, he forced himself to sit up, and Diana followed suit, a worried look on her face. He took one of her hands, brought it to his mouth and kissed the back. "I only have so much control where you're concerned."

The pleasure she clearly took from his declaration sorely threatened it.

"Now, I want to do this properly. Should I get down on one knee?"

Diana's body, so relaxed and pliant just a moment before, grew stiff and unyielding.

"I love you, Di, and now that I know you love me, you can't expect me to let you go. I can't promise there will be no difficulties. You may not have noticed, but we're both stubborn fools." Her lips quirked. Surely that smile, small as it was, deserved a kiss.

His voice was not quite as steady when he continued. "We will doubtless butt heads, or you will throw a plate at my head, and I'm sure I will deserve it. Life is full of disagreements and disappointments, and I want you beside me for those, along with the pleasures and the triumphs. I want for better and for worse with you."

"My parents wanted that too," she said quietly.

"We're not like your parents."

"How do you *know*?" Her voice broke on the last word and that about broke his damned heart.

He took her trembling hands in his. "I know you're scared, love, and if there were some way for me to show you the future and prove your fears are unfounded, I would. The difficulty with constantly worrying about what *might* happen is that it leaves you with no time to enjoy what *is* happening. I don't know what will happen five years or fifty years from now. I do know there are no certainties, and I want however long we have together. Don't deny me— Don't deprive *us,*" he corrected, "of all we already have, of all we could have, for fear of what might be. Please, Di, be brave. I won't let you down."

She gripped his hands. "What if I let you down?"

Henry smoothed his thumbs over the backs of her hands as he thought for a moment. "For a long time, I believed that as long as I didn't try, I couldn't fail. My very wise mother explained, logically enough, that if I never tried, I had no chance of succeeding. In effect, I could do nothing *but* fail. I'm not asking you to banish your fears overnight or be anything other than yourself. I fell in love with you as you are. The only way you could disappoint me is by running away."

Keeping hold of her hands, he knelt before her. "Will you stay with me, Di? Will you agree to be my love, my wife, and the mother of my children? Will you stand beside me and hold my hand as we face whatever adventures life chances to throw our way?"

A choked sound escaped her as she leaned toward him. He didn't know who kissed whom first, and he didn't care. All that mattered was that she'd said— "Di?" He lifted his lips a fraction of an inch.

"Mmm?" She blinked at him.

"I am almost certain that was a 'yes,' but just to be sure, would you mind saying it?"

Her face grew thoughtful as she laid her palm along his jaw. "It."

His jaw dropped. "You can't be serious."

Mischief brought out the gold flecks in her eyes. "I can, and I usually am, but with you, I don't need to be."

A wave of tenderness washed over him, and he brought his hand up to cover hers. Holding her hand in place, he turned his head and pressed a kiss to her palm. "Now tell me what I want to hear," he commanded, adding a little nip of encouragement.

"Oh," she breathed.

"Wrong. Word." He nipped her again.

"Yes!" She laughed. "Yes, yes, yes, yes—"

The sharp rap on the door cut off any further affirmations.

"Go away," he yelled.

"Hal," Isabella's voice carried through the wood. "While she is under my roof, I am Diana's chaperone. Furthermore, I don't think my drawing room is an appropriate place—"

Henry shook his head at Diana, who was turning a lovely shade of rose. "She won't stop talking until I open the door." He went to the door and slid back the privacy bolt. "Izzie," he said as he opened the door, "you may be the first to congratulate us."

"Oh, I'm so pleased for you both!" Isabella flung her arms around him.

He hugged her back. "Where's the other half of the devilish duo?"

"She had to get home to the baby, but she and Jason will come to dinner to celebrate. Tomorrow will be soon enough for you to go see the duke."

Henry raised his brows. "A little sure of yourselves, weren't you?"

"I did have the key, and a refusal was not going to unlock that door." Isabella released him to embrace Diana. "Congratulations. I couldn't be more pleased to have you for a sister, and I have every faith you two will be very happy together." She looked back at Henry, her eyes bright. "Oh, Hal . . ." Her voice quavered.

"Don't cry," he warned her gruffly. "I've had all the female tears I can take today. Thank you for your help. Now, go away." He tugged Diana out of Isabella's embrace and into his. "I want a moment alone with my bride-to-be."

"I locked her in a room with you for well over an hour." Amusement colored Isabella's voice. "It isn't my fault if you can't manage your time wisely. Besides, from the state of Diana's hair, I believe you managed well enough."

As Diana patted at her hair, Henry shot her a glare. "Don't mind her. You look beautiful."

"My maid will set it to rights," Isabella said. "This won't be the first time Becky has fixed someone's hair before dinner"—she winked—"or the last."

Diana laughed, and he couldn't resist kissing her. He breathed in her laughter, happiness, and the utter perfection of the moment. The kiss wasn't long or deep, but his heart was racing when he drew back. Diana appeared just as affected.

Isabella cleared her throat. "You'd best stop looking at my brother with such admiration, or he'll become more insufferable than he already is."

"He's not insufferable," Diana objected without taking her eyes from his.

"Just wait," Isabella advised. "You'll see."

A grin flirted with the corners of Diana's mouth. Henry dropped a kiss on one side, then the other.

"I'm looking forward to it," Diana said with a happy little sigh.

"No more than I, love," he agreed, ignoring Isabella's groans. "No more than I."

CHAPTER SEVENTEEN

If you ever doubt my love, my dearest Diana, know that I have not written a letter to a female (other than my kin) since I was thirteen and fancied myself in love with Emily Hughes, or at least with the portion of her body between her waist and her neck. Mistress Hughes was a maid at Eton and a dozen years my senior; had she been able to cook, I saw a very happy future for us. Unfortunately, she was impressed neither by my billet-doux nor by my poetry. I will have you know, I labored over those lines. Perhaps she took issue with my poor penmanship, because you cannot deny the brilliance of what little I still remember:

As you sweep the dirt from beneath the rugs

I watch, entranced by the sway of your dugs.

The work here continues on both the house and the stables. I am certain the house will be livable by our wedding, and then we will turn it into a home. Ravensfield and I, we are both very much in need of your woman's touch. . . .

—from Henry Weston to
his betrothed Diana Merriwether

Diana had worried that her mother might think Sir Samuel had been mistreated, but he'd made that difficult. He'd called at Lansdowne House the day after she'd accepted Henry's proposal. Henry had visited that morning to obtain her grandfather's permission, and then he'd presented her with a stunning betrothal ring.

When Sir Samuel called, she and her mother received him. Diana broke the news of her engagement to him as gently as possible. He appeared stunned, and for one terrible moment, Diana wondered if she had been mistaken about his feelings toward her. Then he'd smiled warmly and congratulated her, saying that Henry had stolen a march on him. In the next instant, the baronet had turned to her mother to ask if she could recommend another young lady who might suit him as well as had her daughter.

As easily as that, Sir Samuel moved on, and whatever lingering reservations she might have had about Henry, Diana's mother entered into planning the wedding with as much zeal as Lady Weston. With only one month to make all of the necessary arrangements, the two became almost inseparable. The duchess insisted on overseeing all of the wedding preparations, which meant she did none of the work yet managed to express an opinion on everything. And she had an opinion on *everything,* from the flowers at the church (St. George's, as Isabella had predicted) to the color of the silk hangings in the gallery at Lansdowne House, the site of the lavish reception that would follow the wedding.

Besides seeing to her dress, Diana found there was very little required of her. Isabella and Olivia insisted that she go to Madame Bessette for her wedding gown. Though the sought-after modiste already had a long waiting list, she promised *Monsieur Henri* that she would make not only a wedding gown for his betrothed, but an entire trousseau.

Diana tried to protest, but Madame and Henry insisted. Morning dresses, walking dresses, evening dresses, a ball gown—she was to have them all. She also needed matching spencers and pelisses, a heavy cloak, and a riding habit. Madame took the names of Diana's glover and cordwainer and promised to order gloves and slippers to go with her new ensembles. Madame was also to order—Henry was very clear on this—two dozen shifts and nightgowns of the highest quality, all with ribbons as red as the flush on her cheeks.

He *did* like to see her blush. Henry wanted to spend their wedding night—any mention of which made her turn red—at Ravensfield, so he was busy setting the place to rights, but he never stayed away too long. On the days he was in London, they chose furnishings for their new home. Henry had bought quite a bit from the Bedford House sale the previous month, but they still needed a lot. As with the clothes, Diana fussed over spending so much money, but she consoled herself that her dowry would more than cover the expense.

Henry did not seem at all troubled at the cost . . . or by common decency. The first piece of furniture he insisted they buy was a bed, which he claimed was the only truly essential piece. He asked every shop owner whether he had anything larger, which embarrassed Diana to no end.

After he'd dragged her to no fewer than six stores, she lost her patience. Turning to the owner of the store, she asked if there were somewhere private where she might convince her betrothed to see sense. Having perceived that he was dealing with persons of Quality, and still hoping to salvage the sale, the man promptly ushered Henry and Diana into a small room at the back, then quickly made himself scarce.

"You are impossible to satisfy," she declared mutinously, crossing her arms over her chest. "Perhaps you should order a copy made of the Great Bed of Ware and have done with it!"

He grinned and pulled her into his arms, then set about kissing her frown away. Irritated though she was, in less than a minute she had her arms crossed around his neck instead.

"You'll soon find," he told her between kisses, "that I'm no more difficult to satisfy than the next man. Women are the difficult ones to please, but I've always enjoyed that particular challenge."

"How can you say that when I selected a bed for my chamber in the first shop we visited?" she asked indignantly.

"Oh, Di!" He let out a hearty laugh. "I think debauching you will prove the greatest joy of my life. As for the bed you selected, I hope you're not overly fond of it, for I have no intention of letting you sleep there. You will spend each night by my side—once I have utterly exhausted you in this business of pleasure and satisfaction—which is why we must find a bed large enough that we can sleep comfortably together and conceive all eight of our future children."

"Eight?" she exclaimed.

His deep laugh sent streamers of warmth unfurling throughout her body.

He looked thoughtful. "Ten?"

"Henry!" She laughed. "Will you be serious?"

"Not if I can help it," he responded, kissing her again. They were both breathing heavily when he lifted his head. "Well, my dear Miss Merriwether, is the bed we just saw the one in which you want to yell your head off when I give you pleasure, and then again when you birth our eleven babes?"

She blushed and nodded. As they headed back into the store she asked tentatively, "You don't really want so many children, do you?"

He shrugged. "I always thought I would have a large family, but there's no need to worry about that yet. Right now, I can't think beyond wanting you."

Diana held Henry's words to her heart. She refused to let herself think beyond the wedding, beyond the wanting and loving of right now. Well, she let herself think a little bit beyond the wedding. What bride did not think about her wedding night?

When the morning of the wedding finally arrived, Diana stared at her reflection in the dressing table mirror. She might have been looking at someone else. The woman looked like her, only prettier. The stranger's lips were redder, her cheeks pinker, and the color of her eyes was closer to that of dark emeralds than muddy ponds. She glowed with excitement. This was who she wanted to be, who Henry had helped her become.

Unfortunately, the pretty stranger looked no more knowledgeable than Diana felt. Her mother's maternal advice last night hadn't been as instructive as Diana had hoped.

"Your grandmother and I weren't on speaking terms when I married," she had said, "which is as well, since she would only have berated me for neglecting my duty. Your duty is to yourself, your husband, and the family you will have together. Your grandmother would also have lectured me about the mistake I was making. You are making the right choice. I had my doubts about Weston, but I can see he is devoted to you. You have a very happy future before you. Now, I know you must be nervous, but see if you can sleep a little."

"What about the rest?" Diana had asked. "You haven't said anything about the wedding night."

"Oh!" The horrified look on her mother's face had been almost comical. "I don't think that is necessary."

"But—"

"Your husband will teach you what you need to know," her mother had promised her, and that had been her final word on the subject.

Diana had no doubt Henry could teach her a great many things. The man could steal her control and give her pleasure that took her outside herself. She wanted to know if she could do the same to him.

She tilted her head at the mirror, attempting to find her most seductive angle.

"Bouge pas!" A sharp tug on Diana's hair accompanied the reprimand, warning her of the consequences should she keep fidgeting. As Diana's maid, Ellie, had traveled to Ravensfield earlier in the week along with Diana's trunks, the duchess had tasked Martine with dressing Diana's hair for the wedding. *"Qu'est-ce que vous faites?"*

Diana sighed. If Martine couldn't tell what she was doing, it clearly wasn't working. "I want to please my husband."

"He wishes you to make faces *dans le miroir*?"

"No, of course n— Ouch!" Diana's laugh earned her another tug on her hair. She watched Martine's reflection thread white and silver satin ribbons through curls she had twisted into a complicated arrangement. Though the woman must be close to her grandmother's age, she looked much younger. Along with her native language, Martine had retained the French *joie de vivre*. Diana wondered just how much life she had enjoyed.

"Were you ever married, Martine?"

"*Hélas,* I had not that pleasure, but I would trade places with you tonight." The older woman's eyes twinkled. *"Il est très beau."*

Diana flushed. "Yes, he is very handsome." She bit her lip. "Martine, if . . . if this *were* your wedding night, would you know what to do? Is it true that all Frenchwomen are born knowing how to seduce men?"

Martine smiled at her in the mirror as she placed the final pins into Diana's hair. *"Et voilà,"* she said, stepping back. *"Ma chère,* it is for your husband to seduce you, *non?"*

"No." Diana shook her head. "I mean, yes, he should, but he . . . He knows just how to kiss me, how to . . . to touch me so I forget everything and everyone but him. I want to be able to do that to him. I know men are always more eager for the bedding than the wedding, but Henry is particularly excited for tonight. He wants it to be perfect. I try not to think about the women in his past, but I can't always help myself. I'm certain all of them knew how to please a man. Mother wouldn't tell me anything, so I—" She stopped when Martine held up her hand.

"Your husband will enjoy your innocence. Men like to teach their women. They feel *plus masculin et plus viril*. But as your *maman* did not prepare you, I will tell you *les essentiels, assez bien*? You will listen as I help you dress."

Martine's information had been more than good enough. Diana only understood about half of the rapid jumble of English and French, though she wasn't sure whether her problem was a lack of vocabulary, imagination, or both. The acts described alternately shocked and intrigued her, but Martine assured her that certain kisses made all men lose control.

Diana felt convinced all of it would make her lose control. The things he would do to her. The things she could do to him. Just listening to Martine left her shivery and tight with anticipation. And those were only the essentials of bedding . . . Heavens, what more could there be? Her face flamed as wicked thought after wicked thought teased at her mind. Her mother, thank goodness, attributed her rosy cheeks to excitement and nerves over the impending ceremony.

Her color was still high as she waited with her brother in the antechamber of St. George's while the guests and parishioners took their seats. Though she regretted her grandfather's poor health, she was glad Alex would be the one to walk her down the aisle. He'd ridden down from Cambridge a few days earlier, and his happiness over the marriage rivaled her own. At times, she thought his enthusiasm actually surpassed hers.

There were days when she'd had misgivings. Loving Henry had not erased sixteen years of doubts and fears. She was happier than she remembered ever being, and that terrified her because she had more to lose. There was no question that she wanted to marry Henry; she wanted every minute she had with him. She was simply less sanguine about the fifty-plus paradisiacal years he foresaw for them.

Alex had no such qualms. He was like a child with the lure of a new toy. Did Diana think Henry would give him pointers in the ring at Jackson's? Would his new brother-in-law go with him to Tattersall's to help him choose a new hunter? Might he stay with them during his Christmas holiday? Diana had laughed and promised to speak to Henry on all accounts. She suspected she would soon see much more of her brother, which pleased her greatly even if Alex would not be coming to see her.

Isabella poked her head in the room. Not having a sister, Diana had asked Isabella to stand up with her. Isabella had burst into tears, but Diana was growing accustomed to that. Her future sister-in-law had already made good use of the handkerchief clutched in her hand.

"They're almost ready," Isabella whispered loudly. "You wouldn't believe how full the church is! I'll be back soon."

"I believe it," Alex announced with brotherly candor. "The *ton* won't believe this match is happening until they've seen— Ouch!" he exclaimed as Diana pinched his arm.

"Do keep in mind that I've promised to speak with the other half of this unbelievable pairing on your behalf," she reminded him.

He grinned at her. He had their mother's coloring, with dark curls and long-lashed gray eyes. Someday, Diana thought, he would break nearly as many female hearts as his future brother-in-law.

Alex squeezed her hand. "Have I mentioned how beautiful you look?"

"Do you suppose flattery will save you?" she retorted, nonetheless warmed by the compliment. Still tinged with the blush of desire and graced by the natural radiance of a woman in love, she knew she'd never looked better than she did at this moment.

To add to her glory, Madame Bessette had created a gown fit for a princess. Made of fine white satin, the dress was simple and elegant, just as Diana had asked. Silver lace peeked out from the neckline and the cuffs of the elbow-length sleeves. The lace was dreadfully scratchy, but it looked so beautiful she was willing to suffer the discomfort.

The modiste hadn't restrained herself very well in terms of embellishing the gown, but Diana didn't mind at all. Madame Bessette's creations were, indeed, works of art. Silver embroidery and glass beads transformed the scalloped hem of the gown into shimmering waves. Swans, also wrought in silver embroidery, glided upon the glittering water, and in their beaks, they carried oak branches. Not only had the modiste included elements from both family's coats of arms, she'd selected the perfect designs for a wedding gown. The Halswelle oak symbolized endurance and strength, while the swans from the Weston crest represented love and fidelity. Diana glanced down at the intricate work for what had to be the hundredth time that morning. Yes, it still stole her breath.

"It's time," Isabella informed them as she stepped into the room. She gave Diana a quick hug. "Brace yourself. Hal is looking very handsome today. Not as handsome as James, of course, but some of the female guests are already weeping into their handkerchiefs, and the only sentiment they're overcome with is envy."

She picked up the bouquets laid on a nearby table and handed the larger one to Diana. "I hope you like your bouquet. Hal was very particular that you must have day lilies and orange blossoms."

"It's perfect," Diana said truthfully. Tears had threatened earlier when she'd first seen it. She hadn't asked for anything in particular because, truly, all she cared about was marrying Henry, but he loved her enough to care for her. She'd known at once that he'd had a hand in choosing the flowers. Isabella carried yellow day lilies, while Diana's bouquet had white day lilies, lilies of the valley, and orange blossoms.

Though she would never admit it to anyone, even Henry, there was a tiny part of her that grieved her father's absence. She didn't actually want him there, and she knew he'd given her away years ago, but she couldn't help missing him on this particular day. The lilies helped; they gave her a bit of him, a happy memory to cling to as she walked down the aisle.

"Come along," Isabella urged. "We mustn't keep the anxious groom waiting." She winked and stepped out into the church.

"Are you ready?" Alex asked as he held out his arm to her.

She smiled at him as they walked to the center aisle. "Wild horses couldn't stop me."

As the organist began to play, Diana reflected that it was nothing short of a miracle that she'd come to this point. Looking back, she could never have imagined this for herself. Looking forward, though, she saw only Henry.

He waited at the front of the church with Lord Dunston standing beside him as the best man. They were both handsome men, but Diana thought Isabella needed spectacles if she considered her husband the better looking of the two. Henry was, quite simply, splendid.

The ceremony passed in a blur. Diana only realized she was married when Henry took her in his arms and kissed her more thoroughly than was proper in a house of God. In contrast, the reception at Lansdowne House dragged on. After more than two hours of standing beside Henry, greeting guests, and agreeing on her remarkable good fortune, Diana had had enough.

When all the guests had assembled in the gallery, her grandfather gave a long, rambling toast to the newly married couple. It was the most Diana had ever heard him speak. Then Lord Weston gave a speech. Lord Dunston followed him. Throughout it all, Henry never left her side, and scarcely a moment passed without his hands on her.

An arm around her shoulders. His palm against her lower back. His fingers twirling the curls at her nape. So, while Diana was very touched by all the wishes for health and happiness and prosperity, she could only concentrate on how Henry touched *her*. On how he would touch her. On all of the touching Martine had described.

She turned to Alex, who sat on her other side. "If you dare make a speech, you can forget spending Christmas with me."

"Beg pardon?" said Henry.

"I'll tell you later. *Alex!*" she hissed as her brother rose to his feet.

"I, too, wish to felicitate the happy couple," he announced to the room. "Though we can't choose our siblings, I've always considered myself fortunate to have Diana as a sister, and her new husband is exactly the older brother I would have picked for myself. I'm certain the newlyweds are anxious to be off to their new home, so I propose we save them the trouble of saying their good-byes and raise our glasses to bid them farewell. To my new brother and my sister, Mr. and Mrs. Weston, God grant you long life and happiness. Now, be off with you."

The guests laughed as they repeated his final words.

"Thank you," she told Alex as she and Henry rose to make their escape.

"Christmas," he replied, raising his glass in her direction.

Diana stopped only to thank her grandparents, then went directly to change into her traveling costume, another of Madame Bessette's exquisite creations. When she came downstairs, she found her mother waiting in the entrance hall.

"You didn't think you could leave without saying good-bye? Oh—" She put her hand over her eyes. "I promised myself I wouldn't cry."

"Stop," Diana pleaded, "or you'll make me cry, too."

Her mother pulled a handkerchief from her pocket and wiped at the tears she couldn't hold back. "I'm so very happy for you and so very proud of you. Your husband isn't the man I imagined for you; he is much more than I hoped. I'd forgotten how to hope for men like him."

Diana wrapped her arms around her mother. "I love you."

"Not as much as I love you. Go on, your husband is waiting outside for you."

Diana beckoned the footman carrying her portmanteau to follow her as Snellings hurried to open the front door. Henry stood by an unfamiliar carriage talking to his manservant, who was in the coachman's seat.

"It's such a fine day," she said, crossing to Henry. "I suppose your phaeton is already at Ravensfield?"

"It is not," he said, handing her up into the chariot. "I sold my phaeton. Now that I'm a respectable married man, I need a more practical conveyance. Besides, I would have to concentrate on driving in a phaeton. That would be no test at all."

Her eyes narrowed. "You consider riding in a carriage with me a test?"

He nodded, a predatory look on his face, as he climbed in after her and closed the door. "The upcoming hours will be the greatest ordeal I've ever faced, my sweet. You are now mine in the eyes of church and country, but I'm determined not to consummate our marriage until we reach that magnificent bed we chose together, no matter how prettily you beg me."

"Here?" She laughed in amusement, but her humor faded as she realized he was very serious. Her gaze dropped to his lap. Very serious and very aroused. Everything Martine had told her rushed through her mind. She pressed the backs of her hands to her hot cheeks.

"I've also determined," he continued, "that from the time the carriage comes to a stop, I can be out the door, inside the house, and in my bedchamber in twenty-seven seconds."

"You— You *timed* yourself?"

"Indeed." He shrugged out of his coat and glanced around before shrugging and shoving it beneath the seat. "Jasper will have a fit when he finds that. Now, I'll have to take care whilst carrying you, so I'll round up to thirty-seven seconds until I have you in my bedchamber. That leaves me only twenty-three seconds to undress you and toss you on the bed, but I shall contrive."

"Why must everything happen in the space of sixty seconds?" She regarded him with suspicion. "Have you made some idiotish bet?"

"Only with myself, and it's more of a promise to both of us." His gloves went the way of his coat. "I was perilously close to taking you on the floor of that dressing room, but you deserved a proper proposal and engagement. I swore to myself that our first time together would be in a bed and that we would be married." A wry smile twisted his lips. "Had I known the hell you'd put me through, I would've just found a bed and thoroughly compromised you. That's the past, though, and we've finally accomplished the married part."

He ran a finger over her lips. "I'm in a bad way, Di. I have been for months. Once we reach Ravensfield, I'll not wait longer than a minute to have you naked in my bed."

"Oh!" An involuntary gasp escaped her.

"Have I shocked you?"

"Well, yes, a— a little."

"I think I'll shock you often. I love when you blush."

Naturally, his words made her blush even more furiously.

He loosened his cravat before taking her hand and tugging off her glove.

She eyed him warily. "What are you doing?"

"The carriage will get hot," he explained. "I only thought to make you more comfortable."

She was a bit overheated, but that had nothing to do with the carriage. If he planned to spend the entire journey saying wicked things to her, she would combust before they changed horses. He pulled off her other glove. "You may not shove these beneath the seat," she warned him. "They're new, and they match my dress. I won't have them ruined."

He placed them in the pocket on the door, and then frowned at her. "Your gloves are purple."

"Madame Bessette prefers *lilac*. My shoes are also lilac." She lifted a foot from beneath her skirts to show him.

"I can see your shoes and your gloves match, but your dress is green."

"Pistachio," she corrected him, "and there are lilacs embroidered on the gown, but they're hidden by my spencer."

"There's no need for you to wear your spencer in here. Show me your gown," he urged.

"I know what you're doing. Do you think taking off my gloves and spencer will help so much in your sixty seconds?" Still, she twisted, giving him her back, and allowed him to help her out of the short coat. She gasped as his fingertips settled lightly on her shoulders and began to explore the exposed skin from her nape to the neckline of her dress.

"Very pretty," he murmured.

"Madame is quite extraordinary. Did you not think my wedding gown incredibly lovely?"

"My attention was on my incredibly lovely bride." He began to pull the pins from her hair.

"Oh, thank you. I do believe that one was embedded in my skull. Surely you noticed the embroidery on my gown?"

"Ah, yes." He chuckled. "The ducks. How did she know—?"

"*Ducks?* Those were swans! Swans, as in the animals in your family crest. Honestly, Henry, why would there be ducks on my wedding gown?"

"I like ducks."

"All . . . All right. I suppose a wife should know that sort of thing. Do you have a favorite color?"

"The color of your hair," he said easily, tossing aside the last of the pins. He began to unbraid her hair, and she sighed as it relaxed from the tight hold. He combed his fingers through the heavy mass, and then massaged her scalp and neck until she groaned with pleasure.

"Heavens, if I'd known you could do this, *I* might have proposed to *you* at the Keltons'."

He laughed and pulled her onto his lap. Beneath her thighs, his erection strained against his breeches.

"I thought we were waiting for the bed," she said breathlessly.

"For the bedding, yes. For touching, no." His fingers fiddled with the top button of her dress.

"You've been touching me all day."

"Di, there's touching, and there's *touching*." His eyes crinkled at the corners. "Let's have a proper greeting, wife."

She flung her arms around his neck and eagerly dragged him down for a kiss. He wasn't the only one who'd lain awake at night, frustrated with unfulfilled longing. He'd introduced her to pleasure, and now she craved it. His taste was addicting, his smell, intoxicating. He overwhelmed her senses, making her forget everything but the need to be with him.

His kisses were slow, lingering affairs. Impatient, she nipped at him and flicked her tongue over his lips. His arms tightened about her as he thrust his tongue inside her mouth. She parried and returned in kind, joining the dance. She moaned as he shaped her breast through her gown.

The carriage hit a rut in the road, and she bounced into the air. Diana made a desperate grasp for the holdings, but Henry caught her and set her back in place. "As much as I like you lying across my lap, I think that position may prove too precarious."

He was doubtless right, but she didn't have to like it. She pouted as she started to climb off him.

"My thoughts exactly," Henry said as he clamped his hands around her waist and held her still. In an instant, he drew the curtains, so the only illumination came from the long octagonal back window above their heads. He must have had this chariot specially built; she imagined the squabs in most carriages likely reached his shoulders. She stopped speculating about carriage construction when Henry picked her up and turned her to face him. He held her there, poised above him, as if she weighed next to nothing.

"Lift up your skirts," he instructed.

"I beg your pardon?"

"Raise your skirts up enough so you can kneel astride my lap."

She hesitated, eyeing him doubtfully.

"So quickly you forget your promise to obey me?" he teased. "Come, may a new husband not show his bride his undying love and affection?"

"Is *that* what you're going to show me?" He made no move to put her down, so she bit her lip and gathered her skirts up to her knees. Despite all that had passed between them, Diana found she was too shy to meet his gaze as he lowered her to straddle his lap. He clutched her tightly as the carriage hit another stone in the road, and they both groaned as she pressed against him.

"Good God," he muttered, "I must be mad to torture myself like this." He set her back slightly and brought one hand up to cup her cheek. The other he left at the small of her back, lest she go flying again.

"The thing is," he explained, "once we arrive, get upstairs, and are gloriously naked in our glorious bed, I need to have you ready for me. With the way you rip at my control, I don't know how long I'll be able to wait, and I don't want to hurt you any more than nature demands."

"What do you mean?" Perhaps she hadn't understood all of Martine's talk, but she would have understood *that*. The Frenchwoman's *essentiels* had covered everything from chewing a sprig of mint before going to bed to the pennyroyal tea she should drink if she wished to prevent a child.

How could she not have mentioned pain, or was this deception forced on all brides? She began to climb off Henry, but he held her in place despite her struggles. He looked uncomfortable. "Will I hurt you as well?" she asked.

"God, yes," he choked out a laugh. "You're killing me right now, and the thought of giving you pain tears me apart inside. Did your mother not explain what happens in the marriage bed?"

"My mother would not tell me anything, so I asked Martine."

His brows rose. "Martine?"

"My grandmother's lady's maid. She's French," Diana told him, as if that explained everything. Perhaps it did. "She thinks you're very handsome, but she said nothing about pain."

"She didn't want you to run before the wedding. No, Di, don't look at me like that. I was only teasing. I should have kept my mouth shut, but I suppose it's too late for that. It will only hurt the first time, and I'll spend the next fifty years pleasuring you to appease my guilt."

She hadn't thought this through very well, Diana realized. She understood the basic principles of the marriage act. She knew Henry was a large man—everywhere. Somehow, she hadn't put the two together. When she added herself into the equation, it didn't add up. His . . . His . . . *That* couldn't possibly fit inside her.

"We will fit together perfectly." Henry's finger lifted her chin.

Oh, heavens, not only had she spoken aloud, she'd been staring down at her lap. Their laps. Her skirts covered everything, but she was going to burst into flames, so she supposed she really didn't need to worry about her wedding night. Unfortunately, once she started worrying about a thing, she had trouble stopping.

"How much will it hurt?" she asked nervously.

He frowned. "I don't know. That's the truth, love. This is a first time for me as well. If I could spare you this, I would. Since I can't, I'm going to do my best, before we arrive, to make you as ready for me as possible. When I race up those stairs with you in my arms, I intend for you to be frantic." His voice dropped. "Fevered. So desperate to have me inside you that you don't care about the pain."

His husky murmur washed over her like a wave of desire, and she met his lips halfway. She lost track of time—of everything—as they kissed, exploring each other as if their mouths had never met before. She arched her head back as he kissed his way down her neck and over her chest until he came up against her gown. He rubbed his cheek against her, and she delighted in the slight abrasion from his afternoon stubble. His palms skimmed the sides of her torso, stopping just beneath her breasts. She shifted restlessly on him, trying to encourage his hands to move higher.

He nuzzled her again. "Your skin is so soft," he groaned. "Softer than velvet, silk, or mink, and I want more." His fingers moved to the buttons at the back of her gown. "I want to see you."

"I want to see you too." She tugged at his cravat as he yanked at the laces of her stays. His rough need made her frantic, but he made no complaint as she jerkily unwound the starched linen and tossed it to the floor. She loosed the single button at his throat; his shirt sagged open, revealing a golden vee of skin dusted with blond hair. She stroked her fingers over his hot flesh, marveling at the thump of his heart, the quick beat of his pulse. Hers was just as fast, if not faster, and—she watched her laces join Henry's cravat—she couldn't blame her shallow breathing on tight stays.

"I want . . ." He was delicious . . . and hers. "I want to taste you."

He sat still as a statue as she touched her lips to the base of his throat. A shudder ran through him when she touched her tongue to his skin. She took a longer lick, savoring the taste of salt and man. Then she nipped him.

The blasphemy that poured from his mouth should have outraged her; instead, it excited her. Her thighs contracted involuntarily, tightening her knees around his hips. The movement snapped the reins holding the rogue's control. He wrenched her dress forward over her shoulders, taking the straps of her stays and petticoat with it. She scrambled to pull her arms through the layers of fabric.

As soon as she freed herself, Henry flung the stays away and shoved the rest down, leaving her in nothing but her thin shift above the waist. He stared at her chest for a long moment, and then released a shaky breath. "Christ," he swore. "I forgot about the damned red ribbons."

"Henry," she pleaded.

His eyes flicked up to her face. "Come," he said. "Taste me again."

The dark challenge in his voice spurred her desire. This kiss was hungry and clumsy. She started at the touch of his hands on her breasts, and their teeth clashed together. Their noses and foreheads knocked as they struggled to devour each other, neither willing to wait and take the other's lead.

A bumpy stretch of road forced them to pause as he steadied himself with the holding strap and she steadied herself with him. Without the support of her stays, her breasts bounced and quivered like an overset dish of blancmange. Henry eyed them with the same greed he would a tasty dessert. Apparently he meant to taste her, too, because as soon as the road leveled, he leaned her back over his arm and set his mouth on her breast.

She squealed from shock, then panted from pleasure as he sucked softly, dampening the fine lawn with the wet heat of his mouth. The rhythmic pull echoed the throbbing pulse that had taken up residence at her core. His free hand plumped her other breast, squeezing, caressing and running his thumb in circles around the aching peak.

She nearly wept with frustration when he removed his hands, then wanted to howl with desire when she realized his intention. He tugged at the condemned ribbon until it came loose. He sat her up only long enough to slip her shift over her shoulders and down past her breasts, then he had her sensitive flesh back in his mouth, seemingly hotter, wetter without the fabric barrier. He rolled her nipple between his thumb and forefinger, lightly pinching, as his teeth clamped gently around the other.

"Yes!" she gasped, jerking at the pleasure coursing through her body, running from her breasts down to her sex. That was where she wanted his hand. Between her thighs. Stroking her. Outside. Inside. Henry wasn't the only greedy one. She wanted the pleasure he'd shown her before.

"More," she demanded.

He lifted his head, one golden brow quirking in amusement. "More? Like this?" He tweaked her nipple harder.

She shook her head, even as a little breathless cry escaped her lips. She pulled her arms free of her shift. She crossed her arms over her breasts, suddenly conscious of her nudity.

Eyes turned dark as midnight locked with hers. "Tell me what you want," he urged, his deep voice laden with desire. His eyes glittered with fierce, molten lust.

Her nerve faltered. "I want you to . . . to touch me . . ." she trailed off helplessly.

"Tell me, Di," he insisted, nipping at her lower lip. "Where do you want me to touch you?"

She drew in a breath and closed her eyes before dropping her arms and letting the truth spill from her lips. She could withhold nothing from him. "Between my legs. Please, Henry, I ache for you."

A low groan rumbled from his chest as he seized her lips in a kiss so heated, so searing, it stole her breath. It stole her heart. It stole her very soul. She couldn't think, could only feel as he widened his thighs, opening her as he did so.

She shuddered as his fingers delved beneath her skirts and found her; the first light touch had her crying out. She broke the kiss and buried her face against his neck. Her hands clenched on his shoulders as she grabbed large fistfuls of his coat.

The only sounds in the carriage were the harsh rasp of his breathing and her partially muffled moans. She bit her lip, trying to keep quiet, as he cupped her woman's mound. Even that gentle pressure overwhelmed her senses.

"I— It's too much!" She jerked up, thighs clenching, but she couldn't close her legs with him between them. His free hand rubbed her back until she relaxed, then settled on her behind to hold her in place.

"Not nearly enough," he murmured as he slid his hand down. He pressed the heel of his palm against her as the tip of one finger eased inside her. "God, Di," he groaned against her ear. "You're so tight."

"Don't stop," she begged. "I need you."

"You'll have me soon," he promised thickly. "For now . . ." He pressed in further.

Diana tensed, and he withdrew. He dragged his finger up her cleft to circle the sensitive nub. When she began to writhe, he returned to the entrance to her body and worked the digit into her with short thrusts. Each pulse of his hand rocked his palm against her nub. She could feel the muscles of her sex expanding to let him in, an oddly satisfying sensation. But she wanted to fly again, to jump off the edge of that precipice and soar into mindless pleasure.

"More," she demanded.

"More here?" He rubbed his palm on her faster, harder. Behind her closed eyes, red flashes began to streak across the darkness like fiery shooting stars. "Or more *here*?" He began to work a second finger inside her. She bucked her hips, driving him in deeper . . . and soared.

He kept her aloft, spiraling higher and higher, like a feather swirling on a windy day. He would let her drift down, but just before she touched the ground, he drove her back up again. She was crying with the overwhelming joy rioting through her body. She didn't belong to herself anymore, but to him. To the pleasure he gave her. She was lost in it, and he was her only anchor to the person she'd been before.

Just when she decided the feelings were too intense and she couldn't bear it any longer, he curled his fingers into her. Again and again and again, until fireworks burst behind her eyes. Her body shook apart, shattered, dissolved into nothingness. She didn't know how long she was gone before she slowly began to come back to herself. She felt her heart pounding in her chest, the blood pulsing through veins in heavy limbs.

She heard Henry's voice from a distance. He sounded anxious. He ought to feel like her, she thought. Much better than being anxious. She would have laughed, but that would take too much effort. Henry's voice was louder now, closer, more insistent.

"Diana? Sweetheart?"

"Mmm?"

"Are you all right? Di, talk to me. How do you feel?"

His voice was rough with worry. That wasn't fair. Not when she felt so delicious. She leaned back her head and blinked lazily at him. "Wonderful," she said, knowing the silly grin on her face would tell him all he needed to know. "But my bones have turned to jelly, and—" She yawned. "I'm afraid I didn't sleep very much last night."

Henry pressed a hard kiss to her forehead before tucking her head back against his neck. "Rest a while, sweetheart. You'll need your strength for tonight. Are you comfortable?"

"Quite." She burrowed into him, loving the heat of him, the smell of him, the sound of his heart hammering away. "Are you?"

He chuckled. "My comfort will come later, minx, but right now I'm happy to have you in my arms, jelly-bones and all."

CHAPTER EIGHTEEN

Lord and Lady Weston invited me to their home after the wedding feast. The entire family gathered there, and I would not be surprised if they are still celebrating today. I enjoyed myself to no end, but you might have warned me. There was never a quiet moment from the time I entered the house. Lady Weston and Lady Sheldon already have a list of at least seven brides in mind for me, one of the twins—a girl still in the schoolroom!—made sheep's eyes at me, I made sheep's eyes at your husband's aunt, and I somehow managed to lose three of the buttons on my waistcoat. Oh, and I overheard Lady Dunston whisper to her sister that she should have given you some warning about the carriage. Given the other things they said last night, I am not sure I want to know. . . .
—from Alexander Merriwether to
his sister Diana Weston

"Wake up, sweetheart."

Diana mumbled her refusal. She was having the most incredible dream. Henry's mouth was on her breasts, kissing, nipping, and sucking, but she felt him everywhere. Every brush of his lips, scrape of his teeth and lap of his tongue echoed out in shimmering waves. They built upon themselves, until desire pounded through her relentlessly.

"Come, wake up and kiss me." A gentle tug on her hair. A lingering caress along her outer thigh. "We're almost there."

She *was* almost there, if only he would *touch* her. She wriggled her hips, trying to show him what she wanted. He licked the curve between her shoulder and neck, then bit her, just hard enough to clear the dream-daze from her brain. He claimed her mouth the second she came fully awake, and then fractured her concentration with another soft stroke on her inner thigh.

He grazed her other thigh, a little higher up, and she melted for him. When he finally touched her where she wanted, his fingers cruised over her slick folds as effortlessly as a wherry through the Thames. He didn't move quickly, though. No, he meandered as he charted his course, changing directions and skimming the banks until she lost patience and sank her teeth into his lower lip.

He grunted, his hips jerking beneath her, as he tore his mouth from hers. His lips curved into a sensuous, wicked grin, and a knowing glint lit in his eyes. "Are you frantic yet, sweetheart?"

"No," she lied.

"I must remedy that." As he spoke, he slid one finger inside her.

She moaned as her body welcomed him without hesitation, only a jolt of pleasure. A second finger joined the first, stretching her a little, and as before, the slight pinch of discomfort intensified her pleasure. She tensed, waiting for the flames to consume her, but they only burned hotter and brighter.

Henry sucked at the tip of her tongue in time with the shallow thrust of his fingers, both matching the rhythmic swaying of the carriage. He swallowed her cries as their tongues tangled—dancing, dueling, daring each other past reason. He barely moved within her, keeping her poised at the edge of the cliff, but careful not to let her fall over the edge.

The sensation was incredible, the pleasure almost excruciating. Every so often, the carriage would hit a rut or a stone and the resulting jolt would drive him deeper. She felt herself slipping, teetering for balance. She never thought she'd pray for a poorly maintained road, but several large ruts in succession would be more than welcome right about now.

"Why are you torturing me?" she moaned. Her voice was breathy, husky with desire. She didn't sound like a tortured woman.

"Are you fevered yet, Di?" he demanded. His tone was rough, his breathing ragged.

She remembered his earlier words. *I intend for you to be frantic. Fevered. So desperate to have me inside you that you don't care about the pain.*

Yes. Heavens, yes. She was all of those things. Frantic. Fevered. Desperate. She didn't care about the pain. She wanted the explosive release she knew he could give her.

"Yes. Please, *yes!*" The last word was a wailed plea. She didn't care how smug her words made him. She'd passed the point of denials.

"Good." He withdrew his hand.

"W-what? No!" she cried.

"Soon," he crooned. "If I give you pleasure now, you'll tighten up. Besides, I'd prefer to have you awake."

She watched in astonishment as he lifted his hand to his mouth and sucked her wetness from his fingers. She should have been appalled, but every draw of his mouth wound her tighter. Her thighs clenched as she watched his eyes darken to a blue as deep and boundless as a summer night sky. "I should've taken you before we left London," he said, his voice strained.

Diana agreed wholeheartedly, but it was too late for that. "Take me now," she urged. "You said you could take me here in the coach. Forget about the bed. Please, I need you now."

"No." He clamped his lips resolutely and lifted her off his lap. He set her beside him and attempted to dress her. Diana didn't resist, but she didn't cooperate either. Her breathing was becoming more regular, but her body was still burning. Dressing seemed counterproductive to dousing the fire raging within her.

Henry twitched the curtains aside and looked out. "In about five minutes, we'll reach the drive," he informed her. "When we reach the house, I'm dragging you out of this carriage, whatever your state of undress. The servants are all away for the night, and Jasper will look away . . ." He tapped a finger against his cheek. "I rather like the idea of carrying you over the threshold bare-breasted."

His words spurred her into action. She hurried to draw her arms back through her shift, petticoat, and gown. There simply wasn't enough time to lace up her stays. She turned and held her hair out of the way so Henry could fasten the garments. He was a very efficient lady's maid. She tried not to think it was due to his having done it so many times.

"What need have I of Ellie when you are so capable of dressing me?" she teased.

"I prefer to *un*dress you." He kissed her nape, lightly raking his teeth over the sensitive skin.

"You are also very skilled at that," she assured him.

He reached out and drew up the curtains. "Look, Di." He pointed out the window at the red brick manor, and Diana had her first glimpse of Ravensfield Hall. She reached blindly for Henry's hand.

"Does it please you?" he asked softly.

She squeezed his hand and nodded, unable to speak. She'd floated through the past month, through the morning's ceremony, through her husband's—*her husband!*—idea of a carriage ride. She'd feared more than once that she'd dreamed everything. Seeing the place where they would make their home together struck her as real, solid, and enduring.

Worried she might cry, she turned her attention to the mess at her feet. She let go of Henry's hand and began snatching up various articles of her clothing. "You might be as skilled as Ellie, but you are nowhere near as neat."

Henry watched her in silent amusement as she rolled up her stays and laces, wrapped them in her spencer, and tied the parcel with the ribbon from her hair. He retrieved her gloves from the pocket on the coach door, and she handed him his cravat in exchange. He made no move to dress.

"Henry?" She gestured to his bare throat before pulling on her gloves.

She frowned as he started to undo the buttons on his waistcoat. "Whatever are you doing?"

His smile turned to a look of fierce, sensual intent. "Since you appear determined to dress, I have decided to compensate." His waistcoat hit the floor. "That's a few seconds saved." He gathered handfuls of his shirt and tugged it free of his breeches.

"Henry, you can't—"

He drew his shirt over his head. Her heart stuttered, possibly because she'd stopped breathing. She'd felt the hard muscles of Henry's shoulders and back through his clothes, seen classical statues in her grandfather's collection and at the British Museum. Nothing had prepared her for this.

He really was the most beautiful man. Diana licked her lips as her gaze wandered the strong, corded muscles of his arms. Hair the color of burnished gold dusted the firm planes of his chest, vanished on the sculpted span of his abdomen, and then reappeared in a line beneath his navel.

Her fingers itched to explore the different textures of his body. Would the hair on his chest prove soft or wiry? Were the small brown points of his nipples sensitive like hers were? What would they feel like beneath her fingertips . . . or the tip of her tongue?

"Jesus, Di, I'll end up taking you on the front steps if you keep looking at me like that," Henry growled as the carriage began to slow. He opened the door and jumped out before they came to a full halt. Diana clutched her bundle of clothing as Henry swung her into his arms.

"Jasper," he said, addressing the man in the driver's seat, "you are as excellent a groom as you are a valet. My wife wishes me to tell you that this is the most enjoyable ride she has ever experienced."

"Henry!" Diana shoved her elbow against the solid wall of his chest.

"You're right, my sweet," Henry agreed. "I'm wasting precious seconds. Jasper, like everyone else, you are dismissed for tonight. I expect some of the grooms are celebrating at the Saracen and Ring in Great Bookham, should you wish to join them. Spread the word in the servants' hall tomorrow that we are not to be disturbed until . . ." He grinned. "We'll ring when we wish for assistance."

"I will never be able to face him again," she groaned.

Henry turned and hurried toward the house. "You won't see anyone else. I've arranged for us to have this night entirely to ourselves."

The front door opened to reveal a short, round man with spectacles and a cheery smile. His smile broadened as he took in their appearances. "Mr. and Mrs. Weston, allow me to offer you my sincerest congratulations."

"Timms, I didn't expect you here." Surprise and impatience colored Henry's voice, but he didn't seem at all perturbed at being bare-chested while conversing with their new butler.

The man chuckled. "I only came by to leave a cold supper out for the pair of you. My wife feared you would go hungry with no one here."

"We thank you both." Henry stepped into the house and resumed his quick pace toward the stairs. Diana tried to look around at her new home, but she only caught glimpses of colors and flashes of light on polished wood. "Your mistress and I will see you sometime next week," Henry called down to the butler as he bounded up the stairs.

"Next week?" she asked.

"I don't plan on letting you out of my bed before then," he replied, his expression entirely serious. "I'm glad we decided my bare chest should cross the threshold instead of yours." His eyes twinkled. "I might have had to give Timms the sack if he'd seen you so."

She swallowed hard as he stopped in front of a door and dipped his arms so she could open it. His bedchamber. He walked inside, kicked the door closed with a booted foot, then strode to the bed and set her down.

"Should you lock the door?" she wondered.

"All of the servants have been dismissed for the night. They all have families nearby to stay with, and Ellie's gone with Mr. and Mrs. Timms. I'm the only one who will hear you yelling tonight," he promised, starting once more to undo the buttons on her gown. From the speed of his progress, she surmised that he hadn't been overly diligent in doing them up.

"Lord, you're more beautiful than I imagined," he murmured as his gaze roamed over her body, naked now, save for her shoes, stockings, and garters, which he quickly removed.

"You're still dressed," she blurted out in dismay.

"Not for long." He laughed, an edge of need to the sound, and bent over to remove his shoes. She glanced away when he started on the buttons on his breeches, and then he pounced, rolling with her on the bed, his bare limbs tangling with hers. She'd only just begun to process the feeling of his naked body pressed to hers when he kissed her, hot and openmouthed, and, in moments, she was back to the place she'd been in the carriage.

Frantic. Fevered. Desperate.

She cried out as he eased his hand between their bodies, arching up into his touch. He circled the sensitive little bud that sent shocks of pleasure echoing through her body, and then dipped two fingers inside her, stroking her until she was just about to topple over the edge.

"No," she pleaded, when he removed his hand. "Not again."

"This time we're going to fly together, Di," he promised.

She kept her gaze fixed on his and saw her emotions reflected back at her in shades of blue. The sharp flash of heated desire that bolted up her spine as he rubbed the tip of his sex against her . . . The fight for composure as he pushed in that first bit . . . The wonder of joining their bodies like this . . . She gasped as he rocked his hips, pressing in a little further.

"Am I hurting you?" he gritted out.

He was much larger than his fingers, and the stretching verged more on pain than an erotic pinch. She saw the lines of control etched on his face, knew the restraint he was employing on her behalf.

"No," she lied, afraid he would stop if she said otherwise. The pain wasn't that bad, just a sharp sting, really.

"Thank God," he muttered. He covered her mouth with his and thrust deep, seating himself within her.

She hissed as the pain intensified.

Henry stilled, his stricken face looming over hers.

"I'm all right," she reassured him, dredging up a small smile. "Truly, I'm all right." She was telling the truth this time. The hurt was fading, replaced by a sense of fullness. "You're inside me," she whispered, marveling at the way their bodies fit together.

He groaned at her words. "You were made for me," he told her, beginning to pull away.

She ran her hands over the smooth muscles of his back, holding him to her. "Don't leave me."

"Never." He pushed back inside her.

"*Yes,*" she breathed as he began to move on her, in her, to a rhythm that stole her reason. Every part of her body was expanding, threatening to burst out of her skin, even as she was tightening all over.

She wrapped her legs around his hips, and they both caught their breath as the movement brought him deeper inside her. She licked at his chest, his shoulder, any part of his flesh her mouth could reach. He was hot, his skin damp and salty with sweat, and he tasted more delicious than any meal that had ever been set before her. Of course, food had never made her feel as good as Henry made her feel right now. She inhaled deeply, the muscles of her sex clenching around him as she breathed him in. Male musk and heavy rain.

"Christ," he swore. "I can't last much longer, sweetheart."

He plunged into her harder, faster, deeper, and she could feel herself sliding closer to that sweet oblivion. His features tight with determination, he shifted his weight to one arm and reached between them. She tracked the movement of his hand to the place where their bodies joined, and even before he touched her, she began slipping over the edge. She grabbed him, trying to hold on. She wanted to go, but not without him.

"Fly with me, Di," he panted against her ear, as he flicked his fingers over the nub at the top of her sex.

She wailed his name as she tumbled into ecstasy, starbursts exploding behind her eyes as her body shook apart into a thousand tiny pieces. She dimly heard his hoarse shout as he followed her, spilling his seed inside her before he collapsed over her in a sweaty heap. When he tried to lift off her, she wrapped her arms and legs around him, holding him in place.

She would keep him inside her forever if she could. He was heavy, but she welcomed the weight, savored the way his heart throbbed in his chest. Her heart pounded too, as if it were straining up to reach his. They were so close right now, and the connection went beyond the physical. In this moment, they were of one mind. One heart. One soul.

Soul mates.

She'd always thought the term referred to like souls, but she'd been wrong. Henry was nothing like her, but he made her whole. She pressed a line of kisses down his jaw. She felt ecstatic and at peace. Complete. Henry fit her as perfectly as he had promised. He'd been referring to their bodies, but he also filled the empty spaces in her heart.

Was this how all married couples felt for each other, or rather, the couples in love? This unceasing whirl of attraction, affection, and need. She wondered now how she could have ever contemplated marrying Sir Samuel. She couldn't imagine giving herself this way to any man but Henry. She couldn't imagine spending her life with anyone but Henry. Fortunately, there was no need.

It still seemed too incredible to be true. He'd given her so much. He'd brought her to life, tending her like a fragile flower until she bloomed. She thought her heart would burst from loving him. She was giddy with happiness, but hard on the heels of that thought came the horrifying realization that she'd tied her happiness to Henry. Once again, it was out of her control.

Her parents had once been married and in love. Did that mean her mother had needed her father like this, that he'd completed her in the way Henry completed Diana? How had she survived the loss?

Her heart ached, and tears welled up and spilled over her cheeks.

"Did I hurt you?" Henry asked worriedly as he wiped her tears away, a frown creasing his brow. "Was I too rough?"

She shook her head. "I'm just so . . . very happy." Her voice caught on a sob.

He slid out of her and rolled onto his side, bringing her with him. He smoothed her hair off her face with exquisite gentleness, and his eyes were tender as he gazed at her. She knew now with absolute certainty that losing him wouldn't just break her heart; it would destroy her. She closed her eyes so Henry wouldn't see the surge of terror that shot through her.

She couldn't know the future, she told herself. She and Henry would be fine. They wouldn't destroy any lives. She suddenly thought of the little packets of herbs Martine had packed in her portmanteau. She had no control over her own future, but she could make certain that, whatever happened, no child of hers would ever suffer the rejection she had. She squeezed her eyes tight against another flood of tears.

"Rest, love," Henry said, tucking her against him, "because as soon as I can manage, I plan on making us both very happy again."

Henry awoke with a smile on his face, happiness in his heart, and an ache in his cock that he knew just how to cure. He wasn't sure if it was the months of enforced abstinence, the church's blessing, or some combination of the two, but bedding Diana had been the most amazing sexual experience of his life. His wife was an innocent—though she was a fast learner—but lovemaking with her had taken him to unimagined heights. Making love—perhaps that was the difference.

He rolled onto his side to look at her, pride and possessiveness filling him. His *wife*. He was beginning to understand why some of his friends seemed so happy with their shackles. With Diana, he saw shackles in an entirely new light. He envisioned her shackled to the bedposts, helplessly awaiting his every desire . . .

He reached out and ran a finger down Diana's back, tracing the delicate line of her spine. She lay on her stomach, her head pillowed on her arms, that incredible hair spilling around her. Early morning light sneaked in around the heavy curtains casting a glimmer glow on her porcelain skin. His mouth had learned every sensitive inch of her back last night.

He'd set out to kiss all of her freckles, but he'd become distracted halfway down. If her yells were any indication, she hadn't minded. And he wouldn't mind another taste of her. He felt his smile widening, stretching across his face in an undoubtedly idiotic grin.

He shifted closer and pressed a kiss to one shoulder. She didn't stir, so he hooked a finger in the sheet pooled around her waist and pulled it off her. She had one knee hitched up, and his heart leapt—along with his cock—at the sight. Even in slumber, she offered herself to him.

Henry slid his arm around her waist and rolled her onto her side so her back fitted against his chest. He rubbed his chin against her silky hair as he lightly trailed his fingers over her ribs. She wriggled and batted at him as if he were an insect. The press of her buttocks against his aching flesh had him groaning with wanting to be inside her. His fingers slid to the rounded swell of her hips, over the soft flesh of her belly and then down through those scandalous flaming curls to her core.

"Wake up, Di," he whispered between pressing feather-light kisses to her temple, her cheek, her chin. "It's time for me to love you again."

She made a sound that was at once incoherent and definitely negative, kin to the one he'd heard yesterday in the carriage. His wife didn't like having her slumber disturbed. He made a note of it, and then proceeded to ignore it.

He chuckled as he raised himself up on his forearm. "I'll have to change your mind then." He skimmed his teeth over the shell of her ear and lightly nipped her earlobe as he cupped her sex, rubbing his palm against her. He knew the moment she awoke; her muscles tensed and her breathing hitched.

"Good morning, wife," he murmured against her neck. "And it's about to get better." He probed at her entrance with his middle finger and found her tight, but hot and damp. She gasped as he began to slowly press inside and moaned as he retreated.

"Are you sore?" he asked.

She shook her head. He hadn't seen anything yesterday when he'd bathed her woman's flesh, but she'd been a very unwilling participant in that inspection. He'd never seen her turn quite that shade of red before. Still, he'd torn through something to make her bleed, so after the first time, he'd restricted his loving to his hands and mouth. He'd been a gentleman, and he was proud of himself. He was ready to reclaim his status as a rogue.

He stroked up her cleft to circle the bud at the peak of her sex, setting up a steady rhythm. She rewarded him with an erotic symphony of breathy cries and guttural groans, pierced now and again by the keening wail of his name and a great deal of blasphemy.

Stroking his hand over a sleek, freckled thigh, he caught hold of her knee, lifted her leg and rested it atop his. He placed the tip of his cock against her and rolled his hips, slowly working inside her. He gritted his teeth at the exquisite sensation of being wrapped in hot, wet silk. Her inner muscles pulsed softly with the echoes of her pleasure, trying to coax his seed from him.

His breath caught at the thought of watching Diana's stomach grow round and taut with their babe. He'd teased her about children before, but he'd never thought much beyond conceiving them. Difficult to believe he was thinking past that right now, but mixed with his need was an exuberant joy that took the face of a chubby-cheeked child with copper curls.

How incredible that he'd complained of feeling adrift only months before. His life had direction now. He had a purpose. He had an estate, a stud that would prosper and thrive under his guidance. He had a wife. In time, they would build a family together.

He gathered Diana closer, rocking their bodies in a gentle, easy pace, trying to prolong the pleasure. His hand rose from her curls to toy with her breasts as he nuzzled his face into the curve of her neck. She smelled like orange blossoms and sated woman. *His* sated woman.

"Di," he murmured.

She turned her head to look at him, her hazel eyes reflecting all the need and desire he felt. He'd never seen a more beautiful sight. He leaned forward to kiss her, knowing he would never grow weary of her taste, never tire of hearing the hitch in her breathing when his tongue touched hers.

When she began to push back against him, his fingers sought out that tiny bud once more. He swallowed her moans as he drew lazy circles. Diana writhed in his arms, torn between the need to press back and take him deeper or to press forward against his fingers. He made the decision for her as he pulled himself from her velvet grip and urged her onto her knees. She glanced at him over her shoulder, her eyes wide with yearning and a touch of apprehension.

"Trust me, love. You know I would never do anything to hurt you." He placed a tender kiss at the base of her spine, just above the lush swell of her bottom. She nodded, her hips tilting in a subtle invitation that he was more than willing to accept. He positioned himself at her entrance, grabbed her hips, and slowly pushed into her. After a few easy thrusts, he pulled almost all the way out, and then slammed home.

Diana cried out, her sex clamping around him like a satin fist. Her arms buckled, and she collapsed to her elbows on the bed. He paused, but she shook her head. "Don't stop." She ground her head against the mattress as she clawed at the sheets. "Don't stop. Oh, God, don't stop."

He surged into her, riding her through her climax. He fought the urge to spill his seed, desperate to make the pleasure last as long as possible, but he knew he wouldn't last long. He placed one hand down on the mattress and molded his chest to her back, wanting to be as close to her as possible. He reached beneath her with his free hand and stroked her nubbin, already swollen with desire.

"Henry—" she gasped. "I can't— It's too much!"

"Again," he insisted stubbornly. He began to pluck at the sensitive flesh, willing her to go over the edge once more. His spine tingled in warning as his ballocks drew up. With one last hard thrust, he let out a hoarse shout and gave himself over to the demands of his body. Diana cried out a moment later, her inner muscles drawing his seed in a rhythmic caress that left him entirely exhausted and utterly replete.

Henry had just enough presence of mind to withdraw from her and collapse onto his back beside her so he wouldn't crush her beneath him as he had before. Even as he struggled to catch his breath, he found himself reaching for her, pulling her near. The satisfaction he knew when she curled into him and laid her head on his chest was as heart-stopping as the physical pleasure had been.

"I think you've killed me," she muttered.

"Likewise." He groaned and patted at her hair, which was all the movement he could manage. "I understand now why marriage is a sacrament, Di. Making babies with you is the closest I'm going to get to heaven on earth."

She let out a shuddering breath, and something dripped against his chest. He brushed his hand over her cheek and touched tears. His heart ached with tenderness, and he needed a moment before he could speak.

"I know, sweetheart," he told her as he brushed the wetness away. "I'm happy too."

All too soon, Diana pulled away from him. Henry watched in amusement as she attempted to leave the bed whilst keeping the sheet wrapped around her. Unfortunately, he had the other end of the sheet trapped very firmly beneath him. With a huff, she grabbed the counterpane and draped it around herself like a cape.

He crossed his arms behind his head. "I don't know where you think you're going, Di. Did you not hear me say I meant to keep you in bed for a week?"

"We went downstairs last night for supper."

"So we did." He grinned. "Heaven help us if Mrs. Polgrey ever learns your bare bottom has been in contact with the top of her new sycamore table. Ah, there's that blush I love so well!"

She shook her head. "I want to see the house in proper light without you distracting me."

He rose from the bed, and Diana's eyes roamed over him with avid interest. He stretched, preening a bit. "I think you enjoy when I distract you." She licked her lips and he started toward her.

Diana held up her hand. "No, we're not going to spend a week in *there*—" She glanced at the bed. "—doing . . . doing *that*. I am already embarrassed to face Jasper and Timms. We will not insult Mrs. Polgrey by ignoring the breakfast she has doubtless cooked for us, and I must meet the rest of the staff."

Henry strode forward and gave her a quick kiss. "I've spent so much time with my daring Diana of late. I am glad to see my dear Miss Merriwether hasn't abandoned me. Someone must keep Ravensfield respectable. Go and wait in bed. I will ring for your maid." He passed through the door that adjoined their rooms and pulled the bell cord, then returned to his chamber. He found fresh water in the basin in his dressing closet, and he washed quickly before donning a dressing gown.

He returned to Diana's room to wait for her maid. He frowned as he glanced around. He'd wanted so badly for the house to be perfect for her, but he wasn't willing to compromise on quality, and there just hadn't been enough time to get everything done. Last night, as they'd explored by candlelight, imagination and shadows had filled in the missing pieces. In the crisp morning light, the unfinished state of the house became glaringly apparent. When Ellie arrived, Henry instructed her prepare a bath for Diana and to have hot water sent up to his dressing closet so he could shave.

"All right," he called to Diana once the maid had gone, "Ellie will be with you shortly. You may as well come and see your room in the light of day." She shuffled through the doorway clutching her quilt about her and began to look around. "It's a work in progress," he said quickly. "I'm sure you will want to choose your own decorations. The bed hangings should be here within a fortnight. The dressing table is in the closet, and there's a large bathing-tub in there as well. I asked Ellie to have a bath prepared for you. As for the curtains—"

Diana returned to him, reached a hand up to the back of his head and pulled him down for a kiss. "I love it. I love everything we chose together, and I love what you chose for me. Do you think I don't see that still life on that wall has lilies, or that the painting there is of the goddess Diana? The porcelain figures on the mantel are masked revelers right out of our night at Vauxhall. When did you find the time to get everything?"

"I enlisted help," he admitted. "I mentioned to my sisters that they should keep their eyes open for some particular pieces when they went about their shopping. I believe they took my words as a challenge, because crates began showing up at the house within the week. If there's anything you don't like, we can have it changed."

"I told you, I love it. The room is perfect. Thank you." Her other arm joined its mate around his neck. The quilt fell to the floor leaving her naked length pressed against him. His sex rose beneath the silk damask robe to nudge at the soft flesh of her belly.

"Don't get too fond of this room," he warned her. "I have no intention of allowing you to make much use of it."

Her lips curled. "There's the rogue I married." She rose up on her toes and caught his earlobe between her teeth. His breath hissed out, and then he sucked it back in when she reached down and tugged at his belt. The two halves of his robe fell apart, and Diana wrapped her fingers around him in an intimate caress. "It's like satin," she said, her voice full of wonder. "At once soft and hard, just like you."

"Di, what are you—?" His voice cracked when her thumb brushed over the sensitive head.

"Martine's talk was not completely uninformative." She ran her fingers up and down his length, then paused. "You *do* like this?"

"I love it. God, don't stop," he pleaded.

She smiled at him, a temptress's smile, so seductive and confident his breath caught. He stopped breathing as she sank to her knees before him, and then muttered an oath as she kissed the inside of his thigh. She sat back on her heels and gazed up at him, her eyes shining with excitement. As for him, well, if he got much more excited, he was going to explode.

"Though Martine forgot, I suspect deliberately, to mention any pain associated with the marriage bed, she was very, ah, explicit about the pleasures to be had."

She seemed to expect a response, so Henry made a noise somewhere between a groan and a grunt, hoping it would suffice.

"She said men like to be kissed all over."

She leaned forward and pressed a kiss to the middle of his thigh.

"Un bisou ici." A kiss here.

She rose up on her knees and pressed another kiss below his navel.

"Un bisou là." A kiss there.

He tangled his hands in her hair, urging her lower. She laughed softly, unknowingly teasing him with the puffs of her warm breath.

"Di," he pleaded.

"Et le baiser d'amants . . ." And the lovers' kiss.

His breath hissed out at the first soft touch of her lips. She kissed him all over, up and down, quick, fleeting touches that proved the most exquisite torment he'd ever experienced. He didn't know whether he wanted to thank Martine for her instructions or strangle her for not being nearly explicit enough.

"You can also . . . That is, sometimes . . . If you want . . ." It was a struggle to put any words together, let alone think of how to suggest his wife perform such an indelicate act.

"Yes?" She looked up at him expectantly.

"I—" he faltered. He wanted her mouth on him so badly he hurt, but he couldn't bring himself to ask her. "I want you."

"Oh?" she asked a shade too innocently. "I thought perhaps you wanted *this*." She licked him from the base up, then swirled her tongue around the tip.

His head fell back as his world narrowed to the hot, wet heaven of her mouth. When she reached between his thighs and cupped his bollocks, he knew the end was near. He clutched at her shoulders until she raised her head, confusion clouding her eyes.

"Want . . . to be . . . inside you," he explained between heavy breaths.

She nodded eagerly and tugged at one of his hands as she lay back on the rug. He shrugged off his robe and followed her down. He took her mouth as he probed her sex. He found her wet and ready for him, and it was a good thing, because there was no finesse, nothing of the skilled lover in his actions.

Gone was his vaunted control. A need so desperate and fierce it was almost savage governed him now. Her sweetness, her desire to please him, undid him. She gasped his name as he slid a finger inside her. The sound of her pleasure drove him wild.

He levered himself up, added a second finger, and she rewarded him with a deep moan. Even as her hips rose to draw him deeper, she shook her head.

"You," she demanded. *"You."*

She needn't have told him twice. He entered her in one long, hard stroke. He stilled when she cried out.

"Di?"

"More." She flexed her hips, moaning as the action pushed him still deeper inside her.

He growled his pleasure as the ability to speak deserted him. Everything around him dissipated into a haze of passion. All that existed was the red-hot thrust and glide, as he withdrew until only the tip of him remained inside her, and then drove back into her silky depths.

His tongue flicked out to lick her salty tears as she contracted around him, drawing him deeper and demanding all he had to give. He could no more stop from giving it to her than he could stop the seasons from changing.

He rolled them so she lay on top of him, a limp, sweaty blanket. He stroked his hands over her back and down to her derriere. "I thought we weren't going to spend all day doing this," he murmured. "Or did you object to confining ourselves to the bed?" He chuckled. "Not that I'm complaining, mind you. I have a great deal more affection for this room than I had before, but the water for your bath should have been brought up by now; it would be a shame to let it get cold."

She scrambled off him, her horrified gaze fixed on the closet door. "Oh, heavens, do you think they heard?"

He laughed. "If our servants don't have selective hearing, they'll quickly acquire it. I mean to make love with my beautiful wife whenever the opportunity presents itself." He got to his feet and pressed kisses to her flushed cheeks, then took her lips once more. Her eyes were glazed and dreamy when he lifted his head.

"Go to your bath, love, before I decide to test whether the tub is large enough for two." He patted her bottom. "I'll see you downstairs for breakfast." He gathered up his dressing gown and returned to his chamber, leaving her to Ellie's care. He found a fresh basin of water at his dressing table, only lukewarm now, but as his blood still simmered, that mattered little. He washed again and shaved himself. He'd nearly finished dressing when Jasper made an appearance.

Henry took one look at his valet and sighed. "Found a way to celebrate last night, did you?"

"Oh, aye!" Jasper grinned cockily. "I could tell you tales such as you wouldn't believe."

"I would have little trouble believing them, but if you're hoping to romance my wife's maid, this escapade had best be your last."

Chastened, Jasper nodded. "I saw Mr. Kingsley this morning. He wants to speak to you as soon as you've the time. He says there's nothing wrong, but I have the sense it's important."

Kingsley was Henry's head groom, a gruff old man who'd been in charge of the stables at Weston Manor until Henry had stolen him and brought him to Ravensfield. If Kingsley needed to speak with him, that would be his first order of business. His stomach rumbled. Very well, it would be his *second* order of business.

"I plan to eat breakfast with my wife," Henry told his valet, "but tell Kingsley I'll meet him in the stables afterward. Then, for God's sake, go back to bed." He glanced longingly at the rumpled sheets of his own. "One of us, at least, should spend the day there."

CHAPTER NINETEEN

I hope you believe me when I tell you how pleased I am by this turn of events. After our meeting, you will not be surprised, I think, by what accompanies this note. Think of Penelope as my wedding present, free of any conditions or expectations. I only ask that you consider what I asked of you. By this time next year, you may be in possession of a future champion.
—from Thomas Merriwether to
his son-in-law Henry Weston

A small crowd met Diana when she came down to breakfast. She might have fled in the face of all the curious looks, but Henry met her on the stairs and took hold of her arm. She blushed as he introduced her to the butler, Timms, whom she'd seen briefly the day before. His wife, Mrs. Timms, was the housekeeper, and she was as tall and thin as her husband was short and fat. Diana thanked the woman for sending her husband over with the basket of food; though she knew how to plan a dinner party during any month of the year, she hadn't the faintest notion how to execute any of the recipes in the cookery books.

Mrs. Timms then presented the cook, Mrs. Polgrey, followed by the three footmen, the two housemaids, the kitchen maid, the laundry maid, and lastly the scullery maid. The housekeeper rattled off their names in such rapid succession that Diana knew she had no hope of remembering any of them save for the last. She and Tilly, the scullery maid, were off to an excellent start.

The room cleared as Mrs. Timms dismissed everyone, and Diana looked around the hall. What she saw pleased her. The fluted columns and finely carved mahogany staircase were impressive without being ostentatious. The Gainsborough, Cuyp, and Teniers pictures hanging on the freshly painted walls had come from the Bedford sale, as had the ormolu chandelier. She glanced up toward the skylight and noted that the plasterwork needed repairs.

"You're thinking much too hard before breakfast," Henry told her as he slid his arm around her waist. "Mrs. Timms will take you around the house after we eat. For now, content yourself with the morning room."

Over breakfast, Henry told her that, other than Jasper and Ellie, the house staff all came from local families. He entertained her with all of the village gossip he'd gathered over the past weeks. She nodded and laughed when he seemed to expect it, but inwardly she began to count the days since her last flux.

She thought she had close to a fortnight before she needed to start taking the pennyroyal, but her courses weren't always regular. If she and Henry continued as they had started, she couldn't afford to miscalculate. She decided to drink a cup of the tea every day, and then, as Martine had instructed, a few cups a day in the week before her courses.

"Di?"

She blinked, realizing she'd been staring abstractedly at her empty plate.

"This doesn't bode well for the future," Henry teased. "This is our first breakfast together, and I'm already boring you."

"I beg your pardon." She smiled serenely at him. "I get distracted when I'm tired and, for some reason, I didn't sleep much last night. Perhaps I might rest better in my own bed tonight."

"I doubt it."

"Oh?"

"I've heard—" He leaned toward her and lowered his voice to

a confidential whisper. "I've heard spiders often invade the beds of newly married women. You'd best sleep with me again."

"Spiders, you say?"

He nodded. "Big, scary spiders. And newts. The newts here in Surrey are ugly, Di."

She raised her brows. "Are there pretty newts?"

Henry shrugged. "Some are uglier than others."

"I believe I could manage the spiders; some mint and lavender beneath the mattress ought to send them running. Newts, though? I guess I had best sleep with you, just to be safe. As far as I'm concerned—" Her lips began to quiver, and she knew she couldn't hold her laughter much longer. "As far as I'm concerned, no newts is good newts."

Henry was still chuckling as he made his way to the stables. He entered the small office where he kept all the records and paperwork on the horses. He found Kingsley waiting there for him. The man had to be close to sixty, but he remained as imposing as always. Tall and strong enough to rein in the wildest stallions, the groom's hair color was all that had changed, mellowing from coal black to dark silver.

Accustomed to Kingsley's brusque manner, Henry wasn't surprised when the man simply nodded, picked up a letter off the desk, and held it out. Henry took it, broke the seal, and began to read. He grew more furious with every word. How had his father-in-law been so presumptuous as to send Penelope to Ravensfield?

He was desperate, Henry thought, *and desperate men acted like fools.* If Diana hadn't agreed to marry him that day in Isabella's drawing room, he would have resorted to tactics far worse than bribery. As it happened, he actually agreed with something Merriwether had said to him at Tattersall's. There were things Diana and her father needed to say to each other. She needed to face him as an adult, but that would keep until she felt ready. Henry wouldn't pressure her.

"I thought it best to keep the mare here," Kingsley said, "not knowing what you'd wish me to do. The groom that brought her said she was breeding. Sending that little beauty all the way back to Suffolk would have exhausted her, besides which I can't spare a groom to take her."

"You did right," Henry assured him.

"You mean to keep her, then? I don't like to overstep, Master Henry, but you'd be a fool to let her go. She'll produce champions, that one."

"That does seem to be the popular consensus," Henry muttered. "Granted, I wasn't one for the books, but I do recall that bad things come of accepting gift horses. She'll stay until she foals, for I don't wish to risk her health, but I bloody well hate having my hand forced like this."

"She comes from your wife's pa. Could be he means you to have the mare as her dowry," Kingsley suggested.

"I know what he means by this, Kingsley, and I can't accept her. I'll buy her from him, or he'll take her back. I'd appreciate if you and the other grooms would keep quiet on the subject of Penelope's background. We'll call her, um, Penny for the time being. My wife and her father aren't on good terms, and I don't want to upset her with this."

"Of course, Master Henry."

"For God's sake, call me Henry or, if you prefer, Weston. 'Master Henry' makes me feel like you're about to saddle up my pony."

Kingsley snorted. "You would crush a pony. Come to the paddocks. Some of us have been busy while you were off getting yourself leg-shackled."

Henry shoved the letter into one of the desk drawers and wished he could deal so efficiently with his father-in-law. He followed Kingsley downstairs and out the back of the stables. Pride welled in him as he watched one of the grooms working a frisky colt on a *longe* line. Mares and fillies grazed in one of the larger paddocks, and he caught sight of Penelope's—*Penny's*—gleaming auburn coat.

Past the paddocks, grooms put two stallions through their paces. He and Kingsley made their way out to watch the grooms' progress. Henry had great hopes for the big bay. The stallion was coming along nicely; he might even be ready to race this year.

He discussed the possibility with Kingsley as they made their way back to the stables. "I don't want him to have a bad first race. He'll take it to heart, and we'll never get another good run out of him. We need to start by taking him to some of the smaller races. That way he'll . . ."

"That way he'll what?"

"What?" Henry asked. He grinned stupidly at Diana, who'd just come through the stables and was walking toward them, an equally stupid smile on her face. He lengthened his stride, leaving a grumbling Kingsley behind.

"Henry, the stables are incredible!" Diana exclaimed as he reached her. "Is that my Tulip out there?" She threw her arms around him. "Oh, thank you! I thought she'd been sent back to The Hall." She pulled back as Kingsley caught up to them, but Henry caught hold of her hand and refused to relinquish it.

"Kingsley, allow me to introduce you to my wife. Diana, this is Kingsley, our head groom, who taught me to ride and knows the distaff line of every winner of the Oaks, the Derby, and the St. Leger."

"I'm very pleased to make your acquaintance, Mr. Kingsley. When I was young, my favorite bedtime story was that of the Godolphin Arabian and his faithful feline companion, Grimalkin, but if that failed to put me to sleep, my father resorted to reciting pedigrees."

Henry saw a flash of pain cross her face when she mentioned her father. Thomas Merriwether and his bribes could rot in hell. He wouldn't allow the man to upset Diana.

"Well, my love," Henry said, "should sleeplessness ever plague you, I now know the cure." He sidled closer and whispered against her ear, "Though I daresay I can think of more enjoyable ways to exhaust you."

Kingsley gave a choked cough, and Diana's cheeks turned as pink as the flowers printed on her gown. In an effort to avoid looking at either man, Diana turned to gaze out at the horses. "Who is that gorgeous creature—the chestnut mare? Look at those lines! Did you get her recently?"

"Ah. You must mean Penny. She is, in fact, our newest arrival."

Kingsley cleared his throat. "If you'll excuse me, I'll be about my work. A right pleasure to meet you, Mrs. Weston." Kingsley beamed approvingly at her. "I couldn't want more for Master Henry—"

Henry sighed, imagining a pony collapsing beneath a very, very overgrown boy.

"—than a wife who knows the foundation sires and has a keen eye for horseflesh. If I were twenty years younger, I'd steal you away and marry you myself," he declared, kissing the hand Henry wasn't holding.

Henry stared, bemused by this gallantry from a man who'd only ever displayed interest in females of the equine variety. "Stop flirting with my wife, Kingsley, or you'll make me jealous," he joked, but he found himself disturbed by the slight bit of truth in his words.

"What a dear man," Diana said as Kingsley left them. "He reminds me of the grooms at The Hall. I'd escape to the stables whenever I could. It was the only place at all familiar to me amongst all that perfection. I used to sneak books from the library and read in the hayloft. The grooms never told me to mind my manners or watch my clothes, and they always had a kind word for me."

"It's rare for anyone to receive a kind word from Kingsley," Henry informed her as he led her upstairs, "especially a woman. I've never seen him take to anyone as quickly. For that matter, this is the first time I've seen you take such a quick liking to someone."

Diana laughed. "You can't possibly be jealous of an old man!"

"Of course not." Henry scowled.

"You won't—" she said suddenly, looking up at him anxiously. "You will never be jealous over me, will you? I promise you, there is no need."

He ushered her into the office. Midday light slanted through the window and poured over her fine features. He traced his index finger over the delicate arches of her eyebrows. "Di, I know you would never stray to another man's bed. Of course, I never plan to let you out of mine long enough to give you the opportunity."

He expected her to laugh or, at the very least, blush. Instead, she worried at her lip, reddening the soft flesh. Hunger rose up in his gut. "I won't get jealous, love," he assured her. "Is there something else troubling you?"

"It's that mare, Penny."

Henry tensed. "What about her?"

"She must have been terribly expensive," she fretted.

"Since my father purchased the stud, I can put all the money from the investors into the stables and the stock." She didn't look convinced. He sighed. "Will it set your mind at ease if I tell you that she cost me nearly nothing?"

"How can that be?"

"Just think of her as a wedding gift," he advised as he locked the door. When he drew her up against him, she tilted her head back and parted her lips. Being an obliging sort of man, Henry kissed her soundly. And then he set out to prove that an office in the stables was no less worthy of consideration than a linen closet or a dressing room when it came to seducing Diana. He rather thought she agreed.

CHAPTER TWENTY

I am not one for writing letters, but your mother says she will not come to bed until I have added something. She seems to believe I can offer you indispensable pieces of marital wisdom. I am no wiser than is the next man, but if this will please her, you and I will suffer through it. That is my best advice to you: Be good to each other. Make time every day with her to talk, listen, and laugh. Quarrels are inevitable, but only fight about things that truly matter. Right or wrong, you will have to apologize, so it is best to walk away before saying something you will regret. Try not to go to bed angry, but if you cannot, at least sleep in the same bed.

—from the Viscount Weston to his son Henry Weston

Married life suited Henry very well. He and Diana quickly settled into a satisfying routine. He woke in the morning when one of the maids brought in the hot water, which he let grow tepid as he set about rousing his wife. He'd fast learned Diana wasn't an early riser by nature. Rather than have a grumpy wife, he took it upon himself to see she started each day with a silly smile on her face, which usually resulted in an equally foolish grin on his own.

He smiled like a loon even when he wasn't making love to his wife. He and Diana ate breakfast together and then he went off to the stables. He spent the remainder of the morning answering correspondence, settling accounts, and doing whatever it was that needed doing. He couldn't say he enjoyed those tasks, not in the way he enjoyed working with the horses or making plans with Kingsley, but he took satisfaction in them.

Or rather, he took satisfaction in knowing he tried his hardest every day to make the right decisions. He'd only ever been responsible for his own sorry hide, but now he had investors to please, staff dependent on him for their livelihoods, and a wife to provide for. He *needed* the stud to be successful for them; he *wanted* success for himself.

He found he enjoyed taking on the responsibility of seeing to the estate's well-being. He also enjoyed the responsibility of seeing to Diana's well-being. He saw to it often. Henry had always been possessed of a happy disposition, but never in his life had he been as content as he was now.

Another man, encountering such a plentitude of good fortune, might have been nervous that it couldn't continue. The idea never crossed his mind. With only minor exceptions, his life had always gone smoothly. Naturally, he assumed his business pursuits and his marriage would prove similarly easy. Thus, his first marital spat came as a particularly unpleasant shock.

They had been married for a little less than a month when, at the dinner table, he announced that he was going to London.

"I received a letter today from one of my investors in London; he wants to meet with me. I would put it off, but there's a sale at Tattersall's I should attend. If it were one or the other, I wouldn't go, but I may as well combine the two. I also have some business around Newmarket I've put off too long. It will only take me a week, ten days at most."

"When is the sale?" Diana asked. She cut a piece of fricasseed chicken into miniscule pieces and pushed her peas into a pile.

Her plate remained mostly full, while he'd already helped himself to seconds. He told himself not to fuss over her. She'd been indisposed for the better part of the week with her courses. Courses—hell, more like *curses*. He'd wanted to send for the doctor, but Diana had vowed to bring the wrath of God down upon him. Some months the pain was worse than others, she'd told him, but this month wasn't bad enough to allow a man other than her husband to examine her *there*.

He'd acquiesced, but he hadn't let her move into her bedroom. His wife slept with *him*. Lord, if he never saw another bad month again, it would be too soon. He didn't like it, but he could manage going days without making love to Diana. No, what unmanned him was seeing her in pain and being helpless to do anything.

He'd suggested slipping a few drops of laudanum into the special mint tea she favored, but Diana told him the drug made her anxious and irritable. He'd been tempted to dose her anyway. Then, at least only one of them would have been anxious and irritable. Eventually she'd taken pity on him, or perhaps herself, and banished him to his office.

"Henry?"

He dragged his gaze from her growing mountain of peas. "Are you feeling ill again?" He gestured to her plate.

"I told you earlier that I feel fine. I'm simply saving room for the orange and almond tart that Mrs. Polgrey made for dessert. I warn you," she challenged him, "you will have to fight me for every last bite."

"It's not almond tart I'm hungry for tonight, but *I* should warn *you,* after six days, I'm very much looking forward to *my* dessert."

Damn it all, that blush would be the death of him. Henry glanced at the table, wondering how many things he'd have to throw to the floor in order to lay Diana out upon it. She could have her treat later. He wanted her *now*.

"When is this sale at Tattersall's?" she prompted, obviously trying to change the subject.

"Uh, this Monday," he replied distractedly. Perhaps if he just pushed everything to one side of the table . . .

"*This* Monday?" Diana's fork clattered against her plate. "It's Saturday evening! I shall have to stay up all night packing if we're to leave tomorrow. This is too bad of you to give me such little notice."

"I plan to keep you awake tonight, sweetheart, but there's no need for you to pack. I'll go alone."

"Alone?" she demanded. "You would leave me here by myself? For ten days?"

"You make it sound as if I were abandoning you forever in some desolate place. I'm hardly leaving you on your own. The servants will be here, and I plan to ride, so you'll have the carriage should you wish to pay any calls. Taking you with me would add days of travel, love, and I'm not such a beast that I would rattle you about when you've just been ill."

Not to mention, his overdue business near Newmarket was seeing her father, and he didn't want Diana anywhere near the man. Thomas Merriwether was a lit bit of kindling waiting to blow up in his face. If the man thought he could send a horse, what was to stop him from posting a letter or, heaven forbid, arriving unannounced at their door?

Henry needed his father-in-law to understand, beyond a shadow of a doubt, that he wasn't welcome at Ravensfield. Henry planned to offer the man a fair sum for Penelope and her foal, and then they need have no further contact. If the day came when Diana wanted to see her father, Henry would support her in her decision. Until then, he would do his best to see that the man kept his distance.

Diana smiled at him, part seductress, part shy maiden, and all too enticing. "I'm perfectly well now and, if you remember, we pass time very well together in a carriage."

He groaned. "You tempt me, Di, but everyone has gone from London. I don't want to trouble with opening the townhouse for such a short visit, especially when I haven't given the servants any warning. I'll put up at a hotel unless I run into a friend with a spare bedroom. It will be easier if I go alone. In any case, I find you much too distracting. I would never get any business done."

"I don't mind a hotel, and Newmarket is only a few miles from Cambridge," Diana pointed out. "I can surprise Alex with a visit while you see to your business."

Henry laughed. "Young men at university don't wish for their sisters to surprise them, but I'll look in on the young scamp if that will make you happy."

"Halswelle Hall isn't so far from Newmarket either. I could visit my mother. I've never gone so long without seeing her."

There was a wistful note to her words, and it pricked at his pride. He knew he was being foolish, that Diana's wish to see her mother didn't mean she loved him any less, but he couldn't suppress the small surge of jealousy. He dearly loved his parents, but he had no overwhelming urge to visit them. A month into marriage, he had no need for anyone other than Diana . . . and Mrs. Polgrey. He wanted to be enough for Diana, to provide everything she needed. And he could recognize that he was selfish enough to want her as fixated on him as he was on her.

"Your mother is welcome to visit us here," he said tersely. He immediately regretted his sharpness and gentled his tone. "We can visit in a few months when the stud is less busy, but this isn't a good time. I'll conduct my business with all due haste and return home as soon as possible."

"Perhaps we should go to The Hall before you purchase any more stock at Tattersall's. I thought I might ask my grandfather about the horses there. The breeding program mostly fell off without my father's guidance, but there are still a handful of beautiful Arabians. With Alex and me both away, they'll turn fat and lazy. I could ask for them as a wedding present, and—"

He held up one hand to stop her and scrubbed the other over his face. "I know you're trying to be helpful, and I wouldn't want a wasteful, spendthrift wife, but somehow you've got it stuck in your mind that we're impoverished. We may not live in a ducal mansion or piss in gold chamber pots—" He stopped himself when Diana winced at his crude language.

Christ, he needed to get up and walk away. He was already on edge from not having slept well for nearly a week. Diana was one of the few people who could push him to lose his temper, and tonight it wouldn't take much. He took a deep breath. "I am more than able to provide for you. I can afford my own horses. I don't need your family's charity to succeed."

"It wouldn't be charity—" Diana began.

"No!" Henry slammed his palm down on the table. Damn it all, he didn't need her help, and he didn't need gift horses from every damned member of her family. He got to his feet, and tossed his napkin onto his plate. "I've lost my appetite. I'm going for a ride. At least the horses don't doubt me."

Diana stood as well, clearly not willing to let the conversation rest. "I don't doubt your ability to succeed or to provide for me," she said quietly. "I never meant to suggest otherwise. I only wanted some reason to accompany you."

Some of the tightness left his chest. "I'll only be gone a week, Di. If I were going away for longer, I'd force you to come with me. This time, though, it's better if I go alone."

She frowned at him. "You're keeping something from me. You're hiding whatever is making you so determined to go alone."

He forced out a laugh. "I'm not hiding anything from you. I simply want the trip over quickly and for you to regain your health so I may ravish you to my heart's content."

"Did you know the tops of your ears turn red when you lie?"

"You're being ridiculous!" he blustered.

"Am I? Tell me why you don't want me with you. Oh . . ." Her face blanched suddenly, and she reached out for the back of her chair to steady herself.

Henry was at her side in a heartbeat. "Di? What's the matter? Do you feel ill again?"

She shook her head slowly. "Do you have a . . . ?" She moistened her lips. "Are you going to London to see a . . . a woman?"

"What the devil are you talking about?" he demanded.

"There's some reason you don't want me along, something you don't want me to know about—"

"And you believe I'm keeping a mistress?" he asked incredulously.

She wouldn't meet his eyes.

"Apparently your faith in me doesn't extend very far," he said coldly. "I won't lie to you. There *is* some business I'm involved in that I'd prefer not to share with you. I can't tell you more than that at the moment, but I swear that it's nothing scandalous. Since we first began courting, there has been no other woman in my life. There never will be. I can tell you I won't stray, but I can't make you believe me any more than I can change my past."

"I'm sorry," she whispered. "Henry, please, you know I love you."

He shook his head. "That's not enough."

"What more do you want from me?" she cried brokenly.

"Your trust. You need to trust that your happiness is my own, and that I will always keep your heart safe. You need to know in your soul that I meant every vow I made to you on our wedding day. Yes, there are women in my past, but there was never any talk of love or commitment. I have only ever wanted forever with you, Diana, but if you can't let go of my past, you'll destroy us both. You have to trust me. Can you do that?"

"I . . . I don't know. Please, if it's nothing bad, just tell me why I may not go with you," she begged.

"God damn it!" His chest heaving, he grabbed a wineglass off the table and hurled it at the wall, needing some outlet for the storm that had built within him. It shattered in a satisfying cascade of crystal shards. The small bit of wine left in the glass streaked down the wall in bloody rivulets.

The sound of a sob had him spinning back toward Diana. All the blood had leached from her face. She stared at him with haunted, accusing eyes, as if he'd committed some atrocity.

"Christ, don't look at me like that," he muttered. "It was only a glass. I promise we can afford another."

She closed her eyes and sucked in a breath as she pressed a white-knuckled fist to her chest. Did her heart hurt as much as his did? Tears began to roll down her cheeks as she drew in another choppy breath.

"I . . ." She opened her eyes, and her gaze darted to the door. Her muscles tensed to bolt, and he knew she was trying to run from something he couldn't see. He wished he could. If he could see the dragons and slay them for her, this would all be so much easier. He didn't know what to do about their argument, but his anger stepped aside in the face of his need to comfort her. Even if she broke his heart, the damned thing still wanted to take care of her.

He cursed as he closed the distance between them and caught her before she'd taken more than two steps. She resisted for a moment, and then sagged against him. He rubbed one hand up and down her spine as the other urged her head against his chest. He touched the delicate skin at the base of her neck; her pulse pounded hard and frantic against his fingertips. "I'm sorry, love. I didn't mean to frighten you. There's nothing to fear. Just take deep breaths."

He wished he could take his own advice. Seeing her like this chilled him to his marrow. Knowing he'd done this to her . . . Guilt wrapped him in a crushing embrace, wringing the air from his lungs, so that his breathing wasn't much steadier than hers was.

"Keep talking . . . please."

Diana's whispered request brought a lump to his throat and, for a moment, Henry wasn't sure he could do what she asked. He pressed his lips to her hair, breathing in orange blossoms, Diana, and sweat-dampened skin. He usually loved that particular combination of scents, but something wasn't right. No sweetly feminine musk infused the air because he hadn't made Diana sweat with desire. Tonight, the slightly acrid stink of fear overlaid Diana's natural sweetness. He'd promised to keep her happy and safe, and then he'd gone and terrified her. Little wonder she didn't trust him.

Henry swallowed past the painful knot in his throat. "I have you, Di. I won't let anything hurt you." He murmured nonsense to her as he lifted her into his arms and sat down with her cradled on his lap. "Come on, sweetheart," he whispered. "Open your eyes, and I'll tell you about the time my father took me to see Highflyer race."

As inducements went, his storytelling clearly lacked a certain something because Diana didn't open her eyes until after he'd offered her a dozen pairs of lilac gloves, a lengthy visit to her mother, the stars, the moon, and whatever she bloody wanted. He hovered somewhere between desperate and frantic by the time she lifted her hand and cupped his cheek.

She dredged up a tired smile. "I'm all right. The arguing and the . . . It brought back a bad memory."

"It was the glass, wasn't it? It upset you when I threw the glass." He searched her face anxiously. "Di, if I'd known . . . You know I would never . . . Tell me you know I didn't mean to scare you."

Her mouth opened in shock. "Sometimes *I* don't know what brings this on. How could you have possibly anticipated this?"

He shrugged and held her a little tighter. "I hate seeing you so upset."

"I can't say I enjoy it either, but having you with me makes it easier." She tucked her head beneath his chin and snuggled into him. One of her hands rested against his chest, her fingers spread wide as if to claim as much territory as possible. Didn't she know she held his heart in her hands?

"I'm not going to London," he told her as he stroked her hair. "There will be other sales at Tattersall's, and the rest of my business can hold a while longer."

Diana raised her head. "No, you need to go and see to business, and I . . . I'll miss you, but I need you to go." She sighed. "The part of me that can think clearly knows I'm being ridiculous, but there's a small piece that's beyond my control. That small piece of me is terrified for you go to London without me. I don't think you would seek out a woman, but I've seen the way women throw themselves in your path. Perhaps the unmarried ones will step aside, but the rest won't care that you're married. They think you're foolish to have m-married m-me, and t-tonight I agree w-with them."

She laid her head on his shoulder and sobbed. He let her have her cry and, after a few minutes, she quieted and raised her head. She turned her face away from him. "Don't look at me. I'm all red and splotchy."

"You're beautiful. A bit deluded, but beautiful. Courting you was the smartest thing I've ever done."

She sniffed loudly. "Be serious, Henry."

"I am serious. I'm not— I don't consider myself a particularly intelligent man. I was never any good at my studies, not like James.

Before I decided on the stud, I never tried very hard at anything. If I happened to be good at something, I kept on with it. If I wasn't, I walked away, because I couldn't stand to try and then fail. It was easier by far to be a self-indulgent fool than find out I'm nothing but a mediocre man. Can you imagine my father failing at anything?"

"I'm sure he must—"

"No, he's never failed at anything. Both of my parents are incredible. The thought of disappointing them terrifies me. The thought of disappointing you—" He shook his head. "Do you know what you do to me every time you suggest you're somehow unworthy of me? You tear me apart inside. I'm the unworthy one. There you were, right in front of me for so many years, but I was too blind to see you." His hand trembled as he cupped her cheek.

She placed a finger over his lips. "Don't waste time being sorry. We have each other now."

He took hold of her wrist and pulled her hand away from his face, then brought his hand back up to cradle her head. He gently pressed his lips to her temple, her cheek, her lips . . . paying homage and making promises of forever. "No, I'm not smart," he whispered against her ear, "but I was wise enough to fall in love with you and clever enough to convince you to marry me. I hope I'm not so stupid that I would ever let you go."

Henry helped Diana upstairs and turned her over to Ellie's care. Most evenings, they sat in the library for a while after dinner, but the sooner this night was over, the better. He made his way downstairs to fetch Diana's novel and, for himself, Taplin's *Compendium of Farriery*. If the book didn't put him to sleep immediately, it would at least prevent him from attacking his wife. Reading about cures for mange had a way of cooling a man's lust.

He poked his head into the dining room and found that in addition to clearing the table, someone had already swept away the broken glass and cleaned the wall, though it would likely still need repainting. He was about to head back upstairs when Mrs. Timms entered the room through the opposite door.

"Oh, I beg your pardon, sir! I thought you and Mrs. Weston had retired already. Is there aught I can get for you?"

"As a matter of fact, there is." He crossed the room so he wouldn't have to shout. "My wife is feeling poorly again, and she needs a good night's rest. If you will bring up hot water, I'll prepare some of that special tea she likes. Bring me the laudanum as well. She's fretful, and a few drops will help her to fall asleep."

The housekeeper's mouth pursed with displeasure.

"Is there a problem, Mrs. Timms?"

He didn't expect the woman to say anything, but after a moment's indecision, she took a few steps closer to him and lowered her voice. "Will you forgive me for speaking plain, sir?"

Henry inclined his head.

"I'll have you know I don't pass any judgment. There's no harm in letting a marriage settle before there's babes crying all the time, but there's other ways than the pennyroyal—ways that are easier on a body. If you've fixed on it, though, you should know there's no need for her to drink it every day. 'Tis an unpleasant tea, I've always thought. It leaves a bitter taste in the mouth."

It did, indeed. Henry had no idea how he kept his face impassive during Mrs. Timms's revelation. Shock, perhaps. He knew the ways to keep from getting a woman with child, and he was familiar enough with the herbs women used to rid themselves of unwanted babes. He hadn't expected Diana to know of such things, let alone make use of them.

Her fear of his betrayal no doubt stemmed from a guilty conscience. She'd sat beside him so many times, drinking her special "calming blend," lying to him with every sip. God damn her, he'd given her all of himself, held nothing back. He finally understood what James had meant all those months ago when he said he trusted Isabella with his heart.

Henry had trusted Diana with his heart. He'd shared everything he was, good and bad, knowing she would accept all of him—*want* all of him. He wanted all of her. He'd meant what he'd said before. He needed more than her love; he needed her to trust him with her heart.

She didn't even trust him with her fears. He needn't have understood his Oxford professor's ramblings about logic to understand Diana's reasoning. If she didn't believe he would remain faithful to her, she obviously didn't think their marriage would last. Any child of theirs would end up torn between the two of them, or maybe she thought he'd abandon his children as well.

"Mr. Weston?"

He forced himself to focus on the housekeeper. "Thank you for telling me, Mrs. Timms. I hadn't realized the tea might be causing my wife's ill health. I'll speak with her. Please, don't say anything; she would be terribly embarrassed."

"I wouldn't want that, sir. Shall I make a cup of chamomile tea instead?"

"Chamomile, yes, that's fine. I'll be in the library. Let me know when it's ready, and I'll take it up to her."

"I can have one of the maids bring it up, sir," Mrs. Timms offered. "There's no need for you to wait down here."

"It's no trouble," he assured her. He needed time to compose himself before he faced Diana. He paced around the library, his thoughts disordered and discordant. His mind leaped from the fiercest outrage to a tender understanding, from resentment to pity, and he alternately wanted to reassure her and rant at her.

When he went upstairs, he found his room mostly dark. A single candelabrum remained lit on the table, and Diana was asleep in his bed. As he set aside the tea and the books, he glanced at the door to Diana's room. He considered sleeping there, but he heard his father's voice in his head: *Try not to go to bed angry, but if you cannot, at least sleep in the same bed.*

He quickly undressed, doused the candles, and climbed into bed. He turned on his side, facing away from her, and decided he'd leave for London at first light. As he stared into the darkness, listening to Diana breathe, dawn seemed damned far off.

CHAPTER TWENTY-ONE

As you know, James indulges Bride's every whim. Yesterday morning at breakfast, I asked him what he thought I might have been like if my father had given in to my every demand. He grew very pale at the thought, I must say, but his solution is simple. We cannot be at war with France much longer, so by the time Bride is sixteen, we will place her in a French convent—preferably one surrounded by a moat containing carnivorous fish. Naturally, I told him the plan is both brilliant and flawless, and I encouraged him to put it down in writing. Someday I will show it to Bride and we will all laugh . . . assuming Bride has not already thrown her father to the sharks.

—from the Countess of Dunston to
her sister the Marchioness of Sheldon

If she'd known what lay in wait for her on the other side of sleep's gates, Diana would never have allowed herself to pass through. The monsters from her past captured her before she could put up a struggle. They dragged her back to Swallowsdale, back to her hiding place beneath the desk. She pressed her palms against her ears, but they didn't dim the sound of her parents shouting at each other. Two more angry voices joined the fray—Henry's and her own.

"Stop," she whispered. No one heard her. She couldn't hear herself over the clamor of accusations and denials. "Stop!"

Something shattered in a bright clash and the room fell silent. Her breath caught on a sob. The pitiful sound echoed into the empty quiet. Henry called her name. She wanted to go to him, but she had to hear the rest of it. She wrapped her arms around her legs, rested her head on her knees, and braced herself for the words she knew were coming. She'd relived this nightmare so often that its power over her should have diminished.

It hadn't. She flinched as her father gave her up without a second thought, and then exploded out from under the desk with a cry ripped straight from her heart.

"No!" The word burst from her lips, at once pointless and poignant in this room full of broken people with fractured dreams. Just another accusation, another denial. One more plea for love that would go unanswered.

Behind her, someone moved; the heavy tread ground pieces of pottery and glass with every step. Henry called her name again, but she only had eyes for her father.

"Please, Di," Henry pleaded. "I'm here. Come on, love."

She shook her head. "I hate you!" she yelled at her father.

"Diana!" Henry's voice demanded her attention.

She took a step back in his direction, but she couldn't look away from the man who'd sired her.

"You can't decide between us," her father said. "You're stuck between going back and moving forward. You'll choose me, you know. You always come back to me—"

"Leave me alone. I don't want you. I want Henry." She turned, but he was gone.

"Did you think to go with him?" her father asked. "It's too late for that. Don't you know by now that this can only end one way?"

She clapped her hands over her ears and ran from the house. She ran into the woods, farther and farther, until she found a safe place. A place so secret, no one would ever find her again.

She felt cold inside, and as night came on, the chill spread until she shivered uncontrollably. If only she had Henry beside her. He always radiated such heat. He would stave off the chill, but he'd left her. Oh, why hadn't she gone with him when he'd asked? Now she was alone again, in hiding once more.

She thought she heard Henry call her name. The desperate imaginings of an unhinged mind, or—? She heard him again. She scrambled to her feet and spun about in a circle. She couldn't tell which direction his voice had come from, or how to get back to where she'd been. She was well and truly lost, but she wanted Henry to find her. She *needed* him to find her. She shouted his name.

"Diana, wake up!"

She came awake in a rush. Henry's anxious face hovered over her, filling her vision. A sob of relief escaped her as she threw her arms around his neck, toppling him back on the bed. "Oh, God. Oh, God," she whispered. "It was a dream— just a dream. Don't leave me. Please, don't leave me."

She molded herself against him, and then struggled to get closer still, grabbing at whatever parts of him she could reach. She wanted to burrow inside him, to bury herself in his strength and his warmth. She needed to hold him and reassure herself that she hadn't lost him, and she needed him to hold her and reassure her that she wasn't lost.

As she pressed and wriggled against him, his sex hardened between them. A shiver of desire ripped down her spine. *Yes.* She needed this—the elemental joining, the primitive act of claiming and belonging. She reached between their bodies and clasped his hot length. He started at her touch and began to set her away.

"No," she protested. "I need you. Please, Hen—"

He flipped her over onto her back without a word. Her eyes had adjusted to the darkness, and as he came over her, his face was set in harsh, determined lines.

"Is something wr—?"

"I don't want to talk, Di. We've said enough tonight."

Diana's breathing came fast as she struggled to pull her nightgown up over her head. Henry eased back as she stripped away the last barrier between them and tossed it away. She reached out her hands, beckoning him back, and groaned in satisfaction when he settled between her thighs.

He muttered something blasphemous when he tested her and found her more than ready for him. She gasped as he entered her, fast and sure, and took her over, body and soul. Some nights he made love to her gently, taking his time with tender touches. This wasn't one of those nights.

Henry acted like a man possessed . . . or a man determined to possess her. There was a wildness about him as he ravished her, and the wanton in her gloried in it. He didn't coax her body's response; he demanded it. Repeatedly. By the time he took his own release, she was sated, sleepy, and . . . settled.

Right here, right now, she belonged. She belonged to the moment. She belonged to Henry. And she began to see that he belonged to her. They'd fought, and she'd made him furious, but he hadn't walked away. At her most vulnerable, he'd reassured her of how much he loved her. Henry was hers to lose. No, he was hers to *keep*.

When Diana woke, she reached for Henry, but she found only empty air beside her. She heard noise coming from his dressing closet, so she hurried over. If he hadn't dressed yet, she would drag him back to bed. To her disappointment, she found Jasper rifling through the clothespress. Henry's portmanteau lay at his feet.

"Has he already gone down to breakfast?" she asked.

Jasper wouldn't quite meet her gaze. "He left for London early this morning, my lady," the valet informed her. "I'm to follow him. He wanted to make an early start of it. The sooner he leaves, the quicker he can come back, I'm sure."

"Oh yes, of course, he said as much last night. So silly of me to forget, but I never can think straight when I first wake up," Diana lied, trying to hide the fact that her husband hadn't seen fit to inform her that he'd changed his plans. He hadn't even said good-bye. She told herself he hadn't wanted to wake her, but she wasn't very convincing.

Ellie tried to cheer her as she dressed, suggesting they might try styling her hair in different ways so she could surprise Henry on his return. Doubtless, at least one of the servants had overheard their quarrel, and if one had heard, they all knew. Given Henry's early departure, they probably all thought she'd chased him off. Diana scowled and instructed Ellie to tie her hair back with the ugliest ribbon she could find.

Her week without Henry was off to a poor start, and Diana doubted it would get much better. She'd spent most of her life at The Hall and Lansdowne House, and her education had prepared her to run a similarly large household. The relative simplicity of Ravensfield posed no difficulty, and she had quite a bit of time on her hands.

She liked being in the stables, but they didn't need her there. There were three grooms in addition to Kingsley and, at this point, relatively few horses. By the third day of Henry's absence, she knew she must do something or she would drive Kingsley mad, following him about and asking him to recount stories of Henry as a boy.

The older man was patient with her for he was fond of her, but she could tell his nerves were wearing thin. She needed a project, she decided. Something to occupy her mind and her hands, so she wasn't thinking about missing Henry. Worrying about their argument. Wondering what he might be doing that he couldn't tell her about.

The nights were worst. After the first night sleeping—or rather, trying to sleep—alone in Henry's room, she'd moved to her own, where the bed wasn't quite as big and lonely. She still couldn't sleep well. As she lay in bed, Diana wondered if she ought to fetch Kingsley to tell her some stories about the great champions of the turf or recite the long litany of their dams. She grinned. The man would likely suffer apoplexy if she appeared at his door at this hour, and she liked him far too much to kill him.

As she contemplated distaff lines, she suddenly knew what her project should be. She would write out pedigree charts for some of the horses at Ravensfield. She'd meant to order some prints for the office in the stables, but this would be much nicer. She wasn't a particularly good artist, but she had endured enough years of drawing lessons that she thought she could devise some passably handsome ornaments as embellishment. She fell asleep full of plans.

The following morning, she sought out Kingsley. "You needn't look as though you wish to flee," she called out to him. "I haven't come to pester you for more tales of my husband. I want your help." She explained her purpose, and he agreed to aid her in any way possible. After he assured her that she wasn't taking him away from any important work, he went with her into the office. She sat down behind the desk, trying not to blush as she remembered how she and Henry had made use of it.

"I think it will be best," she said, "if I take notes as you speak. Then you can look over it and make sure I have everything correct before I write it properly. Let me get some paper." She pulled open the desk drawer. There wasn't much in it, only a couple of quills and a penknife. The only paper was a folded letter. The bold scrawling handwriting teased at her memory. She knew she'd seen it somewhere before. She looked at the sender's address—

No, impossible. Henry would have told her if he'd received a letter from her father.

"Is everything all right, ma'am?" asked Kingsley.

"No," she whispered, shaking her head as she scanned the contents of the letter. *After our meeting . . . consider what I asked of you . . . next year, you may be in possession of a future champion.*

She scrambled to find some explanation that protected Henry, but it was clear that he was acquainted with her father. She doubted Henry had ever intended for her to find out. He hadn't intended to tell her about the mare—*Penelope*—either. He'd told her to think of the horse as a wedding present, but he certainly hadn't mentioned the sender was her father!

A father who didn't want her, didn't love her, but had gone to the trouble of buying her a husband. What cruel twist of fate had led him to settle on Henry, the one man capable of breaking her heart?

So many things began to fall into place.

Like many men of their class, Henry wanted to found a dynasty. For that, he needed a good brood mare. Not in the sense of a wife to bear him heirs—though he needed that, too—but an actual brood mare.

She had known there must be some reason Henry had started to pay attention to her after so many years of casual indifference. Oh, God, had everything that passed between them been a lie? How long had he been under her father's thumb? Had he come up with the idea of the false courtship to spend time with her after she had expressed her distaste for rogues? Had every word, every gesture been calculated to win her confidence?

She had to know if everything had been some elaborate lie, and she couldn't wait another week for Henry to return. But even if she went to London and found him, how would she know if he were telling the truth? If he took her in his arms and kissed her, Henry could persuade her of anything. If she couldn't ask Henry, there was only one other man she *could* ask. Her stomach pitched at the thought of confronting him after all this time, but what choice did she have?

She focused her gaze on Kingsley. "I need the carriage readied." Her voice wobbled, betraying the frantic storm churning inside her. Waves of emotion raged up and surged over the ruins of the walls that had once stood around her heart. Henry had torn down those walls, smile by smile, kiss by kiss, until her heart lay exposed and vulnerable—his for the taking.

But what if he'd never wanted it—never wanted her? Had she been the price he'd paid to get what he truly wanted? She needed the truth, and then she would decide what her next step should be. If the worst were true, she wouldn't be the first woman in her family with a failed marriage. At least she knew how to handle rejection.

While she ached for what might have been, part of Diana was . . . relieved. This, at least, was familiar. To a certain extent, she'd even expected this. She hadn't held back from loving Henry. She wasn't strong enough for that.

She *had* held back from believing and trusting, though. In him. In them. In their marriage. He'd asked her to let go of his past and trust him. But it wasn't his past that she couldn't let go of . . . it was her own.

Only years spent with the duchess, who disapproved of emotional displays, allowed Diana to regain her control. "I will be traveling to Suffolk," she told Kingsley in a much calmer tone. "I'll take my maid, along with whomever you can best spare. Tell the man to prepare to be gone a sennight, and have him make haste. I wish to reach Romford by sundown. There's a good inn there with edible food and comfortable beds."

A deep frown creased Kingsley's wrinkled brow. "I think you had best wait for Master Henry's return, my lady."

Diana shook her head as she stood. "I'm afraid this can't wait. 'Master Henry' should be glad I've set my sights in another direction. There's a small chance I will be in a better frame of mind by the time I see him." She held up a hand. "Don't try to stop me, Kingsley. I'm holding myself together by a very fragile thread. Unless you wish to see a hysterical woman . . ."

They were on the road by noon.

Swallowsdale Grange hadn't changed at all from the last time she'd seen it, Diana thought as the coach lumbered up the drive. Only when she got closer did she see the small signs of disrepair. Weeds had overtaken the flowerbeds near the door, once lovingly tended by her mother. Was there no one to look after the house? And what of the owner—did he need looking after as well? Not that she cared. After today, she planned to put her father out of her mind—and her life—completely.

A lad came running from the direction of the stables to take the reins from Kingsley. The groom had tried to dissuade her from leaving Ravensfield, but when she'd proven firm in her resolve, he'd insisted on accompanying her . . . though not without a fair bit of grumbling. Diana could hear him muttering as he got down from the coachman's seat and came around to help her and Ellie down from the carriage.

The door to the house opened then, and a short, wiry man stepped outside. There were streaks of gray in his sable hair, but Diana immediately recognized Barnaby Ramsey. The trainer's friendship with her father went back to his trick riding days, and he'd been as good as a member of their family.

Bar addressed Kingsley, who stood protectively in front of Diana, blocking her from his view. "Beg your pardon, but Mr. Merriwether is not at home. If your mistress would care to leave her card or return tomorrow, I—"

"Bar," Diana said softly as she stepped around Kingsley.

His eyes grew wide. "Miss Diana?"

She nodded, her throat tight.

"Saints be praised!" He broke into a wide grin and dashed forward, pulling her into a quick, hard hug. "Let me fetch your pa. Tom," he yelled, hurrying back to the house. "Tom, come quick!"

"Please, wait." Diana reached out to try to stop him, but it was too late. She followed Bar's path to the house, but she hesitated at the front door. Bar had left the door open, and a peek at the entry hall showed her the house also remained unchanged. If she crossed over the threshold, would she once more be the frightened, betrayed child who'd left here? She nearly laughed at herself. Had she ever *stopped* being that child?

She'd come to confront her past, and she ought to be ready. Since finding her father's letter, she'd nursed her anger and indignation, but now, when she needed them most, they deserted her. Looking into a house she'd lived in a lifetime ago, she didn't know what she'd hoped to find there.

Adrift, uncertain, and terribly alone, she considered running back to the carriage and ordering Kingsley to drive off. Her hesitation took the choice away from her. Two pairs of footsteps, one heavy, the other light, hurried toward her. Diana closed her eyes, took a deep breath, and tried to brace herself. It was time, past time, for this particular reunion.

"Diana?" Her father's voice was thick with uncertainty.

Her heart thudded in her chest, willing her to run, but her body was stuck fast to the spot, focused on the sound of his voice. She forced herself to open her eyes and look at her father.

He was older than she had expected. Logically, she knew he must have aged, but she'd lived with the memory of him for so long; her mind had kept him frozen in time. He was thinner, the lines on his face were deeper, and his hair—*her* hair—was shot through with silver. He approached her, one arm outstretched in greeting, reaching for her. Diana stepped back. A flash of hurt crossed his face as he halted, his arm dropping to hang limply by his side.

"I'm sorry," she began.

"No need for apologies." Her father's voice was gruff. "You're here. I have no right to ask more from you."

"I—" she began and floundered.

"It's all right." He took a hesitant step closer to her, his eyes wistful. A short cough sounded from behind him. He shook his head, a rueful smile on his face. "I am not the only one eager to see you." He glanced over his shoulder. "Set out tea in the drawing room, Ingham. Bar, move aside. You will have time to fuss over her later."

Her father turned and took a few steps into the entry hall, then looked back at her. He stopped when he realized Diana hadn't moved. She couldn't. She couldn't do this. She wasn't ready. She'd been a fool to think she could handle this on her own.

"I don't— That is—" She swallowed and drew in a shallow breath. "I won't be staying long enough for tea," she said in a rush. Her skin felt chilled and feverish all at once, and her heart was racing inside her tight, aching chest. Everything in her screamed *run to the carriage*.

Please, not again. Not in front of him. She'd come here to prove she was strong and independent. She clenched her sweaty palms into fists and willed her roiling stomach to settle down. She imagined Henry's big hand rubbing her back, his ever-present heat seeping into the cold nothingness threatening to envelop her.

"Diana?"

She heard the concern in her father's tone and forced her eyes open. "I beg your pardon. I must have got a touch overheated in the carriage." Over the buzzing in her ears, she heard her voice, thin and trembling. "I think I'd like to sit for a moment after all."

Her father lightly touched her arm and guided her to the oak bench in the hall.

"Thank you," she mumbled, not looking up at him. The fear was beginning to recede, leaving profound embarrassment in its wake.

He pressed his handkerchief into her hand.

Diana untied her bonnet and set it aside, then blotted her face and throat. She fanned herself, sighing as the light breeze cooled her damp skin. She leaned back, exhausted, as her father seated himself beside her. She busied herself with smoothing out and folding the handkerchief to avoid meeting his gaze.

"Does that happen often?" he asked gently. "The spells, I mean."

"Spells?"

"Well, it's not a spell exactly, not like a fainting spell, but I don't know what else to call it. It doesn't happen often, but it's a terrible feeling, with your heart pounding and your head spinning, and you feel as if you've been kicked in the chest."

"I get hot and cold . . . and my stomach pitches about," Diana replied haltingly, "and every time it happens I wonder if I'm not slowly . . ."

"Going mad?" her father finished for her.

Diana tilted her head to the side and regarded him out of the corner of her eyes. Understanding filled his clear green eyes. Understanding and . . . guilt?

"As you may have guessed, I've had a handful of those spells. My mother had them as well, and I wondered if my children might suffer them. I don't think Alex does, but I generally don't see him more than once a year. And Cl—" He drew in a quick breath—too quick—and began coughing. "And clearly," he said, once he'd recovered, "you do suffer from them. If it's any consolation, I find they come less frequently the older I get."

"It helps to know that I'm not alone in my suffering," she said quietly.

"No, in that you have never been alone," he responded. "I thought in time you'd think yourself well rid of me. I always knew you were meant for finer things than I could give you. You deserve the best, just like your mother. I can hardly believe that one day you will be a viscountess. The duchess must be pleased."

"She is. More importantly, I'm pleased. Not because I want a title. That doesn't matter to me. Henry makes me happy, happier than I've been since the day . . . the day you . . . you said—" She bit her lip hard, trying to control all the pain that had welled up inside her and now threatened to spill over. She focused on the sharp bite of teeth into soft flesh, but the hurt wasn't enough to distract her. She couldn't hold back the tide any longer. "Why?" she whispered brokenly. "Why didn't you want me?"

"Diana—"

She didn't give him the chance to speak. "Do you know why I'm so happy with Henry? Because I love him, and I thought—" She took a deep breath. The journey to Swallowsdale had given her time to think, especially since Ellie was more prone to catnapping than conversation. Aside from the letter that had led her here, Henry had never given her any cause to doubt his affection. He cherished her with every word, every touch, and every kiss. Deep down, she believed that he loved her, and she trusted that he would keep his promises of forever.

Henry wasn't the problem. She was. She'd always thought that there was something wrong with her, something that made her unlovable. If she'd just been better behaved or more ladylike or prettier, then her father would have wanted her, her grandmother would have approved of her, and hordes of suitors would have pursued her.

Oh, she had her mother's love, but everyone knew a mother's love forgave any number of faults. Alex loved her as well, but Diana knew her status as a perpetual wallflower had distressed him. She'd believed that a woman who couldn't make others happy didn't deserve happiness for herself.

The more she'd doubted her worth, the more unhappy and withdrawn she'd grown. Unable to break free of the cycle, she'd slowly turned into the worst imaginable version of herself—mistrustful, cynical, and guarded. She'd become unlovable.

Somehow, none of that had stopped Henry. He saw through to the heart of her. So deeply had she buried her need for love, she'd convinced herself she didn't need it. Henry knew better and, with him, she had discovered the woman she wanted to be—a woman full of laughter and love. But she was so accustomed to believing herself unworthy that the negative thoughts had continued, no doubt bolstered by Society's general conviction that she *was* unworthy of such a prince among men.

Diana had lain awake all last night, thinking hard as she listened to Ellie's soft snores. She'd decided that she'd had it all wrong. It wasn't through pleasing others that she became deserving of love. By believing herself worthy, by accepting and loving herself, she could be her best self. And if she was happy, she could make others happy, too.

As she'd reflected on her life, Diana realized that she'd always been worthy of love. She couldn't change herself in order to make someone love her, and she didn't want to. On the day Henry had first told her that he loved her, she remembered he'd said, *I'm not asking you to be anything other than yourself. I fell in love with you as you are.*

Maybe she wasn't her best self—there was always room for improvement—but she deserved the happiness she'd found. Yes, she'd made mistakes. She'd allowed her doubts to rule her marriage. It was easy to listen to those familiar voices, and rather than share her fears with Henry, she'd kept her emotions to herself, just as she always had.

She had tremendous guilt over drinking the pennyroyal tea. She didn't mind that she'd prevented a possible child as much as that she had lied to Henry. Fortunately, all she had to do was announce that she'd tired of mint tea, and Henry need never know.

Perhaps she would tell him someday, after they'd had a few children. Mind, she wasn't having more than four, or maybe five. She shouldn't need both hands to count them. Heavens, they might have created a child that last night together. The thought excited her and scared her, but her fears had to do with her health and her aptitude for motherhood. Then, too, there was the concern all women must have upon realizing that birthing should not be possible. Given the size of a baby and the size of . . . She squeezed her legs together.

She could face it. Any pain would be worth a little girl as precious as Bride or a little boy with Henry's eyes and a smile that would always get him out of trouble. With Henry by her side, she could face anything, and he wouldn't be anywhere else. Forever, he'd said, and she believed him. She trusted him with her heart.

Actually, her heart had trusted him all along. When she got lost in her dreams, he came looking for her. When she needed to lose herself and escape from those dreams, she instinctively turned to him. She'd tried to rely on logic and reason in her relationships, but there was nothing logical, nothing reasonable about love.

She loved Henry, and he loved her. She knew it in her soul, and nothing her father said today could change that. She would say what she needed to say here, and then she was going home, where she belonged.

She stood and faced her father. "I am happy with Henry because I love him, and he loves me in return. That's all I've ever wanted. I couldn't care less about wealth and privilege. You claim that you couldn't give me what I deserve. You're right. I deserve to be loved. Do you think that because you couldn't love me, no man could? Is that why you thought you had to bribe a man to marry me?"

Her father grabbed her hand. "Diana, stop, please. I have loved you every day of your life."

She tried to pull her hand away, but he held tight as he got to his feet.

"You are my daughter. How could you ever believe, for a single second, I don't love you?"

"How can you ask me that? I heard you. You wanted Alex to live with you. Not me."

"Alex was always going to go off to school. Your grandparents and your mother would have insisted upon it, and I wouldn't have denied him a fine education to save my pride. I didn't know how to raise a girl, and I could never have given you the advantages you've had with your grandparents. I love you enough to want what is best for you, even if I had to cut out my own heart to let you go."

She jerked her hand away from him, and this time he let her go. "How was it in my best interest for you to buy me a husband?"

He looked at her blankly.

"Penelope," she bit out, "or did you forget offering your champion racehorse to Henry as an incentive for marrying me?"

Understanding lit her father's face, and a twinkle of amusement flashed in his eyes. "As it happens, I offered the mare to Weston if he agreed to stay away from you. I thought to protect you. If Weston's only interest lay in building his stud, he would have taken Penelope and let you alone. Not only did he refuse, he had some choice words for me." He shook his head. "There's nothing like a young fool in love. I sent the mare shortly before your wedding."

"Oh," she said softly. Her father's confession lit a warm glow around Diana's heart. She hadn't *needed* the words from her father, but she liked hearing them.

Her father nodded. "Your young man married you for the right reason."

"I suppose you think marrying for love is the right reason?" she mused.

His brows drew together. "You don't think so?"

"It didn't work very well for you," she pointed out.

"I married your mother for all the right reasons, and I lost her for all the wrong ones. I've made mistakes in my life, some too grave to be corrected, but loving isn't among them. I know now that staying away from you was a mistake. You've gone so many years thinking I didn't care, when I have missed you every day. I don't want to spend the rest of my life missing you, Diana. Tell me I'm not too late."

The hopeful expression on his face wrenched at her heart, and she looked away. She busied herself with taking off her gloves as she thought of what to say. "I've missed you, too," she finally admitted, "but it's not that easy." She set her gloves beside her bonnet, then straightened and forced herself to meet his eyes. "I can't simply forget the past—"

"I don't expect you to forget. I just want the chance to know my daughter again. I can't go back and make up for all the years I missed, but I can be there for you from now on. We can move forward as slowly as you want." His eyes roved over her face, trying to commit her to memory. "Oh, my precious girl—" his voice cracked. The sound broke her heart open. Her chest flooded with a chaotic rush of emotions as he whispered, "Finally. You've finally come home to me."

And then somehow her arms found their way around his chest, and his strong, capable hands held her close as she laid her cheek against his shoulder and wept. She cried her hurt and her fear, her grief and her anger, until she had nothing left to cry. She eased back, a little embarrassed at her outburst until she saw the wet tracks on her father's cheeks. He'd been telling the truth when he had told her that she hadn't suffered alone. They had hurt alone and apart, but perhaps they could heal together.

"Surprise!" A girl's voice sounded through the house.

Diana looked up from her book. She was reading in her father's study while he attended to business. They planned to ride around the estate later, so Diana could see all the improvements he'd made over the years. She'd spent two nights at Swallowsdale, but she and her father hadn't spoken of the past again since her arrival. Though that was the reason she'd come, Diana couldn't bring herself to bring it up just yet. For the first time since her parents had separated, there was a tentative peace between her and her father, and she had a flicker of hope that it might grow stronger, provided she treaded carefully.

She'd often wondered how her mother had been able to forgive her parents after they had turned their backs on her. *I was hurt and angry,* her mother had said when Diana had worked up the courage to ask, *but so were they. They wanted the best for me. They couldn't understand that their idea of the best wasn't necessarily what was best for* me.

Diana was still struggling to accept her father's reasons for staying away, but there was no doubt that their long separation had hurt him as much as it had hurt her. She glanced over at her father, but he was engrossed in the papers on his desk, oblivious to anything else. She got to her feet, hoping to see to the intruder before she interrupted her father, when the door to the study flew open and a girl of about fifteen, all gangly limbs and a mass of copper curls, came charging in like a tempest, talking as she moved.

"Didn't you hear me? Mary Seymour came down with measles, so Headmistress Paxton sent all the girls away from school."

"Claire." The name escaped Diana's father in a strangled gasp. His face was ashen.

She sighed. "I know I ought to have sent you a letter, and then waited for you to send someone or fetch me yourself, but I didn't want to wait. I brought Mrs. Covington's maid and manservant along, so I was perfectly safe and well-chaperoned. Besides, Papa, Bury St. Edmunds isn't more than ten miles from—"

"Claire!"

The girl started at his shout, then caught sight of Diana. Her eyes grew wide. "Oh, I beg your pardon. I didn't realize anyone was in here but, um, Uncle Merriwether."

Diana's breath caught in her lungs.

"Claire," Diana's father rasped, "what are you doing here? Why aren't you with Mrs. Covington?"

"You don't remember? No, of course you don't as it's nothing to do with horses." Fondness overlaid the exasperation in her words. "Mrs. Covington's daughter just had a baby a few months back. You told her she could have this month off to go to Yarmouth to visit her. Of course, you thought I would be in school, and I would be if not for Mary Seymour and her measles. I didn't think you would want me to stay in Mrs. Covington's rooms all by myself, so I told Harriet and John we should come here. I thought it would be a nice surprise." Her face fell and she scuffed one of her feet against the carpet as she snuck glances at Diana.

"Claire, I am always glad to see you. You're my— This is just— I didn't expect—"

"Before, you said 'Papa,' didn't you?" Diana asked. She kept her voice remarkably even, given the thoughts racing through her mind.

The girl—*Claire,* Diana reminded herself—shook her head

even as her cheeks flushed in a way Diana found all too familiar. "You must have misheard. Mr. Merriwether is my uncle."

It was possible, Diana thought. Her father did have a younger brother who'd joined the army. They'd sent him to fight in the American Revolution and, as far as she knew, that was the last anyone had heard of him. It was possible he'd survived and come back to England, but as she regarded the girl whose tall, coltish body and wild red curls were so like her own she very much doubted it.

The girl braced her hands on her hips in a defiant stance. "Who are you?" she challenged.

"Claire—" Diana's father began.

"I'm his daughter," Diana shot back, then her voice softened as she added, "and unless I'm very much mistaken, your sister."

CHAPTER TWENTY-TWO

I thought you would wish to know as soon as possible—your wife found the letter in your desk from Merriwether. She says she is going to Suffolk and, unless I wish to deal with a hysterical woman, I will not stop her. I knew I would deal with difficult fillies when I took this job, but I thought they would all be horses! I will take her myself and keep her safe, of course, but this reminds me why I never married. . . .

—from George Kingsley to
his employer Henry Weston

When the butler informed Linnet that her son-in-law was waiting in the Small Library, she didn't imagine he'd come to pay a social call. A knot of worry began to build in the pit of her stomach as she hurried downstairs. Henry rose as she entered the room. With growing concern, she noted the dark circles beneath his eyes and the weary, wretched air about him.

"Is she refusing to see me?" he asked bluntly.

"I beg your pardon. Did you wish to see my mother? She is—"

"Not the duchess," he cut her off. *"Diana."*

Linnet shook her head. "Diana isn't here. I haven't seen her since your wedding day."

He raked a hand through his blond hair, already windswept and disheveled from hours spent in the saddle. "I was in London on business when I received a message from Ravensfield that Diana had left for Suffolk. I thought she must have come to you. We . . . we fought before I left."

"Please, won't you sit down? You look like you've been riding all night."

"Since dawn," he mumbled as he sank down wearily into a chair, but he was on his feet again before she had seated herself. "My God," he exclaimed. "If she's not here, then she's with *him*."

"Who?" A thought crossed Linnet's mind, a face flashed across her memory, but she dismissed the outlandish notion. There was no reason to think Diana was with . . .

"Her father."

"But why would she go to him?"

Henry met her eyes, and the grief and regret Linnet saw staggered her. "Your husband sought me out before Diana and I wed. He offered me his champion horse if I would bring Diana to see him after we were married. I refused, but he went ahead and sent her. The mare is breeding so there was no way for me to send her back safely.

"After my business in London was finished, I meant to go to Swallowsdale and purchase the mare. I didn't want your husband to think he had any hold over either of us. While I was gone, Diana discovered that her father sent the mare, and I'm afraid she believes that's why I married her." His expression was bleak. "I told her to trust me. I told her to trust me, but I didn't have enough faith in her to tell her about this. Now she's hurt and alone, and I've sent her running to him. I've got to get to her and explain."

"You're going after her?"

He nodded. "I'll need a fresh horse."

"I'm going with you." The words were out of her mouth before she knew what she was saying, but somehow she knew this was right. "I expect we'll be there overnight. It's more than thirty miles from here to Swallowsdale. Will you order the carriage readied while I pack?"

"Lady Linnet—" he began to protest.

"Please, Diana may need me."

He acquiesced at that, but she could tell he wasn't happy. He slept for most of the journey, waking when they changed horses to make certain he hired the fastest teams available. Upon reaching Bury St. Edmunds, their final stop before Swallowsdale, he took her hand. "I'll get to her faster if I ride. Will you be all right with only the coachman?"

"Go," she told him. "I will be fine."

He was out of the carriage before she finished speaking. Nearly two hours later, when her old home came into sight, Linnet realized she'd spoken too soon. She fought the urge to pound on the roof of the carriage and demand the coachman turn around. She was alone. Flight was possible, even practical. There was no good reason for her to have come.

Despite what she'd told Henry, she wasn't worried that Diana needed her. Her daughter had a husband who loved her, and they would sort through their problems together. Linnet wouldn't let Diana run away and repeat her mistakes.

That was why she had come, she admitted to herself. She was tired of living with regrets. No, she wasn't living; she simply *existed*. With both of her children grown and on their own, she needed to learn if there was any living left for her.

She caught her reflection in the glass and straightened her bonnet. She pinched her cheeks, disliking the pale, tired face that stared back at her. She could do nothing about the wrinkles at the corners of her eyes or the strands of silver threaded through her dark hair. She knew, of course, that Thomas had aged as well, but she doubted the added years would diminish his looks. The realization that she would soon find out made it difficult for her to breathe, and she needed all her courage to knock on the door.

"Mrs. Merriwether." The butler's eyes widened at the sight of her.

"Good day, Ingham." She stepped past him into the entry hall. Nothing had changed, but everything was faded and slightly shabby in a way that would only bother the mistress of the house. Relief swept through her at the thought. Thomas could not have remarried, of course, but she'd wondered so many times if there might be a woman in his life.

She untied her bonnet and pulled off her gloves, then handed them to the butler with an uncertain smile. She didn't know what her reception would be in her old home. "It has been a long time."

He bowed. "Too long, madam." As he straightened, he met her eyes. His gaze was warm, but she sensed his discomfort. She supposed there was no clear etiquette for dealing with a visitor in her own home.

"We are all the rage today, Ingham. Claire tells me my son-in-law has come to retrieve his wife. Who is here now?" called a voice she hadn't heard in sixteen long years, except in her dreams. "One moment, I'll come see for myself."

Linnet tried to brace herself for the sight of her husband, willing her heart to stop its frantic gallop. She failed miserably.

"Linnet," Thomas croaked. "What are you doing here?" He looked as though he'd seen a ghost.

Her voice only wobbled a bit as she said, "I came to make certain Diana was all right."

It wasn't a complete lie, but she couldn't tell him the truth: that she'd seized the excuse to return to Swallowsdale one last time. She'd thought if she could just see Thomas again, she wouldn't live so much in her memories; perhaps in the one place she'd known true happiness she could find the measure of peace she needed to face all the long, lonely years ahead.

The second she saw him, though, she knew she'd erred. He looked older, leaner than she remembered, but her heart still leapt, and every cell in her body strained toward him. It had always been that way between them. She guessed it always would. Her love for him wasn't something she could control. Short of cutting out her heart, she was stuck with the feeling.

"Will you not welcome me?" she asked softly, her heart pounding so loudly she could barely hear herself.

"You are always welcome here." He glanced behind him into the library. Linnet followed his gaze. Diana stood in the doorway— No, that wasn't Diana, but the girl was very like Diana at that age, and Diana was very like her father. Thomas had another child. Another woman. Oh, God, she couldn't bear it.

"Please, excuse me," she gasped. She was going to be ill. She stumbled forward, heading for the door to the small parlor that lay behind the more formal dining room. She hurried inside and locked the door. Oh, thank heaven the pot cupboard was still in the same place. She pulled out the chamber pot, blessedly empty, and retched.

There was a knock at the door. Thomas called her name.

"Go away," she managed, before she was sick again. She sank to her knees, heaving over the porcelain dish.

He rattled the door handle, and she was grateful she'd had the presence of mind to lock the door.

"Let me in, Linnet. I must speak with you."

What did he think he could say? She had nursed a broken heart, while he'd moved on with his life. He'd found another woman, conceived a child with her. She wiped the back of her hand against her clammy forehead, bitterly regretting the impulse that had brought her here. Before, at least, she'd been able to imagine that he had missed her, too.

Her head jerked up as the door at the other side of the room began to open. The door led to Thomas's office, but the only way to that room was through this one. He'd often complained that it was impossible for him to get work done knowing she was so nearby. He'd made excuses to go in and out of the room, especially after she'd claimed the price of the toll was a kiss. The door to the office opened and he stood in the doorway, her memory come to life.

"I had a door built between my office and the dining room," he told her. "Cutting through a wall was easier than passing through here every day." A sad smile tugged at his lips, then vanished when he took in her position, the pot clutched in her hands. He paled and started toward her.

Linnet scrambled to her feet and hurriedly replaced the pot in the cabinet, but it was too late. He had seen just how much he'd upset her. He pulled a handkerchief from his pocket. She held out her hand to take it from him, but he ignored her. He wiped her brow, gently cupping her jaw with his free hand. Linnet trembled at his touch. It felt so right, even after all this time. She began to relax into him, and then she remembered and wrenched herself away from him.

His face tightened. "Wait here. I'll return in a minute."

"That's not necessary. As soon as Diana has collected her things, we'll be on our way."

"We need to talk," he insisted. "You must allow me—"

"There is nothing to talk about," she snapped.

His voice was gentle as he asked, "Why did you come, Linny?"

She closed her eyes, fighting tears at hearing his pet name for her. "It doesn't matter anymore," she whispered. There was no response, and when she opened her eyes, she saw she was alone in the room. She unlocked the door to the hall, as there was clearly little point in leaving it locked, and then sat on the needlepoint-covered bench beneath the window. She'd worked the piece herself in the first year of her marriage. Everywhere she looked, memories assaulted her. What had possessed her to come back to this place?

Thomas reentered the room, an apple in his hand. Without saying a word, he took a penknife from the escritoire, deftly sliced the fruit, and then walked over to hand her a piece. She thanked him and ate it, glad to remove the bitter taste of being sick. He'd done this for her every morning when she'd been sick in the early months of being pregnant with Diana and Alex. She hadn't suffered from morning sickness during her last pregnancy. That should have been her first sign that all was not as it should be.

Her heart ached fiercely as it always did when she thought of the child she'd lost. The doctor had warned her that the baby was small, that the heartbeat was too fast. Strain on the mother's body, he'd claimed, would weaken the child within her. She must keep her appetite up and not let herself get overexcited. She'd tried. She'd tried so hard, but she'd failed, and that failure had cost Linnet both her child and her husband. Her stomach churned, and she shook her head when Thomas offered her another apple slice. Had he done this for Claire's mother, she wondered?

"How old is she?" The question slipped out of her mouth before she knew she was going to ask it.

He sighed, setting the apple and knife aside. "Claire is fifteen. After you left with the children—" He rose and began to pace around the small room. "I went a little mad, I think. I drank to try to dull the pain. When that didn't work, I drank more. I wasn't drunk, Linnet. I was a drunkard. It was so bad that Bar took the key to the wine cellar from Ingham. I don't know how I managed to ride to Newmarket without breaking my neck.

"Maybe it would have been better for everyone if I had. I went to the public house. There was a woman who worked there, a widow whose husband had been a trainer. Marjorie Crofter. She always smiled at me whenever I came in for a meal." He swallowed before continuing in a broken voice. "I have no idea what I said to her. I know I kissed her, and I . . ." He took a deep breath. "I asked her to come upstairs with me—"

"Stop," she begged.

"I didn't want her, Linnet. I wanted to forget you, to stop hurting just for a little while. God help me, I don't remember what happened next. I was alone when I woke up. I thought—I prayed—I had been unable and nothing had occurred.

"I was disgusted by myself, and even more horrified by what you must think of me if you learned what I had done, what I had become. I left what money I had on me in the room, came home, and vowed not to let another drop of alcohol pass my lips. And I haven't, Linnet, I swear it to you."

Linnet sat stiffly as he paced the small room, his expression tortured. She saw, in the lines on his face that had not been there before, how he must have struggled. Although he had hurt her, although he had rejected her, thrown away their marriage, she still ached to think of the pain he must have endured—alone. She had turned to her family, taken solace in Diana and Alex. He'd had no one. He had been slow to trust her, slow to trust his feelings for her, having been alone for so long.

"Marjorie left Newmarket a few months later. I avoided the place she worked, so I didn't know until much later. I hadn't heard from her for close to two years when I had a letter asking me to meet her in

London. I knew—" He raked a hand through his hair, setting it on end. "Well, you saw her. There was no denying she was mine. I looked into that little face and knew I had a second chance. I offered to raise Claire, but Marjorie only wanted some money to leave London.

"With my help, she set up in Swaffham as my brother's widow. I visited when I could, but when Claire was seven, Marjorie died of a wasting fever. I brought Claire here until I found a good girls' school in Bury St. Edmunds where she could board. Everyone there—and most people here—believe she's my niece.

"Claire knows the truth, and Bar must as well—my brother has been gone more than thirty years now—but they both understand the need for the pretense. She stays with a woman in Bury St. Edmunds and only visits here a few times each year. I never want to cause you hurt again, but I can't regret her, Linny. She kept me sane, gave me something to live for. After what had happened at The Hall, I knew I had lost you—"

"You left me," she corrected him in a shaky voice. "You left me, Thomas. I asked for you when I woke up and was told you were gone."

"How could I stay?" he asked harshly, coming to stand before her. "How could I stay after—" His voice broke.

"I needed you," she shouted, unable to control her anger. All the hurts of so many years had risen to the surface, and she couldn't contain them any longer. She got to her feet, her entire body trembling with the emotion struggling to break free. "You were there. You knew what was happening, and you walked away. She was your daughter, too." The tears spilled down her cheeks but she made no move to wipe them away. "Whatever you choose to believe, I swear by all that is holy, she was your—"

"Yes, she was my daughter," he roared, a sound of such awful pain that Linnet flinched. "She was my daughter," he repeated, this time in a choked whisper, "and I killed her. I killed her, and I nearly killed you as well. Oh, God, Linnet!" he cried, sinking to his knees. He pressed his face into her skirts and wrapped his arms around her as great sobs began to shake his big body.

For several moments, she was too stunned to move. She'd always believed so strongly that she was responsible for losing their baby. It had never occurred to her that Thomas might hold himself accountable. She couldn't deny his anguish, though, or her need to soothe him.

"What happened was not your fault," she said softly, stroking his hair as her own tears rained down on him. "It wasn't your fault."

She wept for the child they had lost. For shoulders that should have been cried on, but had stood apart, burdened with blame. For all the time she had endured without a single word from him. For the years she had needed him but had been too proud, too scared to try.

"Hush, now." She leaned over to run her hands over his back, trying to calm him. "Don't blame yourself. She wasn't—" She swallowed the lump in her throat and tried to remember the words she had used for Diana and Alex. "She wasn't meant to be ours. I know it goes against what we're taught, but I have to believe that her soul was born into another child, that someone needed her more."

"If I hadn't come— If I hadn't upset you— Your mother was right to tell me to leave. . . ."

She could barely make out the muffled words, but she understood his pain, and he was ripping her heart apart. "She was too small. I . . . I didn't . . ." She faltered, not wanting to speak the words she knew would make him push her away. "I didn't take care of myself as I should. I was too miserable, too weak, and I failed her."

He raised his head at her words, his expression stricken. "No, Linnet!"

"I did. I failed her. I failed you. I failed Diana and Alex."

He rose and enfolded her in his arms where she'd dreamed of being for so many long, lonely years. And now she was finally there, only to have learned that another woman had borne him a child when she had not been able. Had this other woman loved him?

Tall and handsome, Thomas had always attracted notice from women. Linnet had seen the covetous glances sent in his direction when she went with him into town to do a bit of shopping. He'd always laughed at her, claiming he had no interest in any invitations but hers. But he had gone to this woman, and she had taken him into her body. His seed had taken firm root in that woman's womb, not hers. Had he loved her when she had presented him with his daughter? How could he not?

She held herself rigidly within the circle of his arms, crying from the pain tearing through her, worse by far than any physical pain she had ever endured. When she'd begun to lose her child, when she'd realized what was happening, she had been terrified and heartsick. She had clung to the knowledge of Thomas's presence. Whatever happened, he had come for her. The doctor had told her he saw no reason she could not have another child. She had tempered her grief with the belief that, just as Thomas had come back to her, so too would the spirit of this babe.

And then she'd awakened to learn that he had left.

"He said he never should have come," her mother had apologetically related in a tone that conveyed no regret whatsoever, "and he was quite right. Look what that man has done to you. To cause you such distress in your delicate condition—" she broke off, dabbing at her dry eyes with a lace-edged handkerchief. "But then, what has he ever brought you other than pain? What has he brought any of us other than pain?"

"He is the father of my children, and there is no greater joy in my life than my children," Linnet had told her with as much anger as she dared show.

"You must know I did not mean to overlook my dear grandchildren. I have every hope of making a splendid match for Diana, and the continuation of the family line may well fall to young Alexander. You and the children are better off here, with your own people. Now let us not speak on this any further. He has chosen to walk away, and in time you will accept that this is for the best, for you and the children."

She had never accepted that Thomas's leaving had been for the best, because it hadn't been. Not for her children. Not for her. Thomas's words earlier came back to her. She thought he'd said that her mother had told him to leave. Though it made Linnet ill, she had little difficulty imagining it.

What would her life have been like if her mother hadn't driven

Thomas away that day? She couldn't place all the blame on her mother. Why hadn't she found the courage to return to Swallowsdale before today? The past was the past, she told herself. What mattered now was the future. Did they have a future?

"This Marjorie . . . D-Did you love her?" she whispered, terrified to hear his answer.

He pulled back so he could look into her eyes. His big hands trembled as he cupped her cheeks, brushing her tears away with his thumbs. "I swear to you with all that I am: You are the only woman I have ever loved."

A strangled, wounded sound escaped her throat. She wanted to speak, to tell him that he was the only man she'd ever loved, that she loved him still and always would, but the muscles in her throat wouldn't cooperate.

"I have thought of you, missed you, needed you and loved you every day. I know I don't deserve you, and I know you can never forgive me. I will never forgive myself—"

"Stop," she choked. She was so tired of accusations and blame, of guilt and grieving, of recriminations and regrets. They had both hurt each other, both made mistakes, but by some miracle, they both still loved each other. The only mistake now would be continuing to stay apart.

She rose up on her toes and leaned into him, wrapping her arms around his neck as she closed her eyes and let instinct guide her. Now that she was back here in his arms, finally home, she would never leave again.

Thomas stiffened in shock at the first feather-soft brush of Linnet's mouth on his. He forced himself to stand still, fearful that any movement on his part might break whatever enchantment held his wife in thrall. He had never thought he would hold her again, except in his dreams. To have her pressed against him, kissing him . . .

She trailed her lips down to his chin, then up the side of his jaw to his cheek. Her light touch was curious and reverent, at once so much more than he had dared hope for and so damned far from what he needed. It had been so long. He groaned when her tongue darted out to taste his skin. She hummed in approval as she dragged her lips back to his.

His heart slammed painfully against his ribs as his body stirred to life. He never had been able to control that portion of his anatomy around her, he reflected ruefully. He tried to step back, but Linnet tightened her arms around him.

"Don't you want me?" she asked, her voice filled with a combination of need and confusion.

"You know I do," he gritted out, "but—"

"What?" She drew away from him, a flash of hurt in her beautiful gray eyes.

Everything inside him demanded that he pull her back to him, kiss her the way he needed, claim her so thoroughly that she would never think of leaving him again. His hesitation was due to wanting her too much.

"Are you certain this is what you want, Linny?" His hands clenched into tight fists at his sides as he fought the urge to reach for her. "Are you certain *I* am what you want?" He swallowed hard. "Because I won't let you go again. I *can't*—"

His voice broke, but she was there to heal it, to heal him. She launched herself at him and he caught her, trapping her in his arms as he kissed her with all the heat and hunger he had stored through too many lonely years. He wanted to go slow and savor her, but his patience was stretched thin. It snapped at the first dainty flick of her tongue against his. Her taste exploded through his senses and ignited his blood. The fire coursed through his body, burning along his veins and driving him past reason.

Her head fell back as he palmed her breasts through her gown. "Thomas. Oh, God. It has been so long."

"I can't wait any longer, Linnet. I need you *now*." He nearly growled the last word.

"Here?" Eager desire infused the breathily uttered syllable.

"Here." He arched his brows, silently daring her to disagree.

Instead, she nodded and licked her lips. "What about Diana and Henry?"

He strode to the door that led to the hallway and locked it, then crossed the room and did the same to the door connected to his office. "They are perfectly capable of sorting through their problems on their own," he assured her as he stalked toward her.

"And the— And Claire?"

"Later." He came up behind her and nipped her earlobe, then set to work unfastening her gown.

"I want to know your daughter. She is part of you, and—"

"Hush." He moved in front of her and captured her face in his hands. "You are the most astounding woman."

She beamed at him, her eyes sparkling. "I love you," she told him, raising her arms and placing her hands along his jaw.

Her words simultaneously soothed him and inflamed him. He saw the girl he'd given his heart to, and the woman who had kept it safe, despite everything that had come between them—including him.

She was his heart. The only true home he had ever known.

"Not as much as I love you," he vowed. "Forever, Linny, and it still won't be long enough for me to love you."

They were the right words, and she rewarded him with a slow, sweet kiss. "You said forever, Thomas. That's what I want. Forever. With you."

Forever.

With Linnet.

It definitely wouldn't be long enough, but damned if he wouldn't love every moment.

CHAPTER TWENTY-THREE

Be patient with each other. As your marriage grows, so will you. The qualities you love most about your wife will be the same traits that will drive you insane, but when you feel ready to tear out your hair, remember how you felt on your wedding day. Marriage may seem effortless in these early weeks but, like any precious bloom, you must tend it. If married life suits you half as well as it suits me, you will be a very happy man.

—from the Viscount Weston to
his son Henry Weston

As Henry thundered up the drive to Swallowsdale Grange, he tried to prepare himself to face his wife. There was a possibility that she'd already left, but he didn't think so. With his daughter back in his grasp, Merriwether wouldn't let her go so quickly.

He rode past the stables around to the paddocks. Sure enough, Kingsley was talking with a middle-aged man who stood at least a foot shorter than him.

"Kingsley," he called. "This noble steed is now a valued member of our stables. Will you see he gets a proper rubdown and extra oats?"

He dismounted as Kingsley came over to take the reins. "You took your time getting here," the groom grumbled, "and now you bring me a hack?"

"Is she all right?" Henry demanded. "Rutland and Bess were still in London so I stayed with them. I didn't go to my club until yesterday evening, or I would have been here sooner. You might have given me more direction than Suffolk. I went to her mother's house. Damn it all, I'm sorry, Kingsley. It's a bloody mess, but you watched over her and kept her safe, and I can't thank you enough for that. Do you know where she is?"

The short man approached them, casting an unimpressed look in Kingsley's direction. "So he's finally come for Miss Diana, has he? You still owe me a crown. You said he'd be here yesterday morning at the latest."

"That's Mrs. Weston," Henry said tightly, "and I'll give you a guinea if you can tell me where she is."

The man slowly took his measure and then pointed toward the house. "Follow the path behind the garden. She's picking flowers with Claire."

Henry didn't know who Claire was, but he hurried in the direction the man had indicated. He'd gone about half a mile when he heard girlish laughter. At the sound of Diana's voice, relief speared through him. He couldn't make out what she was saying, but she sounded calm and cheerful, which was a long way from how he'd imagined he might find her.

Then he turned a bend in the path and she came into sight. His heart tripped as she laughed at something the girl said. Henry looked at the girl, then at Diana, and then back again, and he actually tripped. He crashed to the ground like a felled tree. Feminine shrieks rent the air as they rushed over to him.

"Henry!" Diana yelped.

"Oh my goodness!" exclaimed the girl.

"Are you all right?" Diana asked. "What are you doing here?"

"I'll bet he scared away all the animals for miles."

Diana began to pat him all over. "Where are you hurt?"

He groaned as he drew in a breath.

"Claire, run to the house and fetch—"

"No." He hauled himself to his feet. "I just had the wind knocked out of me."

"But—"

"Leave be, Diana. Now, who is this?"

Diana placed her hand on the girl's shoulder. "I have a sister." There was wonder in the words, along with a note of protectiveness and warning, as if she were worried he might spurn the girl for her illegitimate birth. Or perhaps she was reminding him of the unspoken rule that one didn't quarrel in front of children or servants. "Henry, this is Claire."

Henry smiled at this younger version of Diana. "If Diana has a sister, then it appears I have a sister as well. I daresay you can't be more trouble than the ones I already have. Now, I would like to spend time getting to know you, but I must speak with your sister right now. Alone," he added, when she made no move to leave.

The girl regarded him with suspicion.

"It's all right, Claire," Diana assured her. "Here, let me get the flowers for you to take back to the house."

As Diana strode off to retrieve the basket of flowers they'd picked, Claire turned on Henry. "If you make her unhappy or hurt her, I'll— I'll—" Her face grew red and pinched as she scowled at him.

Henry's heart twisted at the fierce display of loyalty. "Two of my sisters are married," he told her, "and if either of their husbands hurt them, I would beat him to a pulp and then put a bullet in his black heart."

Claire's face brightened. "Then that's what I will do to you."

"You needn't sound so eager," he teased.

Her smile was like her sister's—a ray of sunshine breaking through the clouds on a cold winter's day.

"How old are you?" he asked.

"I was fifteen in February."

"I have twin sisters just a bit younger than you. Lia and Genni will be fifteen in November." He watched as her eyes lit with interest.

"Do they look alike?"

"Identical. Strangers can't tell them apart."

"But you can?"

"Lia has a freckle right here." He tapped the skin just above his left temple. "Genni's is over here." He moved his finger to the right side of his head. "Identical, but opposite. Of course, that only works if at least one of them is wearing her hair pulled back. You will see when you meet them."

She chewed her lip, the same way Diana did when she was nervous or puzzling out a problem.

"What's the matter?" he asked as Diana approached them.

"The girls at school think I'm an orphan. They all believe my father is my uncle."

So that was the story Merriwether was using. That would work well enough, he supposed, so long as Merriwether had seen to all the details. Henry would make certain of it; he didn't want Diana vulnerable, and though she'd only just discovered her sister, he could tell she wouldn't give her up.

Claire took a breath, slowly exhaled, and then forged on. "Your sisters would know the truth, though, wouldn't they? If they know Diana is my sister, they'll know I'm a bastard. They might not like me."

His chest tightened. Lord, this one would wrap him around her finger as easily as her sister had. "No, they will love you." He reached forward and tugged on a red curl. "Among strangers, it's probably best to keep pretending that you are your father's niece, but we are family now. With me and with my family, you never have to worry about being anything other than yourself."

Claire surprised him with a hug just as Diana reached them. She looked at him questioningly.

He shrugged. "Merriwether women find me irresistible. It must be something in your blood."

Diana muttered something that sounded like, "Hardly," while Claire giggled.

"I expect those arithmetic problems to be finished by the time I am back," Diana told Claire as she handed her the basket of flowers.

Claire made a face. "Will you help me with my French exercises later?"

"Of course," Diana said fondly, and then sent her on her way. As soon as the girl was out of hearing, she turned to him. "I heard what you said to Claire, or part of it, at least. Thank you for being so good to her."

"There's no need to thank me for that." She inclined her head in silent acceptance and began to walk along the path, moving farther away from the house. Henry followed her deeper into the wooded area. Just as well, he thought. They needed to talk, so it was best they had privacy. If Merriwether interrupted them, Henry wouldn't be responsible for his actions. They walked on in silence for nearly ten minutes before some devil prompted him to say, "Though if you truly wished to thank me, I recall a certain French lesson you gave me . . ."

The mutinous look she shot him was neither amused nor interested.

He shrugged. "You can't blame a man for trying."

Diana stopped where she stood. Part of her was overjoyed to see him; she'd missed having his support over the past days. The rest of her wasn't certain where they stood with each other. He'd left her without saying good-bye. She knew she'd hurt him with her lack of trust, and she planned to apologize, but Henry had to admit that he'd made mistakes as well. He should have told her that her father had sought him out, and he shouldn't have left the way he had.

She crossed her arms over her chest. "What *can* I blame you for?"

His hands fisted as he moved to stand in front of her. "Diana, I swear to you, I haven't been with another woman—I haven't desired another woman—since the night I first held you in my arms and tasted your sweetness and your passion. I stayed with Rutland while I was in London."

She shook her head, her arms falling to her sides. "I know you wouldn't be unfaithful—"

"No," he said desperately, even a little angrily, though she knew this big man would never intentionally hurt her. "If you *knew*, I would have earned your trust. If you *knew*, you never would have run. Running away might be the way your family solves marital disputes, Di, but that's not the way it's going be between us."

"But I didn't run away," she protested.

"You didn't wait for me to get home to ask me about the letter you found," he challenged. "You went haring off to Suffolk and led me a merry dance."

"I came here because you wanted me to make peace with the past. I won't pretend that I like all the women in your past, but they weren't the real problem. I thought I would be home before you returned, but I hadn't anticipated what I'd find here. In any event, you were the one who ran away."

"Me?" He gaped at her.

"You didn't say even good-bye. We needed to talk about what happened, but you didn't wait long enough for me to wake up before you went haring off to London."

"I didn't leave because of our fight," he said quietly. "The letter you found . . . You know it's not what it seems?"

"I know. My father told me about his meeting with you." She paused before asking, "Why didn't you tell me?"

He raised his brows. "Why didn't you tell me that you'd discovered a taste for pennyroyal tea?"

She gasped.

"You might have kept me in the dark for quite some time if Mrs. Timms hadn't voiced her concern," he informed her, his tone dangerously calm.

"When?" she croaked.

"That last night at Ravensfield, after I took you upstairs, I thought that I, a caring husband, would bring my overset wife a cup of her favorite tea. I believe you said the blend was calming, did you not? But rather than looking favorably on my efforts, our housekeeper took me to task for attempting to force more pennyroyal tea down your gullet."

"Why didn't you say anything?"

He sighed and raked a hand through his hair, setting it on end. "You were asleep when I came upstairs, and then I had to wake you from a nightmare. Venting my spleen at that point would have been like kicking a whipped dog."

"But after—"

"Christ, Diana, you'd already told me you didn't trust me. Do you think I wanted to hear you admit that you were willing to make yourself ill to keep from bearing my children? You're just waiting for the day I decide to leave you. You think I'm no better than your father."

Oh, God, she'd hurt him worse than she'd known. "It wasn't like that," she insisted, willing him to hear the truth in her words.

His lashes lowered, as if he couldn't bear the sight of her. His Adam's apple bobbed as he swallowed. "Then tell me how it *was*." The words were a low rumble, like distant thunder.

Diana wiped her sweaty palms on her skirts. "The first time you told me you loved me . . . I didn't think I could ever be happier than I was at that moment, but I was wrong. I loved you more every moment I spent with you."

His eyes opened, and that intense, cobalt stare pinned her in place "If you were so damned happy—"

"Please, just let me explain."

He looked like he wanted to say more, but he nodded and motioned for her to continue.

"I thought my heart would burst with joy on our wedding day. That night, well, I suppose it was late afternoon, but the first time we were together, I knew what I felt for you went beyond love."

"What's beyond love?"

"I don't know, exactly, but it's a . . . a need for you that's all the way in my soul. Apart from you, the people I love most are my mother and Alex. If I were to lose either of them, it would be as though I'd lost a piece of my heart. If I lost you, I wouldn't have a heart. Losing you would destroy me. I was so happy, but I was also scared because I was certain it couldn't last."

"You aren't the only one who's scared, Di," he said wearily. "I'm terrified you're never going to let yourself trust me. Your parents stopped trusting each other, and their marriage fell apart. You're convinced that we'll end up like them, so you're trying to protect yourself. But if you can't trust me, it doesn't matter how much you love me. We're like your parents already." He sighed, stepped around her, and began walking in the direction that led back to the house.

Diana's stomach dropped as she accepted the truth in his words.

She hugged her arms around herself, suddenly cold despite the warmth of the day. Henry's exhaustion weighed on her. He'd fought for their marriage, and she should have been fighting beside him. It wasn't too late.

"Wait!" she yelled. He halted, but he made no move to turn around. What could she say to reach him?

"You don't need to be afraid," she called out, hurrying toward him. "I trust you. I've trusted you for a long time in my heart, but my head takes a little longer sometimes."

She stopped a few feet from him. He didn't say anything, didn't move, but there was a tension in his posture that hadn't been there before. She had his attention, at least.

"My parents' marriage made me wary of falling in love, but I was even less prepared to receive love. I had difficulty with the idea that you wished to pretend to court me. Given your reputation, I told myself not to make too much of your flirtations or kisses. I didn't know what to think when I learned you were serious in your affections. I couldn't imagine that anyone, especially someone as wonderful as you are, would want me."

Henry turned around and started toward her, his face grim. Diana held up a hand. "You have to understand, I'd spent my life thinking there must be something the matter with me. My father didn't want me. I know now that I was wrong, but I spent the better part of my life believing he only loved my brother.

"I could never please my grandparents. The duke took little interest in me, but the duchess saw me as her second chance. My mother had foiled her hopes for a brilliant match, but my grandmother hoped to make one for me. Unfortunately, I am nowhere near as pretty or accomplished as my mother. Apart from my marriage to you, I was always a great disappointment.

"Then, too, I was never very popular. I had some suitors when I first came out, but after so many Seasons without a single suitor, it became difficult to remember that anyone had ever wanted me. Heavens, your mother had to force you to dance with me—" her voice broke.

Henry reached her in a moment. He wrapped her in his arms and, just like that, she was right where she belonged. She let him comfort her for several long moments before she pulled away. She drew in a ragged breath. "Do you understand? Aside from my mother, you're the only one who's ever really wanted me. Before you, I had convinced myself that I was unlovable, that I didn't deserve such happiness."

"No, Di—" Henry reached for her again. She was breaking him apart.

"I didn't doubt you. I doubted myself, but I know where I went wrong. I should have told you when I got scared. I'm so sorry."

"I know, sweetheart." He pulled her close, savoring the way she fit so perfectly against him. "I only wish I knew how to erase those doubts. If you could only see what I see when I look at you . . ." He gently eased her back so he could see her face. "You are so very precious to me. I would do anything to keep you happy. That's the reason I didn't tell you about the meeting with your father. I didn't want to upset you. I wanted to protect you, and . . ." He hesitated.

"And?" she prompted.

"And even though I didn't agree with the way he was going about it, I knew your father was trying to protect you as well. For the same reason I was. Because if you hurt, I hurt with you. I told your sister that if either of my sisters' husbands were to hurt them, I would beat him to a pulp before shooting him through his black heart. Claire vowed to do the same to me, and I would hand her the gun, Di.

"When I came up with the idea to run a stud, I was looking to find some purpose in my life. I was drifting along through life and while I wasn't unhappy, I saw my best friend and my sisters and my parents, and I knew there was something more. Something else I was meant to do.

"I thought I could find what that was at Ravensfield Hall and, in a way, I did, because Ravensfield led me to you and that ridiculous pretend courtship. Di, I will give Penelope back to your father if you want me to. I would give up the stud if you asked me. It will never be enough for me without you by my side to enjoy it with me. Ravensfield isn't home for me without you there. Home is with you, wherever you want to be. Do *you* understand what *I'm* saying?"

Her smile wobbled. "Maybe you could say it a bit more simply? There are these three little words, you see, and every time I hear them, the doubts fade away a bit more."

"Then I will say them often." He cupped her beloved face in his hands. "I love you, Di. With everything I am and all that I hope to be, I love you." He wiped at the tears running freely down her cheeks. "Don't cry, sweetheart, or your sister will come after me."

She gave a short, choked laugh. "I love you so much. You are the dream I never believed would come true, the shining star I watched but never imagined I could touch."

His heart expanded until he thought his chest was going to explode. He couldn't speak, so he kissed her. Again and again. Soft, fleeting presses of his lips against hers. As if they had forever. Actually, he thought, they did. The realization eased the pressure in his chest to a comfortable fullness.

Lower down on his body, he felt a different fullness.

He knew Diana felt it too. Not because she couldn't help but notice, pressed up against him as she was, but because she slipped her hand between their bodies and cupped him through his breeches.

"Di—" His breath hissed through his teeth as she ran her fingers up and down his length.

"I've missed you," she said, a husky catch in her voice.

He swallowed hard. "Don't play with fire if you're not willing to get burned, sweetheart."

She dropped her hand, and he fought to control his disappointment. They were in the woods, he reminded himself, and—

She twined her arms around his neck and dragged his head down until his mouth was only a breath away from hers. "Burn me," she demanded.

Her words kindled the fire growing within him. He closed the distance between them, slanting his mouth over hers, angling her head with one of his hands. His other hand swept down to her backside, molding her through her skirts. Thoughts of forever were pushed aside for the burgeoning need of *now*.

When she sucked on his tongue, he swore he could taste her

need. Her hunger fed his own. Her desire made him wild. There was no aphrodisiac as potent as knowing Diana wanted him.

She held his jaw as she broke the kiss. The warm pants of breath from her mouth teased his lips. "You are mine."

"Yours," he agreed.

Her hazel eyes sparkled with happiness as she knelt before him.

"Tu m'appartiens." You belong to me.

She reached for the buttons on his breeches.

"Avec moi." With me.

She wrapped her hand around him.

"Et ne le dis pas à ma soeur, mais je ne parle pas très bien le français." And don't tell my sister this, but I don't speak French very well.

Her mouth joined her hand. He groaned as she licked him—fast, wet flicks of her tongue that sizzled like white-hot jolts of lightning. She built the pleasure in him, heightened the passion collecting between them until the air around them was heavy with it. When she finally took him into her mouth, the storm was close to breaking.

He was close to breaking.

He pulled her off him, lifted her to her feet, and backed her up against the nearest tree.

"If I touch you now, will I find that you're wet for me?" The words emerged as a harsh growl.

She licked her lips. "Yes," she breathed.

"Thank God," he muttered her as he hauled up her skirts. He bunched the fabric in his left hand as his right sought her center.

"Henry, please." Her gasp turned to a moan as he circled the bud at the peak of her sex.

"Put your hands on my shoulders," he instructed as he pressed his chest into hers, trapping her raised skirts between them. He trailed his hand along her thigh, curving around the outside to lift her leg, opening her to him. Her cry of pleasure as he thrust inside her was the sweetest sound he had ever heard. "Wrap your legs around my waist. There, yes, I have you. Let go, Di. Let yourself go."

He raised her up until only the tip of his cock was inside her. He held her there, poised on the edge, poised on him, as his heart beat in hard thuds. There was nothing but the rush of blood through his veins, every drop racing toward the spot where their bodies joined, and those clear hazel eyes, holding his soul captive.

"I love you, Diana."

Her eyes took on that soft, unfocused look as her inner muscles clenched around him. He lowered her onto his length as his hips bucked up, driving him as deep as he could go. She held on tight, clutching her arms around him, chanting his name like a prayer as her release took her, shook her, shattered her and sent the fragments flying. He was right behind her, the pieces of him reaching out for hers, as if even the smallest part of him knew how he needed her. How he was bound to her, heart and soul.

Her face was buried in his neck, her breath rushing against the base of his throat.

"You aren't crying, are you?" he asked, his voice ragged from exertion. "Because your sister really will murder me if I make you cry."

She raised her head, her brilliant smile nearly distracting him from her watery eyes. "These are happy tears," she promised as he withdrew and slowly lowered her to her feet. He kept his arms around her, partly to steady her but mostly because he wanted to hold her. "Besides, you should be more concerned about what my father will do to you when he sees the grass stains on my skirts."

The sound he made was somewhere between a laugh and a groan. "I thought you loved me."

"I *do* love you, so very, very much."

"Even though I'm a rogue?" he teased.

She arched up and kissed him. He would never tire of the taste of Diana and love and forever.

"Because you're *my* rogue," she told him.

And then he kissed her again because she was right.

EPILOGUE

We are anxious for the birth, of course, but one cannot rush nature. I have been thinking of names and so, I suspect, has Henry, but we have not discussed them. If Claire arrives in time, she will doubtless have an opinion as well. I have arranged all the details of her visit, and Henry and I are eager to have her with us, so let your mind be easy on that point. I am delighted that you and Mama are enjoying Harrogate, and you must stay and explore The Dales as long as the weather permits. I will share some further news I believe will please you both...

—from Diana Weston to
her father Thomas Merriwether

A LITTLE MORE THAN NINE MONTHS LATER...

"Come on, sweetheart," Henry urged, gripping Diana's hand so tightly she yelped in pain. "I'm sorry." He released her with a rueful grin. "I'm a little on edge."

A vast understatement, she thought, watching him with equal parts affection and amusement. Her husband had been testy for the past fortnight, ever since Penelope had begun displaying the signs that her time was near at hand. The grooms took turns keeping watch at night and, as per Henry's orders, someone had come to the house to alert them when the mare had shown signs of beginning her labor.

She and Henry had hastily dressed and made their way to the stables where Kingsley and the other grooms observed the mare's progress, content to let nature take its course. Though the birthing process was relatively uncomplicated, there were always risks attendant to both the mare and her foal. Kingsley would intervene at the first sign of a problem, but Henry was the one in distress.

He paced outside the birthing stall, more agitated than Penelope, until Diana guided him to sit beside her on an overturned wooden crate. While the mare was arguably the most valuable horse in their stables, Diana knew monetary concerns were the furthest thing from her husband's mind. While he felt responsible for the well-being of all their horses, he and Penelope had formed a special bond.

"Her water has broken." Kingsley spoke quietly so as not to disturb the mare, but Henry heard him all the same and hurried back over, tugging Diana with him.

"Claire will be so disappointed to have missed this," she murmured. Her sister would arrive in a few days to spend her summer holiday with them. "If it weren't for the possibility of seeing Penelope foal, I think she would have begged to spend her holiday with *your* family." Claire had met Henry's twin sisters, and they had immediately become the best of friends. Henry swore he had nightmares that the three of them were going to try to rule the world.

"Given the choice, *I* would miss this," Henry muttered. "Your sister will have all the fun of playing with the foal with none of the worry beforehand." He turned his attention back to the mare. "You can do this, Pen. That's my brave girl. I'll see you have extra oats for a year."

Henry kept up his encouraging monologue until the foal's tiny hooves came into view, followed by the muzzle. Everyone was silent as Kingsley entered the birthing stall and approached the foal. When he stepped back, Diana sighed in relief at the sight of the small, flaring nostrils and watched in wonder as the mare strained and pushed to finish delivering her foal.

Kingsley moved to make a quick check of the foal. "A beautiful, healthy colt," he announced, a wide grin splitting his face. Diana's heart swelled as the little foal struggled to his feet and approached his mother with wobbling steps, settling in next to her. The exhausted mare nuzzled her son contentedly.

Diana turned to Henry and found him looking at her, a tender smile on his face. She could no more have stopped returning that smile than she could have stopped the stars from shining. "I hope you don't intend to offer me extra oats when the time comes," she warned him.

At his insistence, after they'd returned from Swallowsdale, she'd begun drinking the wild carrot seed infusion that Mrs. Timms suggested. Henry said he wanted her to himself for a while before he had to share her, and he wanted her to be sure she was ready. Diana suffered none of the ill effects she had with the pennyroyal, and she appreciated his concern for her, but she'd finally insisted they let nature take its course.

"No oats for you. I'll remember that . . . when the time comes." He chuckled, as he slid an arm around her waist. "Just don't put me through that again anytime soon."

She canted her head to look into those stunning blue eyes. "What do you consider *soon*?"

As understanding dawned, a dazzling expression of joy broke over his face. "Are you certain?" he demanded.

"I don't think there's any doubt. You go off to the stables after breakfast. I head back upstairs to cast up my accounts."

"You should have told me."

"You were already a mess over Penelope. I didn't want to worry you more." She batted his hand away from her forehead. "I feel fine once it's over. I'm not ill. I'm having a baby. *We're* having a baby."

He caught her up in his arms and spun her around until she felt light-headed. Or perhaps she was just giddy with happiness. "I guess you're not so reluctant to go through this again as you thought," she said as he set her back on her feet.

He cast a glance in the direction of the mare and her foal and shook his head, one hand sliding down to rest against her still-flat abdomen. "I have time to prepare myself."

"Are you truly happy?"

His eyes twinkled. "Did I not say I wished you to bear me at least a dozen babes?"

"Why does that number keep getting larger?"

"Then again, I'm not certain my heart could survive a dozen nights like tonight, especially given the strenuous exercise my lusty wife requires of me nightly."

"Henry," she warned.

"And sometimes before noon."

"Oh, you are impossible." She hovered between laughter and the urge to strangle him.

Kingsley saved him from bodily harm, coughing and clearing his throat half a dozen times before saying, "Beg pardon, but I'll be updating the record book tonight. What name should I put for the foal?"

"What do you think of Telemachus?" Diana asked Henry. "That is the name of Penelope's son in the *Odyssey*."

Henry shook his head. "He may be a horse, but he doesn't deserve a name like that. As it happens, I've given this some thought, and you know I'm not fond of that particular form of exertion. We will call him Rogue, Kingsley, since my wife has a fondness for them."

He placed an arm around Diana's shoulders and murmured, "I will leave the naming of all our future foals in your very capable"—he took her hand and pressed a kiss to her palm—"very beautiful"—a nip—"very *talented* hands."

Kingsley muttered something about marriage making a man soft and walked off.

Diana giggled. "Should I inform him not to worry on that account?"

"Dear God," Henry groaned. "You'll be worse than my sisters soon."

"How could I be otherwise with such a husband?" She looped her arms around his neck. "So, our champion is another rogue, is he?"

He nodded. "In my experience, rogues carry the day."

Her heart swelled at the love in his eyes.

"I thought you were reformed."

"Where you are concerned, my dearest, darling, delightful Miss Merriwether"—he punctuated his words with a succession of light, lingering kisses—"I will always be a rogue."

"I prefer Mrs. Weston," she informed him breathlessly, "and I'm glad."

"Diana." His voice was low, heated now. Her name on his lips an intimate caress.

"Henry," she responded in turn.

As one, they turned and raced through the early morning light, laughing as they chased each other into the house. He closed his eyes and counted loudly as she scurried off in search of her hiding place. She grinned in anticipation as she heard his footsteps on the stairs. A lump beneath the quilts might be obvious, but she didn't want him to waste time looking. Her breath caught as he whisked away the covers, and she laughed in sheer joy as he pounced.

He'd found her, and she would never let him go.

AUTHOR'S NOTE

Anyone who knows me is aware that I like to talk. A lot. I also adore alliteration, as you have probably noticed, and I enjoy researching minutiae entirely too much. I always have more to share after I've finished writing a book, which is why some higher power created the Author's Note . . .

On London's Palladian Palace

When I was revising *Tempting the Marquess*, the second book in the Weston series, I threw in a reference to Thomas and Linnet's scandalous pairing, mentioning them only as the stable master and the Duke of Lansdowne's daughter. Why or how I settled on 'Lansdowne,' I don't know, but I did, and *Tempting the Marquess* went to print. I was finishing graduate school in New York while working on *A Rogue for All Seasons*, and one of my final classes was Museum and Library Research at the Watson Library, which just so happens to be in the Metropolitan Museum of Art.

For two glorious weeks, going to school meant showing up at the Met every day. In my free time, I continually found myself drawn back to the period rooms, especially the ones from the Georgian era. I imagined my characters inhabiting these spaces. The cheery yellow room from Kirtlington Park became a drawing room at Weston Manor. The magnificent green dining room from Lansdowne House—I stopped to reread the label. Yes, it said Lansdowne House.

After learning that there was indeed a Lansdowne House in London in 1800—and it was the epitome of extravagance—I couldn't allow Diana's grandparents to live anywhere else. So, while the Duke and Duchess of Lansdowne are fictional, their house in Berkeley Square is real. Work on Lansdowne House began in 1761 for the prime minister, John Stuart (1713–1792), third Earl of Bute. Just two years later, Bute left office in disgrace, and two years following that, the earl sold the still-unfinished house to William Petty Fitzmaurice (1737-1805), second Earl of Shelburne, who was created the first Marquess of Lansdowne in 1784.

Lansdowne served as foreign secretary, then first lord of the Treasury, and finally for a brief eight months as prime minister (1782-83). His support of free speech, free trade, and American independence made him wildly unpopular with George III, but he counted Benjamin Franklin and Samuel Johnson among his friends. Lansdowne House became one of the leading centers for liberal, sophisticated society in London.

Robert Adam (1728-1792), the leading architect of the day, designed Lansdowne House in the popular Neoclassical style, and it is seen as his finest London house. The house survived largely intact—despite being leased to Gordon Selfridge, the department store magnate, who installed his lovers, the Hungarian Vaudeville performers known as 'The Dolly Sisters,' and hosted wild dancing parties. Sadly, however, in 1929, Lansdowne House was sold, and within a few years, it was partially demolished to make way for a new street. The dining room and first drawing room were shipped to America and installed at the Metropolitan Museum of Art and the Philadelphia Museum of Art. Lansdowne House (or what remains of it) became home to the Lansdowne Club, which opened in 1935 and is still in existence today.

On Pennyroyal

Since ancient Egyptian times, herbal medicines have been used to prevent conception and to induce miscarriage. The use of pennyroyal as an emmenagogue (substance that hastens or induces menstruation) and, if taken in sufficient quantities, an abortifacient, dates back at least to ancient Greece. Aristophanes mentioned the herb in his play, *Lysistrata*, in which the women of Greece plot to withhold sex until the men agree to sign a peace treaty ending the Peloponnesian War.

In Europe, midwives and female healers collected knowledge of herbs that helped—or helped prevent—reproduction. Women shared this information with each other and passed it down from generation to generation. During the 18th and 19th centuries, however, the field of obstetrics emerged, and male surgeons gradually replaced midwives. With men in charge of the birthing process, much of the information about the use of herbal medicine with regard to reproduction, especially for contraception, was lost.

Printed sources, such as Nicholas Culpeper's 17th century herbals, suggest that a number of common herbs were recognized and utilized as antifertility agents. Pennyroyal, rue, savin (juniper), tansy, thyme, and vervain (verbena) were seen frequently in kitchen gardens, having both culinary and medicinal applications. In 1800, the year in which *A Rogue for All Seasons* is set, doctors used pennyroyal to treat illnesses ranging from digestive disorders to gout to bronchitis to menstrual cramps. Prepared correctly and taken in limited quantities, these herbs can be very effective, but in high concentrations, they are toxic; the essential oils should never be taken internally.

The other plant Diana employs, wild carrot (Queen Anne's lace), also has a long history as a contraceptive. Scribonius Largus, court physician to the Roman emperor Claudius, was the earliest medical writer to explore its antifertility properties, but women around the globe have used wild carrot seeds at least as long as they have used pennyroyal. Whereas extended use of pennyroyal can be taxing on the kidneys and liver, wild carrot seeds are safe for regular use. For more information on this subject, I recommend John Riddle's *Eve's Herbs* (Harvard University Press, 1997). Anyone interested in the modern applications of herbal medicine to reproductive health is encouraged to check out the books and/or visit the websites of herbalists Susun Weed and Robin Rose Bennett.

On Self-Publishing

I've always known Diana was Henry's match. He sealed his fate when he complained about dancing with her in *Promise Me Tonight*, the first book in the Weston series. Having been through two books with Hal, I had a firm grip on his character; I knew about his family, about where he'd grown up and gone to school, and about his quirks, his strengths, and his flaws. As I attempted to learn more about Diana, Thomas and Linnet's story emerged, and, through them, I began to understand the girl Diana had been and the woman she became.

Many of the characters in *A Rogue for All Seasons* are struggling to figure out their place. As this is a romance novel, we know they belong with each other, but in order to accept each other's love, they must first love themselves. This book took me on a similar journey. Disagreements with the publisher of the first two Weston novels led them to cancel the series, and I discovered that traditional publishers aren't inclined to pick up a book mid-series. There were discussions about revising *Rogue* so that it was no longer a Weston novel, but I wasn't willing to make that compromise.

The decision to self-publish wasn't an easy one—writers are prone to self-doubt—but I love Henry and Diana's story, and I hope you did as well. I know that this book found its place; it belongs with you. I have always loved fairy tales, and while the iconic words

"And they lived happily ever after" satisfy my romantic side, there's a traditional ending phrase I'm going to use instead: This is my story, I've told it, and in your hands I leave it.

Sara

P.S. I really love to hear from my readers, so tweet me (@sara_lindsey), friend me on Facebook (facebook.com/authorsaralindsey), or email me (sara@saralindsey.net). I know you have stories to tell, and I'm always in the mood to talk! If you'd like to find out when my next book comes out, please sign up for my newsletter on my website (www.saralindsey.net)!

PROMISE ME TONIGHT

Isabella is determined to marry James...
Isabella Weston has loved James Sheffield for as long as she can remember. Her come-out ball seems the perfect chance to make him see her in a new light.

James is determined never to marry...
James is stunned to find the impish girl he once knew has blossomed into a sensual goddess. And if he remembers his lessons, goddesses always spell trouble for mortal men.

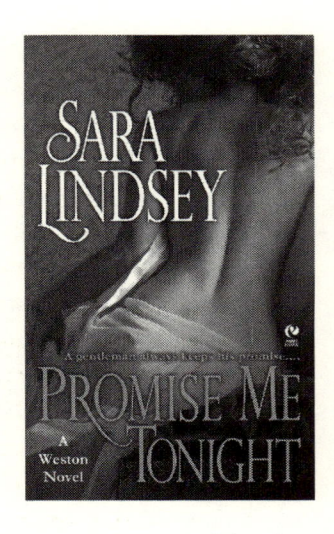

A compromise is clearly necessary.
When Izzie kisses James, her artless ardor turns to a masterful seduction that drives him mad with desire. But, no stranger to heartbreak, James is determined never to love, and thus never to lose. Can Isabella convince him that a life without love might be the biggest loss of all?

Print: Signet Eclipse 978-0451230447
Digital: Amazon · Nook · iTunes · Kobo · Sony · Google Play · Diesel

TEMPTING THE MARQUESS

While Olivia Weston loves matchmaking and romantic novels, she intends to make a suitable match. But first she wants an adventure, and when given the opportunity to visit a reclusive widower living in a haunted castle, Livvy can't possibly resist.

After his wife's death, Jason Traherne, Marquess of Sheldon, shut his heart to everyone but his son, and until now he has succeeded in maintaining his distance. But there's something about Livvy—her unique blend of sweetness and sensuality—that tempts him beyond all reason.

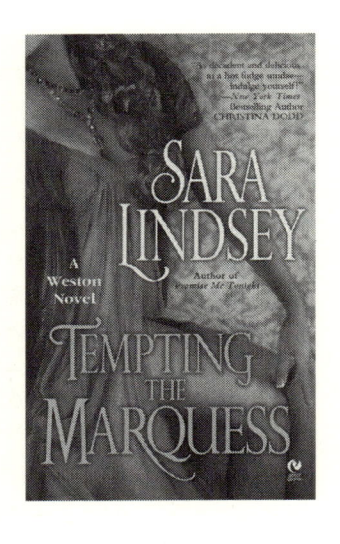

Though there's nothing suitable about the feelings he inspires in her, Livvy can't help falling for the marquess. But can she persuade him to let go of the past and risk his heart again?

Print: Signet Eclipse 978-0451230447
Digital: Amazon · Nook · iTunes · Kobo · Sony · Google Play · Diesel

ABOUT THE AUTHOR

Sara Lindsey began writing during her senior year of college. The rest, as they say, is history . . . or rather, historical romance. Along the way, Sara decided a girl could never surround herself with too many books, so she decided to get a degree in library science. Having read many romances featuring librarians, Sara figures this profession bodes well for someday getting her own happily ever after. In the meantime, she plans to turn as many unsuspecting library patrons as possible into fellow romance addicts.

Sara lives in Los Angeles. If you would like to know more about Sara, her books, her ability to write in third person, and/or her penchant for putting hats on her cats, visit www.saralindsey.net.

Made in the USA
Middletown, DE
31 August 2025